I0522546

Gord—the son of Harry and Brenda, who are long-time friends of Joseph's—has a serious drug and alcohol problem. Joseph tries to help the boy, but to no avail. Suffering from a lifetime of losses himself, Joseph has become a vigilante, determined to eliminate the undesirables of society, something he has become very good at, but he has no idea how to reach an eighteen-year-old boy and make him see reason. When Gord runs away from home after an argument with his parents and joins a cult group, Joseph enlists the help of his friend, Bill, a detective. But Bill has no more luck convincing the boy to come home than Joseph does. Knowing there is nothing more he can do, and hoping the boy will eventually come to his senses, Joseph goes back to what he does best—punishing people who prey on the innocent. It's not a life he willingly chose, but one he was forced into when the system failed to bring justice to him and other victims of these monsters. Resigned to his lonely and secretive life, Joseph searches out and dispatches the most heinous of criminals, until the suicide of a friend and a fatal mistake set Joseph's world spinning out of control into a downward spiral from which he sees no hope of escape…

KUDOS for *The Revelation*

In *The Revelation* by Leonardus G. Rougoor, Joseph is still doing his vigilante work, removing the dregs of society who prey on innocent victims. His friend, Detective Bill Henderson, not only suspects what Joseph does in his secret life, but uses him on occasion to help with difficult cases. But Joseph doesn't trust him enough to confide in him and struggles to keep his shadow life secret. He is very unhappy with this life he was forced into, and feels he can never be forgiven for his sins. Then when a friend dies, and Joseph makes a fatal mistake, his world is turned upside down, and he fears things will never be the same. Intense, compelling, and intriguing, this is one you won't be able to put down. ~ *Taylor Jones, The Review Team of Taylor Jones & Regan Murphy*

The Revelation by Leonardus G. Rougoor is the third book in his Waiting in the Shadows series—the story of a man whose tragic losses in life, combined with the failure of the legal system to bring justice to those responsible, have set him on a path of destruction. Our protagonist, Joseph, lost his mother and two wives to murderers whom the police could not seem to catch, or if they did catch them, the sentences handed down by the court were too lenient to give Joseph closure. Deciding to take matters into his own hands, Joseph sets out to avenge those helpless innocent victims that society fails. Seeking out not only the criminals responsible for the pain in his own life but others as well, Joseph searches online for the scum of the earth, delivering his own brand of justice—swift, brutal, and final. Even those villains he doesn't kill are so traumatized they give up their life of crime and go into hiding. But he can't take them all out, and when a close friend commits suicide because of abuses he suffered at the hands of some criminals, Joseph spirals out of control and makes the one mistake he never thought he would make. *The Revelation* is both a mystery/thriller and the saga of a troubled man living a life he didn't choose but was forced into by desperation and anguish when the people he loved were brutally murdered. Poignant and chilling, it will keep you turning pages from beginning to end. *~ Regan Murphy, The Review Team of Taylor Jones & Regan Murphy*

Other books by
Leonardus G. Rougoor

Waiting in the Shadows Series

Waiting in the Shadows

The Chase

The Revelation

The Clock Series

The Clock ~ Book 1

*The Murderer and the Lost Treasure ~
The Clock ~ Book 2*

The

Revelation

Leonardus G. Rougoor

A Black Opal Books Publication

GENRE: THRILLER/SUSPENSE

This is a work of fiction. Names, places, characters and incidents are either the product of the author's imagination or are used fictitiously, and any resemblance to any actual persons, living or dead, businesses, organizations, events or locales is entirely coincidental. All trademarks, service marks, registered trademarks, and registered service marks are the property of their respective owners and are used herein for identification purposes only. The publisher does not have any control over or assume any responsibility for author or third-party websites or their contents.

The Revelation

Preface

One second nothing, then there it was. The smoke was visible before the noise of the explosion reverberated across the water. When the bilge pump kicked in to pump out the gasoline in the hull area, the new wires spliced in had carried the current to other devices. The next part of the plan then came into play. More explosions, somewhat softer came across the water several minutes later.

The secondary explosives went off, and, as they did, holes were blown through the hull at various places. These had been placed far enough apart to cause the large vessel to start sinking quickly.

Flames poured out of the openings in the luxury yacht. Black smoke billowed into the air as the boat listed slowly over to its starboard side. I guided the boat I was on, closer to the yacht, while I kept an eye on the radar and GPS screens.

So far nothing was in the surrounding waters. Everything on the yacht had been happening quickly. If anyone was attempting to use the life rafts on board, they were in for an unpleasant surprise. I had slit the outer sides, when I was on the yacht, so they couldn't inflate.

The bilge pump must have done its job and activated timers which set the whole scenario into action. The timing had been close to what was planned, but the delay had been nerve-racking.

As I approached speedily from a distance, the yacht slipped under the surface of the water in slow motion. I saw a few people in the water waving for assistance. Guiding the boat I was in to intercept them, I went to offer my assistance, sort of. When I was close enough, I saw the people in the water were mostly big overweight Italians. They called to me for help, expecting me to take them to safety. I was there for another reason.

Chapter 1

Joseph

Bill Henderson and I walked up to the front door of the home where my friends Harry, Brenda, and their kids, Eva and Gord, lived. Brenda opened the door, asking us to come in. It was immediately evident that she had been crying. Stepping into the living room, we saw a house in a bit of a shambles. A couple pieces of furniture were broken, and there was a fist-sized hole in the wall.

My heart sank as I took in the scene. "What on earth happened here?" I asked.

"It's Gord. He's totally out of control. He's gotten involved in drugs and went ballistic when we wouldn't give him the money to pay off a dealer who's after him. This is why we phoned you."

"Where is he now?" I asked.

"He ran away and left his phone behind, so we have no way of getting in touch with him. We don't know what to do," she said as the tears rolled down her face.

Bill knew exactly what to do. He was the police detective who caught Amy's killer. Amy was my first wife.

We had only been married a short time when she was brutally murdered. Her death closely paralleled my mother's.

At this point, Bill took over, introducing himself to Brenda and Harry, who had just come downstairs. "Do you know the name of the drug dealer who supplied your son?" he asked. When she shook her head, he continued. "You have no idea where your son may have gone? Does he have any friends who might shed some light on this situation?"

"Gord has dropped all his old friends and never talks much about anyone he associates with," Harry answered. There was an edge to his voice, one that wasn't usually there.

"This is typical behavior in this kind of circumstance," Bill said. "How long has this been going on? Can you give me as many details as possible, including age, his computer passwords, and anything you feel may be relevant? Just write it on a sheet of paper and show me to his room, please."

"I'll show him up to Gord's room if you like," I said, at which Harry nodded his head.

Up the stairs we went and into a room I had been in many times before. This used to be a boy who was pleasant to be around and respected his parents. Things changed dramatically, right after the first time he got drunk with a few boys from his school. This road had been especially difficult for my friends, and I felt so sorry for them.

Bill found the cell phone that was left behind and with very little effort managed to access the information in it. The two of us read a series of texts between Gord and someone called Jimmy. They spoke of money owed for drugs received. The amount of money was, for a boy in Gord's position, quite high and amounted to several thousand dollars. It would be difficult for him to pay this off.

There also were several texts coming from and going to a person with very strange ideas. There was a phone number attached, and Bill said he would investigate the person. The drug dealer would also be visited and questioned as to Gord's whereabouts.

Bill sat down at the computer and attempted to open it as well, but was stumped. Harry came into the room, handing over a sheet of paper with writing on it and was asked if he knew the password.

"I haven't been allowed to touch his things in quite some time. If you need to take it with you, please do," he said to the detective. "We just want to find him."

"How did your living room get into the condition it is," Bill asked.

"My son asked for a considerable amount of money, and when we told him no, he became quite hostile before he ran away," Harry said with his head hanging down.

Bill continued his search of the room and only came up with a few more items of interest. One of the things he held in his hand was an information pamphlet. He cocked his head to the side and raised one eyebrow. "This is strange. The phone number on the pamphlet is the same as on the phone text. It looks like Gord may have been recruited by a cult leader named Jeremy Baulthus. I've heard of this guy before. He and his sect prey on confused kids, who have gotten themselves into drug trouble, and make some wild promises of enlightenment, enticing them to join," he said. "This is not good, not good at all."

With this, he picked up the computer and pocketed the cell phone. When he got to the front door, he said to the tearful parents, "I'll get the department techs to look into the computer, and I'll handle this case personally."

Harry managed to get out a thank you and asked me to stay for a moment. When we were alone, Harry took me aside and, when he was sure Brenda couldn't hear, said, "There are things about you that I don't know, but I do know that you have helped us before. You dealt with some pretty harsh people for us, and although you wouldn't tell us how, you took care of them. If there is anything that you can do, please do it for us."

"If I am able to do anything, without Bill finding out, I will. For now, we'll have to let him handle things. He is a very capable man, so give him a chance. If anyone can get to the bottom of this, it's him."

With this, I left to head back home. This was not a problem I needed. I just came back from dealing with the man responsible for the death of Kathleen, my second and last wife. I'd made the decision to never get involved with a woman again. Almost everyone that I had ever cared about had been murdered.

Sometimes I thought about the things that made me what I was. I wouldn't wish these things to happen to my worst enemy. The life-altering events that shaped me into a murderer, and worse, still haunted me.

Harry was right, he didn't know much about me, if he did, he would never have had me in his company again, and no one else would either. Part of me lived in the shadows, a part that could never be revealed.

Chapter 2

Looking at me, you would never believe the things I'd done. It all started with the awful death of my mother. Her murderer got away with it for a long while. He and all his friends were paid back in one hot moment.

This deed opened a whole new life for me. Seeing all the pain and abuse everywhere affected me to the point that I started a mission in life—to help the underdog. This mission went on until I met Amy. She brought me back to a normal life, but she was taken from me, just like my mother. The man responsible for her death was dealt with too, permanently.

Pulled once more into the mire, I was forced back into a life I had hoped was gone. I have gone after only the worst offenders, people that didn't belong in this world. The ones that I knew would never turn their lives around. It got a little hairy for me a few times as I almost got killed myself when some of my targets took exception to my endeavors. Some of my encounters, were, to say the very least, strange and even spooky.

Some people, I'm sure would say, "I could never do those kinds of things." Until the buttons are pushed and pushed hard enough, you never know what you are capable of doing.

I worked at Salem Steel Fabrication in Salem Oregon. My job had me wearing several different hats. I was on the safety committee, quality control inspector, did machining and I trained inexperienced employees. The machining aspect of my job gave me the time, materials and the ability to make many of the tools used in my second career, *taking out the trash,* to put it politely.

The men I worked with were pretty good guys, but they knew nothing of what I did away from the job. In order to keep it that way, I found it necessary to become a loner. I was sometimes questioned about this but managed to divert any real probes in other directions. This was most true when I was for a time, in Bill Henderson's sights. It took quite a unique plan to get him off my tail. Since then we became very good friends and a couple of times even partners in crime, strange as that may seem.

For someone who had as much tragedy in their life as I did, I think I'd come through it fairly well, of course, not everyone would share this opinion I'm sure, oh well, on with the task at hand.

Chapter 3

On my way home, I thought about how things had changed so dramatically for Harry and Brenda. They'd been my friends for years and were the ones who introduced me to Amy. Harry was in real estate and helped us buy our first home, waiving the fees. This same home was where I lived on my own again.

I tried to help Gord a few times in the past, but once he started drinking his whole attitude changed. He went from being a nice boy to a surly, unhappy person and later got into the drug scene. Eva managed to stay away from the shit in life and was an honor student at the university.

Harry had relatives that had drinking and mental health problems. Maybe this kind of thing ran in families. I wanted to help my friends but waited to see what Bill could do first. If he solved the problem, I wouldn't have become too involved in something so close to home. This was one of the things that kept me out of prison. It was time for a good work out. That usually helped take my mind off things for a while.

As I lay awake in bed, thoughts of the chase that led me to Dennis Jackson and the heart to heart I had with him went through my head. I was glad I dealt with him the way I did. If I had done to him what I did to Jake Patterson, I was sure I would have been adversely affected again. It took me quite a while to get over the trauma of that incident.

Drifting off to sleep, I had some of the nightmares that had plagued me most of my adult life. As happened to me several times in the past, I was being shot at and wounded by some of the people I was trying to kill. No matter how I justified my actions, there always seemed to be a part of me that had a hard time dealing with it. Why else would I keep having those dreams?

I woke up in the morning and saw out the window that it was a beautiful day. After a bit of yard work, I drove to see Ben and went horseback riding. This helped me organize my thoughts, and gave me the time to look at my future a bit more objectively. Ben owned a riding stable outside of town, on a nice size ranch with lots of trails.

The ride through the grassy fields and along the stream, meandering through the woods brought me to a place of reflection. In order to take my mind off the problem with Gord, I'd gone on the internet and found a suitable next target. Every now and then, a need built up in me to correct a wrong. This involved removing a person that had committed crimes against society and would very likely never change his ways. The research usually gave me a number of choices. There never seemed to be a shortage of assholes that needed an intervention, a permanent one.

Once online I went to the sites that in the past had given me so much information on known criminals. The CDC, *Citizens Discussing Crime*, I had long suspected of having members of the law enforcement agencies. They were the only ones who would be privy to much of what I found there. There were several other sites such as

Seeking Justice, Crime Everywhere, and a special one called V-anonymous, V for Vengeance. Of course, the last one I thought had members on both sides of the law.

Searching, I found the usual suspected rapists, wife beaters, pimps, and drug dealers. My old pals from the Klan were found as well as other hate groups that I dealt with in the past. The Klan had accounted for the highest body count of any of my missions to date. Cartels were still in business, but they were too big for me to tackle. They hired ex-mercenaries who were a bit out of my league unless I could do a hit and run.

Those stinking priests who molested young boys popped up every now and then. Why did people attend that church if there was a chance their child would have long-term damage inflicted on them? I would like to pay a few of those men a visit and make it so their vows of chastity were easier to live up to. Man, those pedophiles pissed me off. I got more irritated each time I heard about them and their perversions.

Finally, a story about organized crime stared out of the screen at me. The head of a major family lived on the west coast. The exact area was not given, but that wouldn't be too hard to find. This group had intimidated, murdered, forced into prostitution, and made life hell on earth for many people. Just for the love of power and money. The accused person's face was not shown, but that also wouldn't be too hard to find.

The story painted a picture of bribes and corruption by a group that had been a real blight on America for a long, long time. I thought that I should look into the problem just a little more. The sites I frequented would help me gather the information I needed to start making my plans.

Mario Castelli became fabulously wealthy on the backs of others. I thought that a substantial withdrawal was in the cards for Mario. How this was going to be done was totally up in the air, but that had never stopped me in the past, so why should it now? The feeling of excitement that occurred in me, when a decision was made, started flowing through me.

Monday, I was back at work, with the job going well for the most part. The strain I was under leading up to the meeting with Dice man, Dennis Jackson, disappeared. The guys I worked with noticed the change in me. The explanation I gave alluded to the fact that I had a great time off. If they only knew, they might not be so happy with me.

Bill called me Tuesday after work and let me know that he had spoken with the dealer. He informed him that Gord was the son of a personal friend. Unless the dealer wanted to have the law on his case every day, it would be best that he absorbed his losses and left the boy alone. The dealer, John Neubert, decided that it was in his best interest and accepted the offer. He knew full well that he would be on the detective's radar more than ever if he didn't cooperate. He would have more trouble than he knew what to do with, something he didn't want.

"I've checked into the possibility that Gord is with the cult and talked to the leader on the phone," Bill told me. "I will be meeting with him tomorrow. I told him if the boy is there, he better have him at the meeting, or I'll get a search warrant."

"Have you talked to Harry and his wife about this yet?"

"I have. They want to go with me when I talk to Jeremy Baulthus, the leader of 'The Light of Promise,' some weird, pseudo-religious organization. I told them no, this isn't the way an investigation is done. I'll keep them informed as to what happens, though. The Baulthus group has around twenty five members at a farm on the edge of town.

"Jeremy inherited it from an off-the-wall uncle a few years ago. He was left with a fair amount of money in a trust fund too," Bill said. "This guy fancies himself a leader along the lines of that wackjob, Jim Jones, who was in the news years ago."

"So what you're telling me is that we should get the boy out of there?"

Bill sighed. "That may be a bit harder than it sounds. I don't think that any laws have been broken, and no one is forced to stay, but it wouldn't surprise me if the members are brainwashing new recruits."

"Let me know how it goes, all right?"

"Will do, Joseph," he answered and hung up.

Chapter 4

Bill

Bill was on his way to meet with Jeremy Baulthus, driving down Conifer Street, where it crossed the Little Pudding River. A plume of dust rose into the air. As he went over the bridge, he turned left down another gravel road for a half mile, leaving a trail in the air, letting anyone who might be watching know of his approach.

Parking his car, he stepped out facing a group of buildings. In the forefront, was a large two story farm house with a wrap-around veranda facing toward the river. The rest of the buildings looked more like bunkhouses, except for one that might have at one time, been an enclosed horse riding arena.

Bill scanned the area, taking in everything in order to be familiar with the place, in case he needed to come back quickly. The sun was hot on his back, as he walked to the steps leading up to the veranda; Bill was confronted by a girl of about twenty years of age. She was slender, had blonde hair, and wore a red T-shirt with the logo, Light of Promise, across the front in black.

"May I help you?" she asked with no warmth in her voice whatsoever.

"I'm here to see Mister Baulthus."

"Follow me," she said as she turned and walked into the house.

A man of about thirty was seated at a desk in the first room off to the right. As Bill entered, the man got up and shook the detective's hand, introducing himself as Reverend Jeremy. There were no plaques on the walls, so he must have been one of those self- professed ministers, the ones without credentials. He stood at five foot ten and had a fairly athletic body. His brown hair was kept short, and there was an intense look about him. His eyes, like the girl's, had no warmth in them at all as he squinted at the detective.

Getting to the point, he asked, "What can I do for you?"

"I'm looking for a young man by the name of Gord, son of Harry and Brenda Motters. I was told he might be staying here," Bill said.

"Has he done something illegal?"

"No, his parents are worried and want him to come home."

"What if he doesn't want to leave here?" Jeremy asked.

"He is underage, and we can have him removed, if necessary. I doubt that you want that."

"I am told that he is turning eighteen tomorrow and that makes him no longer answerable to his parents. I am correct in this, am I not?" Jeremy questioned.

"Tomorrow, that will be true, but not today."

"We aren't going to quibble over one day, are we?" Jeremy asked, frowning.

"Why don't you have him brought here, and we'll go on from there? It'll save some trouble for both of us."

Looking past the detective, Jeremy shouted out through the door, "Melanie, can you bring the new recruit, Gord, here?"

Without a word, she turned and walked out of the house. There had been no further talk between the two men, as Jeremy started writing in what looked like a journal.

Looking up after a few minutes, he said, "We don't force our members to be here, you know? We are here to save these youngsters from themselves. The people of the community should be thanking us, not persecuting us the way they have been."

Bill looked at the man across the desk. "I guess the community worries about how you get the members to stay here, because once they *are* here, all communication with their families is cut off. Most believe that you and your helpers take the youth when they are most vulnerable and twist their heads around. By the time you're finished, they hardly know who they are anymore."

"We do no such thing. We offer enlightenment and a better way of living," Jeremy said, raising his voice angrily.

At this point, a young man walked into the house stopping in the doorway of the room.

Bill got up. "Are you Gord Motters?"

"Yes."

"Could you come outside with me so we can speak in private?" Bill asked.

Jeremy got up and was about to object. But because he was not the boy's guardian, he knew he could not interfere without causing himself more trouble, so he sat back down. Bill and Gord walked outside, and when they were far enough from the house not to be overheard, Bill communicated his concerns to the boy.

"Your parents are very worried about you and want you to come home, Gord."

"If they were so worried, why didn't they help me when I asked for the money?"

"You know that wouldn't have fixed the problem. Come on, you know as well as I do that you would still have been using and back in the same boat soon enough. You would have been back with your hand out, demanding they give you more money. In the end, you would have drained your parents of everything they have worked for all these years. Listen to me, I talked with John, and he has agreed to wipe out your debt, but he never wants to see you again. I hope you know he means it. You could well get hurt," Bill told the surly boy.

"Whatever. I'm still not going back, and if you make me, I'll just come back here tomorrow. You won't be able to do anything about it then."

"How about talking to your parents? I'll call them now if you want," the detective said, trying to get the boy to see reason.

"I don't want to talk to them, not now, not ever. If they cared at all about me, they would have helped me when I asked them for money. I don't care what you say, Reverend Jeremy is my friend, not them. Just leave me alone," he shouted angrily with his face turning red, just as he spun on his heel and ran away, leaving the policeman shaking his head.

On the phone, his conversation with Brenda was not a happy one. The information was relayed and the decision made to leave Gord where he was.

"I know this is not what you want to hear, but I don't think you have a choice. I'm sorry to have to tell you this," he said to the sobbing mother.

Chapter 5

Joseph

Harry, broken-hearted, relayed the information to me and let me know there was little to be done. "How does a boy turn away from his family so quickly?" he asked. "He was such a good boy for so long, and then, all of a sudden, everything got turned upside down."

"This kind of thing is really common these days. I see it at work all too often. Drugs have ruined many lives, and there is little that can be done to prevent it. I'm so sorry, Harry."

I thought about going to see the little goof I'd known for years but remembered our last conversation and how it went. No, this would have to run its course. Maybe he'd get his act together and reach out, but I doubted it. In a few months, I might go see him. In the meantime, Mario Castelli and I needed a rendezvous. These kinds of people pissed me off a lot, and soon my thoughts turned from Gord to a new direction.

Going online, I gathered what information I could, there was plenty on this guy and his friends. He was the head of a crime family, and it looked like he would do whatever was necessary to get what he wanted, and he wanted everything. After requesting information from the sites, I got a lot. This guy must have pissed off a lot of law enforcement members, plus some of his own people.

He lived in a huge mansion outside San Francisco with a few guards always on duty. His list of possessions included a private twelve-seat airplane, a helicopter, and one heck of a nice -looking yacht. Who says crime doesn't pay? It paid off big time for him. I was starting to have second thoughts about taking him on, though. He just might too big, and too well protected for me to go after. The types I usually targeted didn't even know any-one was after them, at least for the most part, but what the heck? I'd tackled some pretty tough people before and survived.

I had to look carefully into it before making up my mind one way or the other. Maybe there was a way to get in close, do what I had to, and get back out quick. I got this itch periodically that had to be taken care of, or I started getting on edge, with people around me wonder-ing what was going on. This probably had to do with the years of waiting, before payback could be exacted on the man that had so horribly murdered my mother.

Castelli's home, I thought, was out, which left the plane, helicopter, and yacht as possible targets. If I could find out a routine or discover some plans he had for his future, I might be able to come up with an idea. With this in mind, I started using my online sources to look for more information on his habits and possible schedules.

I had long thought that some of the members of these online sites were either in law enforcement or criminals who were looking to get even with men like Mario. There were things about the man which only an associate or close enemy would know. That kind of information made the job easier.

Mario Castelli, now and then, like a lot of men, met with a woman at a number of different, upper-end resorts. This woman was not his wife, although he was married. His wife was not the best -looking woman around, but then again, neither was he. Castelli went several times a year to Sicily for meetings with business associates too. Organized crime had its roots in Sicily, as I recalled.

What really piqued my interest was a meeting of several of his kind, the heads of other families, that was likely to happen in the next few months. The location and time of the meeting were not known, but might come to light in the near future, according to the source. I was a bit leery of the source of the information, so I continued my search for another target too.

I found a story on the V-Anonymous site that told of a man in an auto theft ring, Dimitri Barinov, who wanted to get out of the business. He was going to testify for the police in exchange for a new start. The story went on to say that, in order to deter the man from testifying, the gang sent one of its men, who broke into the man's home. The man was masked, but the wife had heard his voice before. He gave the mother the option of choosing which one, of her four children, would be shot.

If the woman could or would not choose, the killer said he was going to execute all four. On the verge of having all the children killed, the wife blurted out the name of the one that was to die. He shot the child in front of the mother, who broke down and had since been inconsolable. A warning was given to the oldest child to give to her father. *Do not testify.*

Presented with this ultimatum, the father vowed to testify and bring down the boss and his gang. A short time later, Dimitri Barinov was murdered too.

I'm not sure why they hadn't just killed him first and been done with it. Just plain viciousness was the only reason I could come up with. The mother had been left with no husband and one of her children dead. Being forced to choose which was to die would have life-long repercussions for the woman. Murdering the child was an act I had difficulty understanding. This rabid dog needed to be put down, and I was the one to do it.

After a bit of digging, I found a name, which I was positive must have come from a disgruntled policeman. This kind of over-the-top crime had to be hard for the cops to handle, too. It was for me. Lazar Pavlov was going to be finding out soon that he would no longer be tolerated in the United States. He was going wish that he had stayed in Russia.

The things I learned about the man showed just how utterly ruthless and dangerous he could be. I was sure the people working with him were just as bad, so my plans had to be refined well, in order to make sure I came out on top.

In the past year when I had been hunting for the Diceman, I had to make certain I stayed alive while terminating my secondary targets. Things like that weren't as important anymore. I didn't have any wish to have my life ended in the foreseeable future, but it just wasn't as important as it had been. Dennis Jackson paid his debt. I had to make sure Bill didn't find this out as he had been feeding me information concerning this man.

The nightmares I had for so long were becoming less intense and frequent. I used to wake up in the middle of the night in a sweat, after dreaming about being hunted and caught by the people I had eliminated or was trying to.

Having a few hours to kill, I headed out to Baskette Slough Wildlife Refuge for a run and ended up in my favorite spot. As I sat on the bank of the lake, watching the clouds drift by, a gentle breeze rippled the water and ruffled my hair.

I sat there, debating whether or not I should use my .300 Winchester Magnum scoped rifle, to take out Lazar Pavlov from a distance. It didn't seem very sporting, but it would keep me out of the danger zone. Plus it got the job done. Of course, this man couldn't possibly give anyone he targeted a sporting chance, so it shouldn't really matter to me either. But I had found, in the past, that whenever I got the itch to do a job, the feeling of satisfaction wore off too quickly if I didn't use the hands-on approach.

Chapter 6

The decision was made, and when I got home, I started gathering details of the area he lived and the man himself. Lazar, I found, lived in the 140th Street area of Seattle. This was a city of over six hundred fifty thousand people, and the auto theft ring stole the vehicles from that city and many other places throughout the state. He had several people working for him, and they all came from Russia too.

I found out lots of things about the guy. If I could do it, why the police couldn't put him out of business was beyond me. I didn't work within the law, and I couldn't believe all the police did either. I sometimes wondered why there weren't more people like me. Oh well, on with the show, as the old saying went.

Lazar had a business in town, which included a warehouse, but I was sure that couldn't be where he operated out of. That would have made it far too easy to be shut down. I had to do what I usually did in these circumstances, perform a little surveillance operation.

Waiting for the weekend, I'd gathered things I needed, packed them up on that Friday right after work, then headed out. I'd called Harry to check in to see how they're doing. I almost wished that I hadn't. I didn't like seeing my friends as despondent as they were. I hated that helpless feeling. I usually tried to take the bull by the horns, but this time I hadn't been able to.

The drive to Seattle was nice, with the warm air blowing into the car through the open window. When I got there, I booked a room, using my fake identification, and paid in cash. I already had a rented car, paid for in the same way, so my own plate number wouldn't be recorded. A drive along 140th street and then on to the side road 55th Avenue got me to where Pavlov lived. The home he resided in was a modest one, all things considered. Maybe he had other residences that weren't in such a family-friendly neighborhood. The people I saw there weren't the same as him at all.

After making my way over to 15th Avenue, I drove slowly past Lazar's place of business. It looked slightly run down and wasn't in the best part of town. Just as I drove by the front entrance, the door opened, and out he stepped. I tried to turn my head away but it had been too late. He saw me looking at him. I wasn't incognito, and if he were to see me in the future, I was sure he would recognize me. Damn!

Looking in my rearview mirror, I saw his head swing to follow the rental car. I was driving past way too slow, and this had caught his attention. I figured that if I made sure I was always disguised from then on, I should be okay, hopefully. After driving back to the room, I went over what had just happened and decided to change cars at the rental place. That would at least protect me to some degree.

Going back to 15th Avenue, I made sure I parked far enough away to escape detection. Watching the building through high powered binoculars for several hours didn't give me any useful information. The only thing I got for my troubles was cramped muscles from kneeling for too long. A few people came and went, but not anyone who looked like they were of any interest to me. I took long-range photos of them anyway, on the off-chance I saw them again. It wasn't until five -thirty that Lazar left, with me following him at a safe distance, always having cars between me and him. After stopping off at a couple of places, he headed out of town.

We were going in a southerly direction and ended up on south 113th Street in the Renton area. This street had nice homes on the waterfront of Lake Washington. The properties there had well-manicured lawns and gardens. There were expensive cars parked in the driveways, and it looked like most had fenced in, in-ground pools in the backyards. I was sure the properties were worth a fortune. Parking his car in the garage, he closed the door, allowing me to drive past safely. This did give me a quick glimpse of the lay of the land. Once done, I left before I was spotted.

Thinking back, I thought out loud, saying, "Shit, why did I drive past his place of business without having some sort of disguise? If he sees me later without anything again, he'll know I'm following him for sure. The guy can't possibly be stupid, or he'd be in prison."

Being on the water's edge would give me two ways to access his home if I decided to take him out there. That, however, might not be the way to go because, being on the water, there were no hiding places. The roads in the area went right around the lake, so if he was in a car, he could easily keep me in sight and take me out when I docked. That didn't appeal to me at all.

The evening brought nothing of consequence. For a few hours the next day, I watched his shop from a hot rooftop. The wind blew the grit on the roof onto my sweaty skin and irritated me all the way back. The shower was a welcome relief, as the water washed away the sweat and grime.

Hitting the computer, I looked over his place of business but found little of use. Being Sunday evening meant I had to work the next day, so once I got home, I relaxed the rest of the evening and then headed for bed.

During the week I contacted Harry and found out that little had changed. He and Brenda were at their wits' end.

"Eva has gone to see Gord at the Light of Promise farm. She talked with her brother and tells us that he isn't the same person anymore. Gord seems to be somewhat brainwashed and, although he looks like he isn't using now, he has told her not to come back." Harry broke down as he said, "I think we've lost our boy."

"I'm sorry to hear that. Bill told me that there is nothing that he can do, but he will go see him periodically."

There was little to be done at that point, so I got back to the task at hand. Watching Lazar had shown me at least one thing. The man was very aware of what went on around him. I knew better than to become careless with this guy. There were two other men with him at his place of business. I needed to get inside the building to find out what I could about him. Maybe some incriminating evidence had been left behind.

Friday evening had me checking into a motel again. I set the alarm for three in the morning, and after getting myself set, I drove over to the shop. After doing a drive-by in the new rental car, I found that all was quiet and parked well away from the building. Carrying a small bag of tools, and a few weapons of choice, I found a back entrance with no security cameras or motion detectors.

Just in case there was a dog inside, I put my ear to the door and listened. Hearing nothing, I rapped on the door and listened again. If there was a dog or someone in the building, the banging on the metal door would have roused them.

A crowbar was the only tool I had that ended up working to open the door. I would have preferred to not make it obvious that I had been here, but unfortunately, it had been unavoidable. Once inside, with the door closed again, I turned on my flashlight and panned the interior. There were a number of large tool boxes and acetylene torches around the shop. There was a small office to the left of the door and a bathroom on the opposite side of the building, but little else.

Doing a thorough search of the premises revealed very little. It was definitely not a chop shop because there would have been far more evidence than what I'd found there. That was all right, though, because I wasn't there to put him out of that business. I was there to take the murdering bastard out of the picture completely.

Going to the back door, I looked it over carefully to see if I could fix the damage I'd done to it. The parts that had been bent and scraped were not repairable enough to hide the fact that there had been a break and enter. In order to divert suspicion in another direction, I went to the toolboxes and took the best and most expensive tools I could find. I placed them in smaller tool boxes that I'd emptied out and loaded the good stuff into.

Back at the car with the tools in the trunk, I drove to the shoreline on the bay, west of the city. When I was sure no one was around, I dumped the load into the salt water and then headed back to the room.

The following day, nice and early, even though I was quite tired, I headed for a spot where I could watch Lazar and his buddies as they entered the shop. I was about half a block away and hiding from sight with the binoculars up to my eyes when I saw them drive up. After they went into the building, there was a fifteen-minute wait while nothing happened. Then the back door flew open, and Lazar examined the lock. Looking around, searching the area he had a snarl on his face. When you looked at some people, you could tell immediately what kind of person they were. This guy looked like a real shit. Ducking out of sight, I headed back to the car.

At this point, I still didn't know how I was going to take him out, or if it would only be him. Lazar would now be on his guard for the next while, so I knew I had to hold off for a while.

I spent the rest of that day keeping tabs on him and a short time on Sunday before heading back home. I did manage to find out that he had a routine that he seemed to follow, but in order to be sure of it, I'd need to observe him for a few more weekends.

During the following weeks, I did as much online research as I could, gathering info on Lazar. I also came across stuff that would help me go after Mario Castelli. I was fortunate enough to have come across the place in the Hamptons he frequently met his mistress. Unfortunately, it was too far away, and the chances of being there when he was were far too slim.

I wondered what the chances were of shooting the helicopter out of the sky. After looking online to see where the crucial points were, I doubted that I could make the shot. The chopper would have to be fairly high up in order to kill him and his buddies, and that would make the shot even harder.

I figured that my best bet would be to find out where his yacht was anchored and then see if I could take care of business there. First, I needed to find out a little about the boat so I could make my plans.

Work was going well, except for some new guy harassing a few of the younger employees. I heard the boys talking during lunch. They were thinking about doing something to stop Mike. Of course, they thought that Mike would probably retaliate, and this worried them.

When Jimmy, one of the younger guys was alone, I headed over and talked to him, trying to see if the problem could be headed off. Being the safety representative in the shop gave me some pull with management, which I could talk to when I found out what was going on.

"Hey, Jimmy, I couldn't help but overhear you boys talking at lunch. You seem to have quite a problem with Mike. What's going on?" I asked.

"Ah, well, we should be able to handle it ourselves, Joseph."

"You and I both know that if you guys do something to him, he will get you back, one at a time. What are you going to do then?" I asked.

He looked at me with a blank stare. It was obvious that he hadn't thought this through too far. I found out exactly what Mike had been doing to the boys.

"Jimmy, hold off doing anything and talk to the others, while I look into this and see what can be done, all right?"

"Sure, we can do that," he replied, looking slightly relieved.

Heading to the office, I talked to Abe, my supervisor. I explained what was happening in the shop. He knew as well as I did that, if an employee was allowed to intimidate others, the shop moral would go downhill fast. It was time to do something about it before it got out of hand. Abe asked me to wait with him while he called Mike into the office over the PA system.

When Mike walked into the office, there was a smug look on his face as he asked what Abe wanted with him.

"We've heard complaints being directed at you. Some of the men say you are trying to intimidate them. I want it to stop, do you hear?"

"I'm not doing anything. They're just a bunch of sissies," Mike said, raising his voice toward Abe.

"Don't bother with the denials. We want it to stop and stop now. Do you hear me? Your job is on the line here, so you better take this seriously," Abe said sternly.

"Right," Mike said, giving me a dirty look.

Out in the shop, while I was working on a machine, Mike came up to me. "Why the hell are you getting me in shit with the boss?"

"Because you're a bully, and it's going to stop. You don't get to push the younger employees around in this shop," I told him.

"You asshole, who do you think you are? I could tear you apart anytime I feel like it, so just stay the hell out of my way, or you'll regret it. You go to the boss about this, and I'll hunt you up when you least expect it, you hear me, shit-head?"

Before I could answer, he turned and left, kicking over a garbage can as he went. When I had a break, I went into the files in the office and looked up Mike's address. The rest of the day went shitty, and I could hardly wait for it to be over. That moron had pissed me off more than I should have let him. Finally, the day was over, and we all headed out the door, going our separate ways. Well most of us went our separate ways. Me, I followed Mike at a distance and saw him head for a bar.

He went in, but I waited for an hour before going in myself. He was sitting in a corner booth with two other guys. They looked like they'd been drinking a fair bit and were quite loud. Taking a seat, I sat at a table across the room with my back to the wall. He didn't see me for about ten minutes, but when he did, he got a nasty look on his face. He talked to the two guys with him, and the group got up together, heading toward me with a swagger. When they stopped, Mike was a step or two ahead of the others and about eight feet away from me.

"Well, if it isn't the guy who doesn't like me picking on the boys at work. Tell you what, how about I pick on you instead, asshole? You made a mistake coming in here, you dumb shit," he said, grinning at me.

"So, you going to teach me a lesson by yourself or do you need the two morons with you?" I said, smiling at him.

I got up before he could move more than half a step. As he came toward me with his arm already starting its swing, I dropped down and let out with a straight kick to the inside of his knee. There was a loud pop, a scream of pain, and the thud of Mike hitting the floor. I was already on my feet, as the other two came at me, one on either side of their friend, who was lying on his back, holding his knee.

Stepping off to the left, I hit the first guy with a right hook that stopped him in his tracks. The other guy, clearly knowing he had made a mistake, was already trying to slow down as if he thought the planned attack wasn't going to be the best idea he ever had. Too late for him. A kick with my left foot connected with his groin. He screamed in pain and dropped to the floor, too.

With his friends out of commission, my attention went back to Mike. With one of his hands on the floor, he tried to move back away from me. I took this opportunity to stomp on that hand, being rewarded with the sound of a bone or two breaking. I don't know about him, but I was having a good time. It felt good to show the guy just how tough he wasn't.

"I don't think you should come back to work anymore. Just call in and tell them you quit and have them send you your pay. What do you think, Mike, good idea?"

He nodded an affirmation.

"You want to keep this between us, or would you like everyone to know what happened here?" I asked.

He just hung his head down and said nothing. I guessed what happened in the bar, stayed in the bar. That would, of course, be in my best interests, too. I wanted to keep a low profile, so it was imperative that as few people knew about this as possible.

The next day at work Abe asked me, "Do you know anything about why Mike just phoned in, saying he quit?"

"Not a clue, but it's good news, isn't it? Maybe he figured he'd be fired sooner or later anyway," I answered, trying to keep the smirk off my face.

"I guess so," he said, looking at me like he thought there might be more to it.

I shrugged and went back to work.

The boys in the shop were a lot happier after Mike left, and things soon got back to normal. The weeks went by with me watching Lazar on the weekends. It looked like the break-in had blown over.

Lazar and his men stayed at the shop late on Fridays, and, because of this, I made plans to interrupt the get-together and take out the whole crew in one shot. Gathering my things, I headed to Seattle, and, after getting a room, I rented a nondescript car.

I laid low, in the vicinity of the shop, in a hidden spot, well away from the front of the building. The front door wasn't locked as I got to it, with my pistol in hand. I opened the door inward ever so slowly. The smell of oil and burnt metal that the torch had been used on hit my nostrils.

The nunchucks were in a long pocket on the side of my pant leg, while I entered the building. I heard voices in the office and a clink of glasses as a toast was being made. So far so good, I seemed to have caught them unaware.

Lazar shouted out something in Russian which ended with the name Ivan. A chill went through me as that meant one of the men was probably not in the room with him. Just as I turned my head to the right, I saw a blur of motion and tried to take evasive action, but it was too late. The lights went out.

Consciousness came back slowly, with a lot of pain in my head. When things started to clear, I realized that I was tied to a chair, with a rope binding my hands behind me. It was evident very quickly that I was in the biggest trouble of my life. Three men stood in a semicircle in front of me.

Lazar opened his mouth leaning close and out came, "Welcome back, you're the man that drove past the front of the shop a couple of months ago, aren't you? Lucky for us, Ivan had to go to the toilet for a piss when you decided to pay us a visit. So why don't you tell me, what makes you so interested in us?"

There was the smell of vodka and a strong smell of garlic on his breath.

I tried desperately to come up with a viable reason for my presence but failed to do so. I couldn't very well tell him I was there to kill him. My silence was taken as reluctance to convey the information he had requested. He stepped forward and hit me as hard as he could on the left side of my head. Even though I saw it coming and swung my head in the direction the punch was going at the last instant, the force almost knocked me out.

I feared this was not going to end well. I dropped my face down feigning unconsciousness, but he wasn't fooled by the ploy. Laughing, he lifted my head and slapped me a few times. He and his men took turns beating up on me. As the blood flowed from numerous cuts, thankfully I finally did lose consciousness.

I was quite surprised when I woke up and found that I was still alive. Pain wracked my body as never before. There were, to my surprise, no broken bones as far as I could tell, but this could easily change in the near future. I didn't have any idea as to how I could get myself out of the situation. I tried not to moan or let them know I was awake. Maybe something would come to me.

"Alexei, go get the car," Lazar was saying. "I think it is time to take our friend for a ride. We'll go to the bush and bury him where the others are. Of course, we'll have a little more fun with him first." At this, they all laughed, and Alexei walked to the door to do as instructed.

I had little doubt as to how it would end at this point. My legs were untied from the chair and retied together. My hands were still bound but not too tightly. As I fell to the floor, I remained still, letting them think I was still out of it, despite the pain running through me as I hit the floor. As I impacted the ground, I felt the watch that I had altered so long ago shift on my wrist. I was very surprised that it was still there. A faint hope entered my mind that this might still work out for me—very faint.

I was manhandled out the door, and my worst fear at this moment was that the watch would be removed. Luckily for me, it stayed on my wrist. No one checked to see how tight the ropes binding my hands were as I was dumped into the trunk of the car. As we drove, I was bumped around a bit, which hampered my task somewhat.

The ropes cut into my wrists as I twisted and turned, attempting to adjust my watch to the position that it needed to be. Many years ago I made an alteration just in case I got into a predicament like I was in now. A small blade, concealed under the tiny thin plate attached to the underside of the watch, finally swung out.

It took around ten minutes of tortuous movements, but the rope was eventually cut. With my handsfree, I untied the rope on my ankles and then searched the trunk for anything I might be able to use. The bruises caused me enough pain to hamper my search. Finding nothing handy, it dawned on me to try reaching the spare tire compartment. One of my targets did this same thing when he was in my trunk.

The ride lasted another half hour, and, as the car stopped, I prepared myself. I lay the rope back over my ankles and placed my hands behind me. Lying on my side as the trunk lid opened, I prepared for a last-ditch effort to save myself. Alexei and Ivan started bending over to pick me up as the tire iron I had managed to get from under the spare tire was brought around. It impacted Ivan's head with a thud and down he went.

"What the hell?" Lazar shouted, jumping back.

Swinging it at Alexei, I only caught him with a glancing blow. This was enough to daze him, and he stumbled backward. Seeing Lazar reaching inside his coat, I knew that a gun was being brought into play. As I exited the trunk, I threw the tire iron, hitting him in the chest.

"Arrgh," he yelled as it hit him.

Too bad the blunt end of the tool was what hit him, but it was enough to put him on his ass.

Alexei was getting up and reaching for a gun too. There would never be enough time to take out both men before getting shot, so I ran past Alexei and struck him hard between the eyes. I didn't have enough time to grab the gun as I saw Lazar's hand coming out of his coat. I was certain that I'd be shot if I waited any longer, so off into the woods I ran, hoping not to hear too many gunshots before I made it into the woods. Using my long-practiced habit of the zig-zagging run, I painfully tried to escape. Unfortunately, the bullets were flying, and I managed to evade all but one of the shots being fired at me. One grazed my side, and, although it hurt, there was no real damage.

I made it in the woods, and the chase was on. Glancing back, I saw Alexei had gotten back in the game too. It was still light enough to see where I was going, but that meant they could too. Trying to look ahead, I almost tripped over a fallen tree but managed to avoid it at the last instant.

The trees in the area were fairly large, and I tried to keep as many of them between me and them as possible. They'd stopped shooting, but I was sure that was only done to conserve ammunition. If I got out of this alive, I'd definitely have to finish the job I'd started. Despite the fact that I came to the shop with no ID, I was sure they would—one way or another—find out who I was and come looking for me.

Taking a moment, I hid behind a large tree and inspected my wound. It hurt a lot, but the bleeding was minimal and didn't need immediate attention. Breathing heavily with my heart thumping in my chest, I looked back to see where they were. A fair distance away, I could see Alexei off to one side, but not Lazar. He was most certainly around but keeping the noise down to keep me unaware of his location. I carefully listened for any sound that would give him away.

Off to my left, there was the snapping of a twig. I ran in a direction that took me away from both of them. The chase continued with me in the open periodically, which allowed the two to follow at a distance, but too far to shoot accurately from. Panting for breath, I constantly looked for a way out. I ended up coming out of a dense section of woods at the edge of a cliff. The drop off at this spot was quite sheer and somewhere near a hundred feet to the bottom.

"Damn, now what?" I muttered.

Listening for sounds, I heard the pursuers come toward me from two different directions. This cut off my escape route, and the only option left was down the cliff, unless I could think of another alternative quickly. They hadn't seen me yet, but that wouldn't last much longer. In a sweat, I pondered what to do.

Come on, think, Joseph. There's usually a way out, think. You need a distraction.

In a flash, it came to me. As quickly as I could, I grabbed a small bush, and after pulling it loose, I tamped down the disturbed soil. Taking off my shirt, I wrapped it around the bush. Over the side, it went. I let out a scream as I tossed a short, thick branch over the side which landed with a thud. Shortly after, the two came running to the edge of the cliff. After taking a quick look around the area, they looked down.

"It looks like he fell off the cliff. I think that's him down by the big rocks at the bottom. Saves us the trouble of having to throw him off," Alexei said, laughing.

"I'm not so sure of this," Lazar said, while they were looking over the side.

I picked that moment to drop out of the large tree behind them. As I was almost to the ground, I shot my arms straight out and knocked Alexei over the side. Lazar reacted almost immediately swinging his gun hand in an effort to strike me with the gun butt. His instincts were better than I had hoped.

Having come down fairly hard caused me to drop almost completely to the ground, and the swing passed over my head. Leaning forward, I sent a straight punch to his groin and swung my free hand up to block his hand from coming down.

As he doubled over, I grabbed his gun hand as my other hand came up and hit him in the throat. The pistol dropped to the ground. Picking it up, I stepped back and waited for him to recuperate enough to have a chat. He kneeled on the soil, holding himself up with one hand.

It took a few minutes before he was able to talk and when he did, he asked, "Why did you come to the shop in the first place?"

"You murdered Dimitri Barinov and one of his children, leaving his wife to raise the surviving three herself."

"He was going to testify against us. We would have gone to prison, and I have no desire to go there," he said.

"Why didn't you just kill him instead of his children?"

"He had to be made an example of, so others would be deterred from doing the same. He left me no choice," he replied.

"You should have killed me when you had the chance, now it is you that will die."

"Surely there is something we can do to work this out. I have money, I could give the wife enough to live her life out in comfort," he pleaded as his hand closed on a fistful of dirt.

Knowing he might try something, I saw this and shot his hand as a way of preventing the dirt from being thrown at me. He screamed in pain, cursing at me in Russian. Enough time had been wasted, so I stood him up at the edge of the cliff. He realized what was about to occur and begged for mercy.

"Sure, you can have mercy," I said as I kicked him in the lower midsection, which pushed him off the cliff. "But not from me."

Looking over the edge, I watched as he flailed his arms and legs in an attempt to right himself, on the way down. After the impact, he lay at the bottom, with his blood staining the rocks. There was, however, one problem that I could see. My shirt was wrapped around the bush lying at the bottom. This would give the police a DNA sample if it was left there, so I looked for a possible way down.

I found the easiest way down a short distance away. Being in pain slowed my decent considerably, but I finally made it to the bottom and retrieved the article of clothing. Making sure the two were dead, I started the hard climb back to the top and headed for the car. On the way back it occurred to me that Ivan had been left by the car unconscious, and I wondered if he was he still there. I took care as I approached the vicinity of the vehicle.

Much to my surprise, I found him sitting in the car still in a daze. I must have hit him pretty hard. There was a look of shock when he saw me with his boss's gun in my hand.

"What the hell? Where are my friends?" he asked.

"Get out of the car and walk," I said, pointing the direction he was to take. This he did, stumbling now and then because of the effects of his head wound. Blood slowly dripped from the cut on his forehead.

When we reached the cliff, I asked him to look over the edge. He did this very reluctantly, and when he saw the two at the bottom, he started to turn around. I picked this time to give him a push that sent him sailing through the air. The sound of the scream and the resulting impact finished my work there.

Having taken the keys to the car from Lazar, allowed me to drive it back to the shop and park it inside. I searched the premises thoroughly. With what I found there and the money removed from the bodies, the total added up to a tidy sum. Collecting my pistol, nunchucks, and everything else of mine, I exited the shop just as the flames caught hold. To get rid of any DNA in the trunk, I poured a lot of gasoline in it.

By the time I was back in my car and driving away, the flames could be seen from a considerable distance. Off to my room I went for some much-needed rest and medical attention. It was dark by that time, and that helped me not to be seen by anyone as I walked to my room.

Except for the gunshot, which I patched up, most of the cuts were superficial. The bruises resulted in no broken bones, so at least I got lucky that way.

By the time I got home, I was pretty sore, and because it was Saturday, I had a couple of days to start recuperating. I contemplated calling Abe the following day, seeing if I could have an unscheduled week off. If I came back to work Monday, there would undoubtedly be questions as to what happened to me. I made the call and was relieved to hear him tell me that, although he needed me for a job, I could have off until Thursday. I planned to relax for a few days at home but wouldn't answer the phone, just in case someone wanted to see me. They could always leave a message if it was important.

Chapter 7

Thinking back, I realized just how lucky I was for having made the alterations to my watch so long ago. The thin plate, with the swinging blade between it and the watch, took some careful work to get right. I had been tempted to remove it because the changes made the watch slightly uncomfortable, but eventually, I got used to it. The predicament I found myself in with the Russians was exactly why I did it in the first place. Without it, I would have been dead by now.

As the week went by, there was a story online about the destruction of the shop, but nothing concerning Lazar and his two associates. That meant they hadn't been found yet, but I was sure it wouldn't be too long before they were.

Having had the extra time off allowed me to heal up, and the pains were subsiding. Since Mike no longer worked there, the shop was running smoothly. The job gave me just enough challenging work to keep it interesting. My sideline had, through the years, made me feel like I had been able to make a difference. So with this in mind, I made another trip to Seattle and found myself parked down the street from the home Dimitri's widow lived in.

The money I'd taken from Lazar, his two men, and his shop was in an envelope beside me. I disguised myself and waited for the right moment to make my move. The lady with her three children exited the building which was located in a modest end of town. As she walked down the street, I intercepted her and handed her the envelope.

At first, she was reluctant to accept it. "What is this? I don't know you, do I?"

"No you don't, but I knew your husband, and I owed him some money. I hope it helps," I said.

There was a look of surprise as she opened it and saw the contents. By that time, I was already walking away but not to my car—not while there was a chance that she could take down my plate number. When she was gone, I left town and went back home, feeling a little better about things.

Despite the fact that I knew I helped people who had been wronged, I sometimes felt conflicted. Maybe it had to do with the fact that I periodically watched Billy or Franklin Graham on the television. Maybe I should quit doing that. The only problem was that there was a nagging feeling deep down inside that I needed to occasionally hear the messages. It was possible that they gave me, at least, some semblance of a conscience. I wasn't sure where I would have been if I had just let loose completely.

I was thankful for people like Harry, Brenda, and Bill in my life, giving me a sense of normalcy. My job had not only allowed me to build many of the devices that were used to eliminate the undesirables of this world but had let me live a partially normal life. A normal life, however, was not in the cards for me—that much I knew.

Every time I had come close, the rug had been pulled out from under me.

With that in mind, I tried to focus on the positives. That last episode taught me once again that proper preparations were necessary. It wasn't the first time I'd almost died, but that one was closer than ever before. When would I learn?

Just to stay on top of things, I kept an eye on my online sites. I had gotten wind of a big meeting, involving the heads of the major crimes families from around the country. Try as I might, I hadn't been able to find out where, or even when, it was to take place. I tried to push the sources, but they claimed not to know the answers.

So with this being a dead end, for the time being, I moved on to other possibilities. Criminals abounded. There were so many choices available. Of course, I only went after the worst, so this reduced the list considerably. There were several suspected rapists, as usual. Drug dealers were also high on my list, and there were even a few that made it to the top ten.

There was a person that piqued my interest greatly. Darrel Thompson lived near Palo Verde, California, along the Ben Hulse Highway. He employed many illegal immigrant workers. The authorities had tried, unsuccessfully, to connect him to the bodies of several workers found dead in the desert.

Apparently, the bodies were found to have been fairly severely hurt by what appeared to be farm machinery. It had been suspected that when the men were hurt on the job, they were driven into the desert and left there to die. It seemed, according to my sources, that it was cheaper to get a replacement than to wait for the person to heal. Anything for a buck. The man had to be cruel, indeed, to just leave someone out in the desert to die of thirst and heat exposure.

Thompson's property was along the Colorado River, which separated California and Arizona. The river supplied his farm with water, which grew vegetables on a large scale for grocery chains. On Google, I saw maps of his farm and the small sheds that the workers lived in. These sheds must have been very uncomfortable in the hot climate. I'm sure he didn't supply air conditioning for them.

I went about the task of gathering more information concerning the situation. Before I made up my mind about how or if I would deal with Darrel, I needed to have all the facts. It wouldn't do to remove someone if the allegations were false. That had been one of my main fears, doing away with someone who was innocent—hence, the in-depth investigations ahead of time.

I found stories about another man who had a reputation for greed and bad behavior. He had been convicted of animal cruelty and abuse of his workers. The underground stories online showed a man with a real mean streak in him. Children's services had been called in on many occasions, and his two offspring had been removed from the home long ago. The youngsters were, by then, adults themselves. The face I saw was a particularly unpleasant one. The man was around fifty-five years old, and I was certain there had to be a history of mental illness there.

I didn't see any dog houses or runs anywhere, but that could have meant they were inside, if there were any. There was very little ground cover, and hiding places were minimal. I had to do a little surveillance to find out his habits so I could figure out the best way to handle the guy. To do it right would require at least a week off, so I started dropping hints at work.

In the meantime, I honed my skills. I took my bow, slingshot, and the .300 Winchester Magnum with the scope and headed far out of town. When I had a good spot, I worked with the bow and slingshot for an hour. Packing those up, I brought out the rifle. After setting up a number of targets at different locations and distances, I went to work. I didn't want to stay there too long, in case there was someone in the area. The place was remote, but you never knew if there was someone around. The warm air blew through the trees with a slight whistling sound. The birds sang for a while until the shooting started.

The sights were set up, and I made short work of the targets. With this out of the way, I packed up and moved to another location. After setting up my hand-held GPS so I couldn't get lost, I did a hard run through the bush. This took another hour, and, by the time I was done, I was good and sweaty.

Taking off my shirt, I doused myself with water. After drying off and changing, I headed home. The phone rang just as I finished eating.

"Hi, Joseph," Bill said. "I've paid a visit to Jeremy Baulthus, looking for Gord. It appears that he left the compound, and nobody knows where he is. One of the girls I interviewed said he mentioned something about a camp. She has no idea where it is, except that it is run by a group of priests from the Catholic Church. I've talked to his parents, but they have no idea where this camp could be. For all anyone knows, he may have gone somewhere else. I'll check with his old drug dealer and see if he has heard from Gord."

"Thanks for staying in touch. Let me know if there is anything I can do."

With this, we hung up, and the next day being Sunday, I decided to go see Ben and do a little riding. Ben and I caught up on things, and soon I was on the trail with my favorite horse. The pace was kept slow as I enjoyed the warm sunshine and light breezes. The golden grasses in the field swayed back and forth as the wind blew across the open meadow.

I used this as a way of putting things in perspective. The ills of the world didn't exist when I was riding. Crossing the field, I headed toward a wooded area. At the edge of the trees, there flowed a small stream. Getting off the horse, I let it get a drink while I sat on the bank leaning against a tree. Opening my backpack, I took out a roast beef sandwich. I could have eaten at home, but things tasted so much better out there. Even the horse enjoyed the apple I brought along for her. This little ritual seemed to make the time there a pleasant experience for both of us.

Continuing the ride, we followed the trails through the woods. Squirrels climbed the trees in order to stay away from us as they chattered away. Birds chirped and went about their business like we weren't even there. A cloud in the sky drifted slowly across the sun, and things cooled down dramatically for a short time. On a trail I knew had no potholes or rocks, I got the horse up to a full gallop. This kept the animal in shape, and I just loved the wind rushing past at high speed.

When the ride was over and I was on my way home, I felt like I had managed to have a good day. Those days helped me get over the ones like I had with Lazar and his friends. I wondered just how long it would be before someone I was attempting to eradicate got lucky and terminated me instead. I'd thought about that many times because I knew it was only a matter of time before it happened. I took precautions and played it as safe as I could, but one day, I was certain, it would come.

With information on Mario Castelli at a minimum, I didn't have enough to proceed. This being the case, my need expressed itself to the point where a visit to see Darrel Thompson was in order. During those times, my mood became irritable and social interaction was stressed.

With my internet hunting done, I had asked for and gotten a week off. As the weekend approached, I prepared all the items I thought I'd need. I looked in my trunk at the hidden compartment. Unless you knew it was there, you would never see it. There was a substantial, recessed lock on it to prevent entry, even if someone were to discover it.

Chapter 8

It took me a little under eighteen hours to drive to Brawley and get a room at the Best Western. The drive usually took a lot out of me, unless I took breaks and went for a run now and then.

I did the usual thing and rented a nondescript vehicle with my fake ID. No one ever questioned the fact that I, now and then, had two cars in the lot, if they even noticed. The one time I was asked, I told the desk clerk that I had to travel to places that I didn't want my own car to go. He left it at that and didn't ask any more questions.

Once I'd settled in, I took a drive out to the district where Darrel lived. The farm was nice enough, considering where it was. The entire region would be a desert if it weren't for the Colorado River. The fields were green and spread over a considerable area. Laborers were in the fields with tractors and hand tools, tending to the crops. Pulling out my biggest binoculars, I scanned the fields and found the man I was looking for.

The men he was talking to kept their heads down, as if avoiding direct eye contact with him. When he walked away, a few of the men stared after him. The expressions on their faces would indicate an underlying feeling of hostility. No sense of comradery was found there, that was for certain.

I wasn't noticed at the moment, but if I lingered too long, I might have aroused suspicion. I stuck around just long enough to get a feeling for the area and then left. The heat of the sun had me sweating, and the air conditioning was needed. Darrel had gone to his house and, it being the hot part of the day, he probably wouldn't be out again for a while.

Coming back after the sun went down, I used the night-vision goggles I had purchased for another job. That episode seemed like a lifetime ago. I drove with the lights out, and when I got to where I wanted to be, I used the hand-operated emergency brake to stop the car and turned it off while in neutral. This way the brake and reverse lights didn't come on, and I wouldn't make my presence known.

The small sheds where the workers stayed were well away from the main house. I had my pistol, double-edged knife, and night-vision goggles with me. Keeping an eye out for dogs, I also had a can of repellant in my hand. The heat of the day had gone, and the air turned nice and cool.

Being careful, I made my way around the house and used the goggles to peer through the windows from a distance until I located him. There didn't appear to be a wife living there, but he did have a Mexican housekeeper. He didn't treat her well during the time I was observing him. As she walked by him, he looked at her in a lecherous way and almost reached out to grab her. Sensing this, she moved away, quickly heading for another room.

He yelled out to her in Spanish, demanding another beer. When she came back, she handed it to him from a distance and disappeared, leaving the house. She quickly walked to one of the sheds in the dark, not coming back out.

I didn't think this man was well loved by his workers. He probably wouldn't be missed if he was gone. I was actually tempted to take him out right then and there, but something in the back of my mind told me to wait. I was certain that the accusations about him were true, but I hadn't seen it firsthand. I usually liked to make sure of this before I made my move.

I felt compelled to do a few days of observations before making up my mind on this one. I had a spot picked out along the river that I could watch from, as long as I had the binoculars and a shelter from the sun with me. Luckily I'd brought the one I used when I visited the Carlos brothers.

The next day found me on the shore of the river with camouflage netting above me. Lying on the fairly steep bank kept me out of sight and still reasonably comfortable after I dug a slight depression in it. My backpack had been loaded with the things I'd need to spend the day there. It took me half an hour to hike there and still avoid being spotted. I didn't feel good about being so vulnerable, but I had little choice. Everything was so flat that the car would have stuck out like a sore thumb.

The day went by very slowly with little happening. It had been hot, and the only thing that helped was the netting over me. It at least somewhat diffused the effects of the sun. In the evening, I moved the rented car closer and used the night vision again. Aside from Darrel trying to grope the housekeeper, nothing much happened. That was, nothing happened until one of the workers, walking in the dark, tripped over a piece of irrigation pipe and fell into a disc parked on the other side of it.

He got up, bleeding quite badly from his forehead and staggered toward the shed he had come out of. Hearing his call, a young man came out, and the injured fellow was taken inside, and the door closed, despite the oppressive heat. At that point, Darrel was unaware of the situation, and I doubted anyone would inform him. It was getting late, and I wanted to be around good and early, so I headed to my room.

The long day and evening in the heat had worn me out, so falling asleep in the air-conditioned room was easy. The next day I was back in position quite early. The men were already in the fields, but Darrel didn't come out until later. He took a head count and realized that he was one man short.

Being across the road, I could barely hear the conversation as Darrel asked loudly, "Where is Jose? Why isn't he working?"

After questioning several of the workers, he wasn't told what he wanted to hear. In a huff, he walked to each of the sheds until he found the one with the injured man, named Jose, in it. He questioned the man—at least it looked that way from a distance. The man came out slowly, and when he got outside, he attempted to pick up a hoe, so he could head to the field.

His hand missed the tool, and he almost fell to the ground. Darrel shouted to one of the workers saying, "Get my truck, I have to take Jose to the hospital."

I ran along the bank to my car, after gathering my things, and waited for him to pull out on the road. Maybe the stories were wrong about Darrel Thompson. If he actually drove the man to the hospital, my work there would be done.

The car had been parked in a spot hidden by brush, and, when the truck passed, I waited until it was almost out of sight before following. Turning on the air conditioning helped cool me down from the bloody hot sun I had had to endure. I hadn't had time to erect the netting because of having to get there so early.

He drove toward town, so maybe the guy was all right after all. I had noticed when he passed me that he was alone with the injured man. I would have thought that there would be someone there with him in case of trouble. The laborer looked like he was hurt quite badly.

When the truck was a few miles from what I thought should be its destination, he made a turn and headed toward the desert. What the hell? I was hoping he was misunderstood, but now? He drove for a long time, with me following at an ever-increasing distance. Using the binoculars to see where he was going, I followed him straight into the desert. It had to be almost fifty miles from anywhere when he finally stopped. The soil there was hard packed and, when he stopped, I continued off the beaten track and parked in a low spot.

Getting out of the car, into the baking sun, I could almost feel my skin sizzle. I climbed the slope just enough to use the field glasses to see what was happening. I saw Darrel exit the truck and walk around to the passenger side. He opened the door and forcibly removed the injured worker from the vehicle. He let the man fall to the ground and closed the door. Briefly, he looked at the man, as he seemed to be pleading with Darrel. Darrel just turned, walked to the driver's side, and got in, driving away.

How in the world can a man do this to another human being? I thought. *This will be a horrible death as he has no provisions. Without water, the man will surely die in a day or two.*

What a stinking low life Thompson was. The reports were true. He had hired illegals, and when they were of no use to him, he discarded them like an old running shoe.

Waiting till the sack of shit was gone, I drove to where the abandoned man lay in the sand. Before I got there, I disguised myself so he wouldn't be able to identify me later on. As I got closer, I saw he had a dirty bandage wrapped around his head, obscuring the vision in one of his eyes. He lifted his head up from the sand with an expectant look on his face. He was unsure if I was his former employer or not. I went to the trunk and removed a blanket to cover the back seat with. Then, very gently, I lifted the man and placed him in the car. Not wanting him to recognize my voice at a later date, I spoke as little as possible.

After giving him a cool bottle of water, I started the drive to town. Seeing Jose was a little better than he had been made it less likely that word would get back to Darrel before I had a chance to chat with him.

I dropped the man off at the hospital in Lake Havasu City. When I knew he would receive medical care, which I ended up having to pay for up front, using most of my cash, I was on my way. I'd have to pick up some more money in order to pay for the room and incidentals. It was a good thing I had a special account and cards for this.

By the time I got back to my room, it was late afternoon. Going for a meal at a local restaurant, I made my plans for the visitation that would be coming shortly. By the time it was dark, I was safely hidden near Darrel's house and waiting for him to be alone. I sat back for the wait in the cool night air.

Through the window, I could see Darrel as he had several beers. He must have liked the stuff a lot because he had quite a paunch on him. Maybe he was drinking more that night because of what he had done earlier in the day.

The housekeeper had left several hours before, and, as it neared midnight, he fell asleep in the recliner. It was time to get on with things, so I made my way over to the side of the house. I listened for any noises that would let me know if someone was around. Hearing nothing but a few insects buzzing around, I slowly opened the side door.

Sticking my head inside, I heard Darrel snoring in the other room. Opening the backpack, I removed the industrial zip-ties. Closing in from behind gave me the opportunity to give him a solid rap on the side of the head with the butt of my gun.

Working quickly, I put the fasteners on his wrists behind his back. A towel from the kitchen was tied around his head, covering his mouth, in order to keep him quiet if he woke up. My car was fairly close to the house, but on the opposite side that the sheds were on. Running to it, as quietly as possible, I drove it to the house.

Since Darrel was a bit of a porker, I worked up a sweat loading the overweight swine into the trunk. Wanting him to feel a sense of irony, I drove to the same place where he left his former employee. My GPS got me there easily. Dumping him out of the trunk and on to the dirt, I positioned his leg on a rock. Using most of my weight, I stomped on it, breaking the main shin bone. By that time, he was awake and screamed with pain.

I usually didn't like doing that kind of thing, but this man had left many people out in the middle of nowhere to die of thirst. In my opinion, he didn't deserve to be treated well. He moaned incessantly and looked at me pleadingly. I think he knew by then that it was time to pay for some of his deeds. I was also sure that, one day, I would have to do the same. I hoped my motives would be taken into consideration when it came time. As the sun started to rise in the sky, I took his gag off.

"Why are you doing this to me?" he asked.

"Because of what you have done to the people you left out here in the desert to die," I told him.

"I haven't hurt anyone. I wouldn't do that. I was falsely accused of those things, I'm a good man. I hire people no one else will, I give them jobs and a place to live."

"So you're telling me, you've never left someone out in the desert to die of thirst?" I asked.

"No, no, no. I have never done something so awful."

"Gosh, I don't know how I could have made such a big mistake. Maybe I should just take you back home," I said, almost sincerely.

"Yes, yes, I won't say anything to anyone. Just let me go."

"Sorry, but I followed you yesterday morning when you left your worker here to die, so I know you're lying. You are an awful person, and now it is time to pay for what you've done. I'm going to give you a choice," I let him know.

"What choice is that?" he asked as he winced in pain when he moved the broken leg.

"I'm going to give you the choice of choosing how you are going to die. I can drive away and leave you here, or I can just shoot you and get it over with. Who knows, maybe you can crawl far enough to save yourself. Maybe someone will drive out here and find you. I doubt this very much, but you never know."

I cut the restraints off and let him sit to ponder his fate. He said nothing, but I could almost hear the wheels turning in his head. It was already starting to get hot, so I asked him for a decision.

"Well, what is it going to be? Do you want me to shoot you or drive away and leave you to die the way you have done to so many?"

"I don't want to die, don't leave me here, please. I will change, I promise."

"No, you won't. You would have changed when you were charged before if you were ever going to. Sorry, but that isn't one of the options. Which will it be?" I asked again.

He lay there and said nothing. I should have left him to die a slow death in the hot sun like he has done to so many innocent people. Unfortunately, I still had some humanity left in me and, despite his deserving to be left here to suffer, this thought didn't appeal to me. I pulled out the pistol, and before he could see me and object, I shot him in the back of the head.

He was a man who had caused far too much pain for others. Not just the ones he left to die, but to the families that never knew what happened to their loved ones. As I drove away, the sun was to my back, and I opened all the windows.

When I first started on Darrel, I thought it was going to take a lot longer. Most of the time when I dealt with someone, I had to be spread it out over many trips. As I was driving, I wondered if there was an heir who would take over the farm. If Darrel had relatives, would they be like him or would they be fair to the workers?

Many people really had it in for the illegal workers, but I wasn't so sure that was totally justified. Who else would work for low wages in the burning sun? I know I sure wouldn't do it. If we didn't have these workers doing the jobs they did, prices for produce would inevitably be higher, and no one wanted to pay more than they had to. There were always at least two ways of looking at things, and I could be completely off the mark here, but I doubted it.

I still had a few days off so, taking my time, I headed toward the ocean and slowly worked my way back home. Stopping here and there gave me the time to disassociate myself with the most recent events. Dealing with the worst people I could find became a second job that required doing periodically. I did this, not for the satisfaction of taking an unworthy life, but for the gratification of helping those who were unable to do it for themselves. Right or wrong, I was pushed into a lifestyle I would never have chosen willingly.

Chapter 9

During the following week, Harry phoned me. It was immediately obvious that the incident with Gord was taking its toll on him.

"We received a call from Detective Henderson. He tells me that he has been unable to locate our son. Since he's eighteen now, he doesn't have to let us know where he is. If he is in a camp somewhere, the people running it won't say anything if he has requested them not to. We have no idea where to go from here."

"I wish there was something I could do for you, but I'm afraid this will have to be dealt with by Gord. You can't force him to do what you know is right, only he can do that. Right after I carried him out of that house when he first started drinking, I noticed the change in him. A few of the guys at work have had the same thing happen with their kids. It has created hardships for a lot of people, as you well know. I never thought it would happen to one of yours. You both raised them so well, and you have nothing to feel bad about in that respect," I let him know.

"I know, but we always second guess ourselves, don't we?" Harry said. "I don't expect you to be able to do anything. I'm just using you as a sounding board. Thanks for being there, Joseph."

"That's all right, Harry, if you need me, just call," I said.

The job had its ups and downs for a couple of weeks. A new employee, Bob, was going around starting trouble. I thought this might be a way of keeping eyes off his work. He did little things behind the scenes. The people involved most of the time didn't even realize it was happening.

The only way I found out about it was that I saw him doing quick chit chats with a lot of the guys. I noticed that Jim, our quality control man, was getting into little arguments with the same guys that Bob had the conversations with.

I called Jim over, and because we had a fair bit of history together, I asked, "What's going on, Jim? The guys seem a bit off lately."

"I don't know why so many of the guys are on edge all the time. I make a recommendation to them, and they kick up a fuss. This never used to happen," he told me.

"Have you been checking Bob's work?"

"I have, and it's okay, but just barely. I've had so many issues with the other guys, that I've let most of Bob's stuff pass, even though I probably shouldn't have," he confessed.

"I think I know what's going on. Let me check Bob's work from now on." I explained my reasoning for this.

When I was done, Jim had a concerned expression on his face. "Should we involve Abe in this?"

"Sure, you go tell him of my suspicions, and that I'd like to try to handle this with as little hoopla as possible," I said.

Just at that moment, there was a PA system call requesting a quality check by Bob.

Good timing, I thought as Jim headed for the office. Gathering my inspection tools, I headed over to see Bob.

He looked at me rather suspiciously. "I want Jim to check my work if you don't mind." With this, he turned his back on me, as if hoping I'd go away.

No such luck.

"He's busy, so I'm going to check your work for the next while," I informed him. "Now what needs checking?"

He looked like he wanted to put up an argument but changed his mind, obviously knowing I was a senior employee who wouldn't take his guff.

Grabbing the print and the piece he had fabricated, I carried both over to the inspection table. That didn't make him happy at all. As I went over every aspect of the work, he started complaining.

"Jim doesn't do all this. Why are you?"

"I'm doing a thorough job because this piece is nowhere near being in tolerance. What made you think this would be passed?" I asked.

"Jim would have passed it."

"Yeah, well, I won't. You have to start over, and if you need help come and ask me," I said.

"I'll get Jim to check it."

"You do that, and I'll call Abe the supervisor in, and you can explain the problem to him. Then we'll go over all the work you've done for the last while and see where that leads us." I smiled, and he knew he had a problem on his hands. "And for your information, you make sure you stay at your station for the rest of the day, no chatting with the other employees."

"Why, what are you getting at?"

"I don't need to explain. You already know why. Call me when you've completed the new part. It should only take half an hour, unless you want my help?" I asked.

He turned to his machine and started working as I walked away. I didn't know about him, but I was having a great time. Forty five minutes later, I went over to see how he was doing. I wasn't impressed much by what I saw.

"I gave you fifteen minutes longer than it should have taken. Is there a problem?" I asked.

"These pieces that were given to me are all wrong. I can't make them work."

"Show me what's wrong with them," I said as I scooped up several pieces.

We headed over to the inspection table, and I checked the parts against the prints. Everyone was well within tolerance. "What is giving you so much trouble," I asked.

He mumbled some stuff and headed back to his work area. It was obvious that the man didn't have the knowledge to do his job. I asked him to wait while I went to see Abe. When I was done, Abe and I gathered some prints and corresponding parts and called Bob into the office.

"Joseph tells me that you're in a bit over your head. Is this true?" Abe asked.

"I never had any trouble when Jim checked my work," Bob retorted.

Jim got called in and asked to assess Bob's work.

"It has always been a bit substandard, but because the shop has been in such turmoil, I've let his work slide. I should have rejected most of it but didn't have the time to keep running back and forth to check his parts," he said.

When Jim left, Abe looked at Bob and told him his services wouldn't be required any longer. Bob was about to say something but knew it was a moot point. Fifteen minutes later, he walked out the door with his tools. Nobody there was too upset at seeing the man go.

The rest of the week went by without any further

problems. The men were back to normal, and work resumed the way it should.

It was mid-summer, and my garden had been doing well. The occasional rain kept things green, and since a few months had gone by, the itch to do some extracurricular activities was building. Darrel Thompson had been found long ago. The police still had no suspects, and the farm was taken over by a nephew. According to reports online, things at the farm were running much better, and the workers were treated fairly well.

While online, I saw a few reports about a construction contractor who was a suspected drug dealer. During hard times, he had been accused of using one or more of his uncompleted renovation projects for the manufacture of illicit drugs. There again was a story of a priest accused of molesting young boys in his charge. There was an attempt to keep it out of the news, but it was revealed, nevertheless, online. That one really got my goat, I wanted to go and fix this problem, so the offender didn't have the ability to reoffend. The only thing that stopped me was the fact that I was raised by my mother to respect the clergy, whether they had earned it or not.

Another story was told of a father brought up on charges of sexually molesting his daughter for years. She, then sixteen when the story hit the airways, committed suicide, unable to endure the public humiliation. The father had been let go because the only person willing to testify was then deceased. I had just found my next target. That type of activity turned my stomach, and since he was out and probably felt he caught a break, his guard would be down.

He had professed his innocence, but the police seemed convinced of his guilt. The person online had a lot of inside information. He put the knowledge to a group that followed these cases through the network. Gathering as many of the details as possible, I started working on a plan to have a meeting with Horace Buchanan. He lived in Santa Rosa, California, on Country Club Drive in a reasonably modest home. There were lots of nice trees in the area, and the properties were well kept.

His home wasn't far from Hall Road. At the intersection, there was a vineyard of considerable size. I wondered if the sprays used on the plants had an adverse effect on the locals because a short distance away was a school and more farms. The district was quite nice and would be a pleasant place to live. That was, it would have been without Horace being here. I wondered if his neighbors tolerated him well.

It took less than nine hours to get to Santa Rosa. I drove around the streets where Horace lived, familiarizing myself with the area. I could smell a faint aroma of insecticides in the air as I toured the suburb. After that, I got a room and a rental car, all with cash and false identification, which I always did.

Getting a good night's sleep prepared me for the day ahead. His car wasn't in the driveway all day or in the evening. I couldn't see any movement in the house that night or see any lights on at any time. I started to wonder if he was even home.

With no other recourse, I came back at three in the morning to investigate. Parking the car in an out of the way spot, I worked my way over to the back of the property, avoiding any properties that likely had a dog. Dressed in dark colors and staying in the unlit areas, I was well hidden. As I got near the back door, I peered through the windows. Not seeing anything, I carefully went over to the side of the garage. With the double-edged knife in one hand and dog spray in the other, I looked through the small window.

To my surprise, I saw a car parked inside. Was it possible that he had gone somewhere and taken a taxi? Going back to the rear, stepping on the gravel, I slowed down, in order to keep the sound down to a minimum, checking the windows and doors as I went. The kitchen was located in the rear, and again, I was surprised when I found that the door was unlocked. Either he was awfully trusting, or he forgot to lock it before he left—if he left.

I was starting to wonder if maybe he had been sick and not left the house, staying in bed the whole time I'd been watching. Taking care, I silently entered the home and slowly worked my way through the kitchen. A bedroom was the next room in line and this I found was empty. Off to the right was the living room, which I was about to forego, until I noticed a form in the darkness sitting in a recliner. Could it be that he had been expecting someone to attempt to exact justice against him? Was I walking into a trap set for another?

Stopping in my tracks, I surveyed the scene. It was then that I noticed a slight odor in the room which had a familiar smell to it. To confirm my suspicions, I had the repellent back in the holder and pulled out a small flashlight in one hand, with my handgun in the other, ready for an attack.

Shining it near the chair but not directly on it, I was able to see my intended target sitting there. Since he didn't move, I shone it on him. Another surprise hit me, because to all appearances, he looked like he was dead. Illuminating the table beside him, I noticed an empty pill bottle and glass. Lying beside him was a piece of paper, folded nice and neat, next to an empty whiskey bottle.

Shining the light around the room first, I walked over to him. I found that he was indeed dead. With my latex-gloved hand, I picked up the note. What I read, explained why there had been no movement in the home.

With the death of my daughter has come the realization of the damage I have done to her. Being left alone, and with all the neighbors harassing me, I feel that there is nothing left to live for. I am so sorry for what I have done.

He had some semblance of a conscience, after all. This came as a bit of a surprise to me. Too bad he couldn't have found it when his daughter was alive. Like many, he didn't see what he had, till it was gone. His neighbors giving him a hard time must have given him that last little push, and that sent him over the edge.

Putting everything back the way it was, I left the way I came. Back in my room, I figured that he must have died earlier in the day. That was why there hadn't been any movement in the home. The smell was the smell of death, which happened when all muscular control came to an end.

The next day, I drove back home in a bit of a subdued state. I recalled all the people I had lost through the years. My mother was taken away at a young age. My father left even earlier and his never having contact with me had left its mark. I'd had to bury two wives and an unborn child. Life, as far as I saw it, had not been good. I wanted, at that moment to lash out, but there was no one to strike against.

Pulling over, I locked the car and went for a hard run, which was the only thing I was able to do right then. Every now and then, things spiraled out of control for me. I had to be real careful not to let it happen. If I wasn't careful, it would take over me. When I was good and tired, I continued the drive, getting home before it got dark. I could have looked at the entire incident as a waste of time, but it had at least put a few things in perspective.

The mood around the shop was normal, and later in the week, I ended up going for a beer with a few of the boys. When I say a beer, that's exactly what I had, a beer. When I was done, they wanted me to have another, but being who I was, and always training to stay in shape, I didn't. After all, the first one took long enough to drink. A second one would have kept me there longer than I wanted to stay. To ensure that I didn't contemplate having a second beer, I always ordered a beer that I was not all that fond of, something with a bitter aftertaste.

Supper was, as usual, eaten alone, but I had long ago gotten used to this. Firing up the computer, I checked up on Mario Castelli. I found that the meeting mentioned earlier in the year was to be held in eight weeks' time. A twinge of excitement hit me. The heads of several crime families were going to be hosted by Mario, but the location of it was still unknown. I tried to find out in as easy-going a manner as I could but found out nothing.

Keeping a low profile would help my chances of success in this endeavor. I didn't know for sure, at that point, whether I would attempt a hit on these men or not. Far too many things had to fall into place yet.

As I was thinking things over, Bill phoned and gave me an update on Gord. "I haven't been able to locate the boy, and I'm starting to think that he left Salem. I've been in touch with Harry and Brenda. They are taking things pretty hard, and although I can sympathize with them, there is little that I can do at this point."

As I sat in a chair, mulling over things, I decided to take my mind off the immediate items affecting me. I picked up a book out the collection given to me by Mark at work. They were written by an author named Isaac Asimov. I'd already read *Caves of Steel* and *The Naked Sun* and been totally captivated by them. The stories had a way of taking me completely out of the present and catapulting me to a time far in the future.

I thought that he wrote around three hundred and fifty

books, an amazing amount. That day, I looked online and found that the number was actually in excess of five hundred books. He was a man who had written in many different fields. To me, that was almost unbelievable. How could one man write so much and still make the stories as wonderful to read as he did?

I hadn't had time to read much for a while and found myself really looking forward to getting into *The Robots of Dawn*. Asimov was the best storyteller I had ever had the chance to enjoy. As the evening progressed, I found myself on a distant planet, in a time when civilization was far in advance of what we lived in. The main character was trying to solve a crime which he felt was far beyond his abilities. I lost track of time, and it was late when I finally got to bed.

The next day found me a little tired at work, with thoughts of being in a far-off future running through my head. When the day was done, I was at home reading again. Soon I was lost to the world. It was almost like being on vacation. For a change, nothing was bothering me, and I was having a ball. I had a feeling come over me like I was actually walking on a different world. The inhabitants seemed close to being real.

Friday evening and back to reality, I checked on the computer to see if any progress had been made as far as finding out the location of the meeting. Low and behold, the place had been narrowed down to two spots. The first was a retreat owned by Mario nestled in the mountains of the Appalachians near the east coast. The second was Mario's yacht, but I didn't know where it was anchored at that point. The search began to get this info so I could do a bit of reconnaissance, just in case that was where the meeting ended up being.

It took two long weeks, on the computer every evening, to find out where the boat was moored. Having finally located the site, I headed to San Francisco and made my way to St. Francis Yacht Club. When I got there, I found that it was the most expensive and elite club in the area. Fabulously wealthy people anchored their prize yachts in the marina. I, of course, couldn't get in, so I didn't even try. I rented a small boat and checked out as much as I could. Just in case things in the area were video recorded, I disguised myself adequately.

The name of the yacht was *Miss Molly*, and she was easy to find. It was one hundred and thirty feet long and about as beautiful as anything money could buy. I couldn't even begin to guess how much the boat cost. I found out that only trusted members of the families would be onboard. One of Mario's sons was to be piloting the yacht. No one who wasn't deeply ingrained in the organization would be anywhere near the boat on the trip. Armed guards were the only extra people who would be onboard, and they would also be taking care of the guests.

It had to be important to these men. Otherwise, they could have met at a home or resort belonging to one of them. I wondered what it was that they would be meeting about. How did a man get to be that rich? He owned so much, and it must have cost a fortune to keep it all going. Oh, well, not my business. I wasn't there to work out that aspect of things.

The yacht was moored in an area with several similar boats. The sea air had a pleasant smell to it as the gulls sailed above me, squawking at each other. There were stains on the walkways from the droppings left behind. The sun shone brightly, and there were only a few clouds in the sky. All in all, it was a beautiful day. I liked being on the water.

The water around these boats was sheltered from the open ocean, but still in a position that would allow them to get to open water quite easily. I thought about it and realized that it could be used to my advantage if I could get all my ducks in a row.

At that point, I didn't know how, or if, I would attempt the mission. First, I'd have to come up with a way for it to be done. I took several photos with the camera Harry and Brenda got me for Christmas two years before. It had a telephoto lens, and I tried to not be too obvious in what I was doing. While I was at it, I took pictures of the entire club.

Taking them one after another, working from one side to the other would allow me to print them out and lay them out on a table. That way I'd have the whole scene before me. There were only a couple of people on Castelli's boat, and they appeared to be a cleaning crew, getting the boat ready for departure.

Just to prepare myself, I checked out the surrounding areas that were adjacent to the club. When I had all the information I needed, I turned in for the day and got back home the following morning. The ride home was uneventful as thoughts of an impending future run through my mind. I wondered if I might be trying to tackle something beyond my abilities.

I'm sure these people had connections in law enforcement and government. Corruption ran rampant through the country. Money paid in large amounts easily bought information and loyalty. I wondered just how much it would take to corrupt an official or a police officer.

I was sure that if I were to leave behind a single piece of evidence, I'd have a hard time remaining free and alive, despite the fact that these people were criminals. Online, I found an update on the meeting. The group was supposed to have their get together in a few weeks, but it had been postponed. The reason why was not given. Now it would happen eight weeks from the present.

That worked out better for me as it gave me a lot more time to prepare and come up with a viable plan of attack. While I was on the internet, I downloaded the layout of the 131 foot Sun Seeker Yacht. Calling it impressive was the understatement of the century. I studied the details and tried to memorize as much as possible. There were numerous staterooms, an up to date galley, and a computer-assisted control room.

The description given said that it was an easy boat to pilot, with all the most -modern features. That must have been why one of his sons could pilot the yacht. Because only seasoned members of the families would be onboard, including the cooks, as everything was to be pre-made and ready to eat. It meant no innocents would be on board, letting me have a wider range of options.

There was no helicopter pad, so once they were out to sea, there would be no way off, except for lifeboats, which were minimal. After studying the control room in depth, I moved on to the galley. After that, I turned my attention to the engine room. I would have thought the engines would all be diesel, but they had smaller gasoline engines included for other purposes.

The beginning of a plan was being worked out in my head. Certain things triggered thoughts from past experiences which would help me with the mission. As the week went by, I set up a board downstairs where I continued to develop the plan. There were things I was going to need, and also abilities I had to acquire, I signed up for classes to help with this.

In less than two weeks, I figured I was good enough to handle the upcoming task. I also continued my training to keep physically fit. With at least six weeks left, I had all the items I needed, and what I couldn't buy, I made. I went over my stock of items several times, in order to make sure I hadn't forgotten anything.

I didn't like the waiting and found myself getting antsy. Because of that, I looked online for a secondary target to keep me occupied. There were several that piqued my interest. Narrowing the list down to two, I weighed the feasibility of being able to complete the job before the big meeting on the yacht, which had, by then, been confirmed.

The first potential was the head of a major corporation. He had spearheaded projects that used natural resources found in pristine areas. When the harvesting was done, the land had been left totally ruined with only minimal efforts made at restoration.

I'd been to some of the most beautiful parks and wildlife refuges imaginable. When I thought of someone destroying these places for the sake of money, it irritated me considerably. I got even more pissed when I found out where the man lived. The trouble was that Malcolm Wright lived quite some distance away, so I'd have to deal with him later.

The other person, who had made life miserable for a lot of people, was an accused drug dealer who manufactured meth and Ecstasy. Some of the products hadn't turned out right, and many young people had died as a result. I still didn't understand the draw of this stuff. If all your friends were doing it, it must be okay, right? Besides, what would be the chance that you'd be the one that got the bad shit? I found some people to be absolute idiots. You'd have to have shit for brains to get involved with some of the crap out there.

After a little research, I found that he had been arrested on a number of occasions. He had even spent time behind bars, but even that hadn't slowed him down much. He must have made a lot of money, because his lawyers, who I'd checked up on, were very expensive. I had no idea where he made his product, and I couldn't seem to get the answers online either.

I'd have to tail him for a while and see if I could catch a break that way. The search helped to settle me down, and I found that I was looking forward to dealing with the lowlife. He lived in Seattle, the same city Lazar did— yeah, did. He no longer lived there. His body and his friends had been found. The authorities hadn't had anything to go on as far as trying to find the person or people responsible, which was a good thing for me.

Marvin Jackson lived on the African-American side of town. Most of the deaths that had occurred involved people of his own race, but not all. He must have had more of a connection with other Blacks, rather than Whites. Most of the information came from online again. In the past, a computer had been the best source to get the inside info from. I learned where he lived and made plans to monitor his neighborhood on the weekend.

Marvin's home was in the central district, and after several hours of waiting, I finally tailed him to the less desirable area away from the downtown. After the knuckle touching, hand slapping routines were done, a little business was taken care of. He went to a few other places in the even-more-undesirable spots around town and finally ended up entering a club. He stayed here until the early morning hours, with me having to wait in the car until he went home. Not wanting to draw attention to myself, I had gotten quite stiff, which would not have been a good thing if I'd been confronted.

After sleeping in the motel room for a while, I parked near his house. Marvin didn't get up until mid-afternoon, and the routine ended up being about the same again. I hung around till late-afternoon and headed home, having learned very little.

During the evenings at home, my plans for Mario and his cohorts were refined. When I got in touch with Brenda, I almost wished I hadn't. She was beside herself with worry and just managed to keep it together. Because of this, my mood went downhill too.

Gord had no idea how adversely his actions had affected the family he'd cast aside. From the conversations I had with him, it was evident that he just didn't care anymore. I had run across this before. Guys at work had gone through similar things, and it left the families devastated. I wasn't sure if it was a sign of the times or if it had been the case for decades. Maybe we just heard about it more now. It made me wonder if it was even a fixable problem.

I had no idea where Gord was, even his sister Eva couldn't locate him. She had asked friends to keep a lookout, with no results. Before he left, Gord took her best things and sold them, in order to support his habit. If he was anyone else, I would have let him go, but I had known the lad for years and wanted desperately to help him. He could be anywhere, at this point, so searching was almost useless.

The weekend found me keeping an eye on Marvin. It was a long two days. When I headed home again, I had little to show for it. The following Saturday gave me the break I'd been looking for. I had to watch from a long way off in order to keep him from spotting me. He at that point, for some reason, had become very wary. Looking over his shoulder constantly, he gave me the indication that he was up to something.

As I followed him through the dirty streets littered with refuse along the curbs, he drove to the outskirts of the city. He parked his vehicle in front of an abandoned building that had some lights on. I thought that the electricity would have been turned off by that time. Maybe a line had been tapped into from a nearby source, so they could cook their crap.

He met several of his friends there and entered the old house. They stayed in there for two hours, with Marvin leaving and the rest staying there. The smell of decaying garbage permeated the air, making the wait even more unpleasant.

After setting my GPS to the address, I followed Marvin back to the center of the city. An old delivery truck was picked up and driven to a few out of the way places. Several pickups were made and loaded into the vehicle. The truck with its cargo was then driven back to the house I'd tailed him to earlier, on Buford Road, and unloaded. I could see why he picked this place. There were no neighbors, and the place was out of the way. The fact that it still had power made me curious.

It was obvious that a batch of illicit drugs was being cooked up. Being late, it was time for me to get back home. On the way, I started brewing a plan to deal with Marvin. I'd seen him intimidate people and beat up on those he had an argument with. The man had a vicious side to him, but then again, would you expect anything different from that type of person? The welfare of his fellow man would be the last thing on his mind.

There was still around four weeks to go before Mario had the meeting on his yacht. I found out from the source that it was going to be piloted into the open ocean into international waters where the coastal authorities would not be able to bother them. Maybe that would give me a bit of leeway in how I could handle the event.

With two missions on the go at the same time, I'd have to be careful. Normally, I didn't do two at once, and it made me wonder if it was a good idea or not. Marvin could wait if it became necessary. For the time being, I planned to proceed, but if any real doubts came up, it would have to be postponed.

When I had the opportunity at work, I made up a couple of items that could be used on the Mario job. I hadn't nailed down the exact method yet, but the things would give me more options to choose from. Having studied the entire structure and operating features of the yacht in detail, I had a few ideas. The job gave me a sense of challenge, which I liked.

The scuba diving lessons I'd signed up for were done. Taking the crash course gave me enough training to do the job, and, hopefully, keep me out of trouble. While I was at it, I brought my swimming abilities back to peak levels. All my rigorous physical training allowed me to swim underwater for longer distances than the ordinary person could. Being in the condition I was in, and all the training I subjected myself to, had in the past saved my life more than once.

The time flew by so quickly that I didn't have time to go to Seattle. Things came up during the next two weekends. Since I would be taking a week off when I went to San Francisco, it became necessary to postpone the visit concerning Marvin.

Working in my basement, getting things together, I found myself in need of a few specialty items. Online, I found outlets in town where I could purchase them. Being disguised and paying in cash gave me the anonymity necessary to make identification impossible. Buying extras of everything, allowed for a mistake to be made, without me having to purchase replacements.

The time came closer and closer. Taking weekend trips gave me a better knowledge of the area and potential mishaps. Just for insurance, I took the scuba gear I rented and did a swim in the club's waterways. Staying out of the places where boats could go, I used an underwater flashlight to do an inspection of the underside of *Miss Molly*. Being careful not to allow the light to hit the surface, I looked for the portion of the hull I might be required to use. The water was cleaner than I had anticipated, but not clean enough for me to be seen from the surface.

When I found what I needed, it took a minute to get my bearings again. Visualizing the position of the yacht, and where it was in the harbor, allowed me to find my way out. If I were to surface in order to get my bearings, it would be entirely possible for me to be seen. I was sure an alarm would have been raised and bring about trouble I couldn't afford at that point.

The meeting on the yacht was to take place in two weeks, on Saturday afternoon. I would have to have all the preparations completed well before that. There would be people on board setting up things for most of the week I was fairly certain.

Taking that into account, I asked for and got a week and a half off. The time should allow me to do the necessary prep-work. My tasks would have to be done the week before the boat was made ready for the short voyage. The main thing that disturbed me was that my prep work could be vulnerable to discovery if there was an in-depth search done. Of course, they would have to know what to look for and where to find it, in order for anything out of the ordinary to be found.

As the time to leave on this so-called vacation got closer, I started getting on edge. It took a lot of effort to keep from letting it be noticed by my coworkers. I'd never undergone a venture like this one before, and there were too many things that could go wrong. If caught, I was sure they would have methods of extracting information from me. That was something I didn't look forward to at all. It's not like I had a cyanide capsule available to me, like the spies in the movies did. Finally, Friday was there, and I was on my way.

Chapter 10

After getting a room nearby and a rental car, I settled in for a day or two in order to wait for the best moment to initiate my plan. From a distance, sitting on a bench behind the shrubbery, I kept an eye on the yacht on Saturday. Using my long range binoculars, I could see what was going on during the day. Going for the occasional walk allowed me to stay limber. Having a large tote bag on the bench dissuaded anyone from sitting on it, providing me with the freedom to continue the surveillance. There was a crew doing a thorough wash up of the entire boat, taking care of every detail.

No expense was spared, nothing but the best for this group of passengers. After all, these were very important people deserving of respect, at least in their eyes. The surveillance used up two days for me.

During the evening there was someone on board till ten p.m., and, after that, it appeared that the yacht was deserted. Sunday afternoon, the crew finished everything they had to do and left.

I had been concerned that someone would be on board twenty -four hours a day, which would have complicated things. With the security at the club making the rounds at intervals of one per hour, it looked like the owner thought extra security was unnecessary.

For what I had in mind, it was going to take more than one boarding. I picked up a waterproof bag that I loaded several things into. The boat was docked with the bow toward the clubhouse and security office. At the stern of the vessel, there was a small platform that allowed me a spot to gain entry to the lower section.

Waking at three in the morning on Monday, I made my way to the jump-off area. Changing into the scuba gear, I made the final preparations and got on my way. Slowly I swam to the end of the docks in the warm water. I held onto a rock at the entrance to the marina until the security man did his walk around. I looked around carefully to make sure no one was out for a stroll. Seeing nothing of interest, I made the rest of the journey underwater.

Knowing the direction and distance I had to swim got me to the stern of the vessel easily enough. The bag was quietly placed on the platform. I did my best to see if there was an extra security system on board. Having studied the lock system online, I used my slip tool to open the lock and then swung the door inward. When no alarm went off, the tanks were removed and hung on a hook inside. The hook must have been used by passengers to hang gear on if they wanted to do some diving, once moored in a suitable spot.

I didn't have a diving suit on so while I was on the platform, I dried off, using a towel in the bag, so there wouldn't be any drips left. Picking up the bag and placing the towel under the hanging tanks, I headed toward the lower level and the engine room. My ears were perked, listening for any sounds of company. Studying the room and locating what I wanted, I got to work with phase one of the plan.

Having gone over the layout of the yacht from online prints, I moved to the fuel tanks. There was one very large one, which held the diesel fuel, and after doing my work on it, I was on my way to the next project. I had brought a series of wires and metal and plastic tubing with me. After locating the lines that fed the gasoline-operated engines, I went to work. In a place totally hidden from view, I made a few alterations, using the accessories I brought with me.

Taking great care to make certain that none of the modifications were visible, I tucked the wires behind the pipes and used putty to secure them out of sight. The next task was a little more difficult, as I had to gain access to the space between the floor and the hull. There were several access plates that needed to be undone. Not knowing which tools would be required, I'd brought several with me. Luckily, I had a socket set with me and the right size socket.

If I hadn't had the right one, I would have had to put that part of the job on hold. As it was, I still had to make a change that could be seen if someone were to look closely. I ran the small diameter copper tube into the gap between the floor and hull along with the wires.

With a small hacksaw, I cut a tiny slot on the edge of the cover plate, as close to a support post as I could, and then replaced it. Looking at my handy work, I wasn't happy with the results.

"Damn, if someone looks at it, they'll know I've been here. I'll have to fix it. The changes are too obvious and stick out like a sore thumb. I'll have to come back with something to paint the tube and wires," I mumbled.

What I used had to be odorless, despite the fact that there was already some engine smells down there. Anything new would be evident to anyone familiar with the area. I was sure there would be an inspection done before the yacht and passengers got underway.

Before leaving the boat, I checked for cell phone reception. It was not great, but it was acceptable. I had done a check online before I went there to see if that was the case and was happy to have confirmation. With this done, I got on my way. I was tempted to take a stroll around the upper areas, just to see what it was like, but thought better of it.

Making absolutely sure that there were no telltale signs of my presence left behind, I left the boat after using the towel to dry off the rear platform. When I got back to my room, it took quite some time to relax enough to fall asleep. I knew I was fortunate that there had been no one on board because some of the changes I made were not done in total silence. If there had been anyone on board, they might have heard me. But then again, I would have changed the way I did things.

In the morning, getting out of bed was a bit harder than usual. The night before had left me short on sleep.

I went to a Home Depot and checked the colors of latex paint, matching it to the photo on my cell phone. I got the smallest amount I could and a tiny brush to apply it with. The paint was quick drying, and I made sure it was completely odorless.

Three in the morning came far too quickly. It took a while to rouse myself properly and get back in the water. All dried off, I waited and listened for any noise or sign of occupancy. Finding none, I headed once more to the engine room and the fuel storage area. Once satisfied with the cover-up, I turned and started back to the stern of the yacht. Out of the corner of my eye, I saw a glint from the flashlight hitting something. Walking over for a closer look, I found a tiny piece of wire that had bounced to the floor when I cut it. Not a big deal but still a sign that I had been there, so it had to be removed.

Looking carefully before I exited the door at the rear platform, I saw some movement. Gently closing the door, I waited for any sign that I had been spotted. Prepared to lash out, I sat with my ear to the door. Faint footsteps sounded from shoes hitting the concrete dock.

It was a good thing I had dried up water on the platform before I entered the yacht. It would have been a dead giveaway if the guard saw water there. Footsteps stopped for a moment as the security guard stopped and turned around, heading back the way he had come. It was necessary to stay put for five minutes. When I was sure that the way was clear, I slid back into the water with the mask and scuba gear on.

Carefully, I used the waterproof light to find my way under the boat. After locating what I was looking for, I finished the last of the preparations. That final phase took almost half an hour, as I worked under various parts of the hull. With a sigh of relief, I drove back to the hotel.

The part of the job that left me feeling a little uneasy, being in the lower section of the yacht, had stressed me out. I'd had too many close calls during those moments when I was under cars or in places where I'd been completely vulnerable.

Phase one of the job ended up being finished a little earlier than I had anticipated, so I headed back home on Wednesday. Calling Abe, I told him I'd be back to work a little earlier than I first thought.

"Oh, why is that?"

"I was visiting a friend, and he got called into his job because of an emergency, so here I am. I told him I'd go back to see him this coming weekend. If it's all right with you, I told him I'd try to stay a day or two longer then. Is it all right with you?" I asked.

"Seeing as how you've come back ahead of time, I don't see a problem with it," Abe replied.

The two days went by fast enough, and Friday evening I was driving back. The meeting was going to start the next day, and I planned to be in the area. I finished the drive to San Francisco, getting there quite late, and going to bed as soon as I got a room. Of course, sleep was a bit elusive, but came eventually, so I slept in later than normal.

The next morning when I finally woke up and had breakfast, I watched the yacht through the binoculars. Late morning saw several of the passengers arrive and go aboard. The men were treated with great respect because of who they were. There was a real arrogance about them as they boarded. You would have thought that they were celebrities, the way they acted. By late afternoon, they were all aboard and, when everything required had been loaded on the yacht, preparations were made to cast off. There was a bare minimum of a crew, and everyone unnecessary had disembarked.

The boat, maybe because of the inexperienced pilot, was pulled out of the dock area by a tug-style boat. When it had been turned toward the open ocean, the engines spun the props as the yacht moved slowly and smoothly away from shore. Possibly with the reduced number of crew members and the fact that the pilot was Mario's son, this seemed the safer way to proceed.

I had already rented a nice size boat—equipped with radar, GPS, and a cuddy—well ahead of time. I had supplies for several days, just in case I needed them. Along with me, I brought a few of my toys, in case of trouble.

The yacht was heading toward the open ocean under its own power. The weather for the next several days was supposed to be pleasant. Using the electronics, I'd be able to keep track of the yacht. I hoped that none of the subordinates were in boats tagging along behind for long-distance protection of the family heads. This could have very well complicated things.

The boat I had rented was a twenty one foot Seaswirl Striper. It was a well made beautiful boat, with a two fifty Yamaha motor. The boat was easy to handle, and I headed in a direction slightly north of where Castelli's yacht was going. The water was fairly smooth, and the boat glided over the surface with ease. I opened the front screen, and the warm ocean air blew through the cabin.

After several hours, the boat had made a fair bit of headway. The trip was, as I'd been informed, supposed to take four days. That would give me plenty of time to complete my plans. As far as I had estimated, the trip should take around six hours before the engines were shut down and the boat allowed to drift.

When the diesel engines were started, an electric current was sent through a newly installed wire to a small reduction transformer. As soon as that happened a switch was activated that started a battery -operated flow switch. The unit would automatically shut down when its task was completed.

This had started the first part of the plan. It was also the crucial portion. Without that working right, other things would have to be done by a secondary plan which wasn't as reliable. I hoped that all the hookups I made were done properly. Things would be questionable as to whether or not the mission would succeed if they weren't. At that point, some of the other mechanisms should have been activated and set in motion too.

At the four -hour point, I sped up and got within two miles of the boat. Being that far away, I could keep an eye on things without being spotted myself—hopefully.

The sun was quite warm, and the time passed slowly as the boat I was in gently rocked. I was waiting for the six-hour point when things should have begun to happen. Many doubts came to my mind as too many things could have gone wrong at that point. If even one of my devices was found, a thorough search would take place, and most of my plan would then probably have fallen apart.

According to the radar unit, there were no vessels in the vicinity, which at least was good for me. The boat I was on had extra cans of gasoline, so I'd be able to get back to shore if I had to spend too much time going to and from the yacht. As I looked at my watch, it showed that one more hour had to pass. That time passed by even slower than the previous hour had. The wait seemed to take forever. The seconds ticked by as I looked at the watch every few minutes.

Fifteen minutes to go. My hands were starting to perspire, and I was getting on edge. You would have thought that I'd gotten used to this long ago. The minutes ticked by slower than a snail going uphill.

Ten minutes left, and I was pacing back and forth. Five minutes, and I had the binoculars to my eyes, peering at the boat in the distance. When a small wave had me going up and down, the curvature of the earth made the boat disappear for a moment.

The last minute passed as I counted down the seconds. Straining my eyes, I saw nothing happening. One minute passed. Two minutes passed. Five minutes passed. What the hell was going on? Fifteen minutes passed, and, still, nothing had happened. I was starting to think the whole thing was going to be a bust as my mood started to spiral downward. I'd have to put the secondary plan into motion if nothing happened soon.

By that time, a fair amount of the gasoline should have leaked out of the tanks. Unless discovered, it should have been working its way between the floors and the hull long ago. That was if all had been done properly and worked the way it was meant to.

"Why has nothing happened yet? Have I done it wrong? I thought I was so careful. Crap, I'm going to have to see if the alternate plan works," I said loudly.

One second nothing, then there it was. I saw the smoke before I heard the noise of the explosion reverberating across the water. When the bilge pump kicked in to pump out the gasoline in the hull area, the new wires I'd spliced in carried the current to other devices. The next part of the plan had then come into play. The sound of more explosions, somewhat softer, came across the water several minutes later.

The secondary explosives had gone off, and, as they should, blew holes through the hull at various places. These had been spaced far enough apart to cause the vessel to start sinking quickly.

Flames poured out of the openings in the boat. Smoke rose into the air as the yacht listed slowly over to its starboard side. I guided my boat, closer to the yacht, keeping an eye on the radar and GPS screens.

So far nothing was in the surrounding waters. Everything on the yacht was happening quickly. If anyone had been attempting to use the life rafts on board, they were in for an unpleasant surprise. I had slit the outer sides so they wouldn't inflate.

The bilge pump must have done its job and activated timers which set the whole scenario into motion. The timing was close to what was planned, but the delay was nerve-racking.

As I approached speedily from a distance, the yacht slipped under the surface of the ocean in slow motion, creating a wave like a big stone thrown into a pond. I saw a few people bobbing up and down in the water, waving for assistance. I guided the boat I was in to intercept them and give them my help.

When I was close enough, I saw the people in the water were mostly overweight Italians.

"Help me, I can't swim too good. The boat, she sink. I need a you help. Why you have a gun in your hand?" one man asked.

"This is how I'm going to help you, you stinking Mafioso," I shouted back as I pulled the trigger.

They called to me for help, expecting me to take them to safety. Instead, I shot each of the survivors, having to reload several times. Their fancy suits didn't look as good wet as they did when they were dry. It took almost ten minutes to finish that part of the plan. When I'd checked every piece of floating debris and was certain everyone had been taken care of, I opened the throttle full and, with a roar of the motor, headed out to sea.

Traveling close to five miles, I turned due north and traveled for around ten miles before turning to starboard and heading back toward land. If a distress call had been made by the crew of the yacht, the coast guard would most certainly have been coming from land. Going to the open sea first would have kept me from being seen.

All told, going by my count as the heads of the families and the few extra people came aboard, there was a total of twenty-four people on the yacht. I doubted there were any survivors. With these men gone, I was sure new people would be jostling for position within the criminal empires. Maybe the power struggles would cause several more people to be killed. One could only hope. The more that died, the merrier—for the rest of the world, at least. These people were a scourge in the world, but far from the only ones.

Once I was near the coastline, I used the extra gasoline containers I brought on board to refill the tank part way. When I was close enough to shore, I threw the empty cans on the beach. That way there was little evidence that I went very far out on the ocean. I learned long ago to play it as safe as I possibly could.

When I brought the boat back, there was quite a commotion on the docks as word of a disaster out at sea spread. The information at that point was sparse. I should have felt bad at that time, but I didn't. I used to, but that was long ago. The people I eliminated were vile and stopped at nothing to get what they wanted. They didn't belong in a world with decent people. I found that I had grown callous through the years. I wasn't sure that it was a good thing. I hoped that I didn't become totally insensitive in my endeavors to correct what I believed were the wrongs of this society. Too many had taken what had been so important to me. They hadn't cared a damn about how it would affect me, and when they were taken out, I cared little about them.

The next day, I traveled north, slowly working my way toward home. It was Sunday, and so I decided to take the extra time to relax a bit. Stopping in a small town, I went for supper in an upscale restaurant, enjoying a meal by myself. That had become the way my life was, alone.

Back at home, the car was unloaded. When that was done, sitting on the couch, I watched the news to see if the story I was looking for was aired. It was, but little information, other than the sinking, was known. All I really found out was that a very expensive yacht with questionable passengers had gone down thirty miles offshore. By the time the coast guard made its way to the scene, the boat had sunk, and the only people found were dead. No details were given and no names mentioned. There was no mention of the deceased having been shot. Maybe that had been withheld to trap any suspects.

Castelli and friends were one group I had been a little hesitant to tackle. The only reason I did was the fact that there was the meeting so far offshore. So many things could have gone wrong, but, fortunately, everything went right. The main thing that started it all was the small electrically operated valve. I had tied it in with the fuel line exiting the gasoline tank, after temporarily closing the shutoff valve.

The crew never knew that, when the engines were started, they inadvertently started the gasoline flow. The valve and tube through which the gas flowed out were a quarter inch in diameter. This caused things to progress rather slowly and gave the fuel time to make its way along the hull between it and the floor. By the time enough was let out to activate the bilge pump, considerable time had elapsed. There was a timer-activated backup system, so which one actually caused the gas explosion, I would never know for sure.

Well placed grenades against the inside of the hull finished the job. These had a string tied to a spring that was kept stretched until the fire burned the string, releasing the springs to pull the pins out. Everything hinged on the gasoline leaking and then exploding, causing the rest to happen.

The backup system I had in place to activate the planted mechanisms used radio frequency remotes. That was a system that I hadn't used before, so I wasn't certain it would work as a primary. The manufacturer claimed it could be used to operate the devices that were not line-of-sight activated. These could be used through walls and hulls. The thing I was not sure of was how close I had to be to make it work, and I might have had to move closer to use them.

Despite this, things went well, and no one had a clue that I was involved in any way.

Chapter 11

In my spare time, I developed a small catapult. This could be used to throw a hand grenade quite a distance. As the spring-loaded arm swung, the pin was pulled by a hook anchored to the base. That job reminded me that I needed to get in touch with the man who had supplied me with them in the past. When I reached him, I ordered two dozen. I was quite sure it must have raised some eyebrows, but it was all done anonymously, so it didn't matter.

While I was at it, I ordered a few other items too. The incendiary bullets for the rifle came in real handy when I dealt with the Carlos Brothers. I hadn't replenished my supply since then.

Later in the week, I found out that Gord had apparently disappeared, and no one had heard from him in some time. Bill Henderson had been to see Jeremy Baulthus several times, with nothing to show for it. Where on earth Gord had disappeared to was a mystery. For the umpteenth time, I wondered what had gotten into the nice young lad I knew.

It was frustrating me a bit to have my friends so upset about their son disappearing. My not being able to do anything about it was not the way things had gone in the past. I would have liked to pay Jeremy a visit myself but realized that if Bill got nothing, I probably wouldn't either.

To relieve some of the feelings of uselessness, I started a new project. I began investigating Malcolm Wright and the corporation he was CEO of. Like many, or most, corporations, these people cared nothing for the environment. They were there to make a profit from it and nothing else.

As I viewed the websites of several groups that were concerned about the way the planet was being abused, I was shocked. The photos of sites, before and after the resources were taken, were absolutely appalling. Land that was once pristine had been turned into little more than a wasteland, with only a few new trees planted. Some of the places they had destroyed they had been ordered by the courts to fix, but it never looked the same. The corporations had interests around the world, not giving a damn about the impact made on third world populations. The rainforests of South America were a prime example.

One of the worst offenders I found was Global Provider, a company that prided itself on being one of the most innovative resource extraction firms in the world. A picture of a smiling Malcolm Wright was in the forefront, and behind him, the devastation left after his company had finished with an area. That photo was not one from Global Provider's files, but one superimposed over the other by the writers of the damning articles.

In another picture, Malcolm's wilderness retreat was shown. A magnificent property and fantastic home appeared on the screen. A custom built twelve-thousand-square-foot home sat on a rise on a plateau. The plateau was on top of a small remote mountain, and the level land itself was reported to be around a mile in diameter.

The slopes of the mountain up to the flat land were rock and free of much growth. The plateau, however, was covered in forest and cleared around the massive home. A helicopter pad was built in the courtyard because the home was otherwise relatively inaccessible.

There were other pictures that had been taken from *Homes of the Upper Class*. They showed the inside of a home built to a standard far above the norm. The opulence was so far over the top it was actually obscene. The view offered by his piece of paradise was absolutely magnificent. It overlooked the entire countryside from its perch far above the common people. Water for the palace was pumped up from a lake, far below the plateau, by generator-driven water pumps. Large solar panels had been erected to supply much of the energy consumption. Batteries were kept charged for times when the sun had set.

It was reported that Malcolm was due to retire, with a huge package, in the next two years. *Forbes Magazine* listed the man as one of the many elites in America. It would be a bit of a trip to get to the Adirondacks. Although his property was out of the way, it wasn't far from civilization, at least not far by helicopter.

As far as I knew, he hadn't killed or caused another person to die. But there should be a price to pay for his unbridled greed. I'd give it some thought and do more research. Maybe he was more accessible, closer to where I lived.

The headquarters for Global Provider was in Washington, DC, with offices scattered around the country and the world. I had no desire to pull off any ventures in the nation's capital, so I had to find a more suitable location. Washington was, however, where he spent most of his working time, and he owned a high-end residence in DC too. The area his home was situated in looked like a district of very influential people. I was sure a lot of the residents in the area had security personnel with firearms who communicated with each other. That could hamper an escape if I was pursued, so that place was out.

This triggered a train of thought. What did I really have to live for at that time? I went fishing now and then with Bill, but when I looked closely at the relationship, we were just friends. Harry and Brenda along with their kids, were fairly close at one time, but that had subsided. There were no female companions in my life, and I was afraid to get one. All my close relationships had ended in tragedy. So what was the purpose of my life? There really wasn't anything, except my pastime.

I tried to correct some of the ills of the world. I felt alive when I was on one of my missions, but that ended soon after it was over. I wondered where I would be in five years. What else did I really have but death? Wow, that line of thought was dragging me down, big time. Except for killing murderers, I didn't have anything of importance left in my life. Shit.

I wondered if things would have been different if I had been home the night my mother was attacked. Thinking back to when the storm was going to hit Salem, maybe if I'd gone home before it hit, Amy would still have been there. Why did I not stay home when Kathleen announced that she might be expecting? All the choices were made, and, no matter what, I couldn't undo them.

Inside, I felt empty. All I saw was the shell of a man standing there in front of the mirror. The memories that I should have had were gone. The life which was so good came to an abrupt end, taken by a man who himself had died. The payment was not enough but would have to do because there was nothing left that could be done to increase the price he paid. The choices were made in life and, once made, you had to live with the consequences. There were no do overs.

I went to bed early that night. Depression was taking hold of me. At work, I snapped at one of the guys I liked and found myself having to apologize. At that time, I was unsure of how to get out of this funk.

Jim saw this and said, "Hey, buddy, what's wrong? You're really out of sorts. Have you ever thought that you should start dating a bit? I know, I know, you haven't had the best results when you've been married. You don't have to get married to a woman in order to enjoy her company."

"I haven't got much in common with any of the women I've seen in a long time. I keep comparing them to Kathleen, and everything goes downhill from there."

"That may be the problem. Stop comparing and just enjoy their company. Don't look at it in a long-term light. Just go out and have some fun. A lot of guys find dates online with people that have similar interests," he said, laying a hand on my shoulder.

A look of revulsion must have crossed my face.

"No, no, it's not as bad as all that. I have friends that have met some really nice girls this way," he said, almost laughing at me. "Think about it, what do you have to lose?"

"I'll think about it, but I'm not promising anything," I said it to get him off my back. I had no intention of looking for a date on my computer.

With the day finished, I headed home to an empty house. I'd gotten used to it a long time ago, but today it seemed different.

I wasn't even sure what started me down this road, but there I was nevertheless. With my mood sinking, what I'd done in the past was go for a grueling run.

Baskette Slough Wildlife Refuge had always been a favorite place of mine to get away from it all. Today it just wasn't cutting it. As I pushed myself harder and harder, I found that all I was doing was wearing myself out. By the end of the run, my mood was still the same.

It seemed like, no matter what I did, the depression had taken hold of me, and there was no way out. After a few more incidents, Abe called me into the office and expressed concern.

"Joseph, what's happening to you is that the tragedies in your life have finally taken their toll. It was inevitable that this would happen. I suggest that you go for some counseling and maybe medication is required to help you through this time."

"Look, Abe," I said. "I've been for counseling and dealt with all this stuff long ago."

"Sorry to have to inform you, but it's come back, and you need to deal with it. The guys in the shop are starting to feel uncomfortable working with you. They remember how you've handled some of the bad employees we've had and are a bit nervous. You're not yourself, and you have to see this. Make the appointment, please. You're too valuable to the company to have you in this condition," he said.

Taking the rest of the day off, I drove to a secluded spot and thought over what Abe and Jim told me. I felt like crying but couldn't. There was anger in me I had no control of, and it was ready to explode. Most things in my life had gone to shit. No matter what I did about it, the end result had almost always been the same.

I was alone and always would be. Going for counseling should have fixed it. What the hell, why was I like this? I didn't see anything much to hang around for. It all started with my mother, and, no matter how I made bastards pay for what they did, my life was still the same. Why was I here?

Going home I tied one on. That was something I rarely did. By the end of the evening, the thought of where I ended up after Kathleen's death sobered me somewhat. At that time, I was a drunk and almost ended my own life. I had no desire to be a drunk again, so I poured the rest of the alcohol down the drain.

It was Thursday, and I'd called Abe, letting him know I wouldn't be in for the rest of the week. Picking up the phone, I called Don Adams, the counselor I saw after Amy's death. I asked if we could have a talk, letting him know things had spiraled out of control. He set up an appointment for the following afternoon.

In the past, I had taken up horseback riding and called ahead, letting Ben know I'd be there shortly. Saddling my own horse created a closer bond with my favorite horse, and, when everything was all set, I took the animal along the trails. It didn't take long to realize that this wasn't helping me either. I got irritated with the animal over absolutely nothing. It was time to call it a day only half way through the ride.

I told Ben something had come up, and I left without unsaddling the horse. At home, I found that the only thing helping me was to have a workout that involved the heavy bag. I pounded away on it till I couldn't pound anymore.

How on earth did it hit me so fast? It seemed like one day I was good, and the next I was completely off track. I went to bed early again and woke up in the middle of the night with a scream.

The nightmares were back. I was being chased by many of the same people I'd eliminated. Heinrich's Doberman finished me off when it latched onto my throat. I got caught in the bathroom by the Klan and fitted with a noose. Finally, I was caught by Bill and sent to prison myself. It turned out to be a long, long night.

Don Adams saw immediately how bad a shape I was in. Because he had no appointment after mine, he kept me talking for two hours. I still wondered how his pencil neck held up that oversized head.

"Joseph, I had no idea that you remarried and moved away. Tell me about what went on after you left Salem."

This I did, and as the story unfolded, I saw the expression on his face change from concern to one of shock. I babbled on about how I ended up at the point where an intervention had to take place. By the time I was done, Don said, "I can't believe how so much can happen to one individual. You have had more tragedy than any three people I have helped."

The two hours went by, and I already felt like the burden had been lightened. Because of the severity of my case, Don had me come back on Monday for another two-hour session. I called Abe, "Abe I'm in counseling and need a little time off. It shouldn't be very long, but I do need it."

"I suggest you take a paid medical leave for two weeks. It will not affect your vacation time, and the company feels that we owe you this for all the times you went to bat for us. Call me when you're time is almost over."

"Thanks, Abe, I'll keep you informed," I said, feeling a relief inside me like a pressure had been released.

Chapter 12

The two weeks went by with me having a total of seven double sessions. Don managed to help me put things back in perspective. I'd been journaling again, and I felt like a new man. It was the second time he pulled me back from the abyss, and I felt I owed him. With the sessions over, I got a gift certificate at an upscale restaurant and mailed it to him. I know he got paid to do what he did, but I felt he had gone over the top for me.

Back at work, I apologized to the men I'd offended and thanked Abe for his help. It didn't take long before things there were back to normal, and I actually started thinking of Malcolm Wright. I'd taken enough time off for the present, but I started looking into ways of dealing with him sometime in the future. I was surprised at how I began looking forward to helping Malcolm pay his debt to society. He did live quite a distance from Salem, so, for now, I needed to find a target closer to home.

I believed that having things back to normal brought back the old Joseph. I was ready to get back into the business of taking out the undesirables. I felt good and was itching to get back into the game. My rigorous training started again, and I even went horseback riding again.

Jim asked me if I ever went online to any of the dating sites.

"I've had so much bad luck with women, I think I might try going gay. What do you think, buddy?" I said as I put my arm around his shoulders.

A look of shock crossed his face. At this, I started laughing hysterically. He realized that I was having one over on him. Gay was the last thing I wanted to be. I didn't care what others did, that lifestyle wasn't for me. As long as they didn't hurt anyone else and stayed the hell away from me, I probably wouldn't hurt them.

A look of relief came over him as he saw he had been taken in. "I guess this means you're not interested in online dating right?" he replied as I smiled an affirmation. Deep down, the thought did cross my mind.

That evening, just for the heck of it, I went online and checked out a site. The one I landed on was called Happy Once More.

Just to see what it was all about, I signed up and, once all the questions were answered, my file was uploaded. A few days later a number of hits showed up. Reading all the responses, I narrowed the choices down to one. A date was made for Friday evening.

I made a copy of the lady's photo, so I'd recognize her when we met.

When I walked into the restaurant, I looked for a young woman who was five foot eight and around one thirty in weight. Her hair should be blonde and shortcut. Looking around, I figured that I must either be early or the lady changed her mind. I moved over to allow a woman to pass, who I figured was going to the bathroom. Instead, she stopped in front of me and introduced herself.

What the hell, this woman looks very little like the photo I have in my hand, went through my head.

"Hi, I'm Sarah, you must be Joseph," she said as I looked at her, stunned.

The woman was close to forty pounds heavier and at least ten years older than the person I was expecting. I showed her the photo and asked, "Is this supposed to be you?"

"Oh, sorry, I haven't had time to get a new one taken."

"I'm sorry too. I made a big mistake getting into this. As far as I'm concerned, you present people with a lie on that stupid site. Good night," I said as I turned around and left.

On my way home, I laughed at how the evening had turned out. I was angry at first but came to realize that I should have known better than to go to the site in the first place. Online, I removed myself from it and, when asked for the reason why, I told them. I decided not to let Jim know what happened, laughing at how people misrepresented themselves and how others were taken in by it.

After getting into another of Asimov's novels, life faded into the shadows once more, and I was off on another planet, far into the future. It felt good to have things at least part way back to normal. I felt I could get on with life again. Maybe I could even contribute to the well being of society. For a while there, I'd lost track of why I did, what I did. I was sure that the people I had avenged wouldn't have wanted me to quit before I'd helped them.

Back online, I searched the sites I had always frequented and found several potential people that possibly deserved a visit. Allen Whickering owned a construction company that had done very well, building apartment houses in Los Angeles. The trouble was, not all his work stood the test of time. One of the apartment buildings, although inspected by the city, collapsed.

Thirty four people died in the disaster. When investigated, it had been discovered that too many corners had been cut. In court, it was found that some of the sub-trades didn't do things as instructed. The owners of these sub-trades insisted they were only following orders given them by Mister Whickering.

Buildings that Whickering Construction built in the past were re-inspected and found to be substandard also. They were condemned, and further investigation revealed the same sub-trades were used. The men owning these companies swore up and down that they were only following instructions issued by Whickering.

Whickering, although fined substantially for building deficiencies, remained in business. I didn't like this man. He was of English descent and seemed unremorseful for his deeds. Although he claimed innocence, there was, in my opinion, too much evidence of his guilt. Why he managed to stay out of jail was beyond me. His high-priced attorney really earned his fee, that's for sure.

Another subject worth having a look at was Samuel B. Alexander. I found out about him through one of the more obscure sites called "Dangerous." Although he was never charged, it was said he was responsible for several deaths. He was an underground fight promoter. These were similar to cage fighting, except there were few rules and no padding. A fighter could strike where he wished, and the fight was only stopped when one of the contenders was unable to continue or was unconscious.

Because the fights were allowed to go as far as they did, several of the participants died. There were photos taken by an obviously concealed camera, showing badly beaten young men. Some were beaten so bad it was a surprise they lived. Most certainly, some had ended up with brain damage.

A picture of the promoter was shown on the site. The person downloading the information said that he was a fan of the underground events until too many deaths occurred.

The bodies were left in the ghettos of San Francisco and dressed in rags, indicating a homeless person. So far no one had been held accountable, and Alexander continued the fights. The man was worth investigating. The accusations may well be unfounded and put online as payback for an inflicted wrong, but they could also just as easily have been the truth too.

Over the next month, I gathered what I could on the three men. Other people came onto the radar, but those three were at the top of the list. Malcolm was a man that had little regard for the environment, and the planet was far worse off with his having been there. It didn't, in my opinion, deserve death, but there had to be some form of punishment. I had an idea rolling around in my head as to how he should be dealt with, but that would be held on to for future consideration.

Allen Whickering needed to be taken to task, but at that point, I was totally unsure of what to do with him. With him on hold, and Marvin Jackson still around waiting for me, it left Samuel B. Alexander, a Black man of sizeable proportions, to be dealt with. I had found some clues to his background. He was, in his youth, a minor-league boxer whose career never went anywhere. Some of his fights were available online and, for the heck of it, I watched a couple. He had plenty of power but didn't have the finesse to be good. So without a proper trainer, he never got anywhere.

I located the run-down residence he lived in and made preparations to do a little spying on the weekend. I'd gotten into very good shape again and was itching to be back in my own game. By Friday, I had what I thought would be necessary packed in the storage compartment of the trunk and was on my way. After getting a room and a rental car the next day, I used the GPS to find the place he called home.

He might have called it home, but I thought it was nothing but a dump. He couldn't be making a lot of money getting the fights together. Either that or he spent it on something else. I parked a few streets away from Ellis and walked toward his home. It was a predominantly Black neighborhood, and I soon rethought the wisdom of that decision. There were far too many groups standing on the street corners.

Trash littered the sidewalks and the gutters along the roads. Every alley and many buildings had graffiti spray painted on them. Rap music could be heard everywhere. Obviously, an area where there was little pride of ownership. Me being White, offense would be taken at my presence. Heading back to the car, I drove past his place and did a quick little tour then went back to the motel.

The episode hadn't been planned out as well as it should have been. I knew he lived in a Black area and should have been better prepared. Going to a thrift store, I picked up baggy jeans, a long tee-shirt, and a hoodie. Finally, I went to a makeup place and bought a dark tone liquid makeup that would allow me to blend in—hopefully.

All prepared, I tried it again. This time I carried a six-foot pole, which should deter any unwanted confrontations, again hopefully. I stayed away from any groups and tried my best to make it look like I belonged there. I hung around an alley for a while, scouting Samuel's place. Luckily, I caught a break and tailed him as he walked the streets, going to wherever. I didn't care to spend any more time in his neighborhood than necessary. It was too unpleasant there.

He headed toward a gym a few blocks away and entered. This gym was used by both Whites and Blacks as it was near the division of a Black and other races area. There I thought I could come dressed a little more White. I didn't feel comfortable being in this kind of disguise at all. Several times while in the area, suspicious eyes followed my movements. If I stayed any longer, I would most assuredly be confronted.

The gym was both boxing and mixed martial arts. Having some training, I had gone to Seattle for a sparring job, the one where I beat the local contender. I thought about going to the gym to meet this guy. I was sure he was there to recruit fighters for the underground competitions. That would get me a location of the fights, and I could then solidify the accusations against him. I had no intention of actually fighting anyone.

I didn't know any other way of finding out where they were held unless I befriended one of the contestants. That would probably take way too long, so I went back to the room and cleaned up. I managed to get back in forty-five minutes, only to find the man gone. I chatted up one of the fighters and found out that Samuel came around several times a week. The place smelled like a sweat box, and there were two raised square rings with people sparring in both.

The manager was busy shouting directions at the two boys in the ring, which was good for me. Looking around, I tried to pick a candidate that might be willing to talk. One guy taking a breather from working the heavy bag looked over and smiled. Taking the opportunity, I walked over and chatted him up. After thirty seconds, I asked about the unsanctioned fights and where to locate Samuel.

"Why you wanna know about the promoter?" I was asked.

"I was thinking I'd give it a shot."

"Yeah, well, these guys play for keeps. The ones who fight are out to hurt you and want to win, no matter what they have to do. You better be really good, because once you sign up, there ain't no turning back. You get picked up, blindfolded, and driven to someplace nobody knows about. That goes for the ones who watch and bet on the fights, too."

"Do you know when the next fight is going to be?" I asked the serious-looking young man.

"As far as I know, it's going to be two weeks from to-night," he told me.

"Do they pick up the fighters from here or someplace else?"

"Our guys get picked up from here. You aren't serious about it, are you? You look tough enough, but these guys fight real dirty, and you don't look like the type. You better think this over if you want to stay healthy," he warned me.

The gym manager started looking at me and must have wondered why I was there. He began to walk over, so I left. The young man I was talking to seemed like a decent enough type. That's why I chose him in the first place. Back in the room, I digested the new information.

If I entered the contest, I'd be at the organizer's mercy. I'd have to fight and wouldn't know where the event was held. I could be forced to fight several guys, one after the other, until I was defeated. I didn't like that idea at all. I'd seen lots of tough guys get taken out and didn't feel like being one of them. The next afternoon, when I didn't get any more information, I went home.

During the following week, I considered ways of finding out the location of the fights. The first idea I had, which involved me participating was discarded. The tracker I'd used twice before would be a good way to find it. That, of course, would only work if I had the opportunity to place it on a vehicle. Barring this, the only other option was to follow one of the cars going there.

Online, I attempted to get the information through the site that made me aware of all this in the first place. As the time drew near, I was no further ahead. The Friday before the fight, I headed back to San Francisco. As I spent Saturday scouting around, I was tempted to go to the gym in order to see if I could learn anything, but decided that I would arouse suspicions. I suspected that the manager must have been in on the activities. Having seen me once already talking to one of his boys, he would be wary if he saw me again, even disguised.

Unsure of exactly when the fighters were to be picked up, I arrived on the scene in the late afternoon. I watched for several hours from the confines of the rental car. At five o'clock, some activity started as a van with the windows blacked out parked near the front of the gym.

A few minutes later, two young men walked out and entered the rear doors of the van. I started the car prepared to follow. At that moment, an extended cab four-by-four parked right beside me, boxing me in. Two big men got out. One walked to my window and signaled me to drop it. The other went to the passenger window and knocked. The one on the passenger side lifted the corner of his jacket far enough away from his body to reveal a pistol in a holster.

Lowering the window, I got ready to dodge a fist. No fist came, but the big Black man with mean looking eyes, bent down to look me in the face.

"Whatcha you doing here, man?" he asked as his breath hit my nostrils, leaving a minty smell.

"Nothing."

"You better not be doing nothin here anymore, you understand? We've been watching you for a couple of hours, and we know you're trying to find out where the van's going. We see you again, ever, and we won't be talking, got it?" he said as he poked my arm with his finger.

I didn't bother to answer. I just nodded my head as he and his buddy left. As he walked around the front of the car, he smashed his fist into the hood, shaking the whole car and putting a nice dent in it. After they were gone, I drove away and did a couple of double backs to make sure I wasn't being followed.

Shit. I thought I was being fairly careful, but these people must have had others try to tail them. I'd rather not tangle with the two visitors if I didn't have to. They looked like they could fight and also carried guns. If I had to take them out, it would be better to use the nunchucks or a gun myself. Those two had actually left me slightly unnerved.

So now I was back to square one. When I first started, I thought it would be easier than it turned out to be. I'd have to wait and see if some other opportunity presented itself in the future. Either that or I'd have to come up with a better plan.

I took the rental car back, and it ended up costing me quite a bit of extra money to pay for the dent in the hood.

Chapter 13

The weeks went by, and other problems took my attention away from the fight game. I figured that, unless I could watch from a distance, I wouldn't make much headway locating where the fights were held. The contestants didn't know themselves, so there was no use talking to any of them. Was Samuel the main promoter or was there another that helped with the recruiting.

I asked myself, *Do I really need to go to the fight location in order to make a call on his guilt? Is there another way to find out for certain, whether he is responsible for the deaths of these young men.*

A situation arose at work which had the company concerned. Supplies seemed to be disappearing. Angle grinders, die grinders, and hand tools were missing. There were a limited number of people with access to the items. We had a tool crib where the tools were kept, and only a small number of people had a key to it. Unless of course, someone forgot to lock it up. That had happened on occasion.

Abe called a general meeting and made an announcement, informing every one of the problems. A reward would be given to anyone who could obtain conclusive information as to who the guilty party was. This all came as a surprise to most of the employees. The guys at the shop were a good bunch, and they didn't like that kind of thing going on there.

The rest of the day had a lot of discussion going on, a few actually had to be told to do their jobs rather than talk too much. I even caught myself watching people to see if the guilty person would give himself away.

No one needed more than one or two grinders. The tools all had the company name stamped on them. A few of the boys headed to the local pawn shops after work. The next morning, there were still no answers because the pawn shops didn't have anything belonging to the shop. After much speculation and time, nothing turned up.

A month went by, and the whole thing had blown over. We had two shifts working there and, after dark, the gates remained unlocked until the end of the second shift. It was discovered one morning by a forklift driver that there was a box behind some material. The material was seldom used so how long the box had been there was unknown.

When he opened the box, he found all the missing tools and items. Abe was notified and, although perplexed, he was also relieved. The identity of the culprit was still unknown, but it appeared that he had a change of heart. The announcement was made, and since everything had been returned, the incident wouldn't be pursued. No one got the reward either.

I'd gone back to San Francisco a few times and rented a room which offered a view of the front of the gym. I'd taken a lot of pictures and finally had one of a fighter who later turned up dead. As far as I was concerned, I now had the proof that Samuel Alexander was at least indirectly responsible for the fighters' deaths. Over the last number of years, seven young men had died in these contests or at least this was suspected. People found dead had injuries that most likely happened in the fight game scenario. The young men had gotten themselves into the situation, but it had been Samuel who set it all up. Now there had to be a price to pay for it.

I hadn't gotten a concrete plan so far, so some thought had to be put into it. I could beat him to death, but I couldn't see myself doing that anymore. I disliked the man a lot, and he did deserve it, but not by me. Looking at the situation, I saw a parallel to a drug pusher in this scenario.

If people weren't so ready to get involved in drugs, the traffickers wouldn't have a market. It looked like the same argument could be made with the promoter. If these fighters didn't get involved in the events, Samuel wouldn't be able to profit from them. But then again, if he didn't set things up, the boys couldn't have gotten into it.

That line of thought just had me going around in circles—if this, if that, didn't solve the problem. Eliminating the man and leaving a message with the body, might slow things down a bit. I started composing a note that would explain things to the underground fight scene. It took several drafts before I got it the way I wanted.

Over the next few weeks, I devised a plan to take care of the promoter. He was six foot two and around two twenty. He had aged poorly, and it was easy to see he hadn't taken care of himself for quite some time. Getting together the things I'd need, I prepared to go see him that coming weekend.

I'd gotten his mailing address and sent him a number of letters. By then, he should have gotten them all and been aware of the situation. I wasn't sure when the next fight would be. Keeping an eye on him, I did notice that he had a routine. He went to the gym, looking for recruits, on Saturday morning at eleven.

That morning, I was sitting in a window that had a view of the gym. I'd been practicing for two weeks and felt fairly confident in my abilities. The front of the gym was close to two hundred yards away from me. The room I had was on the fourth floor, and the field of view was fairly small because of the number of tall buildings around me. My corner room gave me just enough room to do what I planned on doing.

The note I drafted should have been on its way to the manager of the gym. I'd left instructions with the courier to deliver it at twelve noon. It was then ten-forty five, and I had the window open. Sitting in a chair with another high backed one in front of me, I waited.

The time dragged by slowly and, looking through the binoculars, I watched the gym entrance. There was a gentle breeze blowing down the street. Fortunately, it was light and heading toward the intersection I was looking at. Pieces of garbage rolled along the gutters and sidewalks. Foot traffic was light and, with any luck, things would stay that way. The disguise I was wearing didn't hinder me but was a little uncomfortable. The room smelled of stale smoke and whatever foods had been spilled onto the carpeted floor. Not a place I wanted to spend much time in.

Five minutes to go, and all was quiet near the building's entrance. A siren wailed in the distance and faded as it went on to its destination. The flashy vehicle Samuel used pulled up near the front of the gym. He lived in a dump but had a fancy car. Image must have been more important than living in a nice home. I couldn't figure that one out. I'd seen that on other occasions when I went to some of the southern states too. Ramshackle homes with fancy cars parked in the driveways.

The two men in the four-by-four who had given me the warning stepped out onto the sidewalk and redirected foot traffic away from the front of the building. Their eyes panned the area, looking for threats. Seeing nothing, the bigger of the two nodded toward the car. I switched the binoculars for the rifle and rested the barrel on the back of the chair in front of me.

Preparing myself for the upcoming moment by taking a deep breath, I slowly let it out. The promoter exited the car and started walking toward the front door, away from me. Sighting in on him through the scope, making sure there was no one ahead of him, I gently squeezed the trigger on the .300 Winchester Magnum.

Long ago, I made an attachment that fit on the end of the barrel. A tube, filled with soft baffles, having a hole in the center slightly larger than the bullet going through them. The sound coming out the end of the rifle was muffled. The traffic noise completed the cover up, and no one heard anything.

The bullet sped to the target and a small entry hole formed while the exit hole that was much larger appeared on the other side. The mushrooming bullet created quite a mess. Down he went, hitting the sidewalk. The men's eyes, darting here and there, didn't see a thing. I was too far away and already packing up the rifle.

Leaving the room and having paid in advance, I walked out of the building and went to the parking area. The note should have reached its destination shortly after. The messenger would have had to get past the mess on the sidewalk, though.

The note going to the manager read, *If anyone thinks about taking Samuel B. Alexander's place, think again.*

What has happened to him will happen to the next pro-moter. Spread the word if you value your life.

Whether or not it would stop the fights was up in the air. I had done what I could. Maybe some of the partici-pants would clue in. I somehow doubted that would be the case, though.

Chapter 14

The story of the promoter made a small splash and was soon forgotten. It was thought that a bereaved father was most likely the perpetrator of the crime. It didn't look like all that much effort had been expended in solving the crime. Another bad guy bit the dust, and that was all there was to it.

Life went on, and yet no sign of Gord. His sister Eva tried to track him down through old contacts and got nowhere. It had been quite some time now, and the weather was cooling as the summer ended and fall started.

I had a hard time figuring things out because Gord used to be such a nice kid. He and Eva would wrestle me to the ground, and we had such fun when we went to the Zip Line Park. Who would have thought that one drinking session could bring about so drastic a change, and in such a short time? Could this kind of thing have happened to Kathleen and me, had she lived and had children? I turned off that line of thought immediately. From past experience, I knew that it would lead me to a place I didn't want to go.

Marvin Jackson came to mind, and I decided it was time to be taking care of him. Friday evening had me on

Buford Road. That was where I believed he and his buddies were manufacturing drugs.

With the car hidden, I worked my way close to the building. The area was dark and run down, and there was no foot traffic. Staying in the shadows, I listened at an open window as the activity inside continued, the participants unaware of my presence. Going by the number of voices and what I'd seen during my time there, I suspected there were four people inside.

A cell phone chimed some rapper music and was answered. "Hey, yo, Marv. Yeah, we're almost done." Silence for a moment and he continued, saying, "You don't need to come here, but if you wanna, go ahead. Okay, see in a bit."

Great, the whole gang would be there soon. That fit into my plans perfectly. Slipping away, I headed to the rental and made a quick run to my own vehicle. I grabbed what I wanted out of the trunk compartment and headed back.

I drove a bit fast and, seeing a police cruiser parked in a side road ahead, swerved through a parking lot to avoid getting pulled over. Exiting onto another street, I drove to Buford, parking well away from the building which I thought Marvin was probably in by then.

The air was cool and, wearing a coat to carry a few things with me, I worked my way to the same window I was at earlier. It hadn't rained for a while, so the soil around the building was dry. There were voices inside saying, "Hey, Jazz, switch on the pill maker and carry this shit over to it."

The task was done, and more instructions were given to the others.

Taking a quick peek through the open window, I saw the layout of the immediate premises. On one side kettles and heating equipment were on long tables, where

Marvin and the boys were processing the materials already made. There were several machines to make pills of different shapes.

For a moment, I wondered where they would be able to procure this type of machinery. That thought, however, was very short lived as I got on with the plan. Reaching into my pocket, I pulled out two grenades. Pulling the pins from both, I gripped the handles and tossed the grenades through the open window.

One was directed toward the group and the other into the center of the room. Running for cover, I heard yells in the room as they realized what was happening. A moment later, the twin explosions occurred.

At that point, I was on my way back to assess the situation inside what was left of the building. Part of the outside wall had been blown out. There was smoke and dust, making it difficult to see what was going on inside. I covered my face with a respirator, in order to avoid breathing in the chemicals drifting around in the air.

I heard the crash of things falling down inside, but also a door being thrown open and smashing against a stop. Backing up fast, I tried to hide as a figure came running around the front corner. Glimpsing me backing up, Marvin started shooting wildly.

"You stinkin asshole, you gonna pay fo this," he screamed while shooting at me.

One of his shots hit something hard and made of metal, causing it to ricochet. It hit me in the fleshy part of my right thigh. The pistol in my hand almost dropped to the ground as the bullet impacted.

Seeing this, he ran directly at me as I tried to conceal myself behind the corner of the building I was near. He shot two more times, and his gun was empty. He stopped to replace the magazine and, as he did this, I recovered enough to make a shot of my own.

The shot I took was a fatal one. Down he went with a bullet in the center of his chest. He lay still on the ground and, as I looked at the wound in my leg, there was a sound coming from the interior. Where the wall had been blown out, a figure crawled slowly out of the destroyed room. It was obvious that he had been badly hurt. As I stripped off my shirt, I kept an eye on him and watched for any other movement. Wrapping the shirt around my leg, I attempted to stifle the bleeding. Man, did it ever hurt. It took all my concentration to regain my focus.

There was no one else alive after I shot the creeper. I put one more into Marvin, just to make sure, and covered up the blood I'd lost on the ground. There was plenty of garbage there for me to use. Hopefully, the police wouldn't discover my blood. I would have gotten rid of it completely, but the sirens were in the distance, and I had to get out of there.

Using the coat to cover the seat in the car, I drove away. I spent several days in town after I patched up the wound in my leg. I'd had first aid training, which allowed me to stitch up and disinfect the hole where the bullet entered and exited. It was sore as hell, but not life-threatening.

The area around Marvin's drug house had been cordoned off, and, two days later, I went back with an old shovel that I'd gotten hold of. In the evening when the way was clear, I uncovered the place where I bled and dug up all traces of my DNA left behind. On my way home, I stopped beside a river and dumped the contents of the bag into the water. Unless I'd missed something, I should be in the clear.

I had to call Abe to let him know that I'd taken a fall and hurt my leg.

He was sympathetic. "Are you able to go on light duty?" he asked. "If you are, I could use you to do some press work. I'll have someone set up the press, and you can sit on a chair to run it."

"Sure, I can do that, as long as I don't have to be on my feet too much, that will work."

A week later, I was back in good enough shape to take on my regular duties, and things were back to normal—at least as normal as it ever was for one who had been shot at least four times, if memory served me correctly.

The garden was almost empty of vegetables, as most had been eaten. The rest were in the freezer. The last of the tomatoes were now gone with only a few carrots still in the soil. All but a few squash had been harvested and stored. My leg was no longer stiff, and life was okay as I got back into shape.

Friday after work, I sat for a moment on the picnic table in the backyard with a Corona. It had warmed up a little, so I wanted to enjoy it while it was there. Looking at the green space behind the property, I saw some movement. There was something in the bushes, but it was too hidden to make out.

Getting my binoculars, I raised them to my eyes. Lying in the soft grass was a deer peering back at me. It must not have sensed me as a threat and remained where it was. With the sun going down, it looked like it had found a bed for the night. In a tree not far away were a number of crows cawing loudly. I wondered for a moment why they were called a murder of crows. Finishing the beer, I headed inside to make a later-than-normal supper.

Once done, I settled in for an evening of reading. I'd finished the *Robots of Dawn* and the *Robots and Empire* novel. Just having started *Prelude to Foundation*, I was already deeply engrossed in the book. It was another novel by Isaac Asimov that had won great notoriety for an already famous author. Once again, I fantasized about a future none of us would ever see, except in our minds. The world dissolved into nothingness as I was transported into the story.

I wished with all my heart that I could go. There was nothing left to hold me. But alas, it was not to be. I had to be satisfied with going there in my mind. That was exactly what I did for several hours and, when I went to bed, I dreamt, for once, of pleasant things.

Waking in the morning well rested, I made plans to go riding, but a phone call from Bill put that idea on the backburner.

"Joseph, I need your help. I vowed to myself that I'd never do this again, but things have changed. Can I come over this afternoon?" he asked. "I'd like to discuss something with you."

"Of course, Bill, no problem. Two o'clock good?"

"See you then," he said.

I wondered what was up. He hadn't asked for my help in quite some time. The last time he needed me, we did things outside the law, which was highly unusual for him. Bill was one of the straightest people I'd ever met. This had to be really serious and must have had him backed into a corner.

At two on the button, he pulled into the driveway. As he walked up to the front path, I opened the door and let him walk straight in. After I got him a Corona and we were seated, he started talking. "I've gotten a bit of information about your friend's boy. A girl at Jeremy's place let me know where she thinks he went. She says she heard Baulthus talking on the phone about it. It's important not to let him know the girl fed me the news, I might need her again. Gord has gone to some camp run by Catholic priests. I haven't had a chance to go see him because it's quite far from here. Actually, it's in Utah, and I don't have any jurisdiction there. I was wondering if I could impose on you to see him. I've been in touch with them, and the priest I talked to says Gord refuses to have contact with me or his family. He also asked how I knew he was there." He sighed. "This whole thing comes across with a sour smell, if you know what I mean. I'm sure these priests mean well, and since Gord is eighteen, he has the right to make his own choices. It seems funny that they wouldn't put more effort into getting the family back together."

"So what is it you want me to do? If he won't see you or his family, why would he talk to me?" I asked.

"Well, I don't know how to say this, except to be direct with you. There is far more to you than you let on. I don't know exactly what, but there is a side to you that is deeply hidden. You don't have to tell me anything, and I won't ever ask, but I'd like you to use whatever methods you need to talk to the boy."

"All right, give me the address, and I'll see what I can do. It'll have to wait till next weekend, though."

"Okay, thanks, buddy, this will make my job a bit easier," he said as he got up.

I felt there was something else he would like to ask, but that'd happen when he was ready.

After he left, I got on the computer and looked up the area where the camp was. Lincoln Beach Road ran along the eastern side of Utah Lake. The camp was located on the waterfront in a well-treed basin that had a seasonal creek running through it. The camp looked like it had been there for a while. The trees were deciduous and not huge but still of a decent size.

Using Google, I learned that it was a twelve-hour drive. This meant I'd have to take at least one extra day for the trip. I'd probably be wasting my time going to see him. Depending on his state of mind, he could end up leaving that camp too. We would be back in the dark if he ran away again.

Leaving a couple hours early from work on the following Friday got me to Provo, Utah, just after midnight. I slept in till nine-thirty feeling the effects of the long drive. After having the continental breakfast, I took a drive along the lake, watching the water until I reached the camp, then used the binoculars to scan the retreat.

A high fence around the perimeter forced me to use some tools to get into the camp. There was barbed wire along the top. So I would have to snip the wire fence later when I came back. I wanted to twist the ends together again to help delay detection of my having entered the camp. Looking the scene over, I familiarized myself with the layout.

I could see people but couldn't make out details at that distance. They were all dressed very casually, so if I wore the same type of clothes, I'd blend in.

Because it was getting cool in the evenings, I dressed for it, which helped me blend in even more. After leaving and coming back in the dark, and parking the rental car, I jogged across the scrub-brush-infested sand, having to stop to remove the sand in my shoes. The terrain dropped, and the trees became denser as I got closer to the camp. The low basin helped to retain the moisture in the soil, allowing the trees to thrive.

The last hundred yards was traversed when I saw the way was clear. Approaching the fence where there would be little chance of being seen, I used bolt cutters to snip an opening beside a post. Leaving the lower wire and the top two intact would allow me to repair the fence easily when I left with the wire I brought with me. When I was through and had made my way close to the outer buildings, I surveyed the scene.

Off to one side, near the water, was the main building. In rows of ever-increasing distance were smaller cabins widely separated, with a large number of trees between them. In the distance, I heard the sound of water spraying and noticed that the grounds were being watered. That must have been another of the reasons there were so many trees. The water was taken from the lake because there wasn't any other source, except the small seasonal creek.

Staying on the sidelines, I waited for the right person to walk by. There happened to be little foot traffic as it was getting dark, but a slender young man meandered along, shuffling his feet on the sand. As he neared my position, I made my presence known. He stood about five seven and weighed close to one fifty.

He struck up a conversation, saving me the trouble of doing it. He made the usual small talk and asked, "Are you a new counselor? You're too old to be one of the sign-ins."

"I'm here to see how things are going for a friend that's here," I said.

There was a slight lull in the conversation as he was probably wondering why I was there at night, so I used the break to ask, "Do you know where Gord is?"

"Which one, Davidson or Motters?" he asked.

"Motters, I need to see him."

"I think I saw him coming out of the office a while ago."

I limped toward him saying, "I hurt my ankle, do you think you could find him for me and send him here. I'd really appreciate it."

"Ahh, yeah, I guess I could do that." Off he went in the direction of a cabin separated from the rest.

I heard him call out to Gord and when they were close together, their voices became subdued and I couldn't hear anything. A minute later, I saw Gord coming my way. Stepping into the darkness after I knew he saw me, I waited.

"You want to see me?" he said in a flat tone.

"Hello, Gord. Don't walk away. I just want to see how you are."

"I'm fine, I just want to be left alone," he said with his head down. He choked off the last word.

"It's obvious that things really aren't all right. Is there anything I can do to help you?" I asked, feeling a real sympathy for the boy.

Pulling himself together, he glared at me. "What are you going to do, beat up everybody in the camp? I'm fine. I told you. Please don't come here again, I don't need your help."

With this, he turned and walked away. I desperately wanted to go after him, but I doubted I could change his mind, short of picking him up and carrying him back to the car. I felt things had gone terribly wrong for the boy, even worse than I originally thought. I could almost swear there was a look of desperation that crossed his face as he turned away. Because it was getting dark, I couldn't be sure of that. It could have been that he was angry that I had found him. Unfortunately, there was absolutely nothing I could do to help him unless he let me.

On my way out of the camp, I mended the fence and, picking up the tools, headed toward the car. The ride home was a very unpleasant one. The look I thought he had on his face as he turned away kept going through my mind.

I wondered what was going on. I didn't believe this whole thing would end well. The old Gord would have asked me to help him, but that had all changed. I'd known the lad for quite a number of years. We had some great times together. Now he was like another person.

On the way home, I debated the advisability of letting Harry and Brenda know that I'd seen him. For me, it would be better if Bill was the one to tell them, leaving me out of it. I was having a hard time facing my friends in their time of misery.

By the time I walked in the door of my house, I had decided that it had to come from me. Those people had helped me more than any others in my life. Just because it would be tough, I couldn't have Bill do a job that should be mine. Grabbing my cell phone, I made the call, telling Harry I'd be right over.

At his front door, as I walked up the sidewalk, my friends stood in the doorway. I said, "Bill located Gord. I took a trip to Utah and entered a camp run by a number of priests."

"Did you see our son?" Brenda asked apprehensively.

"I did."

"How is he? Is he coming home?" she asked.

"I'm afraid not. He asked me to please leave him alone. He said he was fine." At that point, I wanted to stop but felt it'd be better if they knew the truth. "I don't think they are, but he wouldn't say anything and left me standing there. I doubt that there is anything that we can do to change his mind."

"Maybe if we went to see him, he would talk to us," Harry said.

"To tell you the truth, I know this is the last thing you want to hear, but I really think that if you do, he will leave the camp. With him there, at least you know where he is. The final decision has to be yours, of course. If you think that you can help him, by all means, do it. I don't want to stand in your way."

Brenda looked at me with tears in her eyes. "We lost our boy long ago. I want to see him, but I think you're right. Going there will push him even farther away."

She turned and walked into the house, crying. Harry expressed his appreciation for my help and, with his head down, went in to take care of his wife. The ride home was an unhappy one.

The following week at work was a subdued one for me.

"Is everything is all right?" Jim asked.

I told him the story. He knew Harry and Brenda too and was tempted to call, offering his sympathies. I let him know it might not be a good idea at that time.

The months went by, and the incident affected me less and less as other situations arose. The shop lost a contract with a rather large amount of work not being required anymore. That created a slowdown in the shop, and a number of employees had to be laid off. That type of situation was never pleasant, and most of the rest of the guys were willing to work shorter hours to alleviate the crunch.

Unfortunately, it wouldn't help enough as there was now a real shortage of work, and the company had to scramble to fill the void. It was springtime and, after a particularly mild winter, the existing snows disappeared and the green started taking over. I loved having things warm up. The warmth of the sun shining on my face always helped elevate my moods.

The plant managers found out that the reason we lost the contract was that a Chinese firm could make the parts we built for far less money. Although everyone knew that the parts coming from China were invariably of much poorer quality, the bottom line for many companies, to no one's surprise, was money.

In our quest for cheaper and cheaper prices, we as consumers shot ourselves in the foot. The things we bought broke down faster and needed to be replaced more often. The worker in the USA lost his job and had to take a lower-paying one. That meant less money to spend, and they too had to buy the cheaper products.

Greedy corporations didn't give a shit about the worker. It all boiled down to profits. The CEOs of those corporations raked in huge salaries and bonuses for putting our people out of work. What the hell was wrong with this situation? If we saw the problem, why didn't we do something to stop it? Maybe we should have elected a president with more radical ideas. The one we had, no matter what his color was, just wasn't cutting it. America needed desperately to wake up before it was too late to turn things around. Increasing the deficit didn't help things one bit.

It was a wonder that there weren't any assassinations taking place. Had we become so complacent that we didn't even see this shit happening, or were we getting dumber by the day? I didn't see any of the protests that attacked the real problems, like the ones that used to occur in the past. When the people were not satisfied with the way the country was being run, they used to march in protest. Maybe it was time for a resurgence.

What we saw was a huge rise in mass shootings—most of those being perpetrated by our youth. I heard much of this was due to cyberbullying. Of course, mental illness must have played a large factor in it too. I found that many of the people I knew were wondering what was happening to our country. More and more Muslims were coming to live in the United States. The big question that should have been asked was, weren't the majority of the world's terrorists Muslims? Why, then, were we allowing more and more of them in our country? In my opinion, it was only a matter of time before groups of them were in the country, and another major attack took place. At least screen those people entering thoroughly before they got in, if nothing else.

It was almost as if Muslims wanted to infiltrate and slowly overrun us by marrying our women and raising their children in the Muslim faith. Some claimed our recent president was actually a Muslim, no matter what he said. It certainly seemed that he was, going by the way he treated our ally Israel and how friendly he was with countries in the Middle East that had sworn to annihilate America. What a joke the new prime minister of Canada was. What other world leader marched in gay parades. To me, it looked like he might be gay himself. The man looked like a fool, spending money and running the country into a huge deficit that someone else would later have to fix.

Where was this going to end? Would we ever elect someone who actually wanted what was best for the United States of America? I guess we had more problems than cures. Again, maybe it was time for a new type of president, although that was a scary thought too.

This line of thought brought me back to Malcolm Wright. With the shop being less busy, I was sure that time off would be much easier to get. I started reviewing the photos of his retreat in the Adirondacks. Studying the land from the base to the plateau showed me mostly difficult ways to the top. There were, however, a number of spots that allowed for a somewhat easier climb. When I said "somewhat easier," I meant reasonably easy, compared to the harder ones that an experienced climber would be able to do.

In three places, the approach to the top was far less steep, at least most of the way. They weren't easy, but, with a bit of training, I should be able to make the climb in two or three hours, maybe four. Once I located the best way up, I moved on to the plateau itself. Pride of ownership allowed pictures of the entire estate to be taken, revealing what I was looking for.

After a bit of thought, a plan started developing in my head and, as a result, I started making preparations. Looking up the addresses of outdoor outfitters, I located one in town, not far from where I worked. Since we at the shop were only working three days a week till business improved, I only had one more day left that week. I went to the outfitters the next day on my way home.

The young man I talked to asked me, "What are you planning to do?"

"I want to start climbing some fairly steep terrain. Only short spans will be close to vertical. What do you suggest?" I asked.

"To tell you the truth, I think it would be in your best interest to take some lessons. You can start on your own, but after a bit, you should get experienced help."

Leaving the store several hundred dollars poorer, I headed home to familiarize myself with the equipment. I had a few camming devices for wedging in rock openings as well as belaying ones for lowering myself down fairly quickly. The rope was nice and thin, making it light. The shoes were designed for easy climbing and limited slippage. A hammer would be needed, so I after some online research, I made one at work. It had a steel head and aluminum handle, with excess material, machined out to reduce the weight. Sweet.

Having a few days off, I went to do a few easy climbs to get myself ready for the more difficult ones. Wearing special gloves saved my fingers a lot of pain from abrasion. By the end of the day, I was tired and a little sore. A few scrapes and bruises reinforced the idea that more prep work was needed, and so I took the salesman's advice and signed up for a few lessons.

By the end of two weeks, I'd gotten to the point where I could climb and get back down faces that were at least as difficult as the ones I needed to scale in the next mission. Thanks to some advice from the instructor, I purchased everything I needed to complete the task at hand. Because I'd be carrying everything with me, I managed to keep it light enough to make the climb fairly doable.

It took another two weeks to be able to secure the time off I required and for the scrapes, I'd endured to heal. A rush job came up and, once that was done, the shop could get along without me for a while. The day came, and everything I didn't want anyone to see was loaded into the secret compartment in the trunk.

The mountain passes on the way east were all clear and would present no problems. The plateau in the Adirondacks was free of any ice and snow too, making the climb practical.

The route I would take had me going through many of the states in the middle of the country. The first night brought me to Boise Idaho. The next evening I got to Des Moines. The following day had me driving close to Buffalo New York. That was where I grew up and, although I had nice memories of my mother there, everything else reminded me of her awful death. For that reason, I drove right past the city.

Driving to Warrensburg, I got a room at the Super Eight and rested for a day, enjoying the town. The room was nothing to write home about but would have to do. The area I'd be going to was a half hour drive away, so I got a head start in the morning, nice and early.

The drive took me to higher elevations, and it actually required almost two hours for me to get to my destination. The roads were through treed places that made them into winding trails. Just wanting to familiarize myself with the lay of the land took the rest of the day. I had two weeks to do the job and get back home, so wasn't in any big hurry.

There were no decent car rentals in the immediate area of the Super Eight. That forced me to go to Albany, also making it necessary to leave my car in a secure lot. After transferring my things to the four by four, I was on my way. The SUV gave me better access to the places I wanted to go. I brought my slimline sleeping bag and now picked up lightweight supplies.

The heaviest thing I needed to pack in was water. Having seen several water supply outlets in the pictures of the home on the plateau, I could use some of Malcolm's water. Just in case, I'd carry some part way up the climb and leave it for myself to drink on the way down.

At the bottom where I planned to start the climbing, I looked up at what was ahead of me. There were a few spots that were more difficult than the rest of the trail, but there were handholds, I hoped. I looked through my binoculars to see just how hard it would be.

It was a good thing I bought a number of extra camming and belaying devices. The rope should do fine as I could use it more than once by pulling it free once I'd gone down past each hard part. Going up would be the more difficult of the two hikes, I was sure. Of course, it always looked easier from the bottom than it did from the top. I didn't have a problem with heights, but then again I'd never attempted anything quite so high before.

If I had my information correct, there were no guards, only some maintenance staff at that time. It was somewhat of a concern to me, because I had no desire to cause their deaths. If I played it right, that probably wasn't going to be much of a problem.

In the hotel room, I went over everything thing I intended to take with me on the excursion. When satisfied, I placed the load on the rocking chair in the corner of the room. The anticipation was starting to put me on edge. Never having done a job like this before made me nervous. I'd be vulnerable for a considerable period of time, and I didn't like that at all.

Sleep that night came slowly and, once I did sleep, it wasn't a particularly restful one, so I stayed in bed fairly late. By the time I got up, things were considerably better. Spending the day taking it easy, I prepared to leave at around two in the afternoon.

After parking the vehicle in a suitable spot, I began the hike. At the start of the slope, I looked up at what was in front of me. It was a good thing that I wasn't afraid of heights. Of course, one slip and fall could change that in a hurry. Mentally, I figured out, one last time, my route to the top. There were a couple of ways to go, but I'd attempt to keep to the easiest of those.

With the backpack on and the climbing gloves in my pocket, I was on my way. At first, I was tempted to go quickly up the first part of the climb because the slope was still easy, but that I didn't do. In order to pace myself, I'd have to play it smart.

The beginning portion was fairly steep but easy enough, and the trees grew quite well. There was no one around as I got on my way, making sure to lift my feet so I didn't end up having to stop to empty the sand out of my shoes too often. For the first half hour, I made good headway as the slope increased only a little.

When the trees quickly started thinning out, the slope changed dramatically. The rest of the hike turned into a climb and before me was a rock face that continued to the plateau. There was the occasional outcropping of brush, but, for the most part, it was all rock. I worked up a bit of a sweat, wiping my forehead occasionally.

One stroke of luck was that the rock face was not straight up. For the most part, the angle was ten to fifteen degrees off vertical. This helped a lot, as being almost vertical would have put the climb beyond my abilities.

Stopping for a minute, I took my first good drink of water. I'd brought with me eight, sixteen-ounce-sized plastic bottles. I also brought two extra, one of which I left there at the base of the steep portion. It would be there when I was finished making the descent. There I also left a power bar. I had a pack of supplies that was attached to a long thin abrasive resistant line. As I climbed, I would have to pull the tough pack up and tie it off with a slip knot. The knot could be undone from the next perch by a tug and the pack safely pulled up.

With this done, I marked the spot, put on the gloves, and started the climb. The rocks at the bottom were fairly smooth but as the climb progressed the edges became quite sharp and jagged. One thing I became aware of was the danger of using rocks for handholds that were not secure. As I pulled myself up using a sharp one to help, I felt it shift.

From that point on, I tested each stone I grabbed before trusting it to stay in place. At the forty-five-minute mark, I found myself approximately a third of the way up. Ahead of me was my first real test. Finding a large secure outcropping, I tied off and sat down to rest for fifteen minutes. Here I drank a bottle of water and left one to drink on the way down. This lightened the load slightly.

While I was there, I looked up to figure out the best way to proceed. When this was done, I took a moment to admire the view. After a couple of deep breaths, I was on the move once more. The almost vertical section was about twenty-five feet up before it sloped again. The extra pack was pulled up, placed on a stone sticking out, then tied off. It wouldn't do to have it dislodge and fall with me in a precarious position.

This part of the climb was a bit nerve-racking, as the potential for a fall was at its greatest. Twenty minutes of careful climbing, and a minor slip that had sent my heart racing, found me at the start of the easier section. At this time, I stopped and studied the rock formation. Locating a suitable spot, I used one of the camming devices to secure a rappelling tool.

This would be used to make the descent a lot safer and faster. Once the camming device was inserted in a crevice, it wedged itself tight and was almost impossible to pull out.

Another rest, and I was on my way once more. I found myself relaxing a bit at this point because one of the hard sections was done. My attention was quickly brought back when I felt a shift as I begin to put my weight on a loose stone. A shiver ran through me as I realized the error.

The climb went well till I reached the next almost vertical part. Here there was no outcropping to rest at so I tied off using a camming tool and rested in a web harness while I decided on my route. As I had at various places during the climb, I placed a marker that I would be able to see from above. Otherwise, I could easily go off course and get myself into trouble. The last thing I wanted was to have to re-figure out my descent route.

The next part of the climb was the most difficult of the entire ascent. The climb was about thirty five feet of close-to-vertical rock. My hands were still in good shape, but too much of this type of climbing and I'd need to take the time to recuperate. I could see why most climbers were quite slender. My bulk was proving to be a bit of a detriment and caused me to tire a bit.

The path I wanted to take was memorized, after storing the harness, tools, and leaving another bottle of water behind. It took two short rests and thirty minutes to traverse the short distance. An experienced climber would have made short work of it. Unfortunately, I wasn't one.

When I finally made it past that part, my hands felt the strain of the climb. I had another half bottle of water, and a urinary extraction was required.

At that point, I fastened another descending device and marked it so I could see it on the way down. Looking down, I saw a number of markers showing me where to go. Another half hour, and I made it to the top, pulling the second pack over the edge. The climb had taken me almost an hour longer than I thought it would. In two hours, it would start getting dark, so after a rest, I got started on the half-mile hike to where the house sat on the knoll.

Using a compass, I walked through the woods. The trees were all evergreens in the forest. There was a constant snapping of twigs, so I slowed my pace, looking for the best path. The last thing I needed was one of the help to be strolling in the woods and have them hear me.

The only deciduous trees were located nearer the landscaped property. In an effort to keep the plateau green, Malcolm had had a pump system installed. Water from a good sized lake at the base of the small mountain was pumped up by big water pumps. There were many water cannons placed at strategic points to keep the trees from becoming fire hazards in the dry times.

The locals raised objections to this, but after a rather large donation to the local hospital was made, the objections disappeared. *Who says money can't buy friends.* The water supply for the home was kept in large storage containers and treated before it was used. All this information was included in the article in *Homes of the Upper Class.*

Another excellent piece of information the article gave me was that Malcolm had Cynophobia, which worked in my favor. When he was young, he had been attacked by his grandparent's dog. The experience left him with psychological scars as well as physical ones—so, no dogs.

The plan I had come up with would take most of the next day to complete. If there had been dogs present, it would have hampered my ability to get the job done efficiently. By the time I located what I needed to, it was almost dark. I snuck over to the tanks I required and made a withdrawal from each. I had debated on whether or not to bring along certain tools because of the extra weight. Now I was glad I did because they came in real handy.

Malcom's help lived in the separate quarters with only one couple in the main house. That was all right because I hadn't intended on going into the house anyway. Although I was tired, the next part of the job had to be done while I was hidden in the darkness. It took close to another hour to complete that portion of the plan. Once done, I retreated into the forest.

A light, tough, synthetic material on which I could lay down was unpacked, and I blew up a pillow and thin plastic air mattress. The whole thing only weighed about the same as a bottle of water. As I ate and drank, I lay down, resting my weary body. Being at this altitude seemed to keep the bugs down to a minimum, and a little repellent kept even those away.

Waking in the morning to the sound of chirping birds, and I had another bite to eat. I relieved myself, and, after burying it, got to work. Repacking everything, I marked the tree with a ribbon tied around a small branch ten feet off the ground, so I could easily find it again. Taking the extra precaution of covering my stuff with dead branches and finding a distinctive landmark, I was on my way.

At places that would help take advantage of the natural surroundings, the things I brought with me—and also what I had collected since coming there—were positioned. In order to place the devices and supplies all over the plateau, the entire day was used up. With only one more part of the plan to implement, I made my way over to the edge of the mountain, a hundred yards from the house.

There was an open area that I would have to cross in order to get to where I needed to be. While approaching the edge of the clearing, I heard voices. *Shit!* I wondered why they were there so late. As I crawled closer for a look, I saw two men with a toolbox working on a protective screen that housed an electrical box. On the ground beside them was a nest and broken eggs. Some birds must have decided that this was a good place to raise their young.

The work was done and, after an inspection, the two left. Lowering myself out of sight, I waited until they were gone. When I felt it was safe, I worked my way over to the edge of the fenced-in drop off. The fence, several feet from the edge, was only four feet high so I scaled it, right beside the eight-inch-diameter pipe. A three-inch pipe was three feet away from it. I assumed that the three-inch one supplied the house and grounds, while the larger one was used to run the water cannon. I did what I had come there to do and, after making sure the way was clear, headed back to where my gear had been stowed.

On the way, I heard voices. Hiding behind a stand of undergrowth, I watched as a man and woman walked arm in arm through the woods. This would have been okay, except for the fact that, even though I'd taken care to camouflage the stuff, I'd placed throughout the forest, there was always the chance they could stumble across my things. I didn't bother to hide the backpack and empty carrying pack too carefully, which worried me then. The ribbon around the tree branch would be a real giveaway.

If they continued going in the direction they were, they would have a chance of spotting my stuff. How to detour them was what I needed to figure out and fast. There was quite a breeze, but not enough to create any problems that would have caused them to head back. They were about eighty feet from where my stuff was. I had no desire to hurt them so there couldn't be a confrontation.

Looking around, hoping something would come to me, I saw a tree that was dead and not very stable. It was off to the side and not in their immediate line of sight. As quickly as I could, I made a beeline over to it. With a quick hard push, the tree leaned but swung back. Luckily, I was still out of their line of sight and, as the tree swung back away from me, I gave it as hard a push as I could muster.

This time there was a loud crack, and it continued going—with me almost following it. Regaining my footing, I ducked out of sight and ran along the trail away from them. As I hid in a thicket, I watched as the two came to investigate the crash. Looking at the fallen tree as the dust settled, I heard them as they discussed the reason for it falling. Neither came up with a logical answer, and the woman tugged at the man's arm, wanting to head back to the grounds. Reluctantly he went.

As I went to pick up my things, I realized they had been heading straight toward my stuff. I was pretty sure that if they'd have stumbled across it, there would have been a search and quite possibly my plans would have been foiled. It was close to dusk, so I'd have to wait till morning before heading down the mountainside. I had just enough food and water to see me through the night and breakfast. This night I dreamt of unpleasant things. I didn't like it but was used to it. Nightmares had plagued me most of my life.

In the morning after a few quick checks, I got on my way down. You would have thought that it would have gone considerably quicker than the ascent did. Except for the very steep parts, I went no faster down than I did going up. There was far too great a chance of falling.

At the steep parts that took me so long to climb, I was able to rappel down rather quickly. I quenched my thirst when I got to each of the bottles of water, then flattened them and took them with me when empty. I brought out everything that could have my DNA on it. Although I wasn't in any registry, I didn't want to take any chances on future identification. It took an hour and a half less to get to the bottom than it did going up.

Going back to my hotel room and making a call, I prepared for the next part of the operation. Viewing a map, I checked the location of various places in the area. At three in the afternoon, I pulled in at my next stop. Walking into the office in a carefully thought out disguise, I was greeted by a receptionist and asked to pay up front for the ride I was about to take.

We checked the itinerary, and, when the route was confirmed, she led me out to the back of the hanger. I was introduced to the pilot, and we prepared to fly. This wasn't the first time I'd been in a helicopter, but it was thrilling nevertheless.

It ended up being a lot more expensive to go up in a two-seat helicopter than a group sized one.

I had a camera with a telephoto lens with me and a pocket voice recorder.

The pilot had been informed that I was a journalist doing a piece on the area. I had to pay quite a bit extra to get the flyby of the plateau. He knew that I wanted to see other areas first and then approached the plateau from the side away from the house first. We took forty five minutes touring the rivers and lakes, with me snapping pictures the whole time, and then headed toward the plateau.

"How close can we get to the plateau?" I asked.

"Two hundred yards is customary."

"I really need to be within a hundred feet by the house and around the perimeter of the entire plateau," I told him.

"I can't do that. I'll get into trouble if the helicopter is recognized." He said quite emphatically.

He couldn't—until I handed him five one-hundred-dollar bills. All of a sudden, we got in much closer so I could take pictures through an open window. While I was taking pictures, I also activated a couple of remotes that I had previously set up for different jobs. When we'd made a complete circuit around the plateau, I gave him the all-clear sign.

During the last part of the flight, I saw a few of the workers briefly watch us and then continue their work as we headed out.

The pilot took us back to the landing site. "Do me a favor and don't tell anyone about the close flyby you had me do. If word gets out, I'm in shit, and since I did you a favor, you owe me one, right?"

"No one will ever find out because of me, you have my word," I said as I left.

I drove to an open area that gave me a view of where the two pipes ran up the side of the mountain and onto the plateau. It had been an hour and a half since the flight around the top of the mountain started. Twenty minutes later, I brought out a set of powerful binoculars. At this time, I started keeping an eye on the top of the pipes as they went over the edge.

After five or six minutes, there was a flash of light and a soft rumble coming from very near the edge of the plateau. There was a gush of water as the ruptured pipe released water from the pipe over the level ground at the top. Five minutes later there was another flash, but this one came from the forest two hundred yards from the edge of the grounds around the house.

One after another, flashes occurred and smoke billowed into the air. This continued all around the top of the plateau about one hundred feet from the edge. In half an hour, there was a blaze that created a circle around the top of the mountain. The fire was working its way across the top and would soon consume the entire mountaintop.

By this time the pumps would be working. The water would still be flowing through the smaller pipe supplying the system to prevent the home from burning, but the larger one was now useless. Helicopters could be seen in the air flying toward the home. They landed and were shortly on their way again after most likely having picked up the people at the house. Malcom Wright hadn't been there, so there was never any danger for him personally, and that was one of the reasons I had done the job at that particular time.

By the time firefighting equipment had been brought to bear, the mountaintop was ablaze. At this time, I left and headed back to the Super Eight. Packing my things and placing them in the car, I left town, driving back to Albany and picking up my vehicle. I thought about dropping by my old neighborhood in Buffalo but decided against it. Why open old wounds?

Chapter 15

The drive back home was a little more leisurely than the one to Malcolm's property. On the news, there was a face that was completely distraught. The man's retirement plans had been ruined, and the police knew it had been a case of arson. There were even hints that Malcolm Wright might be under suspicion. That, of course, was unsubstantiated, and he was later cleared of any wrongdoing.

There were before and after photos of the estate. The once-pristine estate had only a beautiful home and grounds amidst an almost completely burnt down forest. The perpetrator of the crime had ruined most of the property. Nothing was mentioned about the fact that Malcom Wright had devastated the environment and had only gotten a taste of his own medicine. It seemed that the general public really felt sorry for Malcolm and wanted the arsonist caught. What the hell?

During the first night on the plateau, I had set up a couple of incendiary devices hidden in air vents coming out of the house. These were phone activated. When I was certain there would be no one around, I made the call just before I left the area. The house caught fire and burned almost to the ground. This story hit the news soon after the first story had.

I wondered if Malcom Wright now knew what it felt like to have the beauty around him destroyed. He had done this same thing so many times in his quest for riches. It was a shame, but this man had never given a second thought to the feelings of others. His pride and joy was now totally destroyed.

During the climb down the mountain, I had retrieved all the markers left to guide my descent. While in the helicopter, I had the pilot fly over the edge just above the forest. This allowed me to spot the yellow ribbons tied to trees. That was where I had placed the plastic bags of gasoline and the remotely activated timers that ignited the fuel. The remotely activated wind-up timer attached to a grenade, a device I had used many times in the past, blew up the water pipe feeding water cannon used to water the forest.

In order to activate the timers, I had had to be within a certain range. If the pilot had refused to go as close as he did, I had another thousand dollars in my pocket. I had my doubts that the pilot would voluntarily come forward. As he said, he would be in a lot of trouble for flying too close to the residence. The staff at the residence might say something, but there were many helicopter services in the area. That was why I chose one located quite a distance from the target that had no markings on it indicating the name of the business.

Should the man have an attack of conscience, my disguise would lead nowhere. On my way home, I stopped in several towns for the night. As I lay in bed watching a little television, flicking through the channels, I landed on another rerun of Billy Graham. Franklin did most of the talking, as he had of late. Billy was getting quite old, and it was clear that his preaching days were coming to an end. Franklin did a good job, but unfortunately, only Billy managed to draw the listener in like few others.

Franklin introduced another famous preacher by the name of Reverend Harold Spencer, who hailed from Arkansas. He spoke for a short time and was very inspirational, before turning things over to Franklin again.

Franklin said that we had a choice in life, and we only had a certain time frame in which to make it. This choice could not be forced on a person. Many came to this point when an out of control life hit rock bottom. Others saw where life would go and made the choice before tragedy struck, thus saving themselves a lot of grief. We were put on this earth for a reason, he said. He was right about that. I was there to help the people who couldn't help themselves. It was all so clear to me.

During my drive through a small city, I looked for a place to stop for lunch. In a school zone, I saw children playing happily in a schoolyard. A man was standing in front of the fence that separated the grounds from the road.

All of a sudden, the children looking at the man screamed and run away. The man laughed and, as he turned to walk away, he zipped up his fly. The dirtbag had just gotten a thrill at the expense of the children. Being in a lesson-teaching mode, I parked the car around the corner, put on a hat, and got out, walking toward the guy coming my way. As he moved over to get by me, I blocked his way.

"What makes you think you can expose yourself in front of the children," I said.

"I don't know what you're talking about, get out of my way."

Shifting position, he started to walk as my foot came up. I kicked him hard in the groin. Down he went with a scream of pain. No one was around, which I had made sure of before I got out of the car.

When I knew he could hear me, I said, "Next time you do this, just may be your last." I raised my cell phone and took his picture. "If I get wind of you doing this again, I'll send the picture to the police and neighborhood watch. Got it, asshole?"

"Yeah, yeah, I get it."

He, of course, had no idea that I didn't live in the city, but that didn't matter. He'd be keeping an eye out for a long time. Just because I didn't like him, I stomped his hand before I left. Because I really didn't like him, I sent the picture to the local police anyway. This done, I threw the disposable phone into the trash, having wiped it clean. I used this type of phone whenever I was on one of my adventures.

Getting home the following Tuesday afternoon, I called Abe to see if he needed me on the job. He said that he could use my help and if I came in he'd make it up to me sometime in the future. This worked out fine for me as I'd need the time to complete some other venture.

I called Harry just to touch base with him. He seemed just a trifle lighter. I think he had come to terms with the situation and was attempting to move on. There were things you could change, and there were things that you couldn't. This was one of those things that we had no control over, and we couldn't let it ruin the rest of our lives. I had found this out the hard way, far too many times already.

The job at work turned out to be a complicated one and took all my attention. I did enjoy this kind of work. It created a bit of a challenge, keeping my mind off distractions. By the end of the week, a lot of progress had been made and the following Wednesday, the completed sections were loaded on a truck and sent to the customer.

That evening, I found myself thinking about an elderly couple that I met last time I went to the Chain of Lakes in Montana. I got to know Linda and George fairly well and wondered how they were. I still had their phone number in a drawer. I hadn't called them because most times I got involved with people, things went south.

The little lady was one of the gentlest, kindest people I'd ever met. It would be really nice to see her again. She reminded me of what I imagined a grandmother would be like. I debated whether or not to make contact. I'd give it some thought over the next few days and then decide one way or another.

I'd packed away the ropes and climbing gear and found that the storage area was getting too filled up again. I'd have to either thin it out or expand in the near future. There were things in there that I made at work and hadn't used yet. The amount of time it took to develop and build these things made it very difficult to discard them. I found that some couples stayed together for that very reason too. They felt they had too much invested in a bad relationship to call it quits. I'm not sure why that was. If you weren't happy and things were unlikely to change, why keep it going?

The remote aluminum dart gun took up quite a bit of space, so I took it apart and tied everything together. This gave me more room, so I looked for other ways to compact some of the stuff. Many of my things were small and lying on a couple of shelves, which took up unnecessary room. Looking the whole scene over, a thought came to mind.

Taking a number of measurements, I grabbed a pencil and paper. By the time I was done, I had plans for another project. Still having some building material, I'd start it on the following day.

The job took a few hours, and when I was done, I had what looked like a series of box openings. I believed the design was called a pigeon hole storage unit or something like that. I wondered if any people still had pigeons. This used to be a popular pastime, but you didn't hear about it anymore.

After placing my things in the openings, I was surprised to find that I had a lot of empty space left over. I should have thought of this before. Cleaning up all the sawdust and leftover pieces of wood, I took them to my burn barrel in the back of the property.

While I was back there, I saw some movement in the bushes a hundred feet away off to the right. Being a suspicious type, I went into the house without making it obvious that I'd seen something. From a window in the house, I used my binoculars to scan the area where I saw the movement, expecting to see a deer or something.

It required a minute before I saw a person hiding in the bushes. He wasn't watching my house but looking at my neighbor two houses away. The guy looked like he was in his early twenties. His being there was kind of peculiar because I lived in an out of the way place. There were a number of houses there, but we were a separate little community of around twenty-five homes.

I thought about possible courses of action to take. I could have gone out and confronted the guy, but this was a too close to home. If I had an altercation with him, it could easily get out of hand. The neighbors would become too aware of my talents. If the guy had friends, my home could become a target.

In the end, I called Bill and explained it to him. He told me he'd send a couple of patrol cars to box the man in, preventing escape, and find out what was going on.

"I'll keep an eye on him till the officers arrive. They won't be using sirens, will they?" I asked.

"No, that would warn him, and he might then escape. If he leaves, just watch where he goes, take down his plate number if he gets into a car," he answered back.

The watcher stayed where he was as he looked through his own smaller set of binoculars at the house. Who was this guy looking at or was he casing the house? He got up moving to another position, but still staying in the tall grasses and remaining fairly hidden. Fifteen minutes went by, and there was a knock on the door. When I opened it, I saw a uniformed officer.

"Detective Henderson asked me to see you, so you can point out where a young man is hiding," he said.

I walked him through the house and to the window, pointing him out. The officer spoke into the radio/transmitter on his shoulder. He gave directions to the other officers as they surrounded the guy in the bushes. The guy panicked and tried to run as the police closed in. It looked like he was so intent on watching the house that he hadn't seen them until he heard a noise.

As he ran, he looked behind him as another officer stepped in front and tackled him to the ground. He was handcuffed and questioned. The area where he had been sitting was searched. A number of items were bagged, and he was taken away.

The homeowners came out of their home to see what was going on at this point. The officer who spoke to me walked over and explained the situation. There was a discussion, and a young girl about seventeen joined the conversation.

A heated discussion took place, with the daughter stomping back into the home. The officer handed the father a card and left. The father and mother looked toward the house with an exasperated expression as they walked toward it.

At this time, I went back to my routine and tried to put it out of my mind. I was sure that the daughter, going by her reaction, knew the guy, and it would get straightened out. At first, I thought the guy, in his early twenties, was casing the homes here, but when he only watched one, I figured there must be another reason for his being there. Because it was still daylight, he couldn't be a peeping Tom.

Bill called me later in the evening and filled me in on the situation. The boy and the girl, as it turned out, knew each other very well. The parents had met the boy and did not approve of him, forbidding their daughter to see him. The daughter, Barbara, and the boy, Jesse, were planning on running away together that evening as soon as the parents went out to a dinner invitation. Jesse, in his eagerness, couldn't wait for her to call him and decided to watch from the rear of the home until the parents left.

Bill almost laughed. "If I had a dollar for each time this has happened, I'd be able to retire." He hung up, and life went on.

When I got off the phone, I almost laughed too. The girl should have waited till she was of age and then there wouldn't be all this trouble. The lad should have known better, too. I'd chatted with the girl's parents a few times, and they seemed like decent people, so maybe this would all work out.

I thought about Gord and the look on his face as he walked away from me at the camp. There was something not right, and it was more than just an alcoholic or drug rebellion. There seemed to be a look of desperation on him. Was it possible that there were severe mental issues at work in him?

On the job, there were always little things that didn't quite work the way they should, but that was normal. The shop had gotten busy again, but a few of the guys who were laid off had gotten other jobs. This had created a shortage, and the company had to hire a number of new men.

Two of the new employees had a background in the industry. Two others were teachers that wanted to get away from the classrooms. Teaching high school kids nowadays wasn't as nice as it used to be. The ones with the experience were fitting in just fine. The teachers required help and, as luck would have it, I was chosen to be the one that had to help them.

Finding out what they knew was a daunting task. I didn't know for sure what the problem was, but because they were teachers, there was an attitude about them. It seemed like they felt they were superior and thought it was beneath them to be taught how to do things. What it boiled down to was that they might have had book smarts, but it wasn't enough. When it came down to actually getting the job done, they were as dumb as a bag of hammers.

The two teachers studied the prints to death, trying to figure out the best way to do things and still couldn't get it right. When the job was finally done, it took three times as long as it should, and it was still only just passable. I guess the old saying was very true. Those who couldn't *do*, taught.

If the company were to keep them employed, it would lose a ton of money. After a couple of weeks, I no longer had a choice. Talking to Abe, I asked them to come into the office. Things were explained to them, and they were given their notice.

"Why would you be letting us go? You do understand that we're teachers and have taken a lot of courses to get where we are, don't you?" Ruprit said rather haughtily.

Ludwig, who was also a wood shop teacher too, shook his head in disbelief. "We have successfully taught many young people how to do things. I don't understand how you can come to this decision."

"Joseph, would you explain to these men what the problem is?" Abe asked.

"I'm sorry that this isn't working out. The two of you may well be good teachers. Of course, we only have your word for that. When it comes down to actually working in a place like this, and probably all other jobs of this sort, you are totally useless. You don't know your ass from a hole in the ground. You nitpick over things that don't matter and spend way too much time thinking about things, rather than doing them. You have spent all your lives studying this and that, and you never learned how to actually do things, even remotely efficiently. Go back to your classes where the kids might think that you actually know what you're talking about. Good day, gentlemen," I said as I opened the door for them to leave.

A decision was made never to hire teachers again.

"You were a touch hard on them, don't you think?" Abe said to me.

"Maybe, but that superiority attitude of theirs pissed me off a bit, especially since it is so unfounded. They really aren't superior to anyone in my estimation."

Back on the job, I felt good about how it went in the office. Time moved on, and new competent workers were hired.

My job sometimes gave me some extra time to make things for my arsenal. I had several of the double-edged knives that were nine and a half inches long and a couple that were twelve.

When I felt the need, I made a set of what people called brass knuckles, only I made them out of aluminum. I made a stick knife a while back too. The handle fit into my palm when my fist was closed, and the three-inch blade protruded between the middle and ring fingers. The blade was sharp on both edges, but only after it came out from between the fingers to keep from cutting me. The knife was meant for penetration rather than slicing but could be used either way. The handle was made so the knife stayed in position and wouldn't let the blade twist, preventing me from being injured.

Chapter 16

After several months had gone by, I felt myself getting a little antsy. The need to do something was building. I'd never been sure why this was. It had been like this since the murder of my mother. I felt that people had to pay for their crimes. Of course, death was only brought to those who had been the worst offenders and more than likely would never reform.

Online, I started looking for targets. There never seemed to be a shortage of these, but there were certain criteria that had to be fulfilled in order to be eligible. There were standards and rules that I liked to stick to.

A person had to have killed or caused the death of another person. There must be no chance for rehabilitation and no remorse. Finally, there must be the chance that they would continue. Of course, there had been exceptions to these rules. Child porn producers, rapists, and beaters were included in the exceptions. These types caused irreparable harm to defenseless youth and women.

This could not be tolerated, at least not as far as I was concerned. This type of target was exactly what came onto my radar. Porn producers were bad enough to be marked for extermination, but child porn was at a level of its own.

There had been ample evidence pointing to Jason Woodworth's guilt. He had already been convicted of production and distribution. I got onto the sites I frequented and started gathering information. He lived in the Sacramento area, and once I found out more about him, I'd pay him a visit. As far as I could determine, he was part of a nationwide network that dealt in this filth.

I believed that I would enjoy helping Jason meet his demise. The exploitation of children like this irritated the hell out of me. Although he had been arrested served time and more than likely interrogated, the network thrived. Just thinking too much about it made my blood boil. Of course, I had to make sure that the facts were checked properly first. The last thing I wanted to do was take out an innocent person.

The people who purchased this stuff were as guilty as the producers, and if I could, I'd gladly remove them too. Certain scum didn't have the right to live, and these people topped my list. How did this business flourish? What had happened to the sensibilities of our nation? We allowed far too much to go on. The rights of the few seemed to supersede the rights of the many. In my estimation, there were way too many bleeding hearts around, and it angered me to no end. I felt like slapping them around, too.

The bastard lived in a nice area of town, and the property was on a fairly well-to-do street. The grounds were separated from the sidewalk by a three-foot-high concrete wall. The property was well treed and had a lot of low maintenance ground cover. On one side, the home was separated from his neighbor by a gravel-covered space about fifty feet wide.

This could have been developed to reduce the chance

of anyone sneaking onto the property or could be a city right of way. There was a camera system around the perimeter with only a couple of blind spots. This limited access to the house, but I was sure a way in would be found. There were a lot of trees in the general area, making it a beautiful place to be living. Too bad this scum bag lived here. I doubted his neighbors were thrilled about it.

I decided to handle this venture a little different than the way I'd taken care of most of my past ones. There were far-reaching tendrils in this business, and Jason Woodworth was only a minor cog in the wheel. Maybe this could be a more in-depth job, but I'd have to find out who he supplied first before I could go any further.

Removing Samuel Alexander had slowed down the underground fight club considerably, but there were people looking to get control of it, according to the online sources. If it was indeed resurrected, I would have to do another takeout.

Allen Whickering still required a visit, but I felt more inclined to deal with Jason first. The garbage this man produced ate away at me. There was a sick feeling in me every time I thought about it too much. What the parents of these children must have felt if they had been aware of this went beyond description.

For the next two weeks, I dug up as much information as I could about Woodworth. There was nothing that I could find as to where he sent the finished products. Getting on Google, I studied Jason's property and tried to locate as many weak spots in his security as I could. There were a few spots that his cameras didn't seem to cover. Of course, I couldn't see everything from the street view. There could be other cameras and motion activated security lights on site.

Right after work on Friday, I headed out for the eight-to-nine-hour drive. Getting into the northern section of the city late, I got a room for the night and was out of it quickly. Waking the next morning a little tired, I got prepared to do a little reconnaissance. Because I wasn't going to drive near his home, I didn't bother with a rental car.

I parked several blocks away and went for a walk in disguise. As I approached the home, I carefully used a video camera to scan the entire property from the street and along the sides. The concrete wall surrounded the property and had a coating of stucco used to make it cosmetically appealing. There were other homes to the rear, which prevented me from getting clear shots in this area. I had the camera hidden from sight as best I could so his security system, if it caught me, wouldn't see it. If I was seen on a security camera, I'd look like someone old out for a walk. The grounds had a number of trees and were nicely landscaped.

After strolling around the neighborhood, looking for escape routes, I headed back to the room where I hooked up the video camera to the laptop. Going over the entire video, I spotted several places where I should be able to get near the house without being seen.

In the afternoon, I stationed myself in the area to see if I could catch him coming or going, but I didn't get a bite till late in the evening. When he came home, he activated the electric gate and drove into the garage. Getting out of the car, he walked toward the door closer mounted on the wall by the door into the home. He stood around six foot, weighed around two ten, looked to be in his late thirties, and had a soft paunch. He looked the type who sat on his butt all day and did little physical activity. The garage was similar to a million others. As I watched him, an idea came to mind.

The next day as I sat in a rental car down the street, I knew I'd stayed too long when a number of people looked at me with eyes narrowed. There was a park far enough away for me to place the car and remain more or less unnoticed. Having just enough of a view of his driveway, I saw him pull out of the garage. Tailing him at a discrete distance, I followed him into town where he went to a coffee shop.

He met with two other guys, and they sat and chatted for an hour. Using the telephoto lens, I took several shots of the three. One man was in his late twenties and the other in his mid-thirties. Both men had a look of being somewhat unsavory. Jason at least looked like he could pass in a decent society.

On his way home, he stopped at a convenience store, picking up a pack of cigarettes. It was getting to be early afternoon, and since I had to work the next day, I headed back to the room, got my things, and drove back home. On the way, I tried to refine a plan of action in my head.

Back the following weekend, I gathered more information. This time, I rented a car and remained in disguise whenever I was scouting. His routine seemed fairly similar to the last time I was there. When he left the cafe, he stopped by a weekly paper dispenser and got out, picking one up. The following week he did the same thing.

When I was at home, I decided on how to proceed. I thought I'd take a couple of days off that coming weekend. Gathering things I needed and a few things I might possibly have a use for, I headed out on Thursday after work. Traffic was light, and I made better time than previously.

Arriving at a motel fifteen minutes from Woodworth's home, I prepared myself for a bit more surveillance work. Sitting in the park down the street from his home, I observed him coming home the next day at four o'clock. He stayed in the house till seven and then left, dressed neatly.

As he drove into town, he stopped to pick up a man waiting in front of a condominium complex. The guy was close to his age, but a couple of inches shorter and a lot lighter. The two headed to a restaurant for an Italian dinner. I brought my own dinner and ate in the car.

An hour and a half later, they drove to a cocktail lounge. Once they were inside, I parked and casually headed in too. Finding a seat near the door with my back to the wall, I ordered a Corona and asked the waiter not to open it. He gave me a look but did as requested. I preferred to open it myself, just to play it safe, I didn't like other people's germs. Too often people went to the bathroom without washing their hands when they'd done their business.

There were a number of tables situated in a position where they all had a view of a small stage where the entertainment played jazz style music. It wasn't my cup of tea, but they were good. There were a number of patrons scattered around the various tables.

Jason and his buddy met two women who were sitting at the bar. They didn't appear to know them and invited them to sit at their table. After a few minutes of conversation, the women got a disgusted look on their faces and left.

I didn't know what was said, but it must have been quite rude. These men must have had crude mouths for these two females to leave, because they didn't look like real ladies themselves. Just for the hell of it, I parked myself at the bar within earshot of the women.

"Those guys are such pigs," one said to the other.

"Why would they ask us to perform in a sex video? Do we look like the type?" the other asked.

"Geez, what the hell is wrong with guys today? It seems like all we meet are assholes. What happened to the decent guys?"

"I think they're all married. Maybe we shouldn't have dumped our husbands. I thought the single life would be more fun than this," the second girl said.

At this time, I went back to my table just in case they tried to talk to me. Jason and his friend seemed to be having a good time with two new girls. These seemed to be considerably overweight but happy enough. At least they didn't walk out on the idiots.

The girls at the bar walked toward the bathroom, and the shorter of the two attempted to make eye contact with me. I didn't her any indication that I wanted her to stop, and she followed her friend into the room. They didn't look like they were having a very good time so, when they came out, they left.

The place was starting to fill up, and it wasn't long before it was standing room only. I took my cue and headed back to the car. Jason and his new-found friends left a short time later. The group was laughing loudly as they got into Jason's car. With the windows open, the shriek of the women laughing could be heard as they drove away toward Jason's home.

After they went inside, I slipped around the property and under one of the cameras. It was a fixed type and, to make sure I wouldn't be seen, I repositioned it to look at a place I wouldn't be if I had to leave quickly. Now that it was safe to move, I got close to a window that had bright lights inside. The exterior was dark so no one would see me in the shrubs from the road, which was a fair distance off.

Peeking in, I saw Jason mixing drinks all around. The girls seemed like they were already half in the bag, as was the other male. While the buddy kept the girls entertained, Jason looked over his shoulder while he flipped a switch that was hidden by a vase.

The only reason I could see why he would do this was so he could record the goings on. I wondered what he would do with the video. The girls were too old for the type of stuff he made for distribution. Could it be for blackmail purposes or just for his personal entertainment? Nobody seemed to be getting hurt, so it was best that I leave. I repositioned the camera so that it wouldn't arouse any suspicions and left.

Sitting in the car, I saw a taxi arrive an hour later with the two girls and his friend getting into it. Indications were that the night was over, so I went to the motel and called it a night myself. Saturday, if everything went the same as the previous ones, I'd make my move.

On the previous Saturdays, Jason stopped by a newspaper dispenser. This happened at around four in the afternoon. This time, I was standing off to the side well ahead of time. As he pulled up in his late-model Ford, he got ready to get out of the car. I tried not to look at him, even though I was in disguise.

He reached for the door handle and stopped. His gaze landed on me and stayed there. For some reason, he shifted the car back into gear and left without getting out. As he drove away, I saw him look in his rearview mirror. Something must have spooked him. What it was I didn't know, but this disrupted my plans.

What I had been planning to do was, follow him to the driver's door, and taken his keys at knifepoint. When we were both in the car I'd force him to drive me into his garage. This seemed like a good plan while I was thinking about it. I wondered what caused him to change his mind about the paper. There must have been something about me that scared him off.

Did I get caught on a camera on his property? It didn't seem likely because I was super careful. Maybe he had been confronted before and was wary of strangers and putting himself in vulnerable situations. The more I thought about it, the more I realized that another approach had to be formulated.

Back in the room, I called Abe and asked if I could come back early and postpone the time off. "My plans have fallen through because my friend had to go back east for a funeral," I said.

"What are you talking about, Joseph? You don't have any friends, do you?"

"You're really funny, Abe, but you're right that I don't have a lot of them."

"Sorry, Joseph, I was only kidding you. Sure, you can take the time off whenever you need it, as long as there aren't any real rush jobs," he said.

Chapter 17

The two men, who had experience in the field and had replaced the teachers, were working out well. These workers could be given a job, and it was done quickly and properly the first time. This made things a lot easier for all involved.

The weeks went by with me having a lot of grueling workouts. I was in peak shape. Problem was that I was itching for some action. Everything that had happened in my life had pushed me in this direction. As I looked back on the things that shaped my life, I felt myself heading down that rabbit hole where darkness prevailed.

It took a great effort to get me back out of it. I'd fallen down this hole before and was not eager to go there again. To help with it, I went to a park and did my mad-dash run. Misjudging the trail, I hit the stub of a branch and scraped my shoulder. This slowed me down and brought my attention back to where it should be.

There was a little blood flowing from the wound, but it was soon taken care of by the first aid kit in the car. It was a little sore for the next few days, but a week later, everything was back to normal. During this time, I pondered how to handle Jason.

By now he had probably forgotten about me if I'd made any impact at all. In my head, I went over the layout of his property and came up with a plan that should work a lot better than the previous one. Getting the time off that I required, I was soon on the road. At this point, I didn't know where or how he produced his product yet. When I was in a position to ask him, he would undoubtedly provide the information I desired. When needed, I could be fairly persuasive.

After I had been watching Jason's home for several hours, the garage door opened. He drove toward the downtown area with me not far behind. It was eight o'clock, and if his past routines were any indication, he wouldn't be back till after midnight.

This meant I would have a long wait ahead of me. Contemplating whether or not to leave for a few hours, I decided it would be better to stay. After it got dark, I took out the things I'd need and several I might have a use for. Sticking to the shadows, I carefully worked my way over to the edge of his yard. When I was certain no one was observing me, I hopped over the wall where there were no surveillance cameras.

I was masked at this point, so if I was caught on camera, there would be little for anyone to go on. Slowly I snuck over to a corner of the garage that protruded toward the street. In a recessed place to the right of the big double garage door and to the left of the front door, I hid. The recess was close to six feet deep and had several large flowering bushes. The main one in the corner was six feet high and four feet in diameter. There was just enough room between it and the next one to move easily. The bag I had was placed on the ground cover. After swatting the resident spiders and other bugs, I was left to myself for the most part. The damp soil smelled of cedar bark, and the flowering bush almost made me sneeze.

Every now and then, I had to swat some insect crawling up my arm or leg.

There was little foot traffic along the street, so I didn't have to be overly worried about being discovered. The time dragged by as I went over things in my head. An old man walking a dog passed. When he was opposite the house on the sidewalk, the dog stopped and barked at where I was hidden. The thing must have had an instinct for intruders. As I peeked out, I saw the owner tugging at the leash, forcing the terrier to follow reluctantly. The time went by ever so slowly, with me having to stand and loosen the stiff muscles in my legs periodically.

My watch showed midnight, and a half an hour later, the remotely activated gate opened. Jason's car approached, and I hoped that he was alone. If there was anyone with him, I'd have to postpone this again. Luck happened to be with me as I peered around the edge just as he drove past. He was alone, and I grabbed the bag, getting ready to make my move. A quick look at the street showed me there was no one about.

The garage door was already open and, as he entered, he parked the car just to the right of center. This gave me enough room to slip in and hide between the car and the wall. Music was playing inside as Michael Buble sang a popular song of his. Sneaking into position before Jason shut the engine off, I lay down beside the rear section of the passenger side. I kept as low as I could in order not to be seen in the outside mirror. The heat of the engine blew into my face as I waited.

The key was turned off, and the music stopped. The driver's door opened, and he exited the vehicle. As he opened the door leading to the interior of his home, he hit the garage door pad, and the big door slowly closed as the interior door slammed shut.

The light stayed on in the garage as the timer on the unit kept things lit for a short time. Quickly I ran to the interior door and put my ear to it. I listened for the sound that would indicate that the alarm system had been deactivated.

The beep sounded, and the system now allowed me to enter the home. Opening the door quickly, I jumped into the hallway and surprised the lone occupant. With a look of fear on his face, he backed up, trying to run. Too late. I kicked his ankle as he lifted his foot to back up. He fell to the floor, tripping over his own legs.

Stepping forward quickly, I landed a fist to the side of his head as he attempted to crawl away. Down he went, lying still. Running back into the garage and picking up the bag, I carried it to the living room. Closing the drapes to shut out any prying eyes, I dragged the limp body over to a chair.

Once he was in the heavy chair, I propped him upright and proceeded to tie him up. One leg was tied to each of the front legs of the chair. One arm went around to the back of the chair, while the other went the other way. From there, a rope was strung under the chair and tied off, holding him securely. He was fastened in a way that would not allow him to wiggle free, no matter what he did.

Once this was all done, I went around the house and closed the rest of the windows and blinds. By the time I was finished, he'd started to come around. He mumbled something, but it was hard to understand him with his mouth duct taped shut.

Sitting in front of him, I left my disguise in place and talked to him. "I'm here for some information. I will get it, no matter what I have to do to you, so my advice is just to give it to me. Do you understand?"

At this, he nodded. His eyes were bugged out in fear, and he was in a sweat. I opened the bag and brought out a number of tools. At that time, he began to moan pathetically. I didn't think he liked what the vise grips, hammer, a collection of knives, and rubber tubing represented.

"If I take the tape off your mouth, are you going to yell?" I asked, at which he shook his head vigorously. "If you do, you won't like what is going to happen to you, Jason."

To really instill the fear factor into him, I placed the hammer on the chair in front of his groin and removed the tape. He was shaking so hard that he could hardly form a coherent sentence.

"What—What do you w—want from me?" he asked, stuttering badly.

"You're a child porn producer. I want to know where they're made, who helps to make them, and who they go to. Plus, I want to know who all your contacts are and the names of any and all other producers of this material."

As I was talking, he was shaking his head wildly. This stopped as soon as I picked up the hammer and rested the head on his knee.

"Please don't insult my intelligence by saying you aren't involved in this practice. We are not going to debate this. Do I make myself clear?" I said.

"Yes, I understand, but if I tell you the names of any others, they'll kill me."

As I put the hammer down and picked up a deadly looking, double-edged knife, the shaking got worse.

"Do you really think these other people are the ones you should be worrying about right now? While I'm gone, think about it," I told him as I put a new piece tape over his mouth and did a search of his home.

Going through each room, I carefully looked in all the closets and anywhere that a hidden compartment could be. There were a few metal cabinets that held various folders, but nothing that would get him into too much trouble. The surveillance system was disabled in short order, and everything on it was deleted. I didn't want to be seen when I left.

In the master bedroom, I found a panel that slid back. It exposed a screen and recording equipment that was hooked up to the camera in the living room. This was tied into the switch he activated when he and his buddy had the girls there.

In the rear of the walk-in sized closet behind the panel was another metal cabinet. In this, I found a lot of pornographic material. Just for the heck of it, I moved the cabinet which had small wheels under it. There, in the floor, was a rather large safe.

Walking back to the living room, I checked the ropes and sat in front of Jason again. Removing the tape, I gave him a warning once more to stay quiet, and then asked, "I want you to tell me the combination of the safe in your bedroom."

His eyes got large again, and his shoulders sagged as he stumbled over his words, "Please don't go in there. If you do, I'm a dead man. I can't tell you the numbers, please."

I put the tape over his mouth and picked up the hammer again. I placed the end of the hammer on his groin area and raised it about eighteen inches up. Swinging down hard, I hit the chair just in front of his junk, missing him by less than half an inch.

He was screaming with the tape over his mouth. His breathing was rapid, and he was sweating profusely.

Very calmly, I said, "This is your last chance. You will give me the numbers, or the next swing will destroy your balls. Have I made myself entirely clear? Are going to tell me the numbers, or do I start using this hammer for real?"

His head began bouncing up and down so fast his teeth almost rattled. When I took off the tape, he gave me the numbers, correcting himself three times. I made him repeat the numbers four times just to make sure he was telling me the truth. Using another piece of tape to keep him quiet, I started to go to the safe.

Before entering the room, I turned around and dragged him, in the chair, in front of the bedroom door so I could keep an eye on him. It wouldn't do to have him manage to free himself somehow, however unlikely, while I was opening the safe. In the hidden room, I spun the dial and was rewarded by the lock opening and the door lifting up and out of the way.

In the safe was a large bundle of cash and a book. Opening the book, I saw names, dates, and amounts of money written down on lines drawn across the paper. At the back of the book were names and addresses, along with phone numbers. I walked back to Jason who had been kind enough to stay put.

"Okay, Jason, I have a few questions about the names in the book. I would really appreciate it if you would tell me who each of these people are and what part they play in the scheme of things. Do you think you could do that for me, or do you need a little persuading?"

I removed the tape, and he trembled as he explained who each person was. There were some very influential people named in the book. At least, Jason said some of them were. I only knew a few of the names. Just to test him, I asked him to repeat some of the answers periodically. The answers were always the same, so I believed what he was telling me.

All through this, I took notes and, when we were done, I asked him where the videos were made in this town and the names of all involved. I almost had to use the hammer to get this last bit of information out of him. What finally got him to co-operate was when I asked him, "Is the money in the safe enough for you to disappear and get out of this business?"

"Yes, yes it is. I'll leave and never come back. I'll tell you anything you want to know."

When he was finished and there were no more details, I put the tape back on. I then took the knife and stabbed him in the heart, making his death nice and quick. There was no way that I could let him go. He would have warned his buddies, and they would have been waiting for me. This person was indirectly responsible for so much harm in our society that there had to be a price to pay for it all. This god-awful garbage had to be stopped. I hadn't used the gun to kill him because of the noise factor.

I still had a week off, and I planned to make use of it. I took the book, notes, and cash with me. I planned to use the money to pay for what this continuing venture would cost me. When all was done, I'd give the rest away. Normally, I just gave away the money I collected from these missions, donating it to needy causes. This time there would be a considerable cost incurred, and so I'd use what I had to.

With the information obtained from Jason and the journal for verification, I went straight to the place where the videos were made. After surveying the scene and studying the area, I worked out a plan.

The building I was looking at was in the suburbs and stood well away from other structures. Being two stories high, it was about the size of a large house. Two vehicles were parked out front, which indicated that there had to be people inside. Along with the other things in Jason's safe had been photos of the local participants of the business, so, hopefully, I would recognize the guilty parties and not hurt any innocents.

The front entrance was fairly sturdy and would require significant force to enter, so I looked for other ways in. The tools of my trade had been strapped in holders and, with a small flashlight in hand, I moved. Checking all the windows and doors, I found one that slid sideways. Gently as I could, using a pry tool, I forced the window open, but the noise awakened someone inside, damn.

As fast as I could, I ran to the front door and waited, standing off to the side of it. It opened and, with the knife in my hand, I stabbed the arm that came out first. The hand had a gun in it. Pulling the man out with my other gloved hand, I stabbed several times in the midsection. The face was one that appeared in the photos.

The scream, unfortunately, had warned anyone else to my presence. Moving inside quickly, with my own pistol, I took out a man coming out of a room off to the left with a single shot. The noise in the confined space was deafening. Lights came on, and I heard the voices of two others yelling. One was outside and the other farther inside the building.

That, of course, didn't mean that there weren't any others. As quick as I could safely do it, I used my run and dash technique to work through the halls toward the rear. A person stuck his head out of a doorway and back in. Taking a shot a foot back from the frame, rewarded me with a scream. Running just past the opening, I fired at and killed the man inside holding his side where blood was staining his undergarments.

A crash at the back door, alerted me as it flew all the way open to a fourth man. Running into the back of the building, he was out of sight before I could take aim. Going by the sounds he made, he was running through the room. This was an indication that there was probably another door leading to a place that he would attempt to ambush me.

The most likely place was just behind me, so I ducked into the room where I just shot the third man. Quietly, I pushed the dead body into the doorway and propped it up, with his hand near the wound. Letting out a fake moan, I waited for the last man to make a move.

"Bill, are you all right?" he asked.

I let out another subdued moan and waited. A second later, the man came out and knelt beside Bill, thinking it was him moaning. Down went the butt of my gun, and he fell to the floor. After a quick search, I found that there were no more people around. I was intending to have a quick heart to heart with the unconscious man, but that wasn't going to happen, because the sirens could be heard in the distance. A bullet solved the dilemma. There were numerous flammable substances in the place so, as fast as possible, I lit the place up. The pornographic materials would burn very quickly.

Leaving, I took as many out-of-the-way routes as I could. Having scouted the area ahead of time, I managed to stay out of the police crosshairs.

Using the scanner I bought when I was pursuing Dennis Jackson helped as I listened to the police reports. The flammable materials in the building had to have hampered the police's efforts.

Just what the four men were doing there was a question going through my head. It looked like there were living quarters there, but no women. Was it possible, that the business was doing so well, that it required a lot of effort to keep supplies flowing? How large an operation had I stumbled into?

When I first decided to go after Jason, I thought it might be a quick in, out mission, with the possibility of a couple of names to pursue. When I found the book, I realized that it was a far-reaching cancer. It made me sick when I thought of what was actually being produced and how much of it. It made me even more upset when I thought of how many people there must be who bought the stuff.

Was it a modern day plague or had this kind of thing always been around? Technology had allowed for easy access and probably caused this rapid spread. The job had become a much larger one since finding the book. The money from the safe would allow me to make a number of trips in the coming week.

For the moment, I had to turn those thoughts off—much easier said than done though. It was tough to distance myself from the content of the products manufactured there. If I failed to do this, it would hamper my efforts and jeopardize my chances of success. It could even put me in a position again like I found myself in with Lazar.

Using that technique of putting my problems in a drawer for the night helped. I visualized them put away, in order to take them back out in the morning. Doing that helped me to deal with them. There was no way that I could solve the world's ills right now, or by my own efforts alone, that was a fact I had to accept.

That thought had me considering another course of action. I wondered if I could or should enlist the help of like-minded people. That would take some of the onus off me. I had for the most part always worked alone, except for some minor involvement with Bill Henderson.

I had yet to find or hear of anyone else taking up the mantle, but that didn't mean that there weren't others like me out there somewhere. How would I go about finding them? Could I really trust someone I'd never met? Would it lead the authorities back to me sometime in the future?

More questions were being brought up than answers, so I had to put it away for the night.

Because of the late night, I slept in on Sunday morning. Waking up groggy, it took a while to get up to speed. Going through the book, I found that the closest target involved in this market I had stumbled onto lived near Los Angeles in San Bernardino. The house the guy lived in was on the corner of Paulson and Oakwood Drive.

According to what I saw on Google, the home had a three-foot-high wall around it like Jason's did. It backed on to a barren undeveloped area, with a few pine trees just behind the property. This was surely not where his base of operations was, but I could find out where it was by asking him "politely."

Brandon Elliot was in his late thirties, going by the photo that came up online. The CDC—Citizens Discussing Crime—site, had only a smattering of info on the guy, but he was known as a distributor of various pornographic materials. His contacts were reputed to be all across the country and Canada.

The drive took just over seven hours, and I arrived at six o'clock. After getting a room and a rental car with Jason's funds, I went for a decent dinner at a steakhouse nearby. A leisurely drive to his neighborhood got me familiar with the area he lived in.

As luck would have it, he pulled into his driveway while I was heading away. Pulling over, I grabbed the binoculars to see if he was alone or not. The car was parked in the driveway and out came Brandon. The door on the passenger side opened and out stepped a really attractive woman in her early thirties.

She walked to the front door along with Brandon. Wearing a form-fitting dress with high heels and a matching handbag, she presented quite a sight. What went through my head was what this good-looking girl was doing with that piece of shit. Could she be involved in the business too? I liked to think women were above that kind of stuff, but looks could be very deceiving, and why would this garbage be limited to males? Still, it seemed unlikely, and she was probably just a date.

I went with the assumption that she wasn't part of the operation until I found out otherwise. Before moving ahead, I'd watch for a few days and then make a move one way or another. It was nine-thirty, and I doubted much would happen that night, so I went back to my room to rest.

Watching the local news, I didn't see anything about Jason or the men I'd eliminated. Switching to the national news, there was nothing much there either. Finally, I pulled out my laptop and checked there. The story of the deaths of the four men and the fire was there. The police statement told the public that it was deemed to have been a targeted hit. There were no theories as to why at that time.

Jason's body hadn't been found so far, which was good for me. That should leave Brandon unaware that he could also be a target. I didn't want to leave this undone for too long. The longer I waited, the more likely that the body would be discovered. If that happened, the empty safe would also be discovered. I'd locked it and placed the cabinet over it again, but a thorough search would reveal it. Of course, to find out that it was empty, they would have to be able to get it open first.

Monday morning, I parked down the road, well away from the home. The bare scrubland to my left and the heat was going to be taxing, to say the least. Brandon's car was still in the driveway. At one in the afternoon, he got into it and started the engine, leaving it running, and went back into the house. The air conditioner was on, cooling the car off. I wondered why he didn't park it in the garage overnight. I had brought along plenty of cold drinks in the cooler, and that helped me deal with the heat of the day.

Ten minutes later, the two, dressed fairly well, exited the house and drove away. They went to a warehouse part of town and entered a building with no markings on it. Loading the address into my GPS for future use, I waited in the hot sun. They didn't come out for three and a half hours. I'd have to come back later to investigate why. Because of the heat, there was no foot traffic to speak of. The vehicular traffic was quite heavy, though. Deliveries and pickups were made continuously in the area.

After the two left the small warehouse, they headed to an upscale restaurant. Across the road was another dining establishment that was geared to the average person. Managing to get a window seat, I ordered a meal that could be made quickly and that I would be able to take with me if I had to leave in a hurry.

The two stayed for two hours. By that time I was already in the car and waiting. I could have broken into their home to scout around while they were gone, but I felt it was more important to visit the warehouse first.

Brandon drove to his place, after dropping the woman off at a home several miles north of his residence. Was she just an occasional stay-over guest or was she visiting someone else for the evening? I wouldn't mind finding out the answer to that question before I visited him. After waiting for an hour, I left for the rental room. I needed a shower and a change of clothes after being in the hot sun most of the day.

At two in the morning, I drove back to the warehouse. There was no traffic in the area, but I attempted to stay in the darkness. Placing a hollow tube against the walls at various spots, I listened for sounds coming from within. Nothing was heard.

Looking for an entry point, I carefully searched the perimeter. Besides a large roll-up main delivery door, there were three other man-size doors that offered a way in. The one in the front was too visible. The other two were well locked with large deadbolts. There were a number of windows seven or eight feet above the ground.

Looking around, I located a refuse bin with wheels under it. As quietly as I could, I rolled under the window. Once on top of it, I peered through the glass. It was dark inside and so I placed the flashlight against the glass to reduce reflection. Inside was a typical warehouse configuration.

There were several walled-off cubicles against the sides. There was also a mezzanine on the back side of the building. On the side of the structure, there was a drop of around three feet to crates stacked by the window I was looking through.

Having found no security system, my best way in was through that window. The only problem was that it didn't open. My only alternative was to break it. This meant that I either had to complete the job there that night or come back at some later date and break in then, in order to finish my task.

Going back to the car, I took with me everything I thought I'd need. Breaking the glass was easy enough. It took an extra few seconds to remove the sharp edges, so I wouldn't get cut during entry. Lowering myself in and climbing down from the crates, I did a quick search of the premises. The smell of the wooden crates filled the air. There were a lot of things there that were totally un-related to my mission. On the mezzanines, however, I found what I was looking for.

After unplugging an electric lift truck, I placed the pornographic materials on the floor in a pile. Once done, I completed the search of the offices and found a hidden safe in the wall. Using the lift truck, I broke away the wall of the office. Cleaning away the debris on the floor, I used the lift truck to bust the wall around the safe. When I had the room, I pushed the two forks to the center of the machine.

The forks were pushed into the reinforced wooden wall just under the safe and then raised to break the safe completely from the holding bolts. The lift truck made short work of the removal. Putting the safe back on the forks after it fell to the floor, I moved it to the window. The safe was around a hundred and fifty pounds, so it was manageable.

The forks were placed just through the open window frame and left there. I went back to the pile of porn materials, opened the crates, and disbursed the contents. Finding various flammable materials around the building, I brought them to the pile of filth. Going back to the forklift, I looked through the window to make sure I was still in the clear and pushed the safe off the forks. It landed with a loud thud on the wooden pallet placed on top of the bin.

I moved the lift truck out of the way and set fire to the flammables. Then it was time to make my escape. Sprinting to the window and jumping on top of the crates, I exited as fast as I could and ran to the car. I drove it beside the bin and popped the trunk then lifted the safe off the bin and placed it in the trunk. I wiped the sweat from my brow. It was time to get out.

Twenty minutes later, I parked the car down the road from Brandon's house. The safe still in the trunk, I waited to see if he got word that the warehouse was on fire.

Half an hour later, the lights came on. Quickly I ran over to the rear of his property.

Through the curtains, I saw a single shadow moving around getting dressed. That meant he was alone, and scene two was about to start. As soon as he left the room, I scurried to the front door standing just out of sight. As the door started to open, I charged, just as he was attempting to set the alarm system, knocking him away. He stumbled backward, quickly regaining his balance. He stood at the six-foot mark and in far better shape than Jason was. Quickly taking up a fighting stance, he came at me with a flurry of punches and kicks.

For the most part, they were easy enough to block, but a couple found their mark. The contacts were only mildly painful, but I wasn't there for a sparring match. A straight kick to the midsection slowed him down. As he dropped his hands, I stepped forward and give him a hard shot to the forehead. Down he went. I could have pointed my pistol at him before the fight started, but I liked having the engagement.

Closing the front door and making sure the alarm wasn't activated, I dragged him to the living room, tying him up with the rope I brought with me. As with Jason, duct tape was placed over his mouth as he came to. He struggled to free himself but soon stopped as I placed the blade of my knife against the end of his nose.

"You're wondering who I am and what I want, right?" I asked. He nodded his head, so I continued. "I want the combination to the safe in your warehouse," I said, to which he shook his head. "Are you trying to say that you don't know it, or that you won't give it to me? Nod once for, you won't give it to me, and twice for, you don't know."

He nodded twice.

There was a look of fear is in his eyes as I took the knife and placed it against the outer part of his thigh, giving it a slight push. It penetrated about an inch. He screamed through the tape, and I waited for him to regain control.

"As you can see, I don't like you or the filthy business that you're in. Do not think that you can convince me that you're innocent. I have Jason Woodworth's book from his safe. Your name and address are in it. How do you think I found you? We can make this easy, or we can make this hard, the choice is yours. Are you going to tell me the combination or not."

His shoulders sagged as he realized that he had no other options. He nodded his head, and after I explained what would happen if he yelled or screamed, I removed the tape. He gave me the combination and told me, "Those numbers won't do you any good. The warehouse is on fire. That's where I was going when you broke in."

"Sorry to disappoint you, but I'm the one who set the fire. I used your lift truck to remove the safe from the wall behind the painting in the office. The painting has a mountain scene on it," I said.

At this point, he realized that what I had said was true because of the description of the painting. Re-taping his mouth and checking the ropes, I did a quick search of his home, not finding anything of use. When I was back standing in front of him, he appeared to know how this was going to end. I asked him about the woman who was with him.

"Her name's Annabelle. She's nobody. I just date her now and then. She knows nothing of the business," he said when the tape was off.

"I find that rather hard to believe. She was with you at the warehouse for a long time. Do you want me to use the knife again?"

Sweat broke out on his forehead even more. There were a complex set of emotions going through his head at the time.

"What will you do if you find out she is involved with all this?"

"I'll turn her in, just like I'm going to do with you after you sign a confession," I said. "That's what I did with Jason."

A look of relief came over him. He obviously didn't know Jason was dead.

"Yes, she's part of the enterprise. She helps with the financial end of it. You won't hurt her will you?" he asked, pleading.

I studied him. "Where are the books kept?"

"They're in the safe. That's why we were so long at the warehouse. Are you going to let me go once I sign the confession?"

"About that, I kind of lied about the letting you go part," I said as the tape was replaced.

His eyes bugged out as he realized this was the end for him. The knife entered his chest, and he was gone. I was exhausted at this time, but the night was not over. There was one more job to do before I could rest.

The drive to Annabelle's home was done in a foreboding mood. I had not eliminated a woman so far in my career. This was something I was not looking forward to. In my heart, I knew she was what upstanding people would call evil, but this didn't make it much easier.

I changed clothes before I got to her house and pulled out a fake detective's shield, an item I had never used before, because I'd decided to handle this just a trifle differently this time. As I walked up to her front door, my hands trembled just a little. I had to take a moment before pressing the door chime button. A sound emanated from inside the home.

It took a moment before a voice called through the door asking who I was.

I flashed the fake police shield in front of the peep hole. "I'm Detective Harrison. I'm here to ask you a few questions about a warehouse fire." I gave her the address of the warehouse, and she opened the door.

We walked inside, and she asked me to sit. As I passed her, I pinned her arms to her sides with one arm and taped her mouth quickly with the other in order to keep her quiet. The rope was placed around her shoulders and torso to complete the job. Sitting her in a chair, I knew that, despite the fact that she was very attractive, she wasn't a lady. The words coming from her taped mouth were definitely foul.

The mouth kept moving as I told her to shut up. Finally, the threat of a backhand quieted her down. Securing her to the chair, I searched the house. What I was looking for were any financial accounts and records. I found nothing and questioned her about it. She knew about the fire but nothing else.

When I removed the tape after a warning, she told me, "The records are all safely locked in a safe. You will never find them, you stinking asshole."

"You mean the safe behind the painting of a mountain scene?" Her expression became a look of shock. "I have the safe in the trunk of my car, and I also have the combination. Brandon was kind enough to give it to me, just before his demise. I also have Jason's journal, that's how I found you and Brandon."

At this time, I picked up a cushion and took my pistol out placing the gun against it. She was about to scream, but it was just a trifle too late. I had never killed a female before, but that day I made an exception. The woman was as bad as her partner. How people could be part of a business as foul as this boggled my mind.

I left, went back to my car, and drove to the motel. Transferring the safe from the rental vehicle to my car, I went to my room for some much-needed sleep. I, as usual, dreamt of horrible things, but I'd gotten used it. By the time I checked out, still groggy, it was time to return the rental and get on the road. A short break from all this was needed. A real vacation was in order, so, after driving to a place where the traffic was light, I checked the contents of the safe.

In it, I found more cash and the financial records I was after. The cash, close to twenty thousand dollars, would be given away. The records and everything else were going to be sent to the proper authorities. I still had close to fifteen thousand from Jason's stash. This I would hang onto for the time being. It was going to come in handy to make the trips I planned to make in the near future. Maybe I could make a dent in the production and distribution of this material. The safe got dumped at a scrap metal recycler.

After packing things away at home and doing a little yard work, things around the house looked nice and tidy. Being Tuesday, I still had the rest of the week off. It took most of that time to get over the disturbing fact that I'd killed a woman. There really was little difference between her and the men. She obviously thought nothing of the children who were abused and exploited, and so deserved no sympathy herself, no matter what she looked like.

Chapter 18

Online in the following weeks, I saw the stories unfold. There was, however, little evidence found at any of the scenes. The reason for the deaths was up in the air at this point, despite the pornographic materials that were found. This was good news as it left me in the clear.

Studying the books that I'd taken, I found out just how far-reaching this cancer had spread. Annabelle's financial records were sent anonymously to a task force I had heard of that was attempting to trace the flow. There were fifteen names in the contact books that I had deemed worth going after. The books could be sent to the authorities, but as I had seen in the past, slaps on the wrist were all that came out of it too often.

This would tie me up for a while, but, then again, I didn't have to kill the entire network in a day. The job could be spread out over several months or more. The thought of what these people made and sold disgusted me to no end. No child deserved to have the sexual lusts of an adult forced on them. If I could find these people, they would all die a nasty death. This included the people who bought this sick shit.

I found I had to get my mind off it because it was starting to bring me down, big time. My mood couldn't be allowed to sink to where it was not all that long ago. Going into that depression caused too much grief for me and those around me.

Harry and Brenda hadn't heard from Gord since he left their house in a shambles. Brenda was taking this very hard as I found out when I gave them a quick call. She asked if there was anything that I could do about it. I relayed the information about going to see him and most of what occurred, leaving out the look.

"Why didn't you say something about this earlier?" she asked.

"I knew it wouldn't help things, and I was afraid to give you more bad news. I'm sorry."

She wanted to say more but stopped herself. The conversation was ended, and I decided to go horseback riding. I hadn't gone for a while and knew it was one of the ways I could lower the stresses. As I rode through a grassy field, I saw the wind blow the grasses around. You could see exactly where it was going as it crossed the field.

As usual, I stopped in a shady area beside a stream. The water tumbled over the rocks and cascaded into a small pool before continuing its journey to the lake a mile or so away. The horse took a drink to wash down the grasses it had just eaten. It would do Brenda a lot of good to come along with me. Once she got used to the horse, I'm sure things would ease off for her too.

Back home, I worried about Gord too. When I went to see him at the camp, I should have given the first lad I talked to some money. If I had done that, he would have called me to let me know of any changes. The way it was, I didn't know if Gord was still there or not. I didn't know anything at all about him.

Gord's rebellion seemed like one of the pitfalls of having kids. In order to get my mind off the problem, I started making plans as to how I'd take action against some of the people in the porn business. When I could take some more time off, that was.

A decision had to be made as to where I would strike next. There were producers and distributors in the southern, eastern, and central states. There were still a few in the western states too, but I made up my mind to suspend action there for the moment. With the three deaths in succession in California, the remaining ones were most likely on their guard.

The southern states would be left for the winter time. The high temperatures and humidity there I found difficult to deal with. I had just taken care of Malcolm Wright in New York State, so my choice was the central area of the US. Looking at the locations and addresses of some of the names in the books, I ended up picking a place farther north. Chicago had four names that appeared to be big in the business.

I found out all this when I went to three of my favorite sites. There was a particularly large network in the windy city. I also found out why it was known as the windy city. Being situated on the southern shore of Lake Michigan, it suffered from gusts of wind coming off the lake. This, however, was not why the city received the nickname. A newspaper editor in the eighteen hundreds once wrote an article about the "full of hot air politicians" in Chicago and used the term windy, the name stuck.

I tried to gain as much info as I could on Bobby Mannetti, Frank Borrano, Al Pastini, and Joe Pesto. According to all the material I'd been able to gather, they were the four top people in the entire region that were involved in the manufacture and distribution of this stuff. According to my contacts, they were also involved in the drug and prostitution trade. It would be a real community service if I was able to eliminate these dirtbags.

Going by the names, the first thought that came to mind was Mafia. This was an organization that had its roots in Sicily, an island just south of Italy. The Mafia had started many years ago and had been a cancer that had proven impossible to eradicate. The love of money and power had proven irresistible to these, and many other, people. I wondered if these men were affiliated with any of the people who died on the yacht.

Three of the faces on the screen had a mean look to them. The fourth, Bobby Mannetti, looked like he could be a friendly lighthearted individual. Walking down the street, you would never think of him as anything but harmless. It showed how wrong you could be in certain instances.

Jim, the quality control guy that I helped now and then, asked if he could talk to me after work. It was Friday, and I didn't have anything planned, so we went for a walk in one of the nearby parks. We met at the park and headed toward a small lake that I used to help me relax. He didn't feel like having a beer or coming over to my place, so we walked.

He'd gotten married a few years ago and had been very happy. "You probably don't know it, Joseph, but Alice is having some medical problems. We got the test results back from the doctor, and he told us that she has terminal cancer."

With a sinking feeling hitting me in the chest, I said, "I'm so sorry to hear this. Alice is such a nice lady. You said terminal. How long has the doctor given her?"

"He told us that she won't last more than six months. The last few months will not be pleasant for her. I want to take her on vacation, but I've used up my time already, and if I take more, I won't get paid for it. We don't have enough savings for me to take care of her the way I want to. I don't know what to do. She's everything to me. You went through some of the most horrible things I've ever heard of, and yet you seemed to make it through," he said with a tear in his eye.

"You'll find a way to cope, too. Counseling is what helped me the most, that and good friends. As far as time off goes, I'm sure the company will give you a couple of weeks, under the circumstances."

"Maybe they'll give me a loan against future earnings, or something. I'm not sure how that works," he said as he sighed.

"Why don't you let me take up a collection and see if the guys want to help? We have a good bunch of people, and I'm sure they would love to give the two of you a hand," I suggested.

"Oh, I don't know. I wouldn't want to be a burden on anyone."

"Let me see what they say, and I'll get back to you on this," I told him.

We continued the walk for a short time, and I let him know that if he had to take time off, I could cover for him. He headed home in a depressed state. If it was me, I'd have felt the same way.

Monday I talked to a number of my fellow employees and management about Jim. A collection got started which I took care of. Everyone chipped in at least something, the company was generous, too. By the end of the week, there was four thousand dollars collected.

At home, after counting the funds, I looked at the money that I still had from Jason's safe. It was a lot of money, but I didn't feel right about giving Jim any of it. That money came from the proceeds of a horrible enterprise and would be used to help bring it down.

Looking online, I priced up a two-week stay at a place Jim told me Alice had always wanted to go. Including the flight and all expenses, it totaled to twice what had been collected. The next day I called Abe, and after talking to him, I made all the arrangements. Because Jim and I went back a long way, I picked up the tab for any extra money needed.

The following week, Alice was called and asked to come to the shop near the end of the day. When the shift ended, a meeting was called. Jim and Alice were presented with the tickets for an all-inclusive two-week stay in Fiji. Included in a separate envelope, was a little extra spending money. Alice, in tears, couldn't thank everyone enough for their generosity. Already you could see that she was starting to show signs of being sick. The trip started the following Monday, so I had to take over for Jim.

Abe walked over to me, and, when no one was within earshot, said, "I didn't think there was anywhere near enough money collected to pay for the trip."

"The guys really came through for Jim and Alice. Jim is well liked, and they feel bad for him and his wife."

He looked at me rather suspiciously then walked back to the office with a grin on his face. The week was finished and, when I got home, there was a message on my answering machine from Alice.

"Fiji is one place I have always wanted to go, and being able to spend two weeks there is a dream come true. Thank you so much for organizing the collection, Joseph."

This gave me a warm feeling and a nice start to the weekend. I wondered if she would feel the same way about me if she knew the things I'd done. Long ago, I'd learned to justify my actions to myself by looking at things from the victims' viewpoint. Unfortunately, many people wouldn't see it this way. It appalled me when I thought about this aspect of things too long. You would think that the victim's plight would be of primary concern. Instead, many sympathized with the poor misunderstood assholes who hurt so many others. I'd love to see their faces when these unfortunates hurt them. Would their opinions change then, or would they still make excuses for the bastards? Some people were so stupid.

The next two weeks went by fairly quickly with no real problems. During the evenings, I gathered information online about the men in Chicago. While watching the news one day after supper, I saw something that happened in Salem which disturbed me somewhat. Two women had been beaten and then stabbed several times in separate incidents, three weeks apart. They appeared to be ordinary housewives with no correlations found tying them together. The two murders had been done exactly the same way, indicating that they were committed by the same person. It was reported that there were no clues as to who had done it, or why it happened.

When Jim and Alice returned, they dropped by my home and expressed their appreciation for my help in getting them this wonderful holiday. They showed me photos of the beaches and the resort they stayed at. Tours that they went on were everything they had hoped for. Alice gave me a T-shirt with *I Love Fiji* on it. I was glad they got to go and felt very happy for them. It had been nice that they at least had a nice time away, before having to face the trials ahead of them.

Since Jim was back, I started thinking about Chicago and the men I planned to visit. Getting a map of the city of Chicago, I highlighted all the relevant addresses. That turned out to be easy because all four men lived on the same street, very near each other. There would be detours put in my path, I was sure. These were not men to be trifled with.

Google showed me the street views, allowing me to familiarize myself with the surroundings. It was a good thing that they all lived on the same street, as this would make the job of keeping track of them that much easier. I did, of course, wonder what the reason for it was, though. Fairview Avenue on the north side of Chicago turned out to be a gorgeous place. The houses there were predominantly brick or stone with some stucco or wood exteriors. Crime here really did pay.

I also wondered if the homes these men lived in had interconnected alarms. If an alarm went off in one house, did it register in the others? If I was in the business they were in and being underworld figures, I'd have this kind of system.

The time went by and, although I had a plan of sorts, I didn't have anything concrete. It would take on-the-scene observations to nail down this aspect. Except for Bobby, they were all married and had children living at home. This would force me to take care of the group in other locations. *Except for Bobby, that is.*

Why would men with families, be in that kind of business? What would they do if someone took their child and made a sex video with them? Would they sell that video too? I doubted it very much. Anger rose up in me, forcing me to do something to take my mind off that train of thought.

Because I'd be using some specialized items, it took time to acquire extras of items that were running low. In a month, the supplies arrived, and I was able to start laying out the things I planned to take with me. As usual, there were too many in the pile, and it had to be sifted through. When it was manageable, everything was stored in a handy place, till I could put it in the storage compartment in the trunk.

Two and a half months had gone by, and it was now mid-summer. I'd booked two weeks off and packed everything. In my spare time, I came up with a couple of ideas for items and made them at work. If the situation arose, the new pieces should come in handy.

Just to keep in touch with him, I went fishing with Bill Henderson. He told me a week before I was to go to Chicago, "Joseph, I am getting worried. There has been another woman found beaten and stabbed to death. The women were all found in different areas of the city. We have no clues as to who the perpetrator is, and no DNA has been found at any of the scenes. I think we have ourselves a serial killer in town. There have been lots of murders but never anything like this."

"I guess the husbands have all been checked out thoroughly, right?"

"Oh, yes, that's the first thing we do. The marriages of two were fine. The third was a bit rocky, but they all have ironclad alibis," he said.

"That's strange for this town," I said, as he got ready to leave.

When I talked to him, Jim told me that Alice's health was starting to go downhill. They still talked about the wonderful vacation they had in Fiji, but I could see that he was very worried about her.

On my way to Chicago, I stayed in the northern states. In Rapid City, North Dakota, after driving for eighteen hours, I crashed for the night. The next day saw me on the outskirts of Chicago. This portion of the trip took twelve hours. When I returned to the room after a meal in a decent restaurant, I lay on the bed and flipped through the available channels.

As usual, there wasn't much on, except for those pay channels with their adult movies. I had no interest in these. There had been guys I've worked with who told me that once they started watching them, it was difficult to stop. Once in your head, the images were there pretty much for good. That was unless you made a real effort or had a good reason to stop. Many of their marriages suffered because of their involvement in adult flicks.

What I landed on, once again, was Billy and Franklin Graham preaching to a huge audience in a stadium. Reverend Harold Spencer was with them again and did some of the speaking. It appeared that he was now part of the crusade team. As usual, he told everyone that you would only have so many chances to turn your life around. He said God was in charge and not us. He would deal, in His own time, with the people doing horrible things.

Well, to tell you the truth, I hadn't been able to wait that long. This was why I did what I did. These people needed to be stopped now, not later. Why I watched him on the television, I wasn't sure. I seemed to be drawn to him and his teachings for some reason.

In a way, I figured that I was helping God correct things here on earth. People, in my estimation, needed help now, and the removal of the undesirables was doing His work, sort of. At least that was the way I justified it to myself. It had worked for me so far, so why stop?

Again, there was this feeling nagging at my insides that this wasn't what Billy thought I should do, and so the television was turned off. If I didn't do it, who would? I was on a mission, and it needed to be completed in order to save countless children and families a ton of heartache.

Chapter 19

The next day found me parked on Fairview Avenue, bright and early. Binoculars in hand and the camera with the telephoto lens on the seat beside me, I scanned the area. This was the camera that Harry, Brenda, and the kids gave me. As I watched, thoughts about Gord went through my head. I wondered what he was up to. Was he still at the camp or had he moved on to somewhere else?

As, one by one, the men I was there to spy on drove away, my attention was brought back to the job at hand. Not knowing which one to follow, I picked the ugliest one. There was no reason to tail Joe Pesto instead of one of the others, except that I didn't like his face. He seemed like he would be the nastiest one of the group. When he talked to someone, his hands were flying all over the place. On the occasions when I was close enough to hear him, his voice had a harsh nasally tone to it. Profanity was like an art to him. Yeah, I didn't like the little shit one bit.

I tailed him around town as he made stops at a few high-rise buildings. He got into an elevator in each and up he went. There were other passengers riding with him, so I didn't know which floor he stopped on.

The one that piqued my interest was the one which turned out to be the city zoning commission. He and the official he met seemed on friendly terms. This led me to suspect that either Joe or the group might be involved in some development scheme.

When he was finished with the running around, he dropped by an Italian Restaurant for lunch. This took an hour and a half. He ate a nice meal while I stood around on the sidewalk, waiting for him to finish. While I was trying to keep from being observed, I had a sandwich from a Deli across the street.

Unlike many of the other areas of this city, there were very few, if any, homeless people loitering around. Some places in the city seemed like they were just crawling with people on the edge of life. These types had no future and not much of a past. As they walked, their eyes were downcast and wary of anyone who might try to take what little they had.

I heard that O'Hare Airport, servicing Chicago, was one of the busiest in the world. Chicago also had another distinction, slightly more dubious. It was one of the murder capitals of the nation, with sometimes up to ten killings in a day. With this in mind, I was pretty sure no one would be overly concerned if and when my targets hit the dirt too.

With lunch finished, Joe headed to a couple of other places, one of which was a small warehouse. It was located near the edge of a district where you didn't go unless you had to. So far, it was the only place that piqued my interest. After putting the address in the GPS, I followed him to one more stop and then back to his house. Nothing much happened the rest of the evening, except that Bobby dropped by for an hour.

With Bobby being single, I ended up following him into town. After a quick trip to the same warehouse, he dropped by an out-of-the-way lounge and parked himself at the long, well-made bar. I picked a seat in the darkest part of the place and waited for something to happen. Bobby had a drink while the bartender made a call. Bobby watched every woman, who walked by, very closely, eyeing their figures. Ten minutes later, a man came out of the back of the establishment and shook hands with him.

The two moved to a more private table. After a short time, the newcomer, a tall, lanky, dark-skinned individual of middle age, reached inside his jacket, pulling out a manila envelope. Bobby took hold of it and placed it on the table. Since he wasn't wearing a jacket, he had no place to tuck it in. The conversation lasted for twenty minutes.

I wanted to know what was in the envelope because it was too thin to be money and so must have had some important papers in it. As Bobby walked out, he carefully held it against his torso as he exited the plush lounge. Not bothering to finish the beer, I walked out of the bar as Bobby got into his Mercedes. Staying near the building, I watched as Bobby scanned the street for potential enemies. His eyes landed on me as I turned my face away.

I was one of the few people walking in the area, hence the interest in me.

As a car drove past, his eyes strained to see who the driver was. Earlier, I noticed a bulge in his pant leg. He must be carrying a handgun strapped to the outside of his right leg, near his ankle.

I really would have liked to know what was so important in the packet. The only way to find out would have been to take it, but to do that I'd have had to kill him. The others would then be on their guard, making things far more difficult for me, so that was out.

Instead, I followed him, at a great distance, to Frank's house where the cars belonging to Joe and Al were parked in the circular driveway. Bobby walked straight into the house without knocking. They must have been expecting him. The entire property being well lit made it impossible to look through any windows except with binoculars. Having parked the car down the street away from any of their homes, I took a quick look to see if I could learn anything as I walked down the sidewalk.

The windows I could look through were dim and showed no one in them. The upstairs rooms were lit with the occasional small figure passing the glass, indicating a child was in there. Bobby and the boys must have been in a room that wasn't visible to me. Whatever they were talking about, I would never know. Then again if they died, it wouldn't matter.

At eleven, the three men who didn't live there exited the front door, walking to their vehicles. All drove to their homes and, at this time, I called it a night. I really hadn't learned much that was useful to me this day. The following evening, if nothing came up, I planned to check the warehouse. I figured there might be something there that would help me deal with the four. Except for Bobby, I couldn't very well take care of them in their homes with families there.

The next day, I planned to tail Frank, but he had the family with him, so I chose Joe instead. Geez, he was an ugly little shit. I shouldn't have thought that way about the little toad, but I just couldn't help it.

Joe left his place at ten in the morning, going to an office building. He got into an elevator which went to two different floors before heading down again. It hit number eight and number twelve. When the door opened on the ground floor, another person got out. That person could have boarded the elevator at either of those floors.

Looking at the directory, I read the names on each of the floors. There weren't any names that gave me cause for suspicion on either. That, of course, didn't surprise me a lot. The names were of businesses and didn't offer much in the way of information as to what they actually did.

Half an hour of waiting and Joe came out, met Bobby, and headed to the Italian restaurant for lunch. It led me to believe that the four owned part or the entire establishment. Aside from the porn business, they probably owned legitimate businesses too.

Later, Joe headed away, with me tailing him to the same warehouse he went to the other day. I was definitely going to have to take a close look at the place. He stayed there for three hours, and the wait was a long one. Trucks drove by me regularly, with the diesel fumes wafting through the car windows as they made deliveries and pickups at warehouses in the vicinity.

Most of the warehouses had names on the front, and the one I'd been watching was no exception. *Samson Enterprises* was written in large black letters across the front. There was a big roll-up door which would allow a cube van to easily enter, but not a tractor trailer. There were windows with a wire mesh in them along the front, as well as metal bars to prevent entry.

There were two man doors in the front and nothing along the sides that I could see. I'd check around back later. There were several windows that indicated there was a second floor. Four windows were high up in the front and three along the side were all that I could see from my position.

Moving the car occasionally, I tried to keep it from being noticed. In my attempts to stay hidden, I left the vicinity of the warehouse completely and came back from a different direction. Finally, after a boring afternoon, he came out with another man. Hopping into Joe's BMW, they drove away.

Joe drove across town to a small printing business, dropping the other rotund, mid-fifties man off. With a full day behind him, he headed home. As he walked to the front door, he was met by his seven or eight-year-old daughter, who hugged him. I guess his looks didn't bother her.

The problem so far with the surveillance was that I hadn't actually found anything that warranted death for the men. If ugly was a crime, Joe would have been dead long ago. Making up my mind, I planned to get into the warehouse that night if possible. With two of the group having gone there, it was my best option so far.

In the evening, I checked their homes before moving on. From what I had been able to ascertain, they were all at home. As I worked my way to my destination, I got cut off by half a dozen different cars, irritating me a bit.

Taking a deep breath, I drove the rest of the way to the warehouse. Before heading to it, I needed to scout the place. Being it was two in the morning, I found nothing to alarm me. Parking the car out of sight, in the dark, I did a quick walk around of the building.

Being careful not to be seen, in case someone happened to come by, I inspected all the doors and lower windows. There was a security system on all the openings, making it a little more difficult to enter.

Going to the side of the structure, I studied the window farthest from the front and stood directly beneath it. That one was a little more in the dark and was a side slider type. In a bag, I'd brought several items, one of which was a grappling hook with a half inch thick lightweight climbing rope. It had been knotted every two feet for handholds, and, at the appropriate spot, I tied a small loop in it. This would offer me a foothold, four feet below the window. The roof was the flat type and just over twenty feet above me.

Placing the rope in a coil on the ground, I stepped on the free end and swung the hook. After it picked up momentum, I let it fly. It flew to the right height but just missed the edge, bouncing off the side of the wall before it ended up on the ground near me with a thud. One more try and it hooked the roof firmly enough to support me.

With the bag on the ground and a light rope tied to it and me, I started climbing. Halfway up I stopped to listen. There was only silence, so I continued the ascent. With my foot in the loop, I worked on the window after checking to see that it wasn't wired to the alarm system.

Shining a light through the glass showed me an office, not big and not neat. Cabinets and a desk with a computer on it pretty much filled the room. The locking mechanism was not fully engaged, making the entry easy. *I guess no one thinks that this window could be used as an entry point because it is fairly high off the ground,* I thought.

With the window open and no signs of an alarm, I carefully climbed through head first. Using the line attached to the bag below, I pulled it up and into the room. I extracted an extendable pole, unhooked the grappling hook from the roof, and hooked it instead to the window frame.

I left the bag and pole on the floor and did a search of the entire warehouse, using a flashlight to guide me. After fifteen minutes of looking, I found exactly what it was that I expected to find. This was a production facility to produce copies of DVDs.

There were descriptive pamphlets in boxes to accompany mail orders and crates of the finished products. I managed to find a few addresses to which these crates were to be sent for further distribution to individuals ordering this filth.

Having the information that I came for, I set about the task I went there to do. It took me an hour to get everything just right. Studying the alarm system to see exactly how it worked, and what type of warning it gave, I was happy to see it worked the way I had hoped.

It didn't look like the regular type that had a siren and alerted a security company. If I was not mistaken, I believed it dialed a series of four phone numbers. I'd studied alarms online for a considerable time and had become quite familiar with them. The most important thing about the system was the fact that there were no motion sensors. It was only activated when a door was opened. The higher up windows weren't wired into the system either, lucky for me. These men would not want the police or fire department coming in and discovering the contents of the building.

Being very careful not to leave any evidence, I gathered my things and went to the room where I had gained entry. Looking out the window, I saw no one about and made my escape. The window had been closed again. It took a minute to disengage the grappling hook. The pole did the job, and I used it to push the window completely closed.

In the hotel room, I had a hard time sleeping. I was anxious to get the ball rolling and dispose of the group. If all went well, they would all be taken care of at the same time. I wasn't too eager about making the children fatherless, but these men trafficked filthy material no one should have access to. How to get all of them there at the same time was going to be the hardest part of the plan.

In the morning I slept in and didn't bother to follow any of them, that part of the job had been completed. I would make my move that night unless something came up. The day passed slowly as I was anxious to finish the mission. To kill time, I checked a few of the places they seemed to frequent. Nothing much came to light, so at the end of the afternoon, I went to a nice restaurant and had a very tasty Italian beef sandwich, something I'd heard about.

After dark, at eleven-thirty, I was back at the warehouse. Having parked well away and in a place I was certain they wouldn't be approaching from, I got ready. Making my way to the door at the front of the building, I used a large crowbar to pry open the door. As soon as it was open, knowing that I had at least twenty minutes, I ran upstairs to the office and broke into anything that looked important. Having done what I'd come there for, I ran down to the main floor. There I broke open one of the crates of DVDs and moved it with a pallet jack to an open area.

I set the contents on fire, got my ass out of there, and ran to the vantage point that I'd selected earlier. Once hidden, I waited. It took another fifteen minutes for Frank and Joe to drive wildly to the front of the warehouse. Both exited the car with guns drawn. Each standing to one side of the door, Frank stuck his head in the opening for a quick look.

Seeing no immediate danger, both ran inside, and, from where I was, I saw them scramble for a fire extinguisher beside the door. A few minutes later, Al pulled up also with a gun drawn and entered after he heard the other two inside. There was shouting from inside, but from my distance, I had been unable to make out what they were saying. But it wasn't pleasant, for sure.

The flickering that the fire made died down and stopped as the flames were put out. The burning plastic must have reeked to high heaven in there. Bobby hadn't shown up yet. I wondered where he was, I would have thought that he'd be there by then.

The three were still inside and should have discovered the trail of debris I'd left going up to the office. Two minutes later the light in the office came on and, by using my binoculars, I saw Frank and Al looking the room over. "*Come on Joe, get into the room with these two*, I thought.

Frank examined the cabinets and the papers lying on the floor. Al looked in the drawers of the desk. *Come on, Joe, move, dammit.*

A shadow finally crossed the threshold of the office, and I pressed the button on the remote I was holding. Ten seconds later while they were all in the room, three grenades went off. Two in the room and one just outside the door, in case they heard a noise and made a run for it.

Leaving as fast as I could, I wondered where Bobby was. I didn't see his car on the roads near the warehouse, but that didn't necessarily mean he wasn't around. I traveled back to Fairview Avenue and found that his car wasn't there. It could be that the alarm system made the call to his house and not a cell phone. I doubted that was the case, but who knew? Maybe he had gotten to the scene late or possibly he was totally unaware of the warehouse incident.

If he was unaware, that would give me the advantage of surprise, but I wouldn't bet on it. Complacency could get me into big trouble. It was late and, as I waited, different scenarios ran through my head. I wasn't interested in leaving the job half done.

After hours of tense waiting, it was three in the morning, when Bobby drove his car home and parked in the driveway. He got out of the vehicle, and I could immediately tell that he knew his partners were dead. He had a gun in his hand and warily made his way to the front door. His eyes scanned the area, constantly looking for a threat. Inside, only a few lights came on and stayed on. He must have been searching the house, room by room.

I wondered what was going on in his head at that moment. Maybe he thought that if he survived the encounter, he would just have inherited the whole business for himself. It could be that he also knew that this could be the end of the line for him, too.

There were various ways that I could handle the situation. The group must have been on the radar of the local police to some degree. If so, would they pay him a visit once the warehouse incident was known to them? How much time did I have to dispose of Bobby? Should I postpone it and come back at a later date?

In the end, I decided to use the sniper rifle. The .300 Winchester Magnum with its scope would allow me to hit him from a fair distance, but only if I could see him. The possibility of waiting a day or two crossed my mind. The choice was made for me as a patrol car pulled into his driveway. The officer talked to Bobby and then took him to the station, presumably for questioning.

Crap. I should have had the rifle ready when he first came home. Things had gotten a little more complicated. Driving back to the hotel room, I contemplated what to do next. Not arriving at a decision before falling asleep, I was faced with the problem the next morning.

In the end, I came to the conclusion that Bobby wouldn't be at the police station long, and I really was in no hurry to get back home either. The thought of having to make the trip again in the future didn't excite me overly much. If I toured the city a bit for the next few days and waited for an opportunity, I might get lucky. Staying away from the warehouse was in my best interests.

Bobby was home the next day only sporadically. Attempting to follow him had to be done at a great distance because I was sure he was on his guard. I lost him several times and had to guess where he was headed. Most of my guesses were wrong, and I ended up having to wait in his neighborhood in order to catch up with him again.

During that time I brought the rental car back and got a new one for only one day. That way it would be much harder for him to spot me. The cash from Jason had come in handy. On the third day of trying to tail him, he went home and seemed slightly more relaxed, but still wary, which was more than could be said about me.

Parked down the street near an intersection, I waited and waited. In the dark, I moved the car backward away from the lights. I continually parked in different places, driving with the lights out as much as possible. I was not eager to attract attention.

At this point, I started wondering if I should just go home and call it a day. It was nine-thirty, and all was quiet. Suddenly, it looked like the waiting was, at last, paying off. Bobby's front door opened and, after peering out and scanning the streets, he walked to the sidewalk. He turned around and went halfway back to his car, stopped, and reconsidered. I was, at that point, in the dark and had a pistol in my hand, but the rifle wasn't handy enough to risk getting it.

He turned around again with a perplexed look on his face in a moment of indecision. Turning around again, he got into the car, started it, and pulled out onto the street. Slowly driving down the road, he pulled into Frank's driveway. In the time it took him to turn into the driveway and park the car near the house, I'd gotten the rifle.

I hoped no one was going to come out of the house, especially one of the kids. At that time of night they were probably in bed, but then again, with the death of their father, that might not be the case. Bobby opened the door cautiously. With a gun in hand, but not too obvious, he exited the car.

I sighted in and, as I was just about to pull the trigger, he made a few sudden moves. It was as if he knew that something was amiss. Maybe he was just being really careful not to present an easy target.

Taking a quick look around proved to be his undoing. He was stationary long enough for me to take the headshot. Down he went as the shot echoed through the neighborhood. Off *I* went, running back to the car. I drove away fairly slowly, with the lights off, from the scene and into the clear. By now the neighbors were aware of the fact that things had gone badly for Bobby.

It was far too late for me to take the rental car back and leave town, so I drove back to the hotel. I lay in bed, attempting to unwind. I lost track long ago of how many people I had disposed of since that time I avenged my mother's death. Had I reached a hundred? I couldn't say with any certainty, but I was sure it must be getting close.

Should I be satisfied with myself for ridding the world of some of its worst occupants? Worst might not be accurate. There were dictators around the world who killed by the thousands. Drug cartels slaughtered anyone in their way and were another scourge on the world. It had been reported on the news that somewhere around thirty thousand people were killed in Mexico in the past year. These were mostly done by the cartels. I couldn't, for the life of me, fathom why anyone would vacation there. In the end, would I have made enough of a difference to change things at all?

Every now and then the enormity of what I did dragged me into a dark pit. Unless I did something about it, I would go into another depression. This, I was determined not to do. For the first time in a long time, I went and looked for some female company.

It was late, and all I found were hookers or women who had difficulty finding a date, no matter how drunk the guy was. I had a couple of drinks and ended up just chatting with the bartender. Things were slow, and he had more than enough time to spare.

He turned out to be quite an interesting guy. He had gone around the world and seen many unique things. He described them in great detail, and soon I found myself laughing at his wild sense of humor. He told me of places that were perfect for the single guy. Not because there were a lot of women available, but because they were easier to see, if you were in good shape and didn't mind the exertion.

"Hey, man, you really ought to go to South America. The Amazon is the most fantastic place you'll ever see. There's Angel Falls, the highest waterfall you'll find. I saw a couple of guys base jump from the top and not open their chutes for the longest time," he said.

"It sounds like an exciting experience, maybe I'll look into it," I replied.

"Do it, you won't regret it. Have a good one."

At closing time, I found myself in far better spirits and determined to take a hiatus from it all in the near future. The bad guys would have to wait. Of course, I'd have to build up my vacation reserve again, but that seemed to accumulate fast enough.

Chapter 20

Leaving Chicago, I headed back home ahead of schedule by a week and a bit, so I planned to go back to work early. When the time came, I'd make my plans for a trip overseas. Soon after I got back to my home on Friday, I called Abe, let him know I finished my trip a week early, and asked if it was okay to come in on Monday.

"How come you're back early?" he asked.

"I ran into someone, and they've been all over Europe. He told me about his time there and what he has seen, so I thought I'd save some vacation time for when I can go."

"Sounds like a good plan to me. Sure, come on in Monday. We can use your help."

During the weekend, watching the local news, a fourth woman's body had been discovered. Like the others that one had also been beaten and stabbed. Her husband, as with the others, had been questioned thoroughly and released. It was definitely looking like a serial killer was in our town. As before, no clues were found. The police were stumped as to who had committed the crimes, or why. I tried to put my thinking cap on, but I didn't come up with any ideas about this situation.

Checking online, I read the story about the three dead Italians in the warehouse containing pornographic materials. The wives, it seemed, were being harassed by reporters trying to interview them. What made things even worse for them was that fact that a fourth man, who was also involved with the three, had been shot dead in the driveway of Frank Mannetti. Frank was one of the men who died in the explosion in the warehouse. No clues there either. Pity.

When I ran into him, Bill told me, "Geez Joseph, the department is at a loss as to how to solve the murders of these women in town."

Despite this problem, we had a nice time during our hours on the water in his aluminum boat with its electric motor.

"How are you and the wife getting along?" I asked.

"Ever since I've started prioritizing my work, we get along much better."

I told him about my plans of trying to take a trip to Europe in the near future.

"My wife wants to do the same thing," he said. "This has been a dream of hers for years."

"I guess we'll both end up there someday," I returned, hoping he wouldn't suggest that we go together.

The time drifted by, and I found myself wondering what my next step would be. I was planning to take care of some more people in the child porn business, but the urgency of that had diminished in me. There was a bit of turmoil building in me. I started to wonder if I should hand off the materials I'd collected to the proper authorities. They had the resources and manpower to go after this infestation, whereas I didn't.

Not that I had any reservations about taking the low-lifes out. There were just too many of them. After much study, I sent the materials that I had obtained to a task force charged with the daunting work of fighting pornography, sending the stuff from Seattle, which would make it more difficult to trace back to me.

Thoughts of checking up on Gord again ran through my mind. It had been quite some time since last I saw him, and it was starting to weigh heavily on me. He was such a nice young lad, and we had some fun times together. The family had meant a lot to me over the years, and so I should at least try to help him, despite the fact that he didn't want it.

It came as a shock when, watching the news, I discovered there was another murder of a housewife in her own home. The husband and she were estranged, and it looked like he was the main suspect. A few days later, however, he was cleared of any wrongdoing, which left the case up in the air again. The only people of interest so far had been husbands, and they, for the most part, had been absolved of any guilt. It made me wonder just who was behind it all.

Needing to get away from all the crap, I picked up another of Isaac Asimov's books. I had finished the novel *Prelude to Foundation* and just started *Foundation* the first of the trilogy. It didn't take long for me to become completely lost in it. I felt like I' was actually living on Trantor, a world far in the future. If it were possible, I would have given everything I had, in order to escape my life and live in that time.

With the book in my hand, I fell asleep and dreamt of things to come. In the middle of the night, I woke up and groggily went to bed. With the weekend here, I went horseback riding and meandered through the fields and trails in the forest. While sitting in the shade of an oak tree, I came to the decision that next weekend, I'd take a run to Utah to see Gord. The situation was bugging me, and I wanted to know what was happening with the boy.

At the mall during the week shopping for groceries, I ran into Bill and his wife. After the pleasantries, I asked how the investigation was going.

"We've got nothing to go on. The two husbands in the troubled marriages have been crossed off the list. The others all have alibis, and the department is at a loss as to what direction to go. Unless the public can supply us with some new information, we're stalled."

There was an idea in the back of my mind, but I couldn't quite get a hold of it. His last statements had triggered something, but I was at a loss as to what it might be. Maybe I'd been watching too many crime shows.

Online, I attempted to check on the task force I'd sent the materials to. A few busts had been made, and a spokesman in an interview said that more were coming. The families of the Chicago four had been disgraced by reporters. Although the wives and families denied knowing anything about the business, the press didn't appear to be buying it. Two of the homes went up for sale. probably in an effort to get away from the unwanted attention.

The following weekend, I headed out for the long drive to see if I could talk to Gord again. Waiting till it got dark, I entered the same way I did the last time. Having repaired the fence before seemed to have paid off.

Once in, it took a while to catch someone who looked approachable. A young man in his mid-teens going for a stroll walked in my direction.

Stepping out well ahead of time made it so he wouldn't be spooked by any sudden appearance of a person who didn't belong there. I flagged him down. He came my way, and I asked, "Do you know Gord Motters?" He nodded, and so I continue asking, "Could you locate him and see if he will talk to me. I'll make it short and quick for him if he wants."

"Yeah, I guess I could find him for you."

Stepping back in the shadows when he left prevented anyone from informing the people in charge that someone had broken into the camp. I waited for fifteen minutes. Gord finally walked over, stopping well away from me.

"Want is it that you want now?"

"Come on, Gord. I'm just concerned about your welfare, as are your parents and Eva," I said.

"You were told before that I don't want anyone coming here again. Why can't you just leave me alone?" he said with his head down, refusing to make eye contact.

"Something is very wrong. I can see it from here. Why won't you let me help you?"

"I don't need your help. I can take care of myself. Go away and leave me alone," he said as he turned and ran away.

Something was terribly wrong with the boy, but he wasn't about to allow me to help him. Had the drugs and alcohol done too much damage? I tried to find the boy I'd talked to the first time I'd come, but he didn't seem to be there anymore, so I couldn't get any information at all. Finally, frustrated, I had little choice but to come back in the morning and talk to one of the priests. Maybe I'd get lucky and find out what was going on with Gord that way.

I came back at nine and got a face to face with the priest in charge. I asked for anything he might know about the situation. "There is something wrong with Gord, I'd like to know what it is."

"Are you his parent or guardian? If not, I'm afraid that I can't help you. Gord has expressed a desire to be left alone, and we are obligated to respect those wishes. You wouldn't be the man who broke in here last night, would you? If you are, I would suggest this not happen again as we will have no choice but to press charges. The safety of our people is of prime importance, and it will not be tolerated again. As far as I know, the young man is having some emotional troubles, like most of the young men here. We are trying to help him, but that is all I am able to tell you. Good day to you, sir. I trust we will not meet again."

With the monolog ended, I guessed that I had been dismissed. I couldn't say that I was particularly impressed with the man. He didn't look like he was a bad man, though. Maybe he really was trying to help Gord. There was a problem, but I had no way of finding out what it might be.

When I got back home, the thought crossed my mind to inform Harry about the visit, but I had doubts about it being a good idea. All that would be accomplished would be to create more grief for them.

A major accident happened at work, midway through the week. A forklift operator carrying a heavy load of long angle iron hit the wrong lever. Everything fell on a completed stainless steel job that had taken many weeks and an immense amount of work to complete.

The truck picking up the job had been waiting for it to be loaded. Only the ends of the angle iron pieces were above the stainless job, but it was enough to destroy the work. The customer was called and told what happened. To say that they were unhappy was an understatement.

The forklift operator was taken into the office, and his employment at Salem Steel Fabrication was terminated. It wasn't the first time the shop had problems with the man, but it would certainly be the last. Another man had to be assigned the job of driving forklift till a new operator could be hired.

A month slipped by with fall approaching. Things at work had quieted, and I began to look for another outlet for my pent-up frustrations. This happened to me every so often. It all started during the long wait for a payback to those responsible for my mother's death. For years I wanted to get even but didn't have the opportunity or the skill. This period of several years, with the anger building, forced me to develop the fighting skills and the knowledge I would require to carry out my first act of revenge.

I needed a release every now and then to rid me of the tension. If I didn't, I got irritable with those around me. A normal life for me was out of the question as almost everyone I had ever cared for had been violently taken away from me. All this caused the continuation of the cycle.

Allen Whickering Construction was back in the news. Shoddy workmanship and poor quality materials used during construction caused another partial collapse of one of his projects. Poor drainage was to blame that time. Even though everything had been inspected by city officials, corners were cut throughout the job. Another investigation was started because three more people perished in the latest incident.

Whickering blamed the subcontractors again for the problems and claimed to be doing everything above board. It was suspected that some of the inspectors may have been paid to look the other way. However, this was only conjecture, and nothing concrete had been found at that point.

Whickering, of English descent, came to this country as a youth with his parents. During his late teens, he started doing renovations and, by the time he was twenty five, had built a thriving business. A lot of the more incriminating things were received from the sites I normally used when investigating criminals.

This man did not own up to being responsible for the deaths of people living in the places he built and would be receiving a visit in the near future. I believed I'd try to make this encounter slightly more interesting for Allen than I did for most.

Chapter 21

The plans were slowly made, and I had driven to Los Angeles. Going to the area in La Habra, North Monte Vista Street I saw a bit of Whickering's handiwork. Standing before me was a cordoned off apartment building, with a section of it having collapsed. Much of it looked like it could fall down without too much effort. There were broken pieces of lumber everywhere. Crushed drywall sheets, along with wiring torn from panels, littered the site. Some of the materials looked like they had been moved to extract dead bodies. These were noticeable because of the dried blood. How could he call himself a contractor and build something that fell down, killing occupants?

Saturday morning, parking down the street from where he lived, I waited for him to make an appearance. Three hours later, he pulled into the driveway and entered the home. I wondered if his fine-looking residence was built to the same standards as the apartment complex.

An hour later, he came out and headed off, with me on his tail. Stopping at a few construction sites, he chatted with what seemed to be other builders. The signs indicated that these were not his projects, and he only stayed a short time at each.

The man drove a Mercedes, which must have set him back a few bucks. He stood around five foot eight and had a slim build, weighing maybe one sixty. His hair was dark brown and thinning. He looked like an average guy and must watch what he ate, as he didn't have a paunch.

Late afternoon, he pulled into an upscale restaurant that specialized in Surf and Turf. As he walked through the door, he was met by a lady who dressed impeccably. She took his offered arm, and the two went in. I already had a mustache on and pulled a pair of glasses out of the console compartment. In the trunk, I got a small suitcase with a change of clothes. Carrying the bag into the restaurant, I asked to go to the washroom so I could change into appropriate attire.

Once done, I entered the dining area and spotted my man. I asked for a table off to one side where I'd be able to keep an eye on Mister Whickering. This was easy enough to get when I handed the young lady seating me a twenty. Whickering and the woman had drinks as they studied the menu, which meant they'd be there for a while.

Having seen the "special" marked on a blackboard on the way in, I ordered a Corona and the surf and turf. At that point, I was unsure what the relationship between Whickering and the lady was. She wasn't his wife, but so far there was little indication that they were romantically involved. They didn't appear to be talking business either.

My dinner had come and gone as I nursed my second beer. The bill had already been paid, and I bided my time, waiting to see what happened with Allen. When the waiter brought the check to him, I left.

Five minutes later, he drove off by himself after he gave the woman a hug and nothing more. Driving home, Whickering stayed there for the evening. During the time he had been under my scrutiny, his manner had been pleasant enough. He hadn't treated anyone badly or looked like he thought of himself as superior.

The only real strikes against him were the poor construction practices he used. This had been an ongoing thing, and it appeared he had little remorse concerning the deaths of many people. The subcontractors all claimed they did their work under his strict orders. All the cutting of corners had been demanded by him in order to save money, according to several of the subcontractors.

Looking at him, you would never think of him as a criminal, but looks were often deceiving. They really were in this case, as far as I knew. A few more hours parked down the street the next day and it was time to go home. It was a long drive, and I got me back later than I liked. Because of that, I forgot to set the alarm and ended up sleeping in the next morning, making me late for work. I probably should have taken the extra day off like I was going to.

After watching Whickering, I had a feeling that I needed to do a little more research on him, just in case the facts weren't quite right. His demeanor didn't fit as well as I'd like. The man just didn't look, or act, like a man who had been the cause of so many deaths.

Could it be possible that Whickering's allegations were true? If they were, that would mean there would have been collusion between the subcontractors. That just might be the case, and if it was, the city inspectors would have had to fit into it somewhere.

Chapter 22

It took a whole lot of digging and calling in of a few favors from site members to find out the names of the two inspectors. The two city employees I found out were the ones that had done most of the inspections on the last job site, and it was looking like they were the ones on the other collapsed sites too. The website member that gave me the information had friends that worked for city hall. Photos and addresses completed that aspect of the search, and the following weekend found me in Los Angeles again.

That time, I took the extra time off so I wouldn't be rushed. It didn't take long to figure out what I was going to do. The hard part was figuring out whether to snag one or both of the inspectors. The choice, however, was made for me as I could only locate one of them. Javier Rodriguez was single and lived in an apartment.

It was Friday afternoon, and the workday would soon end for him. Coming out of the city hall building, he headed for a multi-level parking garage. However, too many people were around for me to make contact with him there. I followed him for a while, but the heavy traffic caused me to lose sight of him. My only recourse was to head to the apartment building, and see if he showed up there.

Half an hour later, he drove his car into a parking spot reserved for tenants and a few guests. He parked very close to the visitor's spots, which worked well for what I had in mind. Parking in the spot closest to his, I snacked on some of my supplies, using bottled water to wash it down.

His car was far enough from the front doors he would have to exit from, to allow me to station myself on a bench under a tree. My disguise was secure, and the rental car had the plates muddied. It had rained earlier in the day, providing me with the opportunity to get the car dirty. All this should help make identification a bit more difficult if something should go wrong and I was spotted.

Having to go to the bathroom forced me to go to the car and urinate in an empty water bottle. Back by the bench with bottle dumped in the garbage container, I waited. The air was becoming chilly as the sun went down behind the buildings. At eight-thirty he came out, all dressed up in party clothes. It was already getting a little dark and, as he walked across the lot, I fell in behind. Javier was humming to himself as he must have been looking forward to a night on the town. Because he was humming, he heard nothing, plus it helped that I was wearing soft-soled shoes.

There was only one other person around, but he was entering the building. At the last minute, waiting for the guy to go through the doors, I had just enough time to make my move. Coming up fast from behind, I stuck a gun into Javier's ribs.

A slight squawk came from his mouth as I told him, "Be quiet, all I want is some information and if you co-operate, nothing will happen to you. Do you understand?" I asked. "Just nod."

That he did as I walked him over to my car. I'd debated over this part of the venture for a while. Would it do to put him in the passenger seat with his hands restrained, or should I have him drive the car with me pointing the pistol at him?

In the end, I decided to have his hands bound behind him and quickly put him in the passenger seat with the seatbelt done up. Looking him in the eye, I said, "You will not say a word and not give anyone any cause to question what's going on, is that understood?"

"Yes I understand that, but what is it that you want?"

"We will go somewhere a little more private first," I said.

With the car being an automatic, I was able to drive and hold the pistol at the same time. He was uncomfortable with his hands behind his back and the belt done up, but it couldn't be helped. Fifteen minutes passed before I got to an isolated place. He behaved himself most of the time, and it only took one smack with the pistol, hitting his shoulder to keep him in line.

When I parked in a green belt area of the city, I turned to face my new friend. From under the steering wheel, I removed a piece of duct tape and placed it over his mouth. His eyes bugged out, and he started mumbling something I couldn't understand. For some reason, it got worse when I took out the long bladed, double-edged knife and showed it to him.

Waiting for him to settle down, which took a minute or so, I said, "I am going to explain a few things to you, and I want you to listen, very carefully. I know that you and another inspector have been paid off. You know what I am talking about, because some of the buildings you and your partner have inspected have collapsed."

There was a look on his face indicating he knew what I meant. His shoulders sagged as if he realized that it would do him no good to deny it. The man was no hard-ened criminal and had probably never had this kind of dealings with one.

I give him time to process things and then continued. "What I want to know is the names of the people who have paid you to look the other way. If you don't wish to feel what it's like to be cut, I suggest that you tell me who they are. I'm going to remove the tape as soon as I know we won't be disturbed, and then you will tell me the truth, right?"

He nodded his head up and down in a defeated fash-ion. Looking around to make sure no one was about, I removed the tape. Beads of sweat had formed on his forehead and were running into his eyes.

Taking a paper napkin, I wiped his face as he began to talk. "We never meant for anyone to be hurt. The con-tractors were very insistent and offered us a considerable amount of cash. My mother was in the hospital, and we were short of money to pay the bills. My friend's son has cystic fibrosis and needed the money very badly too."

"Yes, yes, I understand things were tough, but because of you two, many people died. What are their names?" I asked a little more forcefully.

"Fred Acres of Acres Construction and Bernard Jo-seph of Joseph and Sons Construction are the men who paid us. They told us we would regret it if we ever talked. We will lose our jobs if anyone finds out what we have done. We both regret what has happened," he said as tears flowed down his face.

"If I take you back to your complex, are you going to warn these two men?"

"No, they deserve what they get," he said.

"And you don't deserve what you get? What makes you any different than them?"

"I know you're right, but I swear I will do my job properly from now on, as will my friend, Pedro, I promise."

"I hope you are telling me the truth because if you warn them, I will know. If you ever do your jobs improperly again, you may not live to regret it," I said as I drove back to where he lived.

I stopped on a side street near where he lived and removed the hand restraints, with a stern warning. He walked away not looking back as instructed after promising not to breathe a word about this.

In the morning, I ran the rental through a carwash. It made the vehicle look totally different as I located where Fred and then, Bernard lived. Being Sunday morning, I figured that I might as well head for home. A little research would be needed in order to proceed with this mission.

I felt a real sense of relief at having not dealt with Whickering the previous week. The man had been set up by the other contractors and almost gone to prison for something he didn't do. If I hadn't had this feeling about him, I might never have found out who the real culprits were. If I had killed Whickering and found out he was innocent, I'm not sure how bad it would have affected me.

Life went back to normal and having come back early gave me the opportunity to get more time off later. It took two weeks to get ready to pay the boys in Los Angeles a visit. Preparing the things I'd need took a few days and, when all was ready, I booked several extra days away from work. It was a good thing I was able to break up my vacation time like that. If not, I would be seriously restricted in the number of corrections I would be able to make. It would also make it harder to handle the tensions that built up in me all too often.

Now I was on my way to visit a couple of guys who needed to be shown the error of their ways. The first thing I did, after getting a nondescript car and a room was to visit the site of the last collapse. The area was still cordoned off as the investigation was still ongoing. I looked over the site, wearing a white hard hat. That would give people the impression that I belonged there.

After finding what I wanted, I did a run by Fred's home. He wasn't there, so I drove to Bernard's place. He wasn't home either unless he had left his vehicle somewhere else. There seemed to be no use in waiting there, so, returning to my room, I contemplated my next move. I already had things pretty much planned out, but further refinements wouldn't hurt.

Lying on the bed, I felt a nice run was in order. Keeping in shape was one of the things that had kept me alive so far. When I was finished that, I had a hard work out in the room. Practicing moves kept my timing in tune and helped keep my confidence in line. If the timing was out during a strike, I could easily miss my target, which would leave me vulnerable to a counter shot.

After a nice shower, I relaxed for a while, falling asleep, and not waking till morning. The sun was shining, and the temperature was in the low eighties. Parking down the street from Fred's home, I waited for him to leave. It was Saturday, and there was less traffic than usual on the main roads but more on the residential ones. This forced me to park quite a ways down the street but also kept me more out of sight. At ten, he came out the front door of a rather expensive-looking home, hopping into a truck with Acres Construction on the doors.

Following him fairly closely, but not close enough to arouse any suspicions, I tailed him to a work site. The site wasn't particularly big but was busy. I saw Fred talking to the site supervisor for a while as they toured the job. They stopped here and there, discussing what needed to be done.

Fred was tall and slender of build and had a relatively short, brownish beard, and slightly curly longish hair. His nose was a bit large and seemed to give him the look of a jester you saw on playing cards. Going by what I saw, he really liked talking.

When he was finished there, he went to another site and then back home. Later in the day, he left again, only this time he was with his wife and a chubby sixteen or seventeen-year-old boy. The whole family, dressed in clothes that were more fitting to farm life, got into the car parked in the driveway beside the truck. Having the family with him left me with no choice but to visit Bernard.

The address I had for him put him in an above-average family district. The home on Ventura Drive was stucco with a tile roof. The grounds were well kept, and I saw him tidying the yard. Bernard had quite a paunch and looked like he'd be around the six-foot mark, weighing close to two thirty. I'd guess him to be in his early fifties and balding on top.

Looking at him, it was obvious that he had made the same mistake many men in his position made. In order to hide the baldness, he did one of those silly comb over's, thinking it masked the bare scalp.

Despite his heavy body, he carried himself well. This meant I needed to be careful not to be overconfident with him. He could be fairly quick and cause me some grief if I wasn't prepared. When the chores he'd set out to do were done, he sat in the shade and yelled through an open window. "Hey, Lucille, get me a beer, will ya?"

A mousey little woman thin as a rake brought him the beer without any words spoken between them. She didn't look like a happy camper to me. I got the feeling he wasn't the kindest person in the world to her. Would she miss him if anything were to happen to the dear fellow?

Night time came and, after having a dozen beers, Bernard fell asleep in the lounge chair. His wife turned out the lights in the house and went to bed with him still outside. That development could well be a major break for me.

I had most of my tools with me in the trunk and, when no one was anywhere around, I snuck over to Bernard. Enough time had passed for the little woman to fall asleep. The nun chucks were handy when I got beside him, so I gave him a good whack across the forehead.

Quickly binding his hands and legs, I taped his mouth and then ran back to the car. The back end of the car was as close to his patio as possible. Unlocking the trunk, but leaving it down, I quietly returned to the patio. Getting him up onto my shoulder was a daunting task. A large wheelbarrow would have come in handy. It was a bloody good thing I'd been doing a lot of power training with heavy weights. Despite that, I still had to be careful about throwing out my back if I were to twist the wrong way.

Once he was in the trunk of the car, I drove around the corner and took off the cover I'd placed over the license plate. While driving toward my destination, there was noise coming from the trunk. Pulling over, I opened the trunk and had a quick chat with Bernard.

"If you make any noise, I'll finish you off, here and now, so shut the hell up and don't make any more racket."

He moaned as I closed the lid again, probably wondering what on earth was going on. The rest of the drive was relatively peaceful, for me at least. By the time I got him to where I wanted, it was fairly late. The area was quiet with no one in sight as I parked the car as close as I could to where I wanted to be.

Opening the trunk, I stood back quickly just in case he'd gotten loose. He hadn't and so required help getting out. Under the yellow tape and over the rubble we went, with me holding a pistol. Walking along a path I'd marked earlier, we went inside the partially collapsed building. He tried to make a break for it but tripped over a broken two by four.

Cutting his face when he landed on another piece of wood, he let out a long moan. He tried to shout, what were probably obscenities at me, but the tape across his mouth made it all incoherent.

"Sit down with your back to the post, and shut your mouth," I said.

With his hands zip-tied behind his back, he was fastened to a support post using a rope. He'd sobered up considerably by this time, and as the rope was tightened, it buried itself in the fat around his middle.

His cell phone had been on top of a patio table when I collected him, so I'd picked it up and stuck it in my pocket. When I knew he was secure, the car was moved to a more inconspicuous spot.

Coming back, the conversation began with me saying, "I brought you here after having a nice chat with Javier."

His expression of anger changed to one of, *Oh crap.*

"You're one of the contractors that helped build this complex and paid off Javier and Pedro, so they'd pass the inspections," I said.

At this, he shook his head, not trying to talk.

"I'm going to take the tape off. If you make one loud noise, I'll bust your skull, you understand me, Bernard."

Nodding his head, he settled down. As I removed the tape, he started to scream. The gun butt shut him up immediately, leaving a red mark, which soon turned into another welt on his forehead.

"You want to try this again?" I asked.

The sharp pain had made his eyes water. He mumbled an affirmation, and the tape was again removed. This time, he stayed quiet and asked, "What the hell do you think you're doing? You can't get away with this. I have friends in high places."

"I don't care who you know, but I do know that you and Fred Acres have built sub-standard buildings and paid off the inspectors. Then you ended up putting the blame on Whickering," I said.

"So what? You can't prove anything."

At this time, I lay a beating on the guy, nothing too serious, but enough to let him know that he was in big trouble. I really didn't like the arrogant bastard. When he was a bit more humble, I showed him a printed confession that explained what they had been doing and how the blame was shifted to Whickering. At first, he refused to sign the paper. A little more persuading, and he became somewhat more co-operative.

"I am going to give Fred a call on your phone. I see his number in your list of contacts. This is what I want you to say." I told him what that was. "Do not deviate from what I've told you, and if you try to warn him, I slice you up with this." I showed him the knife and dragged the tip across his cheek.

All the fight had gone out of him by then, and he did as he was ordered to. He told Fred, "Something big has come up. I have to see you at the last place we built, the one that fell down…No, I can't tell you over the phone. Get your ass out of bed and come over here, right now."

Bernard was silenced again with a new piece of tape put over his mouth. After giving him a warning, I moved over to a spot where I'd be able to see Fred coming. Twenty-five minutes went by, and there he was. He parked on the side of the road but stayed in the car. The window went down, and he called out for Bernard.

Standing in the dark so he couldn't see me, I waited for him to call again.

I'd been practicing, trying to sound like Bernard and managed to gruffly tell Fred, "Come into the building."

His brows knit together as he thought about it. Knowing it was Bernard on the phone was enough to convince him to at least get out of the car.

By the time he realized that he had made a mistake, I was beside him with the pistol pressed against the side of his head. Into the building we went, his legs almost buckling under him. I shined my flashlight on his friend long enough for him to see the blood and bruises. His hands started to shake as he thought it might happen to him too.

Forcing him to sit down, I explained what I'd already told Bernard. "Do I have to convince you to sign the paper too, or are you going to sign it now."

"This won't stand up in court. Whickering hired you to do this, didn't he? That chicken shit son of a bitch will get his, you wait and see."

A fist to the side of his head stopped the yakking. A couple more smacks and he too signed the paper. Fred was tied up too and muzzled to shut that never-ending mouth of his. Above where the two were positioned, were two stories of poorly built floors and support walls, partially collapsed. On top of that was an asphalt roof.

Earlier, when I was there, I checked the place out and found a nice unstable spot. That spot was now directly over the two men. Going to the car, I took a come-along out of the trunk as well as a steel cable.

Wrapping the cable around the top of the post and back to the come-along, I tightened it up. The post was the only real support post holding the ceiling up. I stretched it out and attached the come-along to an iron bar embedded in a concrete slab outside the structure. Tightening the cable, I watched the two men struggle.

Before tightening the cable any farther, I went back inside to explain things to the two men. "Innocent people have died because of the way you built things. Now you will suffer the same fate they did."

The two men, seeing what was about to transpire, started struggling to free themselves even more.

Outside, I used the come-along to pull the post out from underneath the ceiling, and the structure fell down on top of the two panicking men. There was a loud crash, and, after unhooking one end of the cable from the come along, I pulled it out of the mess. Taking everything quickly to the car, I left, before anyone came to investigate the noise created by the falling structure. Having worn gloves and a disguise should help to keep me from being found out if by chance either one survived. This was highly unlikely as they would surely have been crushed by the weight of the building that fell on them.

Although it was a very unpleasant way to deal with these men, I truly believed it was fitting. Those two had caused major grief for a lot of people, and I was sure that it wasn't over yet. There were many structures that had been erected by them that were still standing.

On my way back home, I accessed a photocopier and made several reproductions of their confessions. Copies were sent to city hall, local newspapers, and the police. The original letter was sent to Whickering's lawyer. While handling all the items, I wore latex gloves to prevent fingerprints or DNA from being sent too.

After a brief amount of time passed, Allen Whickering was exonerated of all responsibility, and his name had been cleared. Thinking back, it went to show that it bore investigation, no matter what the facts appeared to be. I went to Los Angeles to eliminate the man and found out that he didn't do what everyone was convinced of. The bodies had been discovered, and it was obvious that they were executed in an unusual manner, but executed nevertheless. At first, Whickering was suspected of being involved, but it was soon proven that he wasn't.

The venture came to a successful conclusion, and I felt much better. Having a direct, hands-on approach to solving dilemmas had a lasting effect on me. For a time, I could live a normal life. I would prefer to make this permanent, but I was wired differently than most. This had been caused by the circumstances beyond my control, so there was little I could do about it.

Chapter 23

Jim informed me that his wife Alice was going down-hill fast. He would like to spend some extra time with her before she became totally incapacitated. Before he had the chance to ask, I offered to take over his job whenever he needed to be away.

"Thanks, Joseph. I don't know how much or for how long it will be, but I just want to be there for her."

"Anything I can do to help, let me know. Give Alice my best," I said, patting him on the back.

Online, I did a follow up on the progress of the child porn task force and saw several reports. Much headway had been made, and this gave me a good feeling. The report stated that a lot of the advancement had been made, and was due to information sent to the task force revealing who was involved. Other information sent to the task force included how the distribution was handled and the money trail.

Seeing this lifted my spirits considerably because sometimes I wondered why I was here. It couldn't be just to have everyone important to me killed off.

More and more often, Jim took time off. I filled in for him and saw that the strain was taking its toll on him.

Watching someone slowly die before you was something I would not want. It would be better to have things end quickly. With me taking over for Jim, it gave him the opportunity to spend more time with her, but also made it more difficult. It must have eaten away at his insides to watch her fail before his eyes.

Time drifted by and the summer turned to fall yet again. It had been a hot summer, temperature wise, in Oregon and also throughout much of the country. The Middle East was in turmoil, no surprise there. Refugees were on the move and becoming a worldwide problem, costing some countries in Europe more than they were able to handle. Financial crises in some countries caused governmental insecurities, as the general populace became very unhappy. Terrorist bombings were becoming commonplace as well as roving gangs of Muslims, in Europe, gang raping white girls they thought of as inferior. Too many mass shootings of our young were happening which gave the average American citizen real cause for concern. The way some of the southern states treated the Blacks would soon create a backlash, I was certain.

The world was going downhill fast. I saw news reports showing places like China and India, where the air quality was unbelievable. I'd seen cleaner air during forest fires. Our dependency on oil would, I was sure, one day kill us all. People thought that it was no big deal, that it was only over there in other countries, but what was over there eventually came over here. Just look at the nuclear problem in Japan.

Much of the contamination had reached North America's western shores. The change in weather patterns here was causing more droughts in some areas and flooding in others. We really were like dogs that shit in their own bed, God, we were so stupid.

As I was home that evening, I grabbed the book written by Asimov that I'd been reading. *Foundation* took me away from it all. How I longed to be in a time far away. I was so tired of this place because it seemed like this life had little in it that showed much promise. I'd been thinking about going to see what the rest of the world was like, but with terrorism the way it was, I wondered if I'd actually get there.

I'd have to be content with going to the places I dreamt of in my mind. Greed had always been around, but I doubted that history could compete with the avariciousness of modern society. No one heeded the needs of future generations. CEOs of corporations were focused on one thing, and one thing only—money. The politicians we elected did nothing to fix it. Maybe they should all be exterminated, and we could start over.

This line of thought was counterproductive, so I got back to my book and lost myself in it once more. It took no time at all, and I was back in the zone. I should use it as therapy more often. Only one other thing did the trick as well as this.

The time came and Alice passed away from her disease. Jim, although very unhappy, had learned to accept it. He realized that he'd had more time with her than many others had had with theirs. The trip to Fiji was the icing on the cake and at the funeral—which the entire shop attended—he expressed his and her gratitude.

It took time for Jim to grow accustomed to being alone. Several months passed before he took full control of inspections. In the end, he found that this gave him the necessary diversion he needed to move on. I went to see him now and then but refrained from getting too close. My lifestyle and his were far too alien to each other.

The winter passed as well as another birthday for me. I was in my mid-thirties and, although I stayed in the best shape possible, I sometimes felt like "old" was just around the corner. That, of course, was dumb, but you couldn't help how the mind sometimes saw things.

During the winter, there had been another beating death of a woman. There was one happening every three to six months. I wondered if Bill was getting any closer to apprehending the guilty party. The general populace of Salem had been very apprehensive about the murderer, who seemed to be hiding among them. The women in our city felt very unsafe and wondered who would be next on the vicious murderer's list.

I often found myself wondering what motivated this person. It had to be a man, I felt certain. The force of the impacts indicated this. This man must be horribly angry with women. I sometimes wondered if it was possible, that there might be another reason entirely for him doing this. Again, something in the back of my mind was trying to tell me something crucial. This thought just wouldn't come forward. It had, I thought, something to do with a program I saw on television quite a while ago, but what it was stayed out of reach.

The weather began to warm up as spring came closer. It had been an unpleasant winter, and I was glad that it was leaving. I longed for the excursions into the woods and parks. The weather was supposed to be mild one day, with the temperature going into the sixties. It was only Wednesday, but life seemed too short to miss this kind of opportunity. I called into work and let them know I wouldn't be in.

I packed a lunch and off to Baskette Slough I went. After spending a few hours hiking and sitting by the water then heading to the park, I did some of my mad-dash runs. By the time lunch rolled around, I'd gotten in a good workout.

Again, sitting in a place that overlooked the water, I sat on a dry spot and leaned against a large maple tree. Birds were already working hard at building nests. They flew back and forth, carrying little bits of grass and twigs. The air was alive with the sound of chirps and fluttering wings.

Spring had always been my favorite time of year. Everything started anew, and life began to take on meaning once more. I never cared for fall very much, even though the colors of the leaves were so beautiful. It felt like everything around me was dying. While I was there, I tried not to allow any unhappy thoughts enter my mind.

When I looked across the water and saw the splendor, I was suddenly reminded of a painter that had his own show for many years. Bob Ross, the guy with the fuzzy hair and the wonderful disposition. He could make a canvas come alive in no time at all. He used terms describing things that made life seem a little brighter.

By mid-afternoon, the clouds started to roll in and things began to cool off. I took this as my cue to head home. It had been one of those mental health days that were so badly needed periodically. Refreshed and invigorated, I walked back to the car and, as I drove home, I saw a horse in a meadow. This reminded me that I should go riding as soon as it was nice again. I hadn't seen Bob or my favorite mare in some time.

As the weeks went by, I found myself needing to find a release once more. Gradually it built to the point where I either did something about it, or I started to become irritable. Going online, I hunted for someone who had made life unbearable for others. I found too many stories revealing a part of society that disgusted me. Rapes and murders dominated the news. There was a story that crossed the screen yet again. Another priest accused of sexually molesting young boys. Damn, why did the Catholic Church allow this problem to continue?

One story piqued my interest more than the others. There were gang troubles that infested many of the larger cities. Whenever there were a lot of young men with not enough to do, this situation arose. There had been quite a number of girls allegedly gang-raped by one particular group located in East San Francisco. The Panthers, a Black gang, seemed to feel they had the right to abuse girls of any race. At least this was what the online sources claimed.

Through intimidation and brute force, it was said, the boys had gotten away with this and other crimes for far too long. Although the charges were most often dismissed, my sources insisted they were guilty. Once again, I believed there were law enforcement members making use of the sites I frequented.

This time it was easier than normal to get information on the members of the gang. The more I read about it, the more I believed it. This crime had struck close to home for one or more of the people supplying this information online. A new site, Sweet Revenge, was posting pictures of the gang's members and a record of charges, mostly dismissed.

Double checking every bit of information took time. It was important to verify that someone wasn't just trying to set the group up. After going to other sites, I found that the writing styles of the people posting information varied considerably. After confirming that this wasn't a personal vendetta by one or two people, I was ready to move ahead.

The gang was also accused of drug trafficking, theft, break and enter as well as protection rackets, plus a host of other offenses, including murder. I despised that type of behavior, as it had happened far too often in my life.

Thinking things over for a week, I gathered the items I would be using and tried to make plans for the upcoming weekend.

The group's activities were making me fume. I found myself getting really angry as I drove toward the east side of San Francisco. During my visit to Los Angeles with Fred and Bernard, I found myself getting a bit carried away during the time I was convincing them to sign the papers.

I went way overboard once, long ago and did things that stayed with me for quite some time. After beating a man so badly he wasn't recognizable, I killed him. He had murdered my friends and tortured several girls, so, in my estimation, he had gotten what he deserved. Where had the compassion people were supposed to have for one another gone? Was I heading toward this action again too? I'd have to be careful to watch myself before things got out of hand.

The gangbangers I was looking for were located in the Bay Area. There were parts of SF that were absolutely gorgeous and others that were absolute garbage. Trash, graffiti, and people hanging around selling drugs and sex infested those areas. How did anyone survive in an environment like that? I doubted something like that could ever be cleaned up, short of removing everyone and starting over. No chance of that happening. I'd have to be careful there. It wasn't the type of area I frequented.

Going to a better part of town, I got a room, rented a wreck, and stored my car in a secure, guarded lot. I kept the things I had in the wreck to a minimum. Break-ins of automobiles there were through the roof. Much of the crime in this city was directly connected to gang activity. Violent crime was commonplace there. Geez, why would anyone want to live there?

Silicon Valley bordered areas of homeless people and

must have been a nightmare at times. Looking up statistics, I found that there were an incredible number of gangs and gang members flourishing in various parts of the city. Each gang had its own turf and would fight to the death to keep it. I wondered if this might not be a way of disposing of a lot of these guys. Instigating turf wars might be an option to think about in the future. The only problem I saw at that point was the amount of collateral damage that might be caused.

During the late evening, after I'd done a few hours of spying, I was looking out the rented room's window. The view was of the parking lot and the rental car one floor below. It was fairly dark but still lit somewhat by the street lamp. I noticed two young men scanning the area. Being Black helped them not be very visible. It was quite obvious what they were up to. I got my slingshot out of the luggage and a couple of marbles. With the door open slightly to the balcony, I slipped out and, as they approached the car, I took aim. They had their backs toward me as I let fly. The scream let out by the one and then the other drew a lot of attention as people looked out to see what was going on. The two ran for it, beating a hasty exit. It brought a real smile to my face as I thought of the look on their faces when they were hit.

As I lay on the bed, I had an idea come to me. If I could get access to the electrical panel in the gang's headquarters, I could arrange a surprise. I even thought that I might have an idea as to how I could interrupt the electrical service for a bit. I'd driven past their clubhouse. They were in a building, and I was fairly sure they were the only ones occupying the place. The supply wires were strung on telephone poles, which meant things hadn't been upgraded in the area.

I would need an hour by myself to do what I had in mind. It seemed a bit over the top for me to be able to have the time and equipment to do this, so I thought I'd better think of another way to handle these boys.

Just to see what my options were, I'd go back late that night to see how much foot traffic there was around there. That way, I'd see if I could get a room that was closer but still in the safe zone. It would work well if I could find a place with a window that allowed me to see the front of their building.

It took the better part of three hours before I found a place that wasn't an absolute hole. I boycotted two places because the first had doors thin enough to stick my foot through and the second looked like hookers used it for their service work.

The room I got was on the fifth floor but didn't have a working elevator. The desk person said, "We are working on getting it repaired very soon. The room you have asked for is somewhat quiet and it's secure."

"Okay, thanks. I'll take it for a week, and then we'll see if I need it any longer. I'll pay you in cash now so I'll need a receipt for it," I said.

I kept the other room too, so I had a decent place to sleep. The money I took from Jason was coming in handy yet again. This room "with a view" was far too noisy and run down for my taste, so it would be used for surveillance purposes only.

The spying started again in the evening, and I began to get a feeling for the neighborhood. I had my twenty-by-seventy binoculars, which gave me a good view, and I could see their faces easily. The streets stayed fairly busy until around ten-thirty and then slowed down to a trickle.

The boys hung around a while longer, not really doing anything, but then left too. Trying to memorize the faces of everyone there wouldn't work, so, using the telephoto lens, I took pictures and then downloaded them to my laptop. At that point, I couldn't say with any certainty that there was no one overnight in the building they hung out at.

At my post for the next few days, I watched as they sold their dope and whatever else they had. On the third night, I did a close-up inspection at four in the morning. Dressed in black clothes with a hoodie on, I brought the nunchucks just in case I ended up with company.

Their hangout, I thought was empty, but unless I investigated, I couldn't be sure. The door was solid and had a good lock. Although it wasn't easy I managed to open it without too much noise. Unfortunately, there was a little damage. As I entered part way after waiting a minute, I heard movement inside. The stale air was comprised of cigarette smoke and some strange food smells. Whoever was in there was evidently waiting for me to come in all the way before making a move, so I got the hell out of there.

As I ran down the street, the door flew open and crashed against the building's exterior. The game got underway as two gang members gave chase. They probably had knives and possibly a gun, so it would be best to not get into a fight with them.

Having done all those mad-dash runs paid off. Because I'd familiarized myself with the area, I lost them after a few blocks. At least now I knew there was always someone there.

Things sure didn't work out the way I thought they would. I could have sworn that everyone was out of the building. I also should have checked to see if there was a back door to the place. It would have saved me a hard run. In the morning, I'd scout around to see if I could approach the back of the building from another way. I found another route, one that would keep me a little more out of sight.

The next morning, I got back to watching the goings-on. There was a discussion at the door as it was examined by almost everyone who went through it. Two hours later a man with a toolbox arrived and, after looking things over, fixed the damage. Although paid in cash, he seemed very unhappy with the amount.

He complained to my main target, Jayso Davidson. Jayso took a step forward to within inches of the man's face. What occurred next was typical. The man received a headbutt, and the money was taken away from him. Blood trickled out of his nose as the man picked up the toolbox and left.

Jayso received a round of applause as if he was some kind of hero. What a bunch of assholes. As I watched, I'd noticed that everyone walking down the street gave those guys a wide berth. I thought, *I'll enjoy this job more than I thought I would.* As the day went on, I saw the jerks grope a girl who made the mistake of walking too close to the group.

Laughing like hyenas, the guys tried to remove her blouse. At the last instant, she managed to stomp on a couple of feet and broke free, running down the sidewalk. She almost got hit by a car as she ran across the street. The driver slammed on the brakes, just in time to narrowly miss her. With her blouse torn, she ran into a store, escaping the whooping-it-up assholes.

Studying the situation, a plan began to form in my mind. It would take some preparation and some good timing, but it might work. A smile crossed my face as I worked out the details. The buildings there were built long ago and I doubted very much that many upgrades had been done.

Going to a few supply stores, I browsed through the sections that offered several choices of products that would do the job. After that, I went to a sign shop and had the owner make me a couple of signs that could be adhered to the side of a van. Finally, I picked up extra things that allowed me to complete the job I planned doing.

One thing I was counting on was the fact that the gang members weren't too bright. I had my doubts as to them figuring out what I was going to be up to. Two major things had to be done before I would be able to put the plan into action. Taking a walk down the street near my targets, I checked to see if the plan was feasible the way it was, or if I needed to adjust it some more.

Looking at the power supply, I saw that there were lines supplying each building separately. At the transformer, there was the old-style safety switch—the type that kicked out when there were overloads, such as happened when lightning struck the lines. It was an old type of precaution. Most of the newer installations had put in a more modern system.

The line went to a number of panels inside the building, depending on how many units there were inside. The building I was interested in only had the gangbangers occupying it. This suited my purposes well.

During the evening, I acquired a nondescript, older van from another part of town. After getting it, I swapped plates with yet another vehicle and put the new ones on the van. The owner of the vehicle with the swapped plates would probably not notice for some time.

Using the signs I'd just had made up, I measured the sides and marked the borders. When that was done, taking a large spray can of paint, I got to work.

After the work was done I stuck the vinyl signs to the side of the van and stepped back to see how it looked. It told everyone who would see the truck, that I was the owner of Ace Electrical Services. With this work done in the warehouse district, it gave me the privacy needed to take care of the work undisturbed.

The next part of the plan would have to be done around five in the morning. When the way was clear, I got to work outside the building and sabotaged the incoming power line. Only their place was affected by my work.

A couple of hours later, when the van was loaded with all the tools and parts I needed, I headed out. The gang-banger idiots were on the sidewalk with their arms flying around in the air, trying to decide what to do. That was the moment I had been waiting for.

As I slowly drove by, avoiding people crossing back and forth, I heard a voice call out, "Hey, yo, I gotta job for you."

"Sorry, but I'm on my way to another job, and the boss will give me shit if I'm late," I said.

"I won't be asking you again. You git yourself in here and fix the problem we got, you an electrician, isn't you?"

"All right, but if my boss gives me shit, you straighten it out with him, okay? You are going to pay me, right?"

"Yeah, yeah, just fix it," he said.

Pulling over, I parked the van before going in to see what they wanted.

"Okay, so what's wrong?" I asked.

"The lights don't work. There ain't no power in here."

"Where is the panel?"

"The what?" he asked.

"The power panel is where the electricity is turned off and on, supplying the building, it should be built into the wall with a metal cover," I explained.

"Oh, that's over here in the back," he said as he walked to the back of the structure.

Opening the panel, I looked around inside and asked to see where the power came into the building from the outside. We exited through a door at the back and I looked over the place where I'd done my work earlier. I found out quickly that these guys didn't know beans about electricity. I gave them a bunch of double talk about how the system worked, and they nodded their heads and agreed with everything I said.

"Because the system is so old, a few minor modifications are needed. There is the risk of electrocution and only someone wearing the proper clothes and foot attire can be near the places that I have to work. I don't care if you want to watch, but if you die, don't say I didn't warn you. The electricity can kill you from more than twenty feet away if you don't have the right equipment. What you guys are wearing is perfect for the electricity to kill you. Plus, I can't do the job for free. The things I have to use for this don't come cheap. It'll cost you two hundred bucks, not including labor," I said with a grim look.

"Yeah, yeah, no problem, we can get you the money, just fix it," Jayso said.

"All right, but make sure nobody breaks into the van, or I won't be able to do the job."

"Sure man." Turning he said, "Hey, Ricky, go keep an eye on that busted-ass van out there."

Going to the van, I pulled out a toolbox and a crate of things I needed. I even got one of the boys to carry in the crate and place it on the floor by the panel.

"The dangerous part is going to be done now," I said.

They couldn't get away fast enough.

Left alone, I opened the dead panel, which as luck would have it, was mounted on the wall and not in between studs, leaving the sides accessible. The main breaker had the outside wires coming into it and then into the panel with the individual breakers in it. In the main one, I connected wires to the incoming cable, stripping the heavy insulation, and then connected them to a device I had purchased. I ran them past the on/off breaker. The new line was run through the panel, out the bottom, and along the grounding wire which was connected to the grounding rod.

There was a large beat up rug on the floor that ran up to the grounding rod. Running the new wires along the ground wire, I laid them on the floor and under the rug where I needed them to be.

This completed, I got to work on the next part of the job. Having a ladder already there made this go very quickly. The items I brought with me were in place and, after making sure things had been done right, I walked out the back door with the toolbox. Going to the connection outside that I had installed early in the morning, the next part of the job was completed.

When I first got there at five in the morning, I'd attached a set of, heavy-gauge jumper cables to the incoming lines. That had been done to keep the power flowing when I cut the lines and installed the industrial size breaker.

After installing the breaker, I removed the jumpers and switched the breaker off. Now I had done all the necessary work inside the building, I switched it back on and walked back to the panel and turned it on too.

Seeing the lights turn on Jayso came in and got the guys to carry my stuff to the van. When I turn to collect my fee, the whole gang was standing there.

"Thanks, now get lost Ace," he said.

"What about my money? The boss is going to be mad at me already. If I don't have the money, he'll probably fire me."

"Not my problem, now leave while you can still walk."

Turning around, I got into the van and drove away with the fools standing there, laughing at how they had pulled one over on the ugly white guy.

To myself, I said, "It's been a pleasure getting to know you, assholes. We'll see who has the last laugh."

Later in the evening after I had a nap back at the better of the two rooms, I got to the one near where Jayso and his idiots hung out. Knowing these guys had committed murder in the past and had no reason to stop from doing it sometime in the future, I had no qualms about going ahead with my plan.

When most of the guys were hanging around on the sidewalk, I walked by and hit the switch on the first remote. Following that, I went for a bite to eat a few blocks away to wait things out. After I'd finished, I headed back on the other side of the street and hit a second remote switch. From inside the building, there came loud music. The music, I was sure, was not what they would prefer to hear.

What was blasting away loud enough to be heard on the street was polka music. Even I couldn't stand the stuff, so it must have been really irritating for them. When I was sure most of the gang was in the room with the power panel, I took out the third remote and pressed the switch.

There were a number of screams that ended fairly quickly as the electricity did its job. The wire that by-passed the panel was strung out under the rug. The first button I pressed operated a remotely controlled valve to a tap that got the floor and rug saturated with water.

The second one started the polka music playing on the boom box hidden in the ceiling, which got their attention and should have brought a lot of them into the room.

The high voltage current cooked their asses when the third remote activated the last switch that completed the circuit and electrified the floor soaked with water. Just to make sure it all went to plan, I left the power to the floor on for twenty minutes. Turning it off, knowing I hadn't

left anything half-baked, I removed myself from the scene. After collecting my stuff, I drove the rent-a-wreck
back to the lot and transferred my belongings back to my
car. The van had been taken back and the signs removed.

As had happened quite often in the past, I got home
earlier than anticipated. Still having plenty of time off, I
called Abe and asked if he'd like me to come back early,
thus saving my time off for a later date. He liked the idea
because there was a new job he thought was best suited
for me.

Chapter 24

By the weekend, I was ready to go horse around a bit on the trails.

"Do you mind if I tag along?" Bob asked.

Off we went, having a nice relaxing ride. I liked bringing my lunch with me, so we stopped, and I shared what I had with him. We chatted about life and kids, as well as wives.

He said he was married for years. "The two of us got along wonderfully and, although she is gone, I still have the memories. These are what help get me through the day. We never had children and regretted that part of our life, but thought, it just wasn't meant to be. I enjoy the life I have, and the horses keep me occupied. I don't have many friends, but do have a good rapport with the people that come to ride the horses. Is there anyone in your life?"

"I just don't have the heart for it anymore. The things that have happened to me won't allow me to go that route again." I told him a mere smattering of my woes but left out most of it.

"To tell you the truth, Joseph, life has a habit of making choices for you. I wouldn't call it quits at this early stage of the game. You're a young man, and you have a lot of living to do yet."

"We'll see."

Lunch done, we continued the ride, enjoying the spring weather. The horse and I got along well as it had gotten to know me. After a good rubdown, I sent the animal back to the pasture.

Later at home, I checked into the events that were related to my latest venture in criminal eradication. The story online was about how a gang of criminally active youth had met with fate. A total of nineteen gang members were electrocuted in an execution-style death.

The police thought that the act was committed by someone wronged by the gang members. To find the culprit responsible would be an impossible task indeed. This group had hurt a lot of people and were suspected in the death of several rival gang members, as well as several non-gang members. This is one group that would not be missed.

Once again, I found myself in the clear. I knew that I had to make sure that I always took precautions, because it would be easy to become over-confident. Quite probably I would then make a mistake, and major problems would be on my doorstep.

Thinking about making mistakes, I wondered if the local murderer would make a mistake. In my spare time, I attempted to put myself in his place, in order to see what his motivations might be. There had been something lurking in the back of my mind, but it still wouldn't come out.

Two weeks later there was another murder. A woman had been badly beaten and then stabbed. The husband was, as usual, looked at closely, but found to be innocent. The marriage was having difficulty, but witnesses claimed he was with them at the time of the murder.

Something in my head asked if any of these men might have profited much from the demise of their spouse—if one had an inordinate amount of insurance or would inherit a trust fund. This might be a good reason to rid oneself of a person you weren't getting along with. Of course, a person would not kill a number of others just to take away suspicion from themselves, would they? I was sure that Bill had already thought about this. Just on the offhand chance that he hadn't, I gave him a call.

"Hey, Bill, I was just wondering if you'd given any thought about…" I told him about my theory. I questioned him about some possibilities that would explain what had been happening. I expected him to say that base had already been covered, but he didn't do that.

"To tell you the truth, Joseph, we did a superficial check on insurance policies, but these could be hidden in various ways if one was smart enough. Let me look into it and see what we can find out. I'll get back to you if we find anything."

I wondered if he'd find anything that would incriminate any of the husbands. It was Saturday evening, and I'd already had my workout, so I settled in for a good read. I soon found myself lost in my favorite author's book and zoned out completely.

Monday at work, Jim had a bit of a breakdown. All the months of stress had finally taken their toll. Tears rolled down his face as he recalled the good times he and Alice had and how he was now alone. The guys were sympathetic, but uncomfortable with this. Most of the guys had never done something like this and didn't really want to see another man cry in public.

Abe advised him to take the rest of the week off, and maybe see a counselor in order to work through this time of grieving.

When Jim left the building, one of the guys asked,

"Say, Joseph, did anything like that happen to you when you lost your wife?" Immediately a look crossed the questioner's face, as he realized that he probably shouldn't have asked that particular question. "Sorry, this is none of my business, and I shouldn't have brought it up."

"No you shouldn't have, but since you did, I went through hell when it happened to me. I was in worse shape than Jim. He has actually taken Alice's death very well. You can never understand what it's like until it happens to you. Try to remember that in the future."

We got back to work and started trying to forget what had just happened. Despite the fact that I ended up removing Jayso and his buddies a short time ago, I was already feeling the need again. I wasn't sure why this was. The feeling of release usually lasted several months or more. This time, not even a month had gone by, and the itch was coming back.

At home that evening, I attempted to get a handle on the situation. I checked back over the past year and found that the time between each episode had gotten shorter as time went by. I wondered if this life was taking a deeper and deeper hold on me. The violence had been increasing too, except for the last one with Jayso. Then again, there really hadn't been much chance for anything with him and the rest of the gang. I really had wanted to have a real heart to heart with the little rapist. He had deserved it.

The desire to get into a real fight was getting stronger and stronger. I tried to think about why this was. All of a sudden, Gord came into my thoughts. I started to wonder if he was all right. The turn of events concerning him and my inability to help had frustrated me to no end.

Was it possible that the recent violence was coming about more and more because I had been unable to help the boy who had once meant so much to me? Harry,

Brenda, and the kids had been a big part of my life, and now we hardly saw each other.

I was sure it was affecting me adversely and causing these other things to happen. Now that some clarity had been found, I started using this knowledge to attempt a change in me. I didn't like when things outside my control caused me to react in ways that weren't good for me.

Two weeks later, Bill called. "I'd like to come over and see you for a minute, do you have time?" he asked.

Seeing as how it was Friday and I just got home, I said, "Yeah, no problem. When will you be over?"

"I'll be there in twenty minutes."

"You want to stay for supper at the same time?" I asked.

"Thanks, but I've got to get home, the wife has a dinner for me already."

Sitting at the kitchen table, he told me, "We've made some significant headway in solving the murders of all these women. We looked a lot deeper into all the husbands and found an offshore account for one of them. It appears that one of the husbands had a policy on his wife from an out-of-country insurance company. The money has recently been deposited directly into a new account in the Caribbean. That's why it didn't show up in his regular accounts earlier."

"How did you find out about that?"

"We've been keeping an eye out to see what unusual travel plans they all have had in the past six months, and found several that made us suspicious. When they were studied in detail, one gave us the results we were looking for," he said.

"So now what, are you going after him or have you made an arrest already?"

"He is our main suspect, but we don't have any real proof at this point of the investigation. Having a policy like this is perfectly legal. He could even have had it put into an account in the US and never been taxed on it."

"Have you checked his whereabouts during all the other murders?" I asked.

"We're in the process of doing that now. You know, Joseph, you should have been a cop. You're the only one who thought this far ahead."

"Just lucky. I'm not as close to the problem as you all are, and that probably helped a lot."

"No, I don't think that's it. I've been meaning to ask you for a long time, a certain question, but wasn't sure that I wanted to hear the answer," he said with his eyes staring straight into mine.

"And what is that question, or shouldn't I ask?"

He hesitated for a moment, unsure if he should ask it even then. "Do you remember when I was getting you information on the activities of Dennis Jackson?" I stayed silent and so he continued. "All of a sudden, his robberies stopped, and your interest in him dwindled. You said that you were wearying of the chase and that you just wanted to move on, you remember that?"

"It was a long time ago, and a lot of things have happened since then. I've been for counseling and have learned to deal with it," I said.

"Yes, I have seen a change in you, but it started quite some time before you went for the counseling. If I wasn't your friend, I would say that you caught up with the man when all the law enforcement agencies couldn't. After you said those words to me, there were no more robberies, and he has never been heard from again. Can you explain that?" I said nothing again, and once again he continued. "I think the man is gone, and the world is better off without him. But, considering this, it puts you in a different light as far as I'm concerned. You managed to do something the police couldn't and that, to me, makes you quite an adversary. But I have no proof, and even if I did, I wouldn't use it against you. We are a team of sorts because of the things you and I have done together."

"I consider us a team, also, and because of this, I would never do anything to harm you either, so to answer your question, I'll tell you this and no more. I was tired of trying to figure things out and just wanted to let it go. The reason he stopped can easily be explained. He probably got into an accident and died, or he might have been killed by someone he was dealing with and died under some other name. There are any number of different scenarios about what could have happened. Did you ever have his DNA on record?"

"No, we didn't, but I am having a hard time convincing myself that you're the type that would let it go. I've known you for way too long. To tell you the truth, I think that you're way smarter about these things than I have ever given you credit for, Joseph."

"Thanks, I guess. So, where do we go from here? Are you going to hound me about this for the rest of my life?"

"I've thought about that very thing, and I've come to the conclusion that you're one of the good guys, and I'm going to leave this alone. I won't ask you about it again, even though I'm dying to know the truth of the matter. But then again, I've had to live with not knowing a lot of things and will just have to get used to this too." Bill got up and reached out his hand. "I glad I'm a friend of yours and not an enemy."

I was quite relieved and got a little over-enthusiastic shaking his hand.

"Geez, you've got a grip like iron. I'd hate to get into a fight with you." He left, and I sat there with mixed feelings, yet again.

At times like that, I would have liked to have taken Bill into my confidence. Keeping everything to myself, at times became a burden, and it sometimes weighed me down. If I told him of the things I'd done, he would have seen me in a totally different way. If that was the case, I couldn't see how he would have been so eager to be my friend anymore. Things had to remain the way they were. I had no choice in the matter. If he knew what I had done, it would have become a burden on him too.

Chapter 25

It took a week or two before I was once again comfortable, with the situation between Bill and me. If it weren't for the fact that the two of us had joined forces a few times, would he have let it go? I wasn't sure that he would have. This gave me a bit of cause for concern.

My attention got diverted when there was another beating and stabbing of a woman in Salem. The husband had no good alibi, and it was soon discovered that he was a copycat killer. He and his wife had been fighting for a long time, and she was about to leave and, doing, so she threatened to take him to the cleaners. With him being fairly wealthy, it meant she would have taken at least half his considerable assets. In his mind, he thought that because he had earned the money, he should be able to keep it.

Confessing to the crime, he was interrogated about all the other murders but came up clean concerning those. The real murderer of more than half a dozen women in Salem was still on the loose. I had considered going after him, but Bill would have suspected that I was involved, and I couldn't have that happen. I'd like to have asked him if they had made any headway in the investigation but by then had thought better of it.

In an effort to take my thoughts away from things in my city, I looked online to see what results had come from some of my endeavors.

Malcolm Wright with his estate on the plateau, the one that I had burned, had decided to sell the property. The ruined home and land had been bulldozed down and cleaned up, but it no longer looked even remotely nice. The report stated that he was no longer happy with it and wanted to retire somewhere unspecified.

The Jayso gang's territory had been taken over by several other ones and nothing in the area had really changed. I really hadn't thought anything would come of it. I had just wanted him and some of his boys gone.

The shabby construction companies were out of business for lack of people in the families who could take over. I wondered if that mousy little wife of Bernard's missed him much. At least Fred Acres no longer yacked people's ears off.

Jim had been back to work for quite a while and seemed to be doing better. With me back on my regular job, I had the time to work on a few projects.

I'd thought of getting a crossbow but realized that I would be much faster using my compound bow. It took too long to reload a crossbow. I had quite a number of specialty arrows, and these would have been hard to adapt to a crossbow. Instead, I developed an arrow that I could use to take a light braided fishing line with it. That way I could fire it over a limb or something sticking out from a wall. I could then use it to pull a heavier line over to climb up to places that I would have no other way of accessing.

Cruising through sites online, a number of likely targets came up. There was a Mexican biker club that had been in the news on many occasions. Corruption in politics was always there. Several politicians had been linked to organized crime. Corrupt police officers were also nothing new.

There was one story in particular that grabbed my attention. Running illegal immigrants from Mexico into the USA had been going on forever. Quite often, the money was taken from people looking for a better life, and they were left to die in the desert. Many were shipped in containers used to transport them, and when the authorities got too close, they were left high and dry. Too often many of them died of starvation or dehydration.

All for the love of money, the poor suffered. People with no conscience made large profits by taking advantage of these people. The lowlifes I was sure were drug runners too. If I could find enough information on some of these human smugglers, I thought that I'd take a shot at making a dent in their trade.

I knew there must be preferred routes that were used. Border patrols couldn't be watching the entire US/Mexican border all the time. If there were places where the patrols were not frequenting, I figured that I might just be able to locate some of them through my sources online. Maybe there was someone in the Border Patrol that fed info to the smugglers as to where the safe spots were.

The CDC, Seeking Justice, and Crime Everywhere sites gave me much of what I had been looking for. As I had suspected many times in the past, some of the information I got had to come from people who had firsthand knowledge. The details were far too precise to come from anyone else.

It wasn't the first time I'd tangled with this type. The Carlos Brothers sold young runaway and abducted girls, to be put into prostitution. Another had used them for cheap farm help and, when they were seriously hurt, he would dump them in the desert.

There were quite a number of places that were sparsely patrolled along Texas, New Mexico, and Arizona, where they bordered Mexico. The hard part would be finding where those people crossed. There were lots of spots that would make it fairly easy to walk or drive through, but the authorities knew about these too.

There were places I could see that were far better than others. The reason for this was that when crossing, the immigrants needed to get to large enough cities, so they could hide and blend in when necessary. If they were able to get to a city like that, it would be easier to hook up with other immigrants already settled in the US. Arrangements could then be made to head to places where the network could find them employment.

The search took many hours. Using Google, I scanned all the areas that were within a day's walking distance or an hour or two drive of the border. I limited my searches to cities with a population of a hundred thousand people or more. This cut down the number of possibilities considerably.

Writing down a list of them, I kept in mind that they needed to be near areas that had no monitoring cameras. Fences could be cut and re-mended easily enough. There also had to be cover in close proximity to the point of entry. Las Cruces was a good choice, except that the terrain was very sparse and far too open. South/southeast of Tucson was close enough too, but again the terrain wasn't suitable. Nor was the Yuma area.

The best place I could find was just east of Big Bend National Park. There were mountains and valleys where people could hide while resting. Travel could be limited to early morning and evening. Quite a number of immigrants could make their way to a gravel road to be picked up and driven to a city like Fort Stockton, Texas.

For lack of any better choices, I decided to start in that general area. Once again my search for info on this business was started online. There had been no names in any articles in newspapers or on television that I had been able to locate.

I found trace amounts of what I needed here and there online. There was one source who hinted at knowing some of the people responsible for a container load of dead immigrants. What I found out was that when the authorities seemed close, the stolen container filled with people had been abandoned on a little-traveled dirt road leading into the mountains. By the time anyone found it and investigated, it had been far too late. How anyone could abandon people to die a slow death like that was beyond me.

If I was reading this right, the informant could well have been part of the American portion of the smuggling ring. He didn't come out and actually say it, but it appeared he had an attack of conscience. When I pressed for more information, he stayed offline for three weeks.

I figured at that time that he was either afraid of retribution or had learned to live with it. Once a week, I put out a plea for his help. The problem with the way I was handling things was that I felt I was making myself vulnerable. Having second thoughts about going this route, I stopped pursuing it anymore.

The last thing I needed was for someone to start wondering about me and trying to find out who I was. I never used my own computer for this part of my research, but one could find that I was online in the Salem area. It had crossed my mind to use a remote proxy server, but I didn't know enough about it to take the chance.

This whole thing could have been a setup too. Maybe I was getting somewhat paranoid, but I only had to get caught once, which had already happened. I had very little to go on at that stage, so the best thing for me to do was drop it.

Later in the week, Bill called me. "I thought I'd let you know what's going on. There is an old friend of mine in Salt Lake City. He is on the force there and paid the camp run by the priests a visit. They didn't want to talk to him but relented when he started to make waves. Barney has found out that Gord left the camp two weeks ago and hasn't been seen since. When a few friends of his were questioned, they told Barney that Gord had been very antisocial for quite some time. He had been avoiding most of the other people in the camp, and the only one he ever talked to, knows nothing of his whereabouts."

"Does no one know why he withdrew from everyone?" I asked.

"The kids Barney interviewed claim to know very little about it. It's possible they weren't willing to say much because there was a priest present during all the questioning."

"Was it the same priest every time or a different one?" I asked Bill.

"He didn't say, but I can find out. I'll see if I can get any names. You aren't planning to pay them another visit, are you?"

"No, if Barney couldn't find out anything, I doubt that I could. I'll leave it in your hands. You know how to handle this better than I do. Thanks for telling me this. Have you contacted Harry and Brenda?" I asked.

"Yes I have, and, as you can imagine, it didn't go well. I hate this part of the job."

So, Gord left the camp, and no one knew where he

had gone. I was certain that all was not kosher at the camp. I knew I could be wrong because if there had been something going on, I was sure at least one of the kids would have said something and maybe even asked for help. I wasn't sure what I should do. If a cop couldn't get a location as to his whereabouts, how would I? Maybe nobody actually knew anything.

I didn't like this at all. I felt helpless and useless. Gord had been a troubled boy for quite some time and had acted erratically ever since he started drinking. I wondered why this had taken hold of him so deeply. His wasn't an isolated case by any means, but how could it have happened? It made me wonder why anyone would want to live their lives in a stupor.

There would probably never be an answer to the question. Some people were meant to go down certain roads, and there was little you could do to prevent it or help them out of it.

I found myself in limbo for the next while, concerning life. Then all of a sudden there was some activity on the site I'd been trying to get info on. There was a message posted online by some unknown person. I thought it was the guy that had been hinting around about the immigrant smuggling ring.

The message was short and to the point, *Take a look, east of Big Bend.* And that was it. The idea I got was that there had to be activity east of the park concerning the immigrants. It was the only message I got. I tried to ask questions, but the address at the other end as far as I could tell had been shut down. Either he was afraid of getting caught, or he had been caught and dealt with.

There were two options for me. I could either make plans to go to Big Bend or forget about the whole thing. If I forget about it, many innocent people who just wanted a better life would have died for nothing. The greedy bastards that took their money, and then left them to die would get away with it.

It could, of course, all have been a wild goose chase, and nothing would come of it, but the only thing I'd have lost was time and effort. On the off chance that it was legit, I thought I'd go and see if I could find something. Summer was coming, and it was going to be hot down there. I wasn't keen on being there in the heat, but for the smugglers, it was probably the best time to do it. The best time that was, if there were smugglers there in the first place.

Could this all have been a ploy to throw me off the scent because I was digging around? It, of course, could also have been a trap to draw me out because I'd been snooping. If I went looking for them, they could have been trying to lure me there to eliminate me. The more I thought about that, the more I felt I was way off track. There would have to be some sort of contact in order to find out who I was, and that wasn't happening. Was I getting paranoid? No, I was already paranoid. I was just getting *more* paranoid.

Chapter 26

After all my preparations were made, I asked for and got three weeks off because things were a little slow at the shop. The total driving time straight to Big Bend was around thirty hours, but I stopped in Tucson. There I picked up an all-terrain Jeep and supplies that I'd require for an extended stay in the wilderness.

I had my own tent, air mattress, and sleeping bag, along with a Coleman stove and fuel. There was lots of water with me and food. I even brought my books and laptop with a charger that worked in the Jeep. The steel compartment I made long ago fit in the back nicely. In this were the tools of the trade, plus a few items that might come in handy. Trying to plan ahead as much as possible, I brought more things than I actually needed.

One thing I did bring that could be considered overkill was a magnetic box. I hid it under the Jeep. It contained an extra pistol and ammunition. If by chance I was robbed or caught, I would have something to defend myself with, besides my hands and feet.

When I got to my destination, I cruised around the area in an attempt to find a location that I thought might produce results. My thinking was that I might want to travel along a road where a pickup could be made fairly quickly and at night. The Mexican people would have to make their way with the help of a guide to a certain spot and then wait.

After taking a day and a half, I decided that the best place to pick up the Mexicans would be along the FM 2627 Highway. This choice was made because of two main factors. The first was that the message said east of the park. The second was the fact that a way to stay hidden needed to be used and that road ran just outside the park where there was quite rugged topography. This would allow anyone who wished to stay hidden to do so. They only had to come out when they were close to the spot they were going to get a ride.

I had no way of knowing when or if there was going to be anyone coming into the country illegally. Something like that might only happen once a month or every several months for all I knew. Day after day, I spent looking for some telltale sign that some group had been there. I figured that there would have to be little things left behind, especially if there was a route that was used more than once.

At night, I kept a wary eye out for people in the desert. Using my night vision binoculars purchased long ago, twice I found overnight campers, but nothing else. The heat of the day was oppressive and took its toll. Despite the fact that I was using sunscreen, I got more tanned than I would like. I welcomed the end of each day as the setting sun meant the temperature was going to drop soon. The nights spent laying in the sleeping bag gave me a lot of time to reflect on the events in my life. God, I missed Kathleen. How I wished that I had stayed home instead of going to Salem. How different my life would have been.

Nights were cool and refreshed me to some degree. Two weeks I spent searching with nothing to show for it. By that time, I was starting to think the message may well have been something sent to lead me astray. If this was the area the immigrants used to come into the country, I would have found something to indicate it. At this point, I had found absolutely nothing.

Two weeks had been wasted, and I decided to call it quits. My supplies were starting to run low, and I was getting really tired of being there. On my way back to Tucson, I removed the metal box attached to the underside of the Jeep. Just in case this had all been a ploy to find out who I was, I took major evasive maneuvers to make sure no one followed me back to my car. When I got to the long-term lot where my car was, I transferred everything and took the Jeep back.

Renting a room for the night, I had the first shower I'd had in a while. I spent a long time in it, washing the accumulated dirt and sweat off. I had been near the Rio Grande, but the water in it was dirtier than I was, so I'd stayed out of it.

During my time in the desert, I had checked the laptop, but not getting a signal made it useless. Going online now, I found no new messages from the source that had steered me to Big Bend Park. I had no way of knowing whether the tip was sent to send me on a wild goose chase or if I missed the mark. All I knew was that I went there with little information and got nothing for my troubles. It was nice to get back home.

Chapter 27

It took a couple of weeks to put the wasted trip behind me. At first, I was quite pissed off because it had been difficult to sit put and wait in the heat of the day, getting baked. Then after that, were the cold of the nights, with me freezing. After a while, I just chocked it up to experience.

When last I was online, looking for a quarry, I found a story that I figured was a little off the wall. A number of homeless men in Denver over the past few months had been found burned to death. At first, it was thought that, because of the circumstances surrounding the deaths, misuse of flammables had been the cause. When several more were discovered, the cause of death was re-evaluated.

There was a story told in the local newspaper on the subject. It was then thought that the burnings were a deliberate act of violence against these men. No reasons and no suspects had been discovered at that point. The police claimed that the stories in the papers had no evidence to back them up and should be ignored.

The reporter who broke the news stories claimed to have received his information from an anonymous source. This being the case, he had no way to corroborate the information and provided a disclaimer with it, saying it was only speculation at that point.

It was obvious that the police officer in charge of the case wasn't happy with the reporter. The story did seem a little fictitious. People going around and setting others on fire was difficult to comprehend. And yet, it happened again a short time later.

This time, there was a witness who saw it happen. Unfortunately, she was too far away from the scene for any kind of identification. What had been reported that time was that three people who, going by their actions, seemed to be young men, committed the act. It was only speculation by the witness, but she felt certain she was correct in this observation.

The un-named young woman claimed to have heard the young men taunting the homeless man as they poured what had later been identified as gasoline on him. A few moments later, he burst into flames, and the perpetrators ran away, laughing.

My goodness, what in the world would possess anyone to do something like that? I certainly hope that the police catch up with these despicable jerks. Too bad it can't happen to them.

Unfortunately, there wasn't any information to make them my next targets. Anger began building in me as I thought about it. Man, I felt like beating the shit out of them.

A couple of days later, Bill called, informing me that they had a lead in the case of the beaten and stabbed women. "We checked on the husband with the offshore account the insurance money went into. As soon as we started asking him for his whereabouts during the other murders, he clammed up and got a lawyer. So far we haven't got enough evidence to charge him with, so we can't arrest him."

"Maybe he'll do something incriminating or make a run for it."

"You never know what these guys end up doing. I thought I'd let you know what's happening, see you," he said.

Time went by without a lot happening, so I ended up calling Harry and Brenda. We decided to go out for dinner at a new restaurant in town. As the evening progressed, the topic ended up with Gord.

Harry cleared his throat before saying, "It's been a hard road these past six months. We weren't sure we would make it for a while there. Thank you for going to see our son."

"What are friends for? You two helped me enough, so how could I turn my back on you?"

"Bill called us and said that Gord left the camp. He has no idea where he went, so we're in limbo again with that," Brenda said.

The rest of the evening was turned to other topics, in an attempt to take our minds off the heartbreaking situation. Despite having a wonderful meal, we all headed for home feeling a little deflated. Horseback riding the next day took my mind off these troubles, allowing me to focus on the great outdoors.

The next day Bill informed me of the developing situation. "The husband we've been watching looks like he has made a run for it. We had nothing to hold him on so we had to let him go. One of our men anticipated this move and kept his passport and a small suitcase of clothes handy, and followed him. They landed in Venezuela and booked into a reasonably nice hotel."

"Does he have access to all his money from there?"

"I'm not sure at this point. With financial institutions and real estate being what it is today, he could conceivably take care of everything from a home sale to fund transfers from there," he said.

"Maybe you could create a reason to force him to come back for a quick trip. Is your man going to try and befriend him and get a confession?"

"That's exactly what he is going to do," he replied.

"Let me know how it turns out, will you?"

At work things were good, but the turn of recent events in Big Bend, left me feeling unfulfilled. Doing as much investigating as I could, I found that through the use of street cameras, the Denver Police had three suspects' names. Unfortunately, the three had alibis for the time of the burning. They must have been fairly smart and thought things through. At least two of them always had alibis for each of the times the homeless men were set on fire.

Their saving grace was the fact that the images on the cameras weren't clear. They seemed to know where the cameras were and avoided looking at them. The clothes worn at the time of each crime must have been discarded soon after the events because they weren't found in the homes. Because they had been prepared, they had allowed the investigating officers to search their homes. Unfortunately for me, no names or pictures of the suspects were available through the news or online. At that time they were only suspects as there had been no evidence found that they were involved in any way.

Two weeks later, another homeless man was set ablaze. The way I saw things, it would have been stupid for the guys to have done it again. The police would have had them on their radar, so why take the chance? It was probably someone else that was responsible for the crimes. With little to go on, the case had to be put on the back burner.

When I ran into Bill at the mall on the weekend, he told me, "One of the people that gave Jenkins, the man suspected of murdering his wife, and possibly the other women, an alibi, came forward. He says that Jenkins paid him to say they were together on the night in question."

"Have you gone back and rechecked his other alibis?"

"We have. We are now trying to figure out a way to get him back into the country. We have no real extradition treaty with Venezuela, so we'll have to come up with something," he said.

"If he's selling his house, maybe the realtor can think of a reason for him to be required to come back for a quick trip."

"Maybe…yes, maybe I'll talk to him about it, thanks." He smiled at the thought.

Off he dashed, as he pulled out his phone. I thought back to a comment he had made and thought that maybe I should have become a cop. It would have been interesting. I finished my shopping and headed for home. Putting the groceries away, I thought about the suspects in the deaths of the homeless men. I couldn't imagine being set on fire. The pain must have been excruciating for the homeless people. As if their lives weren't bad enough already, the cretins had to go and make it worse.

In an attempt to find more information, I went to online sites and put out feelers for any thoughts about who might be doing the horrendous acts. I didn't get anything for a few days, but when I did, what I got was most certainly coming from someone in the know. What I found out, I didn't like one bit.

The source had to be involved somehow with the case. The info sent said that the acts were most likely done by the three suspects who were caught on camera. They were students at a school for the gifted. All three had IQs well over the one-forty-five mark. When interviewed, they gave the impression of believing they were very superior to the interviewers.

I got the feeling that the source had had contact with the suspects and was really irritated and frustrated by them. I'd run across people like that on occasion, and at the time I felt irritated too. I would like to have smacked them on the side of their head, so I knew how the source felt.

I still didn't have any of the names and pressed for a little more info. There was silence for a few days again, and then a name came up, Darrel Francis Arlington. There was no address, only the name. Because he was young and attending university-level schooling for the gifted, it had been fairly easy to locate him.

Google got me a map of Denver, and, after typing in his address, I knew exactly where he lived. Martin Lane housed the affluent of Denver. The home turned out to be a beautiful estate-sized stone and stucco residence with a tile roof. The house was large and built to what looked like, exacting standards. Multiple driveways allowed access from several points.

So Darrel comes from a pampered lifestyle. He thinks he is intelligent enough to get away with murder. I wonder what his motivations are. There has to be a reason for doing this. It can't be just to see if he and the others can commit the crimes and get away with it. If that was the case, they would have stopped at one or two and moved on to something more challenging.

How much talent does it take to pour gas on someone and light a match? Is there something personal with the homeless? Other than that, I can't, for the life of me figure out what the reasoning could be. A person doesn't do this just for fun, do they? I think I'll ask him, and if he won't tell me, I'll just ask a little harder.

Studying where he lived allowed me to formulate a plan of sorts. The property had a lot of greenery and places to take cover. Across the road, there were no houses close by, but there were a lot of trees, offering more potential cover.

Things were slowing down on the job, which worked out great for me. I'd already used up quite a bit of my vacation time that year, so this would allow me to take more.

I approached Abe. "I'm willing to take some time off if you want. This will make more work for the other employees. My only motivation in suggesting this is the welfare of the shop, you understand?"

"Do you actually expect me to believe that last line? Ha, ha, ha, ha. It is a nice thought, though. How much time do you want?"

"Two weeks should be fine. I'd like to head to the mountains and relax."

Friday saw me heading out after work. My stuff was in the trunk, and I made it to Denver the following evening. Sunday morning, I did a drive-by, in order to scout Darrel's home base. It really was a nice neighborhood, with his parent's home being the nicest in the area. There was no foot traffic to be seen, so I refrained from doing a walk by.

Leaving his home and going to the city center would require him to drive one way. Going the other direction would just take him out of town. I decided that I'd park later in the evening somewhere in the second direction. This would offer less chance of discovery.

My surveillance so far bore no fruit. Monday morning at seven, I parked down the road and waited to see if Darrel went to school. I saw him leave in a nice looking Porsche. Being bright red, it was easy to follow at least when he drove it slow enough.

I'd have to rent a car with a much larger motor in case there ended up being a chase. While he was in school, I did just that. I got hold of a Ford Taurus SHO. It had the bigger motor and was fast while still handling well. He wouldn't be getting away from me because of his car. Although it was a Porsche, it wasn't the really good one.

After school, I followed him around to a couple of places where he met up with two other guys. They seemed quite chummy and separated themselves from those around them. This, to me, was an indicator that they were probably his partners in crime. They appeared to be very aware of things going on around them, so I'd have to be careful.

An hour later, he went back home, parked in the driveway, and walked into the house. From my vantage point, I tried to watch the house using my more powerful binoculars. To my surprise, when I viewed a window on the second floor facing me, there was a glint of reflection from glass inside the window.

What the hell? I'd been spotted by the guy. I was sure he had a pair of binoculars trained on me. Shortly after, there was a flash emanating from the same window. The bastard was taking pictures of me. How did he know I was watching him? Could he have spotted me when I was following him? It was a bloody good thing that I had been well disguised. The car had been parked sideways and behind the bushes. Plus being quite a distance from the house would have made it more difficult to get an ID on me or the car. He at least couldn't read the plate number.

The figure moved away from the window, so I took the opportunity to motor it out of there before he had the chance to get in his car and see me. Driving away quickly and doing a series of double backs, I made sure I'd lost him. Damn, this guy really *was* smart. I hadn't been caught off guard like that in quite some time and hadn't expected the camera.

I took the car back and went to another rental outlet in order to pick up something completely different. The whole plan was going to have to be rethought. I didn't feel like being the next burn victim, so I'd have to be ultra careful. In order to change things up a bit, I'd have to find out who the other two were and where they lived.

Staying away as much as I could from Darrel, I followed one of the other two the next day after they separated, at school. Watching from a long way off and following at a much greater distance than normal, I located where number two lived. This time I didn't hang around, as it was obvious that even this guy was keeping an eye out for anyone watching him. Darrel certainly must have shown them the pictures he'd taken of me. With any luck, they would think I was the police, doing some surveillance work. After supper, number two left his house, driving over to Darrel's place.

Once I parked the car well away from and out of sight of the house, I took cover in another location and kept an eye out for anyone watching for me. This time, I caught the movement in a window before I myself was spotted and ducked out of the way. Just in case, I looked through the brush with the glasses to see if there happened to be anyone looking from somewhere else. The only one I noticed was the one I had already spotted. Just to play it safe, I used the night glasses to keep an eye peeled for anyone trying to sneak up on me. When I knew that I was okay, I continued to watch the house.

Every now and then, I noticed someone pull the curtain back from the window and use the glasses to check the surrounding area. So far I'd been able to avoid detection. This trio had been super cautious, or I wouldn't have been spotted in the first place.

At ten, number two left and went home, I presumed. I didn't follow because it was dark and being on the outskirts, there was little traffic, so my lights would have given me away. Later I made the trip to the second kid's house just to make sure that was where he went. His car was there, so I went back to my room.

While the three were in school, I scouted the countryside surrounding Denver for any vacant buildings. I had in the past, found that there were always structures that had been abandoned. Those made good places to have a chat with people that interested me. I found a couple and put the addresses in my GPS. Just in case it was ever found, I removed all the info from previous sites in it that could lead someone to me or anyone I knew.

I got back to the school in time to follow number three to his home. All three lived in well-to-do areas. The private university had to cost a lot, so the parents had to be fairly affluent in order for the kids to go to it.

After waiting for an hour and a half, the kid came out and met up with the other two at a mall. The three were very wary as they continually scanned the area for anyone who might be keeping tabs on them. It could be that when they were questioned by the police, they became super cautious, knowing they might be under surveillance.

On this trip, I came prepared in ways that I normally didn't. Because I would be dealing with superior intellects, I thought that I should be ready for any eventuality. It might well have been a good idea because it seemed that they were using binoculars again to check for any unwanted attention. Wow, these guys really were taking no chances. At that time, I decided to do the same. I already had part of a plan together, but some of it needed to be reworked.

These guys were predators, murdering innocent people for the fun or challenge of it. Now they were the ones being hunted. The problem was that their superior intellects might make them resourceful to the point where they might be able to turn the tables on me. I had survived a long time taking out criminals, but one mistake could end that run.

If one of the guys failed to show up at school, the other two would know something was up and take precautions, making the job that much harder. I had yet to come across anyone as wary as these guys. Because they lived with their families, I couldn't break into their homes. Before I did anything permanent to them, I had to be certain that they were guilty. They sure looked like they were—going by their actions—but that wasn't proof.

The three piled into number three's car because it was the only one big enough to fit all three in. Staying way back, hitting side roads, and coming back out, I followed as they drove in a roundabout way to the poorer area of town. There were a number of streetwalkers around. They passed these and continued making course changes quite often, trying to catch anyone who might be tailing them. They ended up driving to an even less desirable area. It was where the homeless could be found. The thought that the police might be monitoring this area too, ran through my mind.

As far as I was concerned, this was the evidence I had been looking for. However, the three only cruised around the area and then left. Could it be that they were only hunting for a potential target? They wouldn't be dumb enough to use one of their own cars when they actually burned someone, would they?

For them to start scouting for a potential victim must

have meant that they might be making their move in the near future. This pushed my plans ahead of schedule. In the back of my mind, there was a feeling that this could also have been a trap to draw me out. It didn't seem like a likely possibility, but you never knew. Maybe I should be a little wary too.

Over the course of the next few days, I saw one of the guys pull into a gas station. He filled his car and then opened the trunk, filling a gas can. It looked like they were going to make their move soon. I wondered if I should grab the kid or not. He could still be only getting the gas for a lawnmower or something, although none of them looked like the lawn-mowing type. I wondered if I should wait until the event was about to transpire, or make my move beforehand? If I were to wait too long, another person could suffer a painful death.

Once I saw what they were going to do, could I get to the scene fast enough to intervene? If I knew, one hundred percent, that they were the guilty people, I'd do it, but I wasn't that sure. The evidence pointed strongly in this direction but still wasn't conclusive.

The rest of the week didn't provide me with much more info, and it wasn't until Friday evening that they got together at a mall on the other side of town. They all parked their cars in a back corner of the lot and started walking around. They didn't go into the mall, but rather looked like they were trying to find a suitable vehicle.

They finally settled for a Ford Fusion, and while the other two kept an eye out, Darrel used a tool to gain entry. After a little fiddling inside the car, he got it started. The other two hopped in and they drove away. The way the car jumped, it was plain to see that it was a standard shift transmission. That was why it had been fairly easy to steal.

After picking up the can of gas from number three's car, they drove off. They did a series of turns and backtracked a few times in an effort to detect if anyone was following. I already had an idea as to where they were going, so I drove to that area instead of continuing to follow them.

That could easily have been a mistake. They might have gone somewhere else entirely, and then another homeless person would have been burned to death. Because of that, I didn't catch up with them until they were already walking toward what I assumed was a man in an alleyway. My lights were out, and backing up slightly put me just around the corner and kept me from being seen. I hoped the backup lights hadn't alerted them.

Grabbing my things as fast as I could, I sat in the car and prepared to move. The only problem was that I only saw two of them at the alley. Could the other one already be in it? For some reason, I didn't think that was the case. Looking in all the rearview mirrors, I saw the third kid sneaking up on me from the rear. I started the car and backed up fast, swerving toward him. There was a bump and a scream as I hit the missing member of the trio.

Jumping out of the car, I rushed the kid before he had a chance to get up. He was about to yell when I pointed my gun at him. His weapon had been knocked out of his hand when he fell. A hard shot with my fist to the side of his head and he was out. Running to the corner of the building, I took a peek.

Darrel and his friend were getting in the car and, having left it running, the tires squealed as they headed my way. Ducking behind a garbage bin that was about fifty feet away, I waited. The guy I hit was still lying on the road behind the car as they pulled up. Each of them had a pistol in his hand, waving it around looking for me.

Being as far away as I was, and with several other places I could be, they searched the car first. The car was locked, and as Darrel had been about to smash the window looking for clues inside, I took aim and fired.

I had practiced my shooting a lot, and now it paid off. The first shot hit Darrel with a glancing hit in the back of the head, and my next one nailed his buddy in the neck. They both screamed, dropping their guns. Running toward them, I kicked the guns away as Darrel started to reach for it. I drove my fist into his head, and he went down. As I went to hit the third, he managed to lash out with a kick that hit me on the side of the knee. Luckily, my foot was off the ground, and as my leg was moving away from him at the time, except for scraping the skin, it had little effect. Regaining my balance, I struck him with a fist to the forehead, and he was out too.

I zip-tied their hands behind their backs, secured their ankles, and then loaded them all into the trunk. It was a tight squeeze, and I had to pack them in like sardines. Driving to the alley, I checked the entrance to see if my suspicions were right. There was the can of gas. Near the back end of the alley lay a homeless man, sleeping it off. With latex gloves on, I picked up the can and put it in the car.

Using the GPS, I drove to the more usable of the abandoned buildings I'd found. Once there, I unloaded my cargo. Two were already awake, and having duct tape over their mouths forced them to be fairly quiet. One by one, they were transported inside. At first, they were a little dumbfounded. Darrel was the last to wake up and only did so as I carried him in.

With the gun in my hand, I asked, "If I remove the tape from your mouth, Darrel, can I count on you to be quiet?" He nodded an affirmation.

After I removed the tape, he asked, "Why have you kidnapped us? How much do you think our parents are going to pay you?"

"Let's not presume that I'm stupid. If you can do that, I won't take offense and smack you in the forehead with the gun butt."

"What did you shoot me with?"

"I nailed the two of you with rubber bullets. You know, the type the cops use. That's the only reason you're not dead. Thanking me might be a trifle premature, though."

"What do you want from us, if not a ransom?" he asked.

"The three of you have been very bad for quite some time. You've been setting homeless people on fire." All the time I was talking, he was shaking his head.

"No, we haven't done anything like that. Why would you accuse us of that? We were just out for a drive."

"Driving around in a stolen car? If not to burn the man in the alley, why did you have that can of gasoline with you?"

He stumbled over his next few words, trying to come up with something. Replacing the tape, I walked out of the room and got the can of gas.

Placing it on the floor in front of them, I asked the other two, "Do either of you want to say anything in your defense?"

They both nodded, and when I let them talk, they claimed that it was all Darrel's idea. Darrel objected as loudly as the tape would allow.

"So the rats desert the sinking ship at first opportunity." Removing the tape from Darrel's mouth, I asked, "Why did you three do this thing? That's what I want to know." He started to deny it all, calling the other two liars, until I smashed him in the nose. "I want the truth. You did it, and you won't convince me otherwise."

He clammed up at this point and, when I had the tape on again, I asked if either of the other two wanted to tell me. One started to weep and nodded his head.

Once the tape was off, he said, "It was Darrel's idea. He wanted to see what was like to set someone on fire. After the first one, we got the idea that we could easily get away with it and started on the next and then the next. It was a challenge, to see if we could outsmart the police. If that witness hadn't seen us and the camera hadn't caught us, we would have been home free. We won't do it again. Who are you anyway? Are you going to turn us in? We can pay you a lot of money."

"I don't want your money, and I'm not going to turn you in. I have spent most of my life taking care of people like you. You think your high IQ makes you smarter than everyone else. It doesn't make you smart at all. If you were that smart, you would have known that you'd get caught sooner or later and quit after the first one or two."

I'd checked their pockets when I put them in the trunk and came across a video camera. I pulled it out of my pocket and viewed the contents. What I saw was the burning of several men, screaming with pain. The dummies even recorded themselves. As they saw me doing this, two of them started to cry. They weren't crying for what they'd done. They were crying because I was pouring gasoline on their legs. They struggled for all they were worth, but it was a bit difficult because I'd bound them all together.

"What's the matter? I thought you wanted to know what it was like."

Just to show them what it was really like, I lit a match and tossed it at them. The gas ignited, and they were screaming, just like the men in the video. Walking out of the room, I grabbed my fire extinguisher and put out the flames. The smell of burnt clothes and flesh permeated the air. It was not a pleasant aroma.

The screaming continued as I said, "So now you have an idea how those men felt. There is, of course, a price to pay for what you do, just like I'll have to pay one day. You are useless people, and you'll always be that way because you feel so superior to those around you."

I pulled out my gun and fired real bullets into each of their heads. I placed the camera on the floor and, after making sure there was absolutely no evidence left behind linking me to the crime, I left.

After bandaging the scrape on my leg, I made an anonymous call to the police informing them where the boys were. Soon I was out of town and working my way back home. By the time I got back, the story had hit the news about an execution and some sort of video found at the scene. What was in the video had not been made clear at that point. The record of their escapades made the situation clear for the authorities. It also showed that all three were active participants during the burnings.

I was glad that I'd caught the buggers red-handed. Why someone thought they had the right to exterminate innocent people made me wonder. Of course, I wasn't in that category. I only removed those that didn't belong in the land of the living. With the three callus individuals out of the picture, life in Denver continued for most of its citizens. An interview showed the parents of the three in shock as they realized what their offspring had done.

Not having used up all the time off, I asked Abe if he needed me. He did because a new job just had just come in and, for the next few weeks, we were going to be busy. Things soon got back to normal, and the shop was humming along nicely. Life, for the time being, was relaxed for me. How long it would stay that way was anyone's guess.

Chapter 28

I hadn't heard from Bill in a while and gave him a call to see if he wanted to go fishing. This we did, and when we were on the water in the little aluminum boat, we chatted about how the investigation was going.

"Oh, I forgot to tell you that we talked to the real estate agent, and he contacted the seller." He paused with a frown. "I didn't tell you his name, did I?"

"Not that I can recall." I thought he did but I said, "It wouldn't mean anything to me, anyway."

"Okay, good. Anyway, when we explained to the realtor what we suspected, he cooked up a fictitious reason for him being required to come back into the country in order to finalize the deal. He came back, and we met him at the airport, hauling him in for questioning."

"Have you made any progress?"

"We've asked him to provide information on his whereabouts when the other murders were committed, but he said all his records were in Venezuela. He just got a lawyer, and we can't get anything more out of him," Bill said, obviously frustrated.

"Do you think that he's the one that committed all those murders?"

"The department thinks that he's the most likely candidate, but we can't prove it yet. If we can't get something soon, we'll have to release him. We can only legally hold him for a short time."

"Then what are you planning to do about it? Once he's out, he'll leave the country, and he'll never come back," I said.

"Exactly, but we haven't got any way of getting him to confess or of making him divulge his whereabouts at the times of the other crimes. We tried to get a judge to take away his passport so he can't leave, but he told us we have no evidence to support our theories, and he refused."

"Where's his passport?"

"When he went through customs, he stuck it into his luggage. Why do you ask?"

"Where's his luggage?" I asked.

"It was delivered to a hotel room he booked before he arrived."

"Why don't you have someone break into the room and steal the passport? If you know anyone at the passport office, you could have them delay the issue of a temporary one," I suggested.

"Shit, why didn't I think of that? The only problem is that I don't want to involve any other officers in this endeavor. I don't want to ask the desk clerk to let me into his room either because he'll claim I stole it, and then I'd have a problem myself."

"Do you have his identification at headquarters?"

"It's there but to remove it would leave me wide open," he stated.

"Get me the address and room number, and his name might come in handy. I'll see if I can get it for you. Just don't ask too many questions, if you don't mind."

Bill got a funny little look on his face and began to

smile. We had done things together before, and he knew better than to pursue it any further. Fishing was concluded, and we went our separate ways. After I cleaned the two perch I'd caught, I cooked them and then relaxed in an armchair reading.

Later in the day, I got the information I required. The Hampton Inn, room four twelve, was where the suspect was staying. Well, he would have been, if he hadn't been in a room supplied by the city. The next morning, Sunday, I went to the inn when the chambermaids were busy cleaning the rooms.

I cruised some of the hallways till I found a room where one of the cleaning ladies had left her passkey on the cart in the hallway, and I borrowed the key. As fast as I could, I went to Arthur Milligan's room. After the door was open, I placed a piece of duct tape over the locking mechanism and tested it to make sure it didn't lock. When satisfied, I ran the passkey back. The maid was still cleaning the room near the cart and hadn't missed the key.

In Arthur's room, with latex gloves on, I carefully searched the luggage being careful to leave everything as it was. I found the passport, and what looked like a key to a safety deposit box. This key started me thinking. I doubted he would have brought it with him if there wasn't something important in the box.

The thing had me wondering. If there was something incriminating in the box, why did he not take it with him when he left for Venezuela? Oh, well, time enough to wonder after I got out of there. Checking my disguise, I walked to the door and opened it just enough to look down the hallway to make sure I wouldn't be observed. No one was in the hallway, so I removed the duct tape and closed the door behind me as I left, letting it lock.

Once at home, I called Bill and let him know what I'd gotten. He drove over in almost record time. "When I find out which bank the key belongs to, I'll go to it," he said. "Using the passport and one of my men who, in a pinch, could pass for Milligan, we'll see what's in the box. Good work, Joseph, thanks."

With this, he left and, in around two hours after having delayed Milligan's release, Bill texted me, saying he had what he needed. I didn't hear from him for three days, and this started me wondering if it had all worked out or not.

The rest of the week went by, and Friday evening, Bill called, asking to drop by on his way home. When he got there, I offered a beer and a chair.

"I'm sorry I haven't gotten back to you earlier," he said, "but we've had one heck of a busy week."

"Not to worry," I said. "I figured you were busy and would call when you could."

"Because you got that key, we were able to get to the safety deposit box. We had to let on that we received the contents of the box anonymously. Milligan claims we broke into his room and then his box. His lawyer has moved to have all the evidence we found inadmissible, because of an illegal seizure. It took all week to convince the judge not to grant bail. The evidence we found in the box was trophy photos of all the women he killed. This case is now going to trial, and because there is no evidence that the police department has done anything outside the law, Arthur Milligan has been charged with six counts of premeditated murder."

"Do you think he'll confess when he realizes that he won't be getting away?" I asked.

"I think so. He's already showing signs of breaking down. He has answered several questions against the advice of his attorney. I can't thank you enough for your help. I really think you should have been a cop. You would have been so good at it."

"Thanks, but I think the law too often works too slowly for my tastes. I like what I'm doing." Immediately, I regretted opening my mouth.

He gave me one of those sideways glances that meant he thought there was more to say but didn't ask, despite his clearly wanting to. We had come to know each other well enough to know our boundaries.

A week later, Bill called again. "Knowing that his case is hopeless, Arthur Milligan has confessed to the murders of the women in Salem. When I asked why, he said it all started when he knew his only way out of his marriage was if his wife became deceased. He hatched a plan to murder her and have suspicion fall elsewhere. He decided to commit a couple of other murders to cover up his wife's. If he could get someone to give him an alibi, he would be home free. He told me that there was only one part of the plan he had not foreseen. The fact that he actually enjoyed the crime so much, he found that he couldn't get himself to stop. The insurance policy paid out, and the proceeds from the sale of his home gave him enough money to relocate. Along with his savings, Arthur confessed that he had enough money to retire in comfort. He was planning to travel and, on these trips, continue his new hobby. If you hadn't gotten that key, the whole case would have fallen apart, Joseph."

"Did you ask him why he hung on to those photos, knowing they could be used to catch him?"

"I did. His answer was that couldn't bear to part with them. He said he would have taken them with him when he first left the country but was afraid of getting caught going through customs with them He told me that he should have found a way to take them. If he had gotten them out of the country, he would have been home free and could have had a great life."

The conversation continued for a time, and before we hung up, he sighed. "You stopped a serial killer, you know."

"Gosh, it's kind of scary when you think about it that way," I replied.

Chapter 29

There was a sense of satisfaction in having been a part of stopping a serial killer being let loose on the world. Who knows how long he would have gotten away with it? It's funny how the need he felt for getting rid of his wife turned into something so much more.

Maybe I shouldn't have been so surprised at all. My life was a living testimony to a similar story. There were, however, two main differences between us. I only took out people that most of society thought of as very bad, and I didn't do it for the pleasure of inflicting pain, at least for the most part. I had taken some pleasure in hurting a few people, but only because it had been necessary.

With another year in my life coming to a close as my birthday approached, I got a call from Harry. Despite all that had been going on in their lives, he felt it necessary to have me come over for a small get together.

"Are you sure you're up to this, Harry?"

"We really want to do this, Joseph. You have been a friend for many years, and Brenda and I feel we've let it fall by the wayside. Eva would like to see you too. She misses you coming over."

The day arrived, and as I walked up the familiar steps to the front door, Eva came out and gave me a hug. Stepping back, I noticed that she had grown up into a nice young lady.

"It's so nice to have you here, Uncle Joseph," she said. "Happy birthday."

"Thank you, Eva, how is university going for you?" I said, changing the subject.

"I'm getting really good marks, and I've made quite a few good friends. How are you doing? Do you still like working at Salem Steel Fabricators?"

"It gives me the stability I need, and I have a few guys I hang out with once in a while," I told her.

At this point, Harry and Brenda wished me a happy birthday too. We went to the patio in the rear of the house. To my surprise, there were a number of people there and a shout of "Happy birthday" filled the air.

I laughed. "I really wasn't expecting this, thank you so very much."

Going around, I shook hands with the guys and got a hug from the ladies. A few of the guys from work were there, and Bill Henderson with his wife, who I'd, met once or twice. It was a small get together of a dozen people, and things soon became a buzz of conversations. There was a cake after a buffet meal that most of the people had contributed to.

The day was pleasant, and I realized how much these people meant to me. I didn't think I'd spent a lot of time cultivating deep relationships with many of them, and yet there they were. As I sat back in a chair and thought about this aspect of my life, Eva sat down and said, "A penny for your thoughts, Uncle Joseph."

"I was just thinking of how nice it is to be among friends. I don't have many, but the ones I do have, mean a lot to me." I reached into my pocket and pulled out an envelope. Handing it to her I said, "I know you have a part-time job to help pay for the books you need for your courses, and maybe this will help. It's a prepaid credit card. All you have to do is activate it."

"It's your birthday, not mine, you shouldn't have." She gave me one of those hugs that had come to mean so much to me. These were the times I thought about now and then when I was by myself.

"I'm glad that you are doing so well. You deserve a bit of a break." I said.

The rest of the day was really nice, and as I walked to the car, Harry and I had a little chat about things that were going on in their lives. I told him I would do what I could to find out where Gord had disappeared to.

Going home, I carried a bag full of gifts. Some of them were the joke type, and others were the kind that friends gave when they wanted you to know that they had put a lot of thought into it. All in all, it had been a good day.

Sunday, I headed for a hike through a park. After an hour of strenuous activity, I sat on the bank of the Willamette River. The water flowed by in no hurry and, as I caught my wind, I remembered a number of online stories. There seemed to be an inordinate amount of bullying going on using the internet. Some of the stupid morons could have used a slap up the side of the head with a two by four. Maybe that would have straightened them out.

Evergreens lined the opposite shore, and I watched as an eagle perched on a branch, tearing apart something it had caught. The sun shone warmly as a few clouds drifted slowly across the sky.

Thinking of Gord, I wondered if there was a way to find out where he had gone. The cop Bill knew couldn't find out anything. It was like he'd just vanished. I was sure that if I went to the priest who ran camp again, that I wouldn't find out anything either.

The following week wasn't a pleasant one at work. The temperature went much higher than normal, and the heat wave really affected the work being produced. The shop fans were unable to cool the guys off, and with the sweat rolling down their faces, tempers were flaring.

The men were told that the shop would be closing until it cooled down a bit. Some of the employees didn't have air conditioning at home, so they weren't real happy about it. It was suggested that they just spend the day at the mall.

By the middle of the following week, it finally broke, and everyone was called back. During this time there had been an increase in violent crime across the state. The high temperatures had caused a lot of people to lose control. Hopefully, things would get back to normal.

During the time off, I did a lot of online searching and found a likely next target. A man named Boris Mezkov was being released from prison shortly. He spent twenty years in jail for abducting and girl and then raping her repeatedly. After he had viciously raped the girl, he cut off her forearms and threw her off a thirty-foot cliff. I couldn't, for the life of me, figure out what would have motivated the man to do this.

The girl, Frederica Jones, had survived the fall and still managed to climb back up to the roadway. A passing motorist picked her up and took the almost dead girl to the hospital. Boris, for years, swore that he would finish the job when he got out. It had been reported that the amputee was deathly afraid as his release date approached. It was believed that Boris, according to a cellmate, was going to attempt to fulfill the threat. Boris, of course, denied all allegations.

Wow, the woman must have been in a panic over this. I had little doubt that he would do what he had said. Even if he wasn't planning on completing his threat, he deserved to die, in my books. I found out all I could about where the victim now lived and as much as I could about Boris Mezkov. I obtained a recent photo from his prison release story and started making my plans.

I was considering, for a short time, whether the punishment should fit the crime. I'd done this before with bad results, so I was a little reluctant to go that route. The tools I'd require were gathered together, and I ordered a gas-powered handgun which I received well ahead of time.

Boris was due to be let out on October sixteenth, and I would have to make sure I was there ahead of time. Unfortunately, Abe told me that getting this time off wouldn't be easy. There was a job, to be completed the week I wanted off, that required my abilities.

I hadn't counted on this happening. I asked to see the prints and the work order. I asked if I could get the parts cut ahead of time. If I worked a couple of Saturdays and overtime during the week at straight time, I should be able to get it done before I had to go see Boris. I asked Abe if this was all right.

"Boy, you must really want to go away. I guess, if it means that much to you, I can okay the work for you."

The next few weeks were really busy for me. Despite all the extra hours, I still managed to stay in shape and prepare everything that I'd need. I actually found myself looking forward to dealing with the shit.

When the day of his release arrived, I made sure that I was parked not far from the gates of San Quentin. Now and then, cars drove by, but none stopped. I just hoped there was no one coming to pick him up. I moved the car a little closer in anticipation of him coming out.

He finally stepped out the main doors and walked into the sunshine. Having looked up the bus schedule, I knew there was one coming in half an hour and with no one there, this was what he would be waiting for.

He stood beside the road for a minute, and then I started the rental car and drove as if I was going to drive past him. He stuck out his thumb and smiled, hoping this would entice me to give him a ride. He stood around five foot ten and looked like he would weigh around one seventy. His hair had been cropped short and was graying. He wasn't a very pleasant-looking man, despite the smile. I frowned, as if I was debating whether or not to give him a ride, and then stopped beside him. His clothes were out of date and must have been the ones he'd had when he was arrested, twenty years before.

He got in and said in a gravelly voice, "Thanks for picking me up, I wasn't looking forward to waiting for the bus."

As we drove, he chatted and almost seemed like an all right guy, and I wondered if maybe I might have made a mistake about him. Maybe all that time in jail had straightened him out. We chit chatted for a time and as we got closer to San Francisco, I asked him where he was headed?

"I'm going to see an old friend in Bakersfield. I haven't seen her in twenty years. We have a lot of catching up to do."

It was a good thing that I had found out where Frederica Jones now lived because that was where she had moved to after Boris went to prison.

"Oh, that's nice. You're in luck I'm going to Bakersfield myself. You want a lift there?" I asked nonchalantly.

"That's great, I don't have money for gas, but I can spare enough for a dinner in a restaurant."

"You've got yourself a deal, as long as you don't mind me taking a slight detour in order to drop by to see a friend for an hour," I said.

"I've waited for twenty years, I can wait an extra hour," he said with a smirk on his face.

Driving south on West Side Freeway, he said he was getting a little hungry and asked if I could find a diner or something where we could grab a bite to eat. There was a service center along the way, which I pulled into it.

I had a wrap and a small salad, while he ordered a double burger with fries and a drink. As he ate, his eyes shifted back and forth as if he was expecting someone to take the food away from him. As he ate, he studied me. "Why did you pick me up? You must have known that I was just released from prison."

"I'm not sure, now that you ask me. I guess you just seemed like an okay guy who needed a ride."

"You haven't asked why I was in prison, aren't you curious?" Boris asked.

"I wasn't until now. So what were you in prison for? You said you were in there for twenty years."

"No, I didn't say that. I said that I've waited twenty years to see my friend, not the same thing."

"I guess I just assumed that's what you meant," I said as he looked hard into my eyes. He must have expected the look to unnerve me, but it didn't, so I continued, "So what were you in for?"

"I set a fire trying to get back at someone, and a man died in it. I never meant to harm anyone, but they never believed me, so I've been away for twenty years."

"So you *were* there for twenty years," I said.

"Yeah, but that's not what I said earlier."

If he wanted to play a game, that was fine by me, I really didn't give a shit.

When the meal was finished, I headed for the bathroom. After I came back, he decided he should go too, before we got back on the road. He left the table and, looking things over, I felt there was something not quite right. Studying the scene, I noticed that one of the knives was missing.

Now, what does he want with a knife like this? It's the type to spread jam on your bread. Does he plan to use it on Frederica or me? I asked myself. *Have I given myself away? Not likely. I'm pretty good at putting on a poker face."*

In the car again we traveled down the road, with Boris apparently enjoying the view. I kept wary, just in case he had plans I didn't know about.

I saw a road in the distance that led away from any civilized places and decided to take Boris there. As I turned off, he asked, "Your friend lives way out here? I don't see any houses."

"A little ways out, the road takes a turn, and he lives just past that. Steve is a bit of a loner, so we'll only stay a short time. Don't worry, we'll get you back on the road in no time at all."

"I'm not worried, I usually make out okay," he said.

"How was your time in prison? Anyone give you a hard time?"

"No one bothers me. Now that we're away from the main roads, why don't you tell me why you were waiting to pick me up? What's the deal here?" he said as he pulled out the knife.

Staying calm, I replied, "I just happened by when you came out and thought I'd do you a favor."

"Bullshit, I saw the car while I was still inside. You were waiting for me to come out. I don't believe you, now if you don't talk, I cut you up, asshole. Pull over while you can."

I figured I was fast enough to grab the knife hand before he could lunge at me with it, but I decided to play for time. I should have seen this coming a little earlier than this. Slowing down, I saw a pothole off to the side and hit it pretty hard slamming the brakes on when I did.

The car bounced around, and he was momentarily thrown off balance. On the side of the seat by the driver's door, I had the gas-powered pistol. Letting go of the wheel, my right-hand grabbed his wrist. He didn't have a seatbelt on and had to use his other hand to prevent himself from hitting the dash.

Grabbing the pistol, I brought it over firing a tranquilizer dart into his neck, just as he started trying to slash me with the knife. I blocked his arm, hitting it near the elbow, while dropping the gun by the door. Knocking the knife arm down and grabbing it, I reached across with my left arm and slammed my fist into the side of his head. He was stunned, but not out, so I shut off the car and pulled out the key.

He tried to lash out at me again, but the drugs from the dart were already starting to take effect. Having hit him in the neck, it allowed the drugs to knock him out much faster. I'd used this method of knocking out a person before, the only difference was a rifle and a longer dart were used.

Standing beside the car getting my breath back and calming down, I waited for Boris to come around. I'd used restraints on him and leaned him back against the seat, tilting it back as far as it went. The restraints were placed, so they weren't immediately visible, which turned out to be a good thing.

Coming from the main road was an old pickup truck. An old man pulled up next to me. "Everything all right, son?"

"Yes, it is, thanks. My buddy fell asleep, and I decided it was time to stretch my legs. Too busy along the freeway."

He left when my answers became shorter and shorter. My disguise would keep him from giving the police an accurate description, if by chance Boris's body was connected to this moment by the old man.

There were several other back roads nearby, so I went about twenty miles away and parked, just as my companion woke up. He was confused at first, but suddenly realized where he was and that his plans hadn't worked out quite the way he'd anticipated.

"What the hell's going on? What do you want from me?" he asked angrily.

"To tell you the truth, Boris, you were right about me waiting for you to come out of prison. I saw your story online and read about your promise to finish the job with Frederica."

"I've gotten over that long ago. I have no intention of doing anything to her."

"Oh, then why are you headed to where she lives? Don't bother lying, Boris, I don't believe you."

"I went to prison for twenty years because of her. She should have bled to death when I dumped her. She cost me my freedom, the stupid bitch."

"No, Boris, you cost yourself your freedom. That girl has lived in fear ever since she heard about your parole. You don't belong here, and I'm going to make it so she never has to worry about you again."

"You don't have the guts, you bastard."

Just to show him that I actually did, I dragged him out of the car. Because I really disliked the man, I decided to give him a good beating. Before I killed him, I brought out my hatchet. Seeing this, he knew what was coming up, and a look of terror entered his eyes as he thought that I was going to do to him what he'd done to Frederica all those years ago. Just to prolong things, I played games with the hatchet, flipping it in the air and giving him a look.

I hated this type of individual. His kind was what was wrong with this world. Instead of chopping his arms off, I just shot him in the head, left his body on the side of the road, and made an anonymous call to the police. That was done in order to let Frederica know that she no longer had to concern herself with the man.

The hands-on approach had left me with a feeling of satisfaction. I went home quite relaxed and in a surprisingly good mood. He could have cut me in the car, but I wasn't overly concerned with this. All had turned out good, and, that night, I had no nightmares, sleeping amazingly well for a change.

Chapter 30

Things were very pleasant for the next several months. I went riding on many occasions and kept fit doing my mad-dash runs through the forest, even during the winter. Life was good, and things seemed to be going my way. During this time, right after Boris's body was found, there was a story about how Frederica was so relieved that the man she had feared would fulfill his promise to finish her was dead. She looked like she had been through hell. I was glad I'd been able to help her.

I still marveled at how badly people treated each other. How many others went through horrible things that the public knew little or nothing about? All I saw on the news was one bad story after another.

At the end of February, Bill, after a long absence, called and asked to come over. His voice sounded grave, and he wouldn't tell me what was going on over the phone. He got to my house an hour later. When he came in from the snowy weather, he looked quite cold. He sat down in front of the wood stove with a grave look on his face.

He took a deep breath and let it out with a sigh. "The

friend I have in Salt Lake City says that a body matching Gord's description has been found in Ogden. It's a small city north of Salt Lake. At this point, he only suspects it might be him. I probably shouldn't even be telling you this, in case it's a false alarm. The reason I'm telling you is, that if it turns out to be him, you'll have time to prepare yourself because your friends will need you. Don't let anyone know I've said anything to you yet. I'd be in big shit if it were to come out. We've been friends for quite some time, and I feel I owe you. That's why I'm here. An autopsy and DNA test will be done to prove one way or another if it's him or not. The reason he only suspects it's Gord is because the face of the corpse is damaged, and he can't be certain it's him. The results will take two weeks at least because there is a backlog."

"Do you have any idea as to what happened to him?" I asked.

"The report I got doesn't give any specifics, and he didn't want to elaborate too much. We'll just have to wait this out. For his parent's sake, I hope he's wrong in his suspicions. I asked why he thought it might be Gord, and he said that some of the identifying features I told him about matched. I've sent the DNA sample I got when we first started looking for Gord to the forensics office in Salt Lake City for comparison. Sorry that I'm bringing this type of news to you." With this, he got up and left.

I too wished he hadn't brought me this news. He was right about me being needed by Harry, Brenda, and Eva, though. I'd have to be ready in case this turned out bad. This family had been there for me in the past, and I had a feeling that it may well be time for me to return the favor.

The time dragged by slowly for the next two weeks. I'd been hoping that this did indeed end up being a mistake. If he was indeed dead, it would have horrible consequences for his family, so I was dreading the results.

To take my mind off things, I searched online for any stories concerning people I had dealt with in the past year. There was nothing new that had been put out that I didn't already know. This was usually a good thing. In the past, I had never been linked to the demise of anyone, and I sure hoped this continued.

One story did bring back memories that put a smile on my face. A vacation resort I had stayed at in Montana was advertising on the web. The last time I went to Thompson Chain of Lakes in Montana, I met a lady named Linda. She was the sweetest little old lady I'd met in a long time. The fish I'd caught, and she cooked, were the best I'd ever had. I hoped she and her husband George were well.

Chapter 31

Two and a half weeks later, Bill called. I could tell by his voice, he was going to say something I didn't want to hear. "Can you meet me in town, Joseph? I'm pressed for time, and I'm going to have to pay a visit to your friends after I see you."

"You can't tell me over the phone?"

"I'd rather do it in person. Please don't push me on this. I want to talk to you first, face to face." He told me where to meet him and hung up.

It was a good thing that it was Friday because if the news turned out to be what I feared, it would give me the weekend to deal with it. I headed out and saw his car in the parking lot he had chosen. Leaning against the front of his vehicle with a folder in his hand, he was waiting for me.

"Sorry I had to insist on seeing you here, Joseph," he said as he opened the folder.

"I take it that the news is bad."

"I'm afraid so. The DNA results are back and there is no doubt that it's Gord that was found dead. By all indications, the evidence points to the fact that he took his own life."

My knees got weak, and it took a few moments to recover. This had been a young man whom I had known for a long time, and his death bothered me greatly. The fact that he took his own life made it even more devastating.

Immediately, I felt guilty at not having been more aggressive when I saw him last. I could have picked him up and carried him out of the camp. It might have given me the chance to make him see where he was headed.

Bill must have seen this. "Don't beat yourself up too much. There are things you can control, and there are things that you can't. I've seen this many times over. No matter what you think you could have done differently, the outcome would have been the same. He was on a path only he had the ability to change."

"How did he die?"

"He managed to jump off a building and died almost immediately."

"You haven't told his parents yet?"

"No, I'm going over there now. This is unusual, but I think it will go better if you are there when I tell them. I know they have been with you when you've gone through the worst times in your life. There is that bond, which may help them over the worst of it," he said.

I wasn't looking forward to this at all, I tried to think of reasons not to go, but with butterflies in my stomach, I went anyways. Bill called ahead and let them know he was on the way. When we got there, and the news was relayed, the scene went every bit as bad as I thought it would be. I stood on the sidelines and felt that I was of no help whatsoever. This was the most devastating moment of their lives, and I was powerless to do anything.

I offered my condolences and let them know I'd be ready to help in any way I could, but it fell on deaf ears.

When Bill and I walked toward our cars, I asked, "Is there any indication as to why he killed himself?"

"I wasn't told, and I doubt that anyone knows at this time. There will be an investigation and possibly something will come to light. I'll let you know if I find anything relevant."

The following week, Gord's body was shipped home. The funeral took place the week after. It was a very somber occasion. When I saw my friends crying, I too broke down. I tried desperately to think of anything that I might have done to help the boy but was at a loss. Harry and what was left of his family retreated into themselves and shunned any contact for the next while.

Bill once again contacted me, and we met at my house. After a few minutes of idle conversation, he said, "The Salt Lake City police found the last place Gord stayed. When a search was performed, they found most of a handwritten note. The bottom portion was ripped off and what he wrote was cut off in mid-sentence. I have a copy of it, and against my better judgment, I've brought it with me."

"Why do you say, against your better judgment?"

"There are things about you, Joseph, that I can't fathom. I know there is a part of you that has the potential to do things that nobody knows about. People who have caused you a world of hurt have died or disappeared. I've never found any direct evidence to support the theory that you were somehow involved, but I know you have never told me everything. The people, who died deserved what they got, and we've even done things together, so I won't ever press it." I stayed silent, rather than express myself one way or another. Bill continued, "The note is rather damning."

He handed me the copy, and I read, *I can't live anymore with the thought of what I have been forced to do.*

During my stay at the camp that the priests run, I was drugged and sexually abused by the bastards. It happened more than once, and when I confronted one of them, Father Masey denied it and said I must have been dreaming. I know I was raped because I could feel it where I shouldn't. I remember seeing his face and Father Thomas's just before I went all funny. There are images in my head of being forced to do awful things. I cannot bear it any longer. Father Masey, that fat pig, did this to me. Father Thomas did...

This is where the note was torn off. I felt a fury in me that must have shown on my face because Bill said, "I think it was a mistake showing the note to you. I should have followed my instincts. I don't want you doing anything to those priests, you hear me?"

"Those bastards have to pay for what they did to Gord. They must have done it to others too. How can they be allowed to do this kind of thing with no penalty? How can the Catholic Church allow their priests to do this and still allow them to be priests? Anyone else would have been put in prison."

"I know what you're talking about. I and many other Catholics feel the same way. They are a disgrace and don't belong in a church. Joseph, look at me. Look at me, Joseph. I don't want you to do anything. The matter will be investigated. I'll make sure of it."

"All right, you needn't concern yourself with me. Just make sure they pay for it. What they did is the same as if they pushed him to his death."

He picked up the note and left. The way he looked at me as he closed the door behind him showed me he had serious doubts about me keeping my word. After he went, I had the need to get rid of the hostility that seethed inside me.

If they had been in front of me at that moment, it

would not have ended well. I had a workout so hard that I was totally drained by the time I was done.

The next week was long, as were the following weeks. Finally, I'd had enough, I had been reacting adversely at work, and I needed to find out what was going on.

I called Bill. "Hey, Bill what's happening with the investigation? Has anything been found out, are they under arrest?"

"It's not as cut and dried as that. The priests were interviewed, and neither admits to any wrongdoing. They both say it's a church matter, and they can't discuss it. The note, although damning, doesn't prove that they actually did anything. The lead officer investigating the incident says that anyone can accuse someone of anything. The fact that the deceased wrote the note doesn't mean the accusations are true. I thought as much when I saw it, too."

"So where does this leave us?

"Detective Morrison told me he was going to talk to the archbishop. He isn't hopeful at this point, but who knows? If I hear anything, I'll let you know." With this, he ended the call.

How anyone could follow this church was beyond me. Was this what their bible said, *Do unto others, as long as you don't get caught doing it, or admit to it?* This was much the same as the Muslim religion. Some small group of them seemed to think that if they killed those who weren't Muslim, they'd be rewarded and go directly to what they thought was Heaven. I really didn't have much of a belief in all this, but even I knew it couldn't possibly be the way it really was.

The anger in me threatened to take over as I thought about Gord. I had a difficult time staying focused at work and a hard time sleeping at night. I realized that the only way I'd get any peace was if I tackled the problem the way I had in the past. Just in case the charges were never brought against those two priests, I started making plans to go visit them.

How to handle this incident was bothering me. Taking out a priest went against the grain. We were raised in a society where priests were held in esteem. Planning to kill two was something I found difficult to comprehend. Nevertheless, it could become necessary. These two had undoubtedly done this to others and so must pay for their transgressions.

With this in mind, I proceeded. I found it impossible to just let this pass. It ate away at me constantly. Gord's face kept coming to mind. The good times we had when he was young invaded my thoughts all my waking hours.

The first thing I needed to do was confirm that they were still at the camp. If not, I would have to find out where they had gone. I didn't wish to leave a trail, so if they weren't at the camp I'd have to devise a way of obtaining the information. I couldn't go beating up on anyone in order to find the two.

I tried to think of a way to locate them if need be. If I didn't hear from Bill in the next two months, I'd go after them. By that time it would be late spring and enough time should have passed to even have Bill not become too suspicious, I hoped that, but doubted it. He was too good a cop and knew me too well.

Chapter 32

The time passed slowly. I made my plans and would be leaving next weekend if no action was taken against the priests. I called Bill mid-week and asked what kind of progress was being made in the case.

"I've been putting off calling you, Joseph. It looks as if there'll be no charges brought against Father Masey or Father Thomas. There's no corroborating evidence to support the note. There's a fairly high turnover in youth attending the camp. We haven't been able to find anyone willing to admit that the two priests have abused any of them. I'm afraid that this is blowing over. The two are still at the camp, and the priest in charge has difficulty believing that they are capable of performing the deeds they have been accused of."

"So they get away with it?"

"To tell you the truth, Joseph, there just isn't anything besides the note to say they're guilty. They could be innocent, you know. It's possible," he said.

"Do you think they are innocent?"

"No, but that doesn't necessarily mean they did it," he said rather unconvincingly.

We said our goodbyes after he advised me to let it go. I told him that I'd try my best. When I got off the phone, I finished my plans and confirmed my time off with Abe. It was a good thing I found out that they were still both at the camp. I wished I had photos of them. It would make it easier to identify them.

Friday after work I was on my way and, at the end of the next day, I booked a room in town. My mood had been foul for too long. I really needed to treat this like I had other incidents. If I didn't, things would probably unravel in a hurry. To do this venture properly, I had to find a place to take them, a spot that was remote and easily accessible. After a bit of exploring, I found an area in a national park in western Colorado. Clear Lake had a number of deserted cabins and, after marking them on my GPS, I headed back to Salt Lake.

I rested up for a day and, in the late afternoon, I started the trip to the camp. As evening arrived, I found that the mended break in the fence was just as I had left it. With the cut in the wire being so close to a post, it hadn't been discovered.

The season had been very dry, leaving the brush near the camp in a state easily burned. As it started to get dark, I made my way inside the perimeter of the camp. Most people there had already gone indoors so it took a bit of time to get a likely candidate to call over. A young man slender and not looking too bright walked by and, as he neared, I stepped out just enough for him to see me. I struck up a conversation with him, after I calmed his fears as to why a stranger was loose in the camp.

"I came in earlier and lost track of time. Do you know where Father Masey and Father Thomas are? I really need to have them meet me here."

"Father Thomas is in the main office, doing the books. I think I saw Father Masey in the supply building on the other side of the camp," he said. His eyebrows were knitted together in an effort to visualize where they were.

"Can you go tell Father Thomas to come see me here and then go tell Father Masey the same thing?"

"I don't know. I was just going to turn in. It's a long walk to both places."

I reached into my pocket and pulled out a twenty. "If you do this for me, you can have this."

He strained his eyes trying to make out what denomination the bill was and when he saw that it was a twenty said, "Sure, I can do that, thanks, mister."

As he left, I prepared myself for the upcoming visit. It took over five minutes for who I believed was Father Thomas, to come close to where I had been hiding. Because it had gotten so dark, there was no one else around. As he walked carefully past the bush I'd hidden behind, I snuck up on him and gave him a solid rap to the back of his head.

He was a beanpole of a man and weighed next to nothing. I restrained his hands and quickly carried him about thirty feet away behind a number of trees. Keeping an eye out for the other priest, I took the time to gag him.

It took almost ten more minutes for Father Masey to waddle near where I was. He stopped at the edge of the clearing and softly called out, "Is anyone here?"

I tried to speak like a younger person to see if I could calm any anxiety he may have had, and said, "I'm over here, Father. I've hurt my ankle. Can you help me get to my room?"

"Why certainly I can help you. What is your name, my son?"

I almost wanted to say, "I'm not your son, you stinking son of a bitch," but I kept myself under control.

I couldn't come up with any name in case there wasn't a boy by the name I used, so I just moaned. This got him moving quickly. Because he was such a porker, I didn't whack him over the head. Instead, I placed my knife to his neck and covered his mouth with my other hand.

"If you yell, I'll slit your throat. You hear me?"

He nodded his head and, as we turned and start walking I quickly scanned the area for possible witnesses. I guessed everyone went to bed early at this camp. When I had him to the car, I zip tied his hands behind him. I then pulled out the dart pistol and shot him as he got into the back seat. The guy had been way too big to be put in the trunk. Once all the way in, I fastened his ankles together with two pairs of zip ties.

Running back to Father Thomas, I found him just as he had started to walk away. Taking care of fatso had almost given Father Thomas the time needed to wake up and make a run for it, with his hands tied behind him. He was unsteady on his feet and that had been enough to slow him down enough for me to tackle him and knock him out again. I carried him to the car as fast as I could and, once he was in the trunk, I shot him with a dart too.

All the way to the destination, I had an eerie feeling coursing through me. Having the two priests confined in the vehicle had me thinking like a youngster that was doing something very bad. I had to fight the feeling very hard in order to not turn back and release them. In my mind, I knew this was a line once crossed, there would be no turning back. This, to me, seemed like a person taking their first shot of heroin. They knew what had happened to countless others and yet they proceeded, knowing full well this would probably the beginning of the end of the line for them.

By the time the two woke up, I was almost to the old cabin near the edge of Clear Lake. Before I got there I gagged the heavyweight too. Just to make sure we wouldn't be disturbed, I drove around to make certain there wasn't anyone camping or anywhere near there for a hike. The place was deserted, so I went to the cabin and unloaded the cargo.

Father Thomas was easy enough to get into the run-down cabin, but I had to wait for Father Masey to wake up. I didn't want to take the chance of throwing out my back. I kept my disguise on because of a habit I'd developed long ago. There was no reason for them to know what I looked like.

With Father Thomas secured and going nowhere, I sat in the car and waited for my captive to regain his faculties. He had been out of the drug-induced state for some time, but the effects lingered for an hour or two.

With Father Masey in the cabin too, I tied a thin noose around his neck and fastened it to a post. This prevented him from getting up. The post wasn't secure enough to fasten him to it, but the noose would be a deterrent against any real struggles.

Soon they were both wide awake and attempting to talk. The first to have the gag removed was the big one, but only after a stern warning. He started talking immediately saying, "Why have you abducted two priests? This is not only a federal offense but a crime against God too."

Taping his mouth shut with duct tape I explained, "Let me tell you the way it is. You had a young man by the name of Gord Motters at the camp a while back." I waited for a reaction and wasn't disappointed.

There was awareness in their eyes as they thought about things. So I continued saying, "Maybe you know, and maybe you don't, so I'll tell you. Gord has committed suicide, and a note was left behind, most of a note at least." Again I waited to see what the reaction was going to be.

There was a look of fear on Father Masey's face as he

thought that he may have been found out. He mumbled with the gag in his mouth restricting him. Father Thomas, however, seemed to slump in resignation.

"The note explains that you drugged him enough to make him incapable of resisting, but he was still aware to a degree of what was going on. You two sexually abused him and made him feel so much anger and shame, that he eventually couldn't live with it."

They were both shaking their head no, but this, of course, was to be expected. Most people denied things like this to the bitter end. I took the tape off the big one and he vehemently denied it all. At this, I decided that a little persuasion was necessary. I hesitated for a moment, but only a moment, before striking him in the mouth. A shocked look appeared on his face when I did hit him. A trickle of blood ran down and dripped off his chin. There was a look of resolution in my eyes, and he must have realized that I wouldn't be convinced by his lies. I looked hard at the two of them and yelled, "You tell me I am committing a crime against God. Are you trying to say that what you two have done to Gord, and who knows how many others, is not a crime against the God you say you serve?"

"We have repented of our ways and confessed our sins in confession. So we have been absolved of our sins." At this, Thomas violently shook his head.

I took the tape off his mouth. He now spoke for the first time. "I was never involved in the practices of Father Masey—"

Father Masey cut him off. "We have both been released from our sins, and our slates have been wiped clean."

"He's lying. I was never a part of it. I spoke to the archbishop about the goings on but, when it was investigated, Gord had already left. Because he couldn't be located and no one else would admit to being abused by him, the file was closed, and nothing came of it."

"What deceit you speak. This man knows we both committed this sin, there was no investigation, and a confession is confidential. We confessed our sin to each other and before the Lord. You have no grounds to hold us captive. Release us immediately, and we will not bring this matter before the police. You cannot possibly think of harming us. We are God's servants."

As I placed the tape over their mouths, Father Thomas was crying and shaking his head no. I expected both to deny everything to the end, but one confession was good enough for me. Looking at these vile men, anger rose in me at the atrocities they had committed against the lad I'd known for years. This kind of anger, I had not felt in a long time. I could hardly think straight at this point. They were guilty and had to pay.

Father Masey had a hard and defiant look in his eye, almost daring me to commit what was considered by many to be an ultimate crime and sin. I had yet to come across many people who were willing to kill a priest. These two I really, really wanted to beat the hell out of. A young man I'd known for years was dead because of them.

I stepped outside for a moment and thought over the situation and my course of action one last time. What came to my mind was a life that had been cast aside and the horrors suffered by an innocent at the hands of men who were trusted by most people. I saw Gord's face as he was years ago. When the three of us went zip lining, we had an absolutely wonderful time. These two men had taken away any chance of this happening again.

Servants of God they claimed to be, but I highly doubted that these men were what God had intended the church to be run by. Having made up my mind, I walked to the car, made sure we were still alone, and then returned to the derelict cabin. As I walked up the creaking step and porch, then through the rotting doorway, they saw the gun and started struggling to free themselves.

"May God have mercy on your soul. You didn't have any for your victim." I shot both of them in the head.

In the forest, I dug a large hole in the soft earth. When this was done, the bodies were placed side by side in the deep excavation. A large bag of lime had been spread over the bodies to accelerate the decomposing process and help keep animals from disturbing the site. The earth was replaced, packed down firmly and covered with leaves and brush to finish the job.

In the cabin, any traces were removed and disposed of by burial in the bush too. Unlike most other times, I did not feel that I had done a good thing. These men were guilty of atrocious acts and needed to be removed, but I did not feel good about it at all.

It was supposed to be the responsibility of the church to deal with these things. It had failed miserably in this task, and if there really was a God, why hadn't he done something to correct this shameful behavior? It made me think that the entire church was either corrupt or turning a blind eye, which to me, amounted to the same thing.

On my way home, I thought about how I would have to handle the situation when Bill asked if I knew what had happened to the two priests. He would find out, I was sure, because my presence at the camp would be made known, once the two men were missed. Although I was totally disguised, my distinctive voice and my size would give me away if they located the boy I had talked to. Having taken days off work at the time of their disappearance would also convince Bill of my guilt in the matter.

I thought, for the time being, I would destroy all the items I used to change my appearance. To protect myself, I'd rent a storage unit under a fictitious name and place all the tools I had accumulated in it. The storage space in the basement would be dismantled and made to look like it originally did.

Bill would suspect me, and I wasn't sure if he would let it go. I was certain he would start to investigate me. His hands were dirty too, but he was Catholic and would feel he had no choice in the matter. He was a man of conviction and principle, no matter the indiscretions he himself had performed.

Chapter 33

As soon as I got home, I went to work. The clothes and items used to conceal my identity were taken to a burning pit I'd found and destroyed completely. My collection of devices and weapons were taken to a storage unit in Seattle. I rented a truck under a fictitious name, and all my purchased identities were also stored for the time being.

Once all this was done, and the basement changed to look like it had never been anything different, life started to return to normal, except that the nightmares had returned. They were now darker than they had been for some time. I was sinking into another depression, and I found that I had to make another appointment with the counselor.

I justified my actions in a dozen different ways, and yet the guilt remained.

The counseling helped and, despite the fact that I couldn't talk about what was actually causing my depression, I had been helped immensely. At work, my bad mood had been commented on more than once before the counseling. This was now also getting back to a more normal state.

Bill had questioned me about the disappearance of the two priests. He could not possibly have bought my explanation of things but hadn't pursued it any further. He pulled away from me, I feared, because he knew the true answers to his questions. His visits had stopped, and we no longer went fishing together. It was all probably for the best. I didn't deserve to have any friends.

I had lost touch with Harry and Brenda too. We no longer called each other. When we did, we were reminded of times that had been so much different. This reminder caused far too much pain for all of us, although mine was caused by other things too. I was trying to forget these things, but they were always there just below the surface. The nightmares diminished but still persisted in reminding me of what I had done. The guilt at times threatened to overpower me.

The months rolled by one by one. I no longer seemed to have the need for release that had plagued me so much in the past. The things I had done and the cancer I had, in the past, removed from our society, I did not regret. This reminder was one of the things that kept me going.

As I lay awake in bed, I wondered if this in time would pass too. I threw myself into my job and started working longer hours, just to keep my mind off things. The work was pretty much the only thing I had left, except for once in a while going out with the boys. I put on a cheery face but as soon as I was alone again, it was gone.

Out of the blue one day, the phone chimed. I could see by the call display that it was Bill. He asked how I was doing and we chatted for a few moments. The conversation turned to a serious side as he said, "I got a call from the police department in Salt Lake City. The tenant, where Gord holed up before he committed suicide, found a scrap of paper."

"Oh, what is it?"

"It's the rest of the note Gord wrote. It was stuck in a joint in the drawer where it was found and tore off when the note was removed by the investigating officer," he said, pausing.

"So what's on the rest of the note, anything of consequence?" My stomach was twisting into knots at this point.

Bill wouldn't be calling if there wasn't something pertinent on the paper.

"Do you remember how the note accused Father Masey of sexual abuse and ended with what we assumed was an accusation against Father Thomas, too?"

"Yeah, I remember all this, what about it?" I asked.

"The rest of the note reads like this," he said. "'Father Thomas did his best to bring the situation to light by contacting the archbishop, but I knew how it would end. I knew I would be forced to reveal all the things that went on, and I couldn't bear the anger and shame, so I left, signed, Gord Motters.'"

I felt sick to my stomach. My mind turned hazy, and it was like a fog had rolled into my head. The gravity of what I had done hit me like a ton of bricks. I told him, thanks for letting me know and hung up.

The thing I had always dreaded more than anything had come to pass. To make it all ten times worse was the fact that the innocent man I had murdered was a man of the cloth. He was actually trying to rectify the situation, just like he said. He was a good man with morals, and I murdered him. I ran to the bathroom and retched into the toilet.

I had in the past become callous to the feelings of taking lives, but the ones I took deserved death. This priest was trying to do right, and because a suicide note tore when taken out of a drawer, he died. There was a queasy feeling in the pit of my stomach, and I threw up again. My head was in a whirl, and I almost collapsed. How could this have happened?

I called in sick the next day and asked for time off. When asked why and for how long, I answered that there had been a death in my family, and I didn't know how long I'd be gone. I was leaving the city and needed a leave of absence.

I was reluctantly given an indefinite leave, and I packed the next day. I got a kid to look after the grounds and told him I didn't know how long I'd be away. I gave him a hundred dollars in advance and told him I expected him to do the job properly. By the end of the day, I was gone.

Chapter 34

I had lots of money in my accounts and could always transfer more from other areas. I drove to no particular destination but ended up going to the site of the grave where I buried Father Thomas.

I asked the dirt in front of me to forgive my rash actions. I actually cried in the realization of what I had done.

I didn't expect anything to come of this and so continued my aimless traveling. As I drove, the phone chimed many times. Each time I looked at the display, I saw that it was Bill calling. I turned the phone off and placed it in the glove compartment. I couldn't talk to him. He would be asking me questions I didn't want to answer.

My life as before was out of my control. I had no idea what I would do or where I would go. I couldn't be at work, and I couldn't continue my life the way it was. For the first time in a long while, I got a bottle of whiskey.

In a room in a fleabag motel, I got drunk. The next morning I woke with a massive headache and knew I could not go down that road again. The last time I did it, I almost died. Not that it mattered whether or not I died now. I just refused to go that way.

After three weeks of indecision, I came to the conclusion that my life in Salem was over. I could no longer face the people I knew and gave Harry a call. After talking to him, I made a quick trip back to sign papers and took a few things I wanted. The furniture and everything else would be sold with the house. After talking to Harry, I called Abe, informing him that I would not be returning to work. Although he was not happy to hear this, he wished me the best.

A quick trip to Seattle, and I emptied the storage container and destroyed everything in it. The remnants were taken to recyclers and the dump. I had no need for the things anymore as this part of my life was done. The only things I kept were the fake IDs. The death of the innocent priest had finished me. There was a constant feeling of anxiety in the pit of my stomach, which made it difficult to eat.

Harry could text me when any papers needed to be signed, and I'd then send him a fax number. The lad taking care of the property had been doing a good job. Brandon was told if he continued there would be a bonus for him. I asked Harry not to tell Bill any more than he had to about me. I hadn't told Harry anything about why I'd packed up and left. By the end of the day, I drove out of Seattle and was on the road again.

I sold the car and bought a truck, which could pull an RV. I ended up buying one of those from an old retired man who was no longer able to use it. The RV was the perfect size for me and in excellent condition. The house sold four weeks later, and the money was transferred to my account. Bill had given up trying to get in touch with me after sending me a text saying, "Contact me when you're ready to talk."

For the next six months, I drifted across the United States. I went from warm places to hot places and then to freezing cold places. I didn't care where I was, I just went. Now and then, I answered an ad in the local paper, asking for farm help and stayed at these for a short time, then moved on. I had no experience in this field, but I was strong and smart enough, and I learned things fast. I stayed in buildings meant for hired hands and made sure I was the only one working for the farmers.

Finally, I found a job on a ranch outside Wapiti, Wyoming, and because I knew how to handle a horse, I got hired. My job was to keep an eye on the cattle grazing in the foothills. There were bears in the vicinity and, if not looked after, the cattle were attacked. I asked what happened if one of the cattle was killed while I was in another place. Did I lose my job, or did I go after the bear and kill it?

The rancher told me to go after the bear. He showed me several rifles and asked if I could shoot.

"Oh, yeah, I can shoot. I'm most familiar with the Three Hundred Winchester Magnum you have."

"Let's go out, and you can show me how good you are."

This we did, and he said, "You've got the job. Where did you learn to shoot like that?"

I just shrugged and let it go at that.

Soon, I had my supplies and a route he wanted me to travel. I had enough ammo for six months of hunting and shown on a map where water could be found. I had a small water purifying unit with me, and all the supplies were carried on the second horse.

I would be on the range for two weeks at a time. I would then work on the ranch for a week, and then go out again. I found it took me a week or more to get used to sleeping in a two-man tent and a sleeping bag. There were patches of evergreens here and there that I kept an eye on. If there were any bears around, that would be where they were.

I camped near water sources, so the horses could graze and drink when they needed to. The rifle was kept in the tent with me while I slept. The night sky had more stars than I had ever seen before. They twinkled, and the planets of our solar system stood out brighter than I thought possible. It all reminded me of the stories Asimov had written. I was glad I had kept my binoculars and a few books. I felt more than ever the desire to be away from this life and in the future he had written about. I had a lot of time to think out there. I thought about how badly my life had gone, and how I had ended up in the wilderness by myself. I was not a happy man.

This was a very different lifestyle than I had ever had. After two weeks, I was back at the ranch for a week. I was actually glad to have someone to talk to. Al Morrison was a down-to-earth kind of man. He was a good twenty-five to thirty years older than me and in his middle sixties. We kept our conversations about farm work, and he respected my privacy, which I appreciated.

"I have a daughter Alexandra, who is three years younger than you and has a boy of six, called Bobby," he said. "They live in Denver, so I don't see them very often. Her marriage fell apart when her husband decided he liked other women more than her. This happened two years ago, and she has had a hard time getting over it. She has since started going to a church and found some peace."

I just nodded.

I lived in my RV parked beside the barn. It was a little tight compared to what I had been used to, but it worked. Four months after starting work on the ranch, I found that Al and I had gotten fairly close. My trips out on the range looking after the cattle were done in two days now, as Al needed my help more and more around the ranch itself.

I had thought about moving on and even discussed it with Al, but he almost pleaded with me to stay. His health was starting to fail a bit and having only had the daughter, couldn't run the ranch all by himself anymore. He didn't want to be forced to sell the ranch and move into a retirement home.

"My daughter has offered to move in with me, but the work is beyond her abilities, so I asked her to stay where she already has decent employment. If you leave, it would prove to be a hardship for me."

So I stayed. I liked it there, away from it all, but I was still haunted by nightmares of what I had done. The weather was warm, and school was going to be out in three weeks. "Alex," as he called her, "is going to come for a two-week stay in July with her boy. I think you'll like them, Joseph."

Al was all excited about this and smiled more than he had since I started working there.

He had asked if I would like to move into the main house several times, saying there was plenty of room in the home. I was going to move in until I heard that his daughter would be coming. I thought that I'd spend some extra time out on the range looking after the cattle while she and her son were there. I could always move into the house after she left.

"I have a friend in Billings, Montana, that I haven't seen for years, Fred Barnhart," Al said. "He asked me to come for a visit because his health is deteriorating too. Joseph, could you do me a big favor and drive me to Billings for an overnight stay? We'll be back soon enough, and you could use a little time off away from the ranch. You still seem like you have some major things bothering you, and a change of scenery might be just what the doctor ordered."

"Yeah, I guess that would be okay. When do you want to go?"

"It's Wednesday now, and Fred asked me to make the trip as soon as possible, so why don't we leave tomorrow morning. He's got a small place, so I'll put you up in a motel overnight," Al said.

"I have more than enough money to pay for it myself. You don't have the resources to pay for any extras, so don't worry about me."

Chapter 35

The drive was done in my truck, which was fairly new, because his old truck probably wouldn't have made it, and I hadn't felt like sitting at the side of the road with a breakdown. After dropping off Al at his friend's home and making sure everything was all right, I'd headed for a motel near the center of town.

Billings had a population of 170,000 and had lots to do. I went for lunch in a nice family restaurant, sitting in a booth behind a young family. The air in the eatery was buzzing with excitement. A big-name preacher was in town and speaking later that evening at the small stadium in town.

Who would have thought that Franklin Graham, son of the world-famous Billy Graham, would be in the same town as me? This man and his father were the only evangelists that I had ever had any respect for. People were also talking about the preacher from Arkansas. He had made a big impact on the folks in the diner. This event was, of course, not for me. My sins were way past forgiving, and I had done far too much in my life on the wrong side of the tracks.

I finished my meal and took a walk around the downtown area. I probably should have stayed in my room, because most of the time I spent walking, I did it with my head hanging down. My mood had, for some reason, darkened, and I didn't think that I should be out in public. I could feel things beginning to unravel for me and had to get away. It hadn't hit me too badly for a while, but I could feel the depression forcing its way into my mind. At this time, I decided to turn around and head back. As I did, there was someone in my way and, as I started to go around them, I was stopped by a voice.

"Say, friend, you seem like you have the weight of the world on your shoulders."

With a sigh, I looked up. I was shocked to see, standing in my way, none other than Reverend Harold Spencer, who traveled with Franklin Graham. All I felt was shame and tried to walk around him. He stepped into my path, blocking my way, and asked, "Do you know who I am?"

"Everybody knows who you are. I've seen you with the Grahams on television several times."

"Then you know why I've stopped you, don't you?" he said, trying to get me to look into his eyes, which I avoided.

"Some people are past saving. There are things that can't be undone."

"Really, are you trying to tell me that what the Grahams have been saying all these years is wrong? That they don't know what they have been talking about all this time?"

"I didn't mean to insult you, Reverend Spencer. I've heard before what they have to say, and I know what I have done. There are things about me which are past redemption. Things no one knows about, things that haunt me constantly. I am going to hell for what I have done, and there is no changing this."

He took a deep breath, letting it out with a long sigh, and then he said, "I have several hours of free time. If you even remotely want forgiveness for anything and everything that you have ever done, please let me help you. Come with me and my friends and tell me what has gone on in your life."

There was no saying no to the man. I wanted so badly to just run, but my feet wouldn't do what I told them. He gently took me by the arm, guided me to a private place, and we talked. Over the course of the next hour, I spilled my guts. All the time his friends made sure we were not disturbed.

I told him the story of my mother and the downward spiral it took me on. I told him about the payback and how it started me down the road of removing many people who had constantly hurt others.

I told him about Amy. I told him of how one thing after another forced me to take the lives of those people that I and society felt needed to answer for what they did. Continuing, I told him of Kathleen and how she took me away from the life I had chosen. How I had found justification for doing what I had done.

Her death was almost my death, and the cycle just continued on and on, until the death of Gord. His death was the last straw. The one that broke this camel's back.

I told him of the one final mistake I made that caused me to make the fatal error, the killing of an innocent priest, which ended everything for me. Since then, I had been living in the shadows. "How can a man be forgiven for living a life like mine?" I asked him.

Most of the time I had been spilling my guts, he remained quiet, only asking the occasional question for clarification. He took a deep breath. "Yes, you have had quite the life. As a matter of fact, it is a life unlike any I have ever heard of before. I can understand why you feel the way you do. It would seem that far too much water has passed under this bridge. I have been studying the Bible all my life. I honestly believe that the Lord has put me on this earth for the express purpose of helping those, such as you, find salvation. What you have failed to see is the fact that there is no sin too big to be forgiven by our God. The creator of the universe can do anything. What so many unbelievers fail to comprehend is that God does truly exist. How could this universe be here if it was not created? People seem to think that it all started with a big bang. How do they think the material for the big bang came to be there in the first place? The next question people ask is one even I don't have an answer for. How did God come into being? We won't find the answer to that until we get to heaven. Yes, there is a heaven because if there wasn't, there would be absolutely no purpose to anyone's life. There would be no reason for any of us to be here, and I for one cannot comprehend this being the case."

I sat there taking it all in. Everything he said made sense to me, so I asked, "What you are telling me is, despite everything thing I've done, I can still have my sins taken away?"

"If you are truly sorry—I don't mean that if you feel bad about it, but if you know you have done wrong and know that it is God who will collect the debt for all the things done by sinners who do not repent, that you believe he sent his son to pay for all our sins, and you want forgiveness—then yes, you will be forgiven. Do you want this with all your heart?" the reverend asked.

With tears rolling down my face I said, "Yes, I want this more than anything, please help me, I can't go on like this anymore. Everything I have done has not helped.

No matter what I did, I still ended up falling into oblivion."

As I had seen him do on other occasions, he led me to the Lord and, when all was done, he asked me to attend the revival that night. He would have someone at the gate to bring me to a seat where I could see and hear everything I needed. I would be given information that would help me continue my journey to salvation.

I had been in tears throughout most of the time it took me to tell him about my life. Now I walked back to the room and got ready to go to hear Franklin speak to the masses. I was met by someone at the gate, just as Reverend Spencer had said. During the course of the evening, I found myself drawn in further and further. When the call was made to receive the Lord, I went forward with the others, even though I had made the decision to follow the teachings of Jesus that afternoon.

He saw me from the platform and smiled. This day had been a long time coming, and I felt like a new man. The past was now really the past. Going back to my room, I read the information packet I'd received. Al had mentioned church a few times during my stay, but up till then, I had not been ready to hear it. I could hardly wait to tell him about what had happened to me.

Chapter 36

Things at the ranch had taken a real turn. Al treated me more like a son than a hired hand. I moved into the house with him and had my own room. He told me that if I wanted, I could paint it a color that suited me better. His deceased wife, he said, would be happy that I was there.

Alex and her boy were coming for a visit that weekend, and I found that I was looking forward to meeting them.

I saw photos of them in the house, and she was an attractive, blonde-haired, blue-eyed girl. Her boy had many of his mother's features and was smiling in most of the pictures I saw.

When they arrived, I made sure I was out of the way, so they had the time to catch up. When the time was right, I walked to the house, and Al introduced me to his daughter.

"Joseph, I'd like you to meet my daughter Alex. This young man is Bobby," he said, smiling.

"I'm pleased to meet you, Alex, and you too, Bobby. Al has told me a lot about you."

They both smiled and said hello. She was a truly pleasant young lady with manners, unlike many of the crass women I had met in the recent past.

Bobby was nice as well, and we hit it off immediately. When I had to do some chores in the barn, he tagged along and helped me. When all was done and we approached the house, I overheard Al say to Alex that I had met the Reverend Harold Spencer, the one who went on the crusades along with Franklin Graham. Al told Alex that I had, because of that meeting, turned my life over to the Lord, just as she had done a few years earlier.

Sunday, we all went to the local community church that Al and I had been attending. There were welcome greetings for Alex and Bobby as people saw her. Some of the folks looked at her and then me, suspecting that I might have had more than a passing interest in her. This could have been because I kept looking at her. Bobby and I played around a lot, and soon we become very good friends. The warm weather made for good horseback riding. Alex and I went for some long rides together. Bobby hadn't learned to ride a horse, so I taught him. He learned quickly, and his laugh could be heard all the way into the house as he had the horse trotting around the coral. We had a great time together.

The two-week stay was almost over, and it would soon be time for the two to go back to Denver. I asked if it would be all right if I came to see her and, without even thinking about it, I found her in my arms. It had been a long time since I felt this way. We had grown so fond of each other in the past two weeks that I already felt an ache inside me at the thought of her going back to her home.

Al saw this in me, and he pulled me aside, asking Bobby to give us a few minutes alone.

"Joseph, I don't like to interfere in anyone's life, but I think you and Alex feel the same way about each other. She has told me that she thinks she is in love. She didn't think this would ever happen again. She is not looking forward to going back to Denver. If you are of a mind, I would be most happy if the two of you got together."

With this said, he walked into the house. Alex and Bobby were in the kitchen finishing off the dishes. I looked out the window and saw the interaction between her, Bobby, and Al as he entered the room. As I stood there, I thought of what life would be like if I let her get away from me. My life alone for the past number of years had been lonely, to say the least. It didn't take long before my mind was made up.

I went to the open window, and she looked out at me with a smile that lit up her blue eyes. There was a flutter in my chest as I asked her to go for a walk. Bobby stayed with Al, despite wanting to go with us. The walk led us to the top of a knoll that overlooked a valley spread out before us. There was a gentle evening breeze blowing through our hair. The sun was setting behind us as I started to explain my life to her.

She placed a finger to my lips and asked, "Is your future going to be affected by what has occurred in your past? We all have baggage that has been dealt with. If you are going to live the rest of your life the way you are living now, you need not explain your past life to me. I have things I'm not proud of too, but they are gone, never to return, so I won't bother cluttering up my or someone else's life with them."

The weight that had just been lifted from my shoulders was like a new-found freedom. No more justifying myself and my actions. Even more at that moment than when Reverend Harold Spencer led me to the lord, I felt that my past life was finally no more. I had regretted doing what I did and would never get into that life again. I knew in my heart that I had been forgiven and had also been given a second chance.

Looking into her eyes, I said what was on my mind, "We've only known each other a very short time, and already I can't bear the thought of being without you. I don't want you to go back to Denver. If you need time to think about it, that's all right. I won't push for a decision, but—" My heart was thumping in my chest as I said the next words. "Will you marry me, Alex?"

There was a moment of silence as she looked at me. Waiting for her to answer made my fingers tingle slightly in anticipation and there were butterflies in my stomach.

She smiled. "Yes, I'll marry you. I feel the same way too. I never thought that I would ever want to be married again, not until I came back here," she said as tears streamed down her face.

We stayed at the top of the knoll for a short time before going back to the house. Al and Bobby were sitting on a swinging bench that hung from the ceiling of the porch. Alex made the announcement, and Bobby ran to me and jumped up into my arms. Al came over and, shaking my hand, and told me how pleased he was.

The three of us went to Alex's home in Denver. It was put up for sale and sold fairly quickly and for a price that left her a tidy amount of money. I had already told her of my resources, and we had more than enough to live a comfortable life on the ranch.

The marriage took place in the Community Church where we were attending regularly. All the ladies of the congregation pitched in and the day was as wonderful as any I had ever had. On our honeymoon, I showed Alex where Amy and Kathleen were buried. She asked what kind of women they were and was pleased when I told her how wonderful they were.

Life on the ranch settled into a routine, and Al and I taught Bobby all we knew about how to run a ranch. The first year went by, and life was great. Bobby and I developed a real bond, and it was almost as if he were my own son. Soon it was exactly that—I thought of him as mine—and we were one big, happy family, with Al being like the father, I never had.

The life I led was gone. I hardly ever thought of it anymore. I felt I was really a saved man. It was truly a revelation. This was reinforced even more when Alex informed me that Bobby was going to have a new brother or sister.

About the Author

Leonardus G. Rougoor was born in the Netherlands. His parents and most of his family moved to Canada to start a better life years ago. He was raised on a dairy farm, which made for an abundance of work. Educated in southern Ontario, he tried a number of different jobs before he ended up in a major tool and die shop, starting a lifelong career.

Having a heart for the underdog, although causing many sleepless nights, has been the driving force in a writing career. He now writes in three genres: crime, young adult mystery adventure and the supernatural.

"If you like rejection, become a writer."